THE
STARS BLUE YONDER

SANDRA
McDONALD

A TOM DOHERTY ASSOCIATES BOOK
NEW YORK

THE STARS BLUE YONDER

A Tor Book
Published by Tom Doherty Associates, LLC
175 Fifth Avenue
New York, NY 10010

www.tor-forge.com

Tor® is a registered trademark of Tom Doherty Associates, LLC.

ISBN 978-0-7653-6020-5

First Edition: July 2009
First Mass Market Edition: October 2010

Printed in the United States of America

0 9 8 7 6 5 4 3 2 1

To Jerian and Nicholas,
Alli and Sydney,
and all the other children, living and lost

ACKNOWLEDGMENTS

This book could not have been possible without the support and love of many people, including Carol McDonald, Wilfred McDonald, Terry Berube, Stephanie Wojtowicz, my brothers, and my nieces.

My enormous gratitude goes out to the members of the Jacksonville Science Fiction and Fantasy Writer's Group, including Steve Covey, Jean Osborne, Brandie Tavrin, Charisse Phelps, Norman Wood, Sherry Czerniejewski, and Stefan Lingonblad. That critique session at Panera's will always be a memorable Sunday in 2008.

Many thanks also to Sarah Prineas and Greg van Eekhout, whose support and truth-telling is much appreciated, and to the team at Tor, including Patrick Nielsen Hayden, Liz Gorinsky, James Macdonald, and Terry McGarry.

Modern Australia was built on the backs of thousands of men and women convicted, imprisoned, and cruelly banished to the other side of the world in an attempt to rid England of her "undesirables." Many of them never again saw their homes or families. At the same time, indigenous people whose ancestors had roamed Australia long before the birth of Rome and Greece saw their land, families, and traditions destroyed by newly arrived Europeans. The vivid, heartbreaking story of this beautiful country cannot be done justice in just a few hundred pages, but I tried my best.

THE
STARS BLUE
YONDER

PROLOGUE

Smoke and dust, and a far-off rumbling like thunder. Choking, Terry Myell rolled over onto his stomach. Burnt skin pulled and tore under his clothes. His throat and lungs ached as he tried to suck in air. He couldn't see clearly.

"Jodenny!" Though he put all his strength into it, his voice came out as a raspy whisper. "Jo!"

No answer. He clawed at the dirt and deck beneath him. Stupid space station, overgrown with jungle plants and ancient gods. He'd never trusted the place. And now something catastrophic had happened, something that left his mouth tasting like ash.

The station groaned and shook around him. The deck heaved. He heard no voices or cries for help. Jodenny, Commander Nam, Anna Gayle, all of the others—they couldn't all be dead. Not after what they'd been through together. Not after he and Jodenny had just found each other again. He hauled himself to his hands and knees and tried crawling through rocky debris.

He didn't get far.

Jodenny, he thought, and now it was an apology.

He was dully aware of a crack as his head hit the ground. The sound of thunder faded in his ears. Breathing no longer mattered. Then a cool breeze washed over him, soft as a pleasant spring rain.

"Teren Myell," a voice said. "Can you hear me?"

He didn't move. The breeze was refreshing and clean, a balm to his abused body.

The voice took on more urgency. "Listen to me. You have to use the ouroboros. The ring. Use it and escape from here."

Myell wasn't sure if his eyes were closed or not. The face before him was blurry, indistinct, as if in a dream. The hands against his skin were thin and cold.

"Go to Kultana," the stranger urged. "Save the human race."

Myell groaned. He didn't want to be responsible for saving humanity. He didn't have the strength for it. He was tired, so very tired, and inadequate to the task.

The stranger paused. Reconsidered.

Whispered, "Save your wife. Save her and the child."

Child? The stranger was wrong. There was no child. But for his wife, Terry Myell would drag himself across a desert, up a mountainside, through hell. Though he had no strength, nor confidence, nor sure knowledge of how to do it, Myell reached out his blistered hands and called the ouroboros to him. Bid it and bent it and thought of Jodenny, only Jodenny.

The blue ring came to him like a lover and carried him away.

CHAPTER **ONE**

N ana," Twig whispered, scared. "They're coming. The Roon."

Commander Jodenny Scott was seventy damned years old. On days like today, crouched in her own living room closet, she felt closer to ninety. The closet was small and dusty, but it was the only viable hiding place they had. She tried to ignore the aching in her back.

"What should we do?" she asked her ten-year-old granddaughter.

Twig waved her finger, bidding her to be silent.

Heavy footsteps approached. Stopped. All else was quiet in the house. Jodenny couldn't bend down far enough to peer out the slit between the door and the floor, but Twig was still small and limber. She leaned close with her blond hair falling in her face.

Another footstep.

Closer.

The door swung open.

Jodenny's daughter Teresa, enormously pregnant and

clearly annoyed, asked, "What are you two doing in there?"

Twig sat up with a frown. "Aunt Teresa! You ruined our game."

Teresa sighed. "You shouldn't go dragging Nana into closets, Twig."

"I volunteered." Jodenny steadied herself against the door frame as she rose on creaky knees. "Someone's got to fight off the hordes of dangerous aliens."

"Why don't you go meet the boys at the creek?" Teresa said to Twig. "They've been there all morning and I bet they haven't caught a fish yet. Show them how it's done."

Twig bounded to her feet and gave Jodenny a quick kiss on the cheek. "Don't worry. Next time I'll save you, Nana."

Jodenny tried not to envy her granddaughter's energy and youth as Twig dashed out the door. "Oh to be a kid again."

"Which you're not," Teresa said. "Come on outside in the breeze and sit down."

"I'm not an invalid," Jodenny grumbled, but she followed Teresa out onto the back porch anyway.

They both sat in the morning shade. Their rocking chairs creaked against the weathered planking. On days like these, under sunny skies and with the landscape so pretty, Jodenny could almost pretend that the planet Providence was home. The fauna, flora, animals, geography, and landscape were certainly just like Earth and her colonies. Gifts of the gods. Though, personally, she would cheerfully strangle the god Jungali, who had given them this gift and stranded them on the other side of the galaxy, cut off from civilization, doctors, hospitals, universities, armies—

"You've got that look on your face." Teresa put both her hands on her baby bump and made small soothing circles. "I knew Twig shouldn't be talking about the Roon."

"The Roon don't bother me," Jodenny said. Which was true. She hadn't seen one in forty years, and didn't expect to see any again. Not in this remote corner of the galaxy.

"Then what is it? You feeling ancient again?"

"I *am* ancient," Jodenny replied.

Teresa made a harrumphing noise. "Not if you can go crawling around in closets. But at least you're not turning seventy-six tomorrow. That's something to be happy about, isn't it?"

Farther down the sloping yard, where the gum trees met the stream, seven-year-old Alton emerged from the weeds. As usual, he'd managed to get himself covered with mud. He had a jar in one hand, in which he'd no doubt stashed the latest lizard, frog, insect, or other small creature unfortunate enough to be caught in his nets.

"Nana!" he yelled up to them. "Mom! Look what I found!"

"Who's turning seventy-six tomorrow?" Jodenny asked Teresa. Surely she hadn't forgotten someone's birthday again. It wasn't enough that her knees ached and her back hurt and when she looked in the mirror, she saw only a wrinkled sack of leathered skin. Now she was forgetting things. Soon she'd be a gibbering idiot, someone they'd have to park in the corner and feed through a straw.

Better to face an entire Roon army than the indignities of old age, she thought.

Teresa rubbed her belly some more. "How many candidates are there?"

Not many. Aside from some officers, some business travelers, and a few elderly immigrants, most of the crew and passengers on the *Kamchatka* had been under the age of thirty when they had been stranded here. Jodenny took a mental head count. Not old Captain Balandra; her birthday was in January. Not Baylou Owenstein. They'd just celebrated his birthday a few weeks ago. That left—

"Sam," Jodenny said unhappily.

"Yes," Teresa said. "Dad's birthday is tomorrow. I knew you'd remember. I'm making a cake."

"Mom!" Alton stomped his foot. "Come on! He's in the water!"

Jodenny said, "Watch your tone, young man."

Teresa made to stand up despite her swollen ankles. "I'll go see what he's going on about."

"You stay put. I'll do it." Even with her arthritis, Jodenny moved more quickly than her daughter. "But if this is another one of his frogs, I'm going to make him kiss it."

She limped down the stairs and past her vegetable garden. Four grandsons and one granddaughter, who would have expected that? Forty damn years spent stranded in this backwater wilderness with the rest of the crew and passengers. Sam, turning seventy-six. There'd be a cake and maybe a banner, lots of jokes about aging that were funny only to the young, and recycled or home-made presents he had no use for. Certainly he wouldn't want her there. She didn't think anyone except Teresa could seriously expect her to go.

Alton had turned and dashed back into the woods. "Hurry up! I think he's dead."

"If he's dead, I don't need to hurry," Jodenny said.

Alton's discovery wasn't a drowned turtle or half-crushed snake or any other morbid find. Instead it was a man lying half in and half out of the stream. He wore Team Space trousers ripped at the seams and a black T-shirt. His feet were bare but he didn't appear injured in any significant way. With her bad eyesight she couldn't tell if he was breathing. If she moved a step or two to the left she might be able to see his face, but her legs wouldn't obey her.

"Did he come from away?" Alton picked up a stick. "What's he doing here?"

"I don't know." Jodenny's voice sounded small in her own ears. Her head filled with a buzzing and her knees went weak. Certainly the man wasn't one of their own. No one these days dressed in a Team Space uniform, or would wander down to this stream to take a nap. He might be from one of the splinter groups that had gone off on their own shortly after their arrival here on Providence, but again, where had he gotten the clothes?

Alton crept closer to the stranger. The buzzing in Jodenny's ears grew worse. The green of the forest was blurring at the edges. She'd fainted only a few times in her life, but the warning signs were clear.

"Run and get the sheriff," Jodenny said.

Alton poked at the man's arm. No reaction. He was probably dead.

"Go get the sheriff!" Jodenny snapped, fear and anger all mixed into it, because the child never listened and here she was going to faint like an old lady. She knew the man in the creek, knew the shape of his head and shoulders, knew him down to the withered fibers of her fading heart. Wasn't it bitter and horrible that he'd returned from death just as she was getting ready to embrace it?

Alton dashed off up the hill, yelling at the top of his lungs.

Jodenny's world grayed out and went silent.

Myell woke in a soft bed without anyone shouting at him, which sure beat most of the other ways he'd been waking up lately.

He blinked at the plastisteel ceiling and pinkish gray walls. Bright sunlight spilled past gauzy curtains over what looked like portholes from a Team Space ship. The furniture seemed like ship salvage as well—the narrow bed, a metal dresser, a round mirror. But there were touches of domesticity in the bright yellow bed-spread and the daisies in a blue vase on a shelf. A smell like bitter coffee hung in the air.

"Caffeine would be nice," he said aloud.

His voice was rusty but otherwise fine. He couldn't say the same about his legs, which were shaky as he swung them out to the floor. The brown rug on the metal floor tickled his toes. He checked his arms and torso. Just a few bruises and scars, and a place on his right arm where someone had recently given him an injection.

He tried to stand up and the room spun out from under him. The next thing he knew, he was flat on his back and a woman was talking to him.

"That was a dumb thing to do," she said. "Come on, wake up again. Don't make me get the smelling salts."

He forced his eyes open. A woman with the same color hair and eyes as Jodenny Scott smiled down at him.

"I'm Lisa," she said. "You're in my house."

Myell nodded, his mouth gone dry. Lisa was as pretty

as Jodenny but with wider shoulders and a longer nose. He knew that nose. Had seen it in the mirror all these years. She was in her late thirties or early forties and had an old-fashioned stethoscope around her neck.

"You patched me up?" he asked.

Her cool hand touched the inside of his wrist. "You weren't too bad off. A bump on the head, a few bruises. You've got some burn scars. Not too old, from the look of them, but someone took care of them. Someone with better medical equipment than mine, but not enough to get rid of the scars."

He shrugged. A few scars didn't bother him.

Lisa said, "Can you tell me how you feel now?"

"Better."

"Good. We do what we can, though the ship's infirmary has been stripped out for years now. How'd you come to be in the creek, anyway? It's not like we ever get any strangers here."

He said, "You haven't asked my name."

"I don't have to." Lisa's smile faded. "I know your name. You still have a dog tag embedded in your collarbone. And my mother's the one who found you. Jodenny."

He felt for his wedding ring, which was still firmly affixed to his finger. If Lisa was about forty, that would make Jodenny nearly seventy. Wrinkled and arthritic and probably hating every moment of it.

"I need to . . ." he said, and gestured toward what he hoped was the bathroom.

"That's the fluids I ran into you," Lisa said. "Come on. Up you go."

She helped him upright and shouldered him to a bathroom equipped with a Team Space toilet. He scrubbed at his face and peered at the bloodshot lines in his eyes and the stubble on his chin. Vanity was a luxury he hadn't had in a while. When he felt steadier, he emerged to find three men sitting in his room on chairs that had been pulled in from elsewhere. Lisa was straightening the pillows on the bed.

"That's Baylou Owenstein," she said, nodding toward a man with white hair and long gray beard. Beside him was a much younger man. "And that's my brother-in-law Brian Romero. And over there is—"

"Commander Osherman," Myell said. There was enough military left in him to nod respectfully. "Sir."

The years had not been kind to Osherman. His face was deeply cracked with wrinkles. His arthritic hands were wrapped around a cane. His eyes were rheumy, his posture hunched. He stared at Myell but didn't nod or smile or give any indication that he'd even heard him.

"Chief Myell," Brian said, leaning forward. "You knew my father, Putty."

"And your mother," Myell said. "We met at Supply School."

Baylou slapped his hand against his thigh. "Never met you, no I didn't. Met your wife, though. She's one of my best friends. You scared the hell out of her, showing up in her creek like that."

Lisa handed Myell a glass of water. His fingers tightened on it. "I didn't mean to."

"We're a tiny bit confused," Brian said. "About how you got there. About how you can be here at all. And why you haven't aged a single day."

Myell wished this part would get easier.

"I don't know," he lied. "It's all blank to me."

Osherman continued to stare at him silently. Baylou

scratched his jaw, and Brian angled himself toward Lisa.

"Amnesia?" Brian asked.

Lisa gave Myell a considering look. "It's possible."

Baylou said, "Mark Sweeney lost his memory for a while. After he fell down that mountainside."

"The only thing Uncle Mark forgot was how much poker money he owed people," Brian said. "I never did get my four million yuros."

"What's the last thing you remember?" Lisa asked.

Myell was feeling unnerved by Osherman's stare but he didn't want to show it, so he drank the water and kept his gaze on the others. "I was living on Fortune with your mother. We were married. She wasn't pregnant."

Lisa's chin lifted. "Nothing after that?"

He shook his head. Lying.

"How about the Roon?" Baylou asked. "Big ugly aliens that look like lizards. Ring a bell?"

Myell gazed helplessly at them. No matter what he said, they wouldn't believe him. The water twisted in his stomach and he put the glass down before he spilled it into his lap.

"No," he said. "I don't remember. I don't remember what happened to me."

Baylou and Brian sat back in their chairs. Osherman's cane scraped on the floor as he shifted his weight. He lifted himself from the chair with the stiff, cramped movements of a man burdened by age. His face was still unreadable, but there was no missing the certainty in his voice.

"Terry Myell died back on Earth," he said. "We buried him here. Whoever you are, you aren't him."

* * *

On the other side of town, Teresa said, "I think you should stay in bed."

Jodenny already had her feet on the floor. "I want to see him."

"He's resting. As you should be. That was quite a faint. You're lucky you didn't crack your head open on a rock."

One of the Taylor boys bicycled past the window, shouting something to his brother. Jodenny's bedroom wasn't much to look at—some furniture, bare walls, a few clothes on pegs—and Teresa was sitting in the only chair. Jodenny reached for her sandals.

"My head's perfectly fine," she said.

The front door to the cottage opened. A moment later Lisa came down the hall, looking thoughtful. She asked, "How are things here?"

"Mom's being stubborn," Teresa reported.

"How is he?" Jodenny asked.

Lisa leaned against the door frame. Though she was several years older than Teresa, and they were only half sisters, sometimes the resemblance between them was startling. "Not so bad. He's back to sleep now. No major injuries, just some bumps and bruises and dehydration. But he says he doesn't remember where he's been or how he got here."

Teresa asked, "You believe him?"

"I don't have any reason to disbelieve him."

"Doesn't mean you have to trust him," Jodenny said. "Don't hurt Sam over this."

The other Taylor boy rode by, casting shadows into the room. Lisa and Teresa exchanged looks. Jodenny knew exactly what her daughters were thinking. The one who'd hurt Sam the most was the one who'd kicked him out of their bed and home.

Briskly she reached for her other shoe. "You're sure he's not carrying a million different diseases?"

"I wouldn't have let him into my house if the scanners hadn't okayed him," Lisa said.

"Scanners that are forty years out of date," Jodenny said.

Lisa shrugged. "If that's the case, you better not visit him. It took you months to get over last winter's flu. Your immune system's not what it used to be."

"I'll take that into consideration, Doctor." Jodenny brushed past Lisa to splash cold water on her face. There wasn't much she could do about the bird's nest her hair had become—gray and stiff, unruly in the humidity—so she pulled on a hat, then took it off again. Forty years, and she was supposed to look good for some impostor who couldn't possibly be her dead husband? Whoever he was, he could damn well take her in her ruined elderly state.

When she came out of the bathroom, Lisa and Teresa had moved to the living room, with its solitary sofa and two flanking chairs. Brian Romero and his sister Alice, the town sheriff, had joined them. Brian was sitting with Teresa's feet in his lap, massaging them for her. Alice was leaning against the front door, frowning.

"Well?" Jodenny asked.

Alice scratched at her sunburned nose. She was a tall woman with long blond hair and broad, dusty hands. "I went up there and checked myself. There's still a body in the grave. No sign that it's been disturbed recently. Or ever."

"So the man didn't crawl out of a grave," Lisa said. "You only have to look at him to know that's true."

"He got into that creek somehow," Brian said.

Brian was a good man, sensible, popular enough to be elected mayor and smart enough to not abuse the position. Jodenny was happy to have him as a son-in-law. But she missed Lisa's husband, Eric, who'd gone on a hunting trip and wouldn't be back for two days. He was more likely to talk sense into Lisa than anyone else.

"Who is he, if not Terry Myell?" Lisa asked. "His biological profile matches the information on his embedded dog tag, right down to the DNA sample. He's a positive match for my DNA. And he knows things the real Terry Myell would know."

"Or he guesses well," Jodenny said. "What did Sam think?"

"He's not saying," Brian said. "I think he'd rather see us lock him up until it's all worked out."

Alice sniffed. "Lock him up where? No one will let me build a decent jail."

Lisa said, "Why would you lock him up? He's not carrying any weapons and he hasn't threatened anyone. You think I'd put him in my spare bedroom if I thought he was dangerous? Around my own kids?"

Brian said, "You might be a bit biased."

"Horseshit," Lisa replied.

Teresa grinned. "Give 'em hell, sis."

Jodenny shook her head at the lot of them. "I'm going to go see him. Get to the bottom of all this."

With Lisa at her elbow she crossed the lane from her cottage toward Lisa's house. The sun had gone behind gray clouds and a wind was kicking up dust. Jodenny tilted her head back, frowning. The weather forecast had been for fair weather all week. When they reached Lisa's, she saw four kids clustered by the side fence and trying to peer through the slats.

"Get on, get going," Jodenny said, shooing them with her hands. "Nothing to see out there."

Seven-year-old Mimi Balandra, her face dirty, peered up with big eyes. "Momma says there's a stranger in there from outer space!"

"My daddy says he's come down from heaven," said six-year-old Luke Owenstein, one finger stuck up his nose.

Lisa ushered them from the fence. "There's nothing to see, and you all go home and tell your folks so."

Inside the house, all was dim and quiet. The ongoing struggle for dominance between houseplants and Lisa's watercolor paintings appeared to have tipped again in the watercolors' favor, with new landscapes and sea-scapes hanging on the walls and refrigerator. Paintings from the kids also adorned the walls. Books from the *Kamchatka* were kept on a high shelf as befitting their rare and precious status. An ancient deskgib, long past its usefulness, was collecting dust in one corner under the watchful gaze of the family cat, Leia.

Jodenny was surprised to see Osherman and Baylou sitting silently in the living room, drinking coffee. Osherman didn't say much these days, but Baylou could usually be counted on to be a chatterbox.

"Anything exciting happen?" Lisa asked them.

"He's sleeping again. Nothing exciting about that," Baylou said.

Jodenny tried to read Osherman's expression, but it was as inscrutable as it had been for the last ten years. He met her gaze for a moment and then turned his head, unwilling to share whatever he'd learned or decided.

"Give us some time," she said to Lisa. "This might take a while."

She went down the hall, her sandals soft on a rug of

woven grasses. The door to the spare bedroom was closed. Her hand shook when she touched the knob, but that was the normal shakes. Not anxiety, she told herself. She had nothing to fear from him, and there wasn't much to lose at this point anyway.

Then she saw Myell lying in bed, the sheets pulled down to his waist, and the shakes began all over again.

CHAPTER TWO

Jodenny snagged a chair for her sorry ass and sat down with a thump.

It wasn't that Myell looked particularly sexy under that sheet. She hadn't cared for romance in a long time and didn't think even a lightning bolt could jump-start her libido. It wasn't his apparent youth, either, though she was envious. She couldn't even look at pictures of herself anymore. Impossible that she'd once had glossy hair and smooth skin. In his sleep Myell projected vulnerability and helplessness but she didn't feel protective of him, exactly. Instead she was struck by what he represented: The past, lost to her forever. Her love, gone like water down a stream.

The shakes continued, even as she sat on her hands and clamped her knees together.

But eventually they passed, as all things did in her life, and when Myell woke she had her limbs under complete control.

He woke up slowly, in obvious confusion. For a long moment he did nothing but stare at her. Jodenny held herself perfectly still. His gaze sharpened with recognition and he made a slight noise that could have been a protest.

"So you know who I am," she said. "That's a start."

"Kay," he said.

She hadn't heard that nickname in close to forever. Jodenny didn't let herself blink or flush, however. "Not anymore. That was a long time ago."

He sat up in bed. "Not to me."

The next words out of her mouth surprised her. They weren't what she was planning to say, and she wasn't sure she believed them, but they came out anyway. "Whoever you are, you're not Terry Myell. My husband's dead."

He didn't reply.

"He died in my arms on Burringurrah," she continued. "I buried him on the hill outside of town. We checked, and the corpse is still in the ground. So whatever or whoever you are, you're not him."

He moved to the end of the bed and sat with his knees barely touching hers. His gaze was intent on her, as if memorizing every wrinkle and liver spot. She wanted to cover herself with a blanket.

"I could tell you something," he said. "Something only you and I know. Our first time making love. What we said to each other when we were trapped in that tower on the TSS *Aral Sea*. But you already know who I am."

Defensiveness crept into her voice. "You're not him."

"You want to believe that," he said, sounding thoughtful about it. "But you don't, Kay. You know me. No matter what, no matter where, you know me."

She left the chair and paced to the window. Through the plastiglass, past Lisa's water fountain and through the slats in the fence, she could see that the neighborhood kids had returned to gawk. Jodenny turned from the window, folded her arms across her chest, and glared at him.

"Where's your dilly bag?" she asked.

He shook his head. "Long gone. But I have this."

Myell held up his hand. His wedding ring was small and circular and instantly familiar to her.

Jodenny shifted her gaze. Her own ring was on a necklace under her shirt, though she wasn't about to admit it. "If you were him, I'd ask where you come from. And I wouldn't listen to any horseshit about a bad memory."

Myell shifted back on the bed. She recognized the signs of being bone-tired, of having little left to draw on, but waited him out anyway.

Finally he said, "I remember Commander Nam forced me on a mission to find some missing scientists. I remember most of the worlds we went to. At the end of it, there was some kind of space station. You were there. But it was . . . I don't know. Destroyed? There were a lot of people there, and then no one but me. The whole place was falling apart. Then someone told me to use an ouroboros to escape and find you."

"You can call one? Control it?"

"No." More strength in his voice now, and grimness too. "I have no control. I don't know how it brought me forty years forward in time, and I don't know how to get back. All I know is I'm supposed to find some place or some thing called Kultana. Ever hear of it?"

"No," she said, but she was barely listening to him now. The prospect of escape had her in its grip. Not so much for her—where would she go?—but for the younger generations, for her children and grandchildren.

With a token ring from the Wondjina Transportation System they could return to civilization. They could enjoy plenty of food, plenty of electricity, plenty of opportunities. No more scrabbling for survival.

But he said he couldn't control it. Maybe that was true, and maybe it wasn't.

"You said someone told you to use it. Who?"

"I don't know. I remember a voice, but not the details. I wasn't in the best shape at the time."

"And now?" she asked. "If you can't control the ring, does that mean you're stuck here?"

Myell rubbed his eyes. "Would that make you happy?"

With more bitterness than she meant to reveal, she said, "It would have made me happy forty years ago."

"Tell me how I died on Earth. On Burringurrah."

She made a dismissive gesture. Those were old, bad memories, not easily resurrected even if she wanted to dig them up. "It doesn't matter."

"It matters to me," he said.

Jodenny turned back to the window. "Do you remember Leorah Farber? You met her on Fortune. She worked for Anna Gayle. Or Teddy Toledo? Her partner? They're gone now. Mark Sweeney too. Hullabaloo, Louise—they're all dead now."

"I'm sorry."

"We were sent here, stranded here, and they lived the rest of their lives waiting for rescue that never came. But here you are. Forty years late."

He stood up and came within touching distance of her, but didn't reach out. "It hasn't been forty years for me."

She kept her gaze on the garden. "Your daughter's here. Your grandchildren. Trying to keep food on the table, keep the power going, keep the sewage from backing up every other day. They fight about who's in charge, about religion, about alcohol. Half of them don't know what it's like to live in civilization and they're never going to find out, because no one knows we're out here."

Myell was silent.

"You're their only chance," she said, and her gaze settled on him with a heavy weight. "Do you understand? You have to save them."

"Save them but not you?" Myell asked.

Jodenny snorted. "Save me for what?"

Three knocks sounded against the door, which creaked open under Lisa's hand. Her face was tight, but also hopeful. "Are you two okay in here?"

"Fine," Jodenny snapped.

Myell asked, "Is that dinner I smell?"

"Yes," Lisa said. "I could use some help in the kitchen."

Jodenny gave her a glare, but Myell said, "You bet," and moved past Lisa down the hall.

"I said you shouldn't interrupt," Jodenny said.

"It's just food," Lisa said, all innocence. "A good hot meal never hurt anyone."

"We were busy talking."

"You were busy haranguing, I bet."

Lisa followed Myell. Jodenny stayed at the window, suddenly tired beyond measure. By the time she joined them in the kitchen Myell was sitting on a stool and shucking small, narrow ears of corn. Lisa was chopping up tomatoes for a salad. The season's crops had come through at last, though they'd lost a lot to fungus.

Osherman was still sitting in the living room. Jodenny knew better than to try and avoid him, so she took the seat opposite. The table between them was one they'd had in their own house, once. It was recycled metal from the ship, scratched and worn over the decades but covered with a tablecloth Jodenny had received as a wedding gift.

"You want something to drink, Mom?" Lisa asked. Behind her, thin raindrops started to splatter down on the window. "Or you, Sam?"

"No," Jodenny said.

Osherman didn't answer. He was staring at Myell and Lisa, who bent close to her father to show him where to recycle the corn husks. His intense concentration was not uncommon these days. He could stare all day at a tree, or a rock, or any old building. Jodenny didn't know what he saw when he looked so long at one thing. He couldn't or wouldn't explain it, not to her, not in these last years of their lives.

"Mom!" A flurry of feet and elbows marked Twig's full-throttle arrival through the kitchen door and up against the counter. She had dust on her face and her long hair was loose from its ponytail. She stared at Myell. "Is this him? You're my grandfather?"

Thirteen-year-old Kyle, who was Teresa's oldest son, came in close on his cousin's heels. Like his grandpa Osherman, he had sandy-colored hair, a long nose, and a narrow face. He said, "Don't be stupid, Twig. You already have a grandfather."

Twig said, "But he was my first one. Right, Mom?"

Lisa put a wet cloth to Twig's dirty face. "You're supposed to be fishing. Where's the catch?"

"We caught a bunch," Kyle said. "Steven's got 'em."

Twig's brothers Steven and David soon arrived, bearing a string of river trout. Alton trudged in after them, his feet filthy up to his knees. After Lisa made the introductions, Alton said, rather proudly, "I'm the one who found you! In the stream."

"Where'd you come from, anyway?" Kyle asked.

Twig poked his arm. "From the grave, doofus."

Myell paused from shucking corn. "Do I look like a zombie?"

"You're supposed to be old." Kyle gave Myell a thorough, scrutinizing look. "As old as Nana."

Lisa corralled the kids and pointed them toward the bathroom. "Go wash up, all of you, and then keep yourself busy until I call for supper. And if you've got homework, you better go do it now. I'll be checking later."

Twig broke free of the gang to duck into the living room. "Hi, Nana," she said, throwing her arms around Jodenny's neck and giving her a quick, sweaty squeeze. "Are you happy your first husband's back?"

"News travels fast around here," Jodenny replied. "How many of those fish are yours?"

"Just one." Twig circled around the table and hugged Osherman. "Hi, Grandpa. It's okay if I have two grandfathers?"

"We'll talk about that later," he said.

Twig dashed off, never content to walk when she could run. Osherman's gaze turned Jodenny's way for the first time since she'd sat down, and he said, "You fainted."

"Hours ago."

"You were that surprised to see him?"

"You're not?"

His nose wrinkled up. "Nothing about him surprises me. Not anymore."

Teresa and Brian showed up a few minutes later bearing fresh biscuits. They would have used the last of their good flour for those, but Jodenny didn't chide them for being so generous. Teresa gratefully sank into the nearest chair and Brian took the fish outside to fry. More visitors arrived, including Captain Balandra on her cane, and her son Malachy, who'd brought his own kids and grandkids, most of them bearing what little food they could spare. Most everyone was in good cheer and curious about Myell. Alice Romero was one of the few ill at ease, and stood in the corner watching Myell with close attention. Osherman didn't move from his chair but instead nodded at those who came over to pay their respects. Jodenny didn't move either, though she felt like fleeing the house and heading for the hills without ever turning back.

Someone put music on. Conversations grew louder. More beer and rotgut liquor showed up, and Lisa grew more frazzled. *Any excuse for a party,* Jodenny thought in dismay. The humid air built up like a sauna even with the fans rattling overhead. The kitchen, living room, and dining room weren't big enough for the crowd, which spilled down the hall and into the bedrooms. It would have spread into the garden but for the rain that was slanting down harder and faster each minute.

Myell, meanwhile, was pestered with questions to the point where he stopped answering and instead retreated to the corner. Brian flanked him, warding off would-be interrogators, and Baylou kept him supplied with wine. Finally dinner was ready, and Lisa shooed off just about everyone who wasn't immediate family.

"Off you go," she said. "I can't feed every single one of you."

The partygoers disbursed cheerfully, some of them stumbling off home to their own dinners, others moving the party to the town's only pub. In the end there were several chairs, stools, and boxes set up around the dining room, with most of the grandchildren eating around the kitchen table.

Wedged between Teresa on one side and Brian on the other, with Osherman right across from her and Myell next to Lisa, Jodenny poked at her food without any appetite at all. Myell didn't seem interested in dinner either, though he dutifully pushed around bits of fish with his fork. Music played softly on an old machine while the rainy breeze sucked the curtains in and out of the window frames. Thunder and lightning rolled through the air, making Jodenny uneasy.

Lisa struggled to keep the conversation going. The party had sucked up all the easy words, leaving only awkward ones behind.

"Tell him about the school, Baylou," Lisa prompted.

"Hmm?" Baylou asked. "Oh, the school. Well, we teach everything to the best we can. The kids, they all have to learn medicine and engineering, and how to keep the fuel cells charged—we used hydroelectric and solar, though it's not easy."

Lisa tilted her head toward the kitchen. "Kyle's very good with engineering."

"Stop talking about me, Aunt Lisa," Kyle said around a mouthful of corn.

"They know all about the colonies," Lisa said. "How all of the Seven Sisters and this planet, too, presumably, were made by the Wondjina to be just like Earth for mankind to colonize. It's important that they don't forget where they came from."

Thunder rolled through the air, as if in agreement. Myell didn't answer. He and Osherman were vying for the Most Uncommunicative award.

Teresa made a faint noise and put her hand on her stomach. Jodenny remembered how her children had kicked and fussed in her womb, and how sore she'd been from little fists and heels poking at her day and night.

"All right?" Brian asked her.

She nodded. "Just a foot under my rib, I think."

Lisa offered a plate to Myell. "More corn?"

Myell ignored the plate and said, "You're not real."

Everyone looked at him.

"What did he say?" Captain Balandra asked, mostly deaf these days.

Jodenny's hands tightened on her cup.

Myell gazed miserably at his beer. "You're real to you. You live here, in this moment, then the next, and it's real to you. But soon I'll be gone and forgotten."

Lisa put the corn down. "Maybe you should go back to bed."

He stood up but didn't move away. Myell's gaze swept the table and then settled on Jodenny, as she feared it would.

"Sooner or later the blue ouroboros is going to come for me again," he said. "When I open my eyes it'll be twenty years ago, or five years from now, or whenever. Maybe I'll be on Fortune. Maybe I'll be right back here. But you won't remember that I was here before. You never remember. After I leave, everything goes back to the way it was. Nothing ever changes."

Jodenny found her voice. "That's ridiculous."

"I've been here before," Myell said. "Seven years ago, when Alton was born. He came out breech. Teresa, you lost a lot of blood."

Teresa stared at him, openmouthed.

"I was here thirty years ago," he said to Osherman. "I showed up in the middle of your wedding, right when Captain Balandra was about to pronounce you man and wife." To Lisa he said, "You were ten years old. You said, 'Are you my dad?' and I said yes."

He turned back to Jodenny. "I was there when you

graduated from the academy. I saved you from the disaster on the *Yangtze,* for at least a little bit. I was here the day after you buried me, and we made love by my grave. But you never remember. Dozens of times I've been here. But only the gods can change time."

Silence hung in the room.

Baylou rocked back in his chair. "Well, now. That's not what I expected to hear."

"Dad." Lisa's hand snaked out to grasp his fingers. "Sit down. We'll find a way to fix this."

He gave her a forlorn smile.

"That's what you said the last time," he said.

Thunder drummed through the air. Lightning lit up the world outside the windows, bright light for a second here, a second there. Myell was trying to sleep through the ruckus when a voice said, "You forgot the most important part, didn't you, Gampa?"

"Go away," Myell groaned. He realized he was kind of drunk. Baylou and Brian and Alice had plied him with a lot of beer in their attempt to get the whole time-traveling story out of him. He might have been a little maudlin there, toward the end, weeping into his glass before Lisa escorted him to bed. He wasn't quite sure.

Homer's voice was slightly chiding. "Everyone was having a good time until you had to go and tell the truth."

"I'm not talking to you." Myell rolled over in the bed. He watched more lightning, and felt the roll of thunder in his bones. He wondered if the children were sleeping through this. "There's nothing for you to document here."

Homer planted himself on the floor lotus-style. He was wearing a ridiculous outfit today—oversized trousers, a scarf, a wild hat. His shining young face was full of eagerness and curiosity. "Gamsa didn't age very well, did she? She's like a whole new species. 'Cantankerous maximus grandmotherus.'"

"You don't know her," Myell said, because Homer didn't. Didn't know what Jodenny had been through, and had no damn right to pass judgment on her. Though it was true she was somewhat cranky. He supposed he'd be cranky too, stranded for decades in the middle of nowhere and facing the infirmities of old age.

Homer cracked his knuckles. "She still hooked up with Sam? Kind of funny, considering how she hated him and all before. After he broke her heart the first time. Love's a strange bird."

Myell closed his eyes. If he somehow blocked out that eager voice, maybe he could just get in a solid block of sleep before the ouroboros came for him again. He figured he had eleven hours left in this eddy. Maybe ten.

"He was grumpy, too, Gampa. You think he'd be happy. He got the girl."

Through gritted teeth Myell said, "Shut up already."

"Though they didn't look at each other much. Or interact much. It was like they don't even know each other anymore. You think they're divorced? I could put that in the file."

Myell pulled a pillow over his head. He didn't want to hear Homer's speculations about Osherman and Jodenny's love life. In a wriggling, uneasy way he still felt guilty for interrupting their wedding. It had been a beautiful spring day in the town square, with white flowers twined in Jodenny's hair and Osherman sweating through his crisp white shirt. A small ceremony, nothing extravagant. Extravagant wasn't in Jodenny's nature, even if it had been possible. Yet the wedding had been prettier than their exchange of vows in the infirmary of the *Aral Sea,* both of them still recovering from injuries.

He was proud of the woman Lisa had grown to be. A doctor, a mother, a wife. Jodenny and Osherman's daughter, Teresa, was always kind to him. And all Jodenny's grandchildren, five of them, sprouting like weeds. He wasn't always sure he could match names to faces except for Twig, who'd latched on to him like a puppy. She was bright and eager and all the things he hadn't been as a child on Baiame.

Homer sprawled backward on the floor and laced his fingers over his belly. "She's obviously still carrying a sweet torch for you."

"She's long over me," Myell said. Getting remarried proved that. He didn't begrudge her happiness, indeed hoped for it, though it was slightly galling she had found it with Osherman and not, say, any of the other men on the *Kamchatka.*

He still hadn't wormed out of anyone how Osherman had come to be on that freighter. The last clear memory Myell had of the commander was losing him in the Wondjina transportation network built by the gods. Maybe in the next eddy he'd see how he and Jodenny were reunited, or see them in love from their first time together, or be there when either of them died.

Homer said, "You should tell her how every trip you make is about her."

"It doesn't matter," Myell said. "She won't remember."

"True." Homer heaved a sigh. "Getting to Kultana would be easier if you could control the ring."

Myell sat upright. "Then for the love of Christ tell me how."

Lightning struck somewhere close outside, so close that the sizzle and snap of it made Myell's teeth itch. The accompanying thunder nearly deafened him. For the first time Homer seemed to notice the weather. He glanced at the ceiling with a flash of fear or worry.

"I can't, Gampa," he said. "You know that. I'm only here to observe. I can't tell you how to get there, where it is, what it is, anything. You have to figure out everything for yourself. But I want you to succeed. I want you to save humanity."

The thunder and lightning subsided as the storm burnt itself out. All that was left was rain steady on the roof. Myell said, "The very fact you're here proves I succeed, right? So you've got nothing to worry about. Tell me what I need to know and let me get it done with."

Homer's eyes were wide and sad. "I wish I could. I do. I really, really do."

The kid sounded sincere.

Then again, he always did.

"Go away, Homer," Myell said, "Go back to school."

Slowly Homer faded from the room. A relief. Myell could finally get some sleep. But the conversation had left him wide awake and restless, and lonely in the narrow bed, and full of regrets he couldn't fix.

His head began to ache in earnest, and he wondered if Lisa had any painkillers in the bathroom cabinet. As quietly as possible he slipped to the door and opened it. Sheriff Alice was keeping watch from a chair in the living room.

She nodded at him. "Chief."

"Sheriff," he said, trying to speak low enough not to wake the house. "You really think I'm going to try and escape?"

"Don't know," she said. "Just being sure."

"I could go out the bedroom window."

Alice stretched her back, producing a distinctive pop. "Got a man in the garden as well."

"Wise precaution," he said.

He didn't find any painkillers in the bathroom but didn't want to wake Lisa, not for a few aches and itches. Everything was quiet but for the rain. Myell went back to his room and closed the door on Sheriff Alice. Standing by the window, he waited for his eyes to adjust to the lone streetlight. There, huddled under a tarp, was Alice's man with a mazer rifle strapped across his chest. It would be a miracle if the weapon still worked.

A shape moved behind the sentry—taller, bulkier, with claws that could kill and red eyes that glowed in the darkness.

A Roon.

Myell opened his mouth to shout for Sheriff Alice and the others. Then a last lonely flash of lightning illuminated the landscape more clearly. The Roon resolved itself into an overgrown bush, bits of twig, some hanging moss.

He stared for a long time, but saw only darkness.

CHAPTER THREE

Power's out, thanks to the storm last night," Lisa said at breakfast. "But I boiled some water for coffee."

Myell peered dubiously into the cup and took a daring sip. Unfortunately, the coffee tasted just like it smelled—like burnt tree bark with some mud mixed in for good measure. He put the cup back down.

"We had real coffee when we first got here," Baylou said, perched on a stool. He stroked his long beard. "Had a hard time replicating it out of the ship's stores. It degraded, generation after generation. The beans refused to grow. Now all we have is swill."

Teresa's kids had come over to walk with Lisa's children to school. Steven couldn't find his homework, Alton wanted more breakfast, and Twig was against the very idea of spending her day in the classroom.

"I want to stay and talk to him!" Twig said, hanging off Myell's arm.

"Is Dad coming home today?" Kyle asked, giving Myell a suspicious look. "I think he should be here."

"Your father will be back tomorrow," Lisa said. "Now, off with all of you. And behave yourselves."

After the kids were gone Myell said, mildly, "I don't think Kyle likes me."

"He doesn't know you." Lisa finished stacking the morning dishes and wiped her hands on a towel. "Now, then, what would you like to do today?"

Sheriff Alice, sitting on the sofa with her hat over her eyes, said, "You're supposed to be down at the clinic, Doc."

"Greg and Sarah can handle it," Lisa said. To Myell she said, "Scraped knees and banged thumbs, that's what we get a lot of. Once in a while someone goes into cardiac arrest, or has a stroke, or a baby gets turned around and won't come out the right way."

Baylou raised his coffee cup. "There was that time Doc Collins drove a nail into his own head by mistake."

"I remember Ensign Collins," Myell said. "Did he survive the nail?"

"Sure did. Doc Lisa here pulled it right out of his skull with a pair of pliers."

"Baylou, as always, has a problem with exaggeration." Lisa sat on a nearby stool and gave Myell a straightforward look. "When's this blue ring of yours supposed to scoop you up and take you away?"

Myell rubbed the side of his head. Sometimes he shared the information and people in the eddy believed him. Sometimes they locked him in the brig or other spaces, as if the ring might not be able to find him in a small enclosure. That never worked. The ring outwitted everyone.

"About twenty-four hours, give or take a few, after it dropped me in the creek," he said.

"There's got to be a way to stop it," Lisa said.

He shook his head mutely.

Baylou checked the clock. "Well, then. Not much time at all. You probably won't even get a slice of cake."

"Cake?" Myell asked.

"It's Sam's birthday," Lisa explained. "Come on, let's take a walk. See the town."

"I've seen it," Myell said.

Undeterred, she said, "Come on, Baylou. You can come, too."

Alice stood up with an audible crack from her knees. "Don't forget me."

Lisa shook her head. "Really, now. What kind of danger is he? Didn't murder us in our sleep last night, did he? Didn't even try."

Alice said, stubbornly, "You never know what trouble is until it shows its ugly face."

"Go get some sleep, Alice," Lisa said. "Doctor's orders."

The air outside was hot and humid, and debris from the night's storms was still littered on the ground. The settlement itself had indeed grown since its early days. The main street of homes and buildings had developed into several short streets around a grassy commons. Lisa said the population was a tad more than three hundred people, not bad considering how many they'd lost in the early years to splinter groups and illness or injury. Recycled parts of the *Kamchatka* were everywhere— bulkheads grown over with moss or rusty with age, plastiglass cloudy from sunlight, railings and porches and posts that had been stripped out of the ship and repurposed. The place had an industrious if worn look to it.

Baylou kicked at a lamppost they passed. "Most of the power conduits are beginning to fail. Damn rain and rust gets into everything. We should have scavenged more out of the ship, but who knew we'd lose her so quick? Goddamned autopilot."

"I know," Myell said. The devastating and unexpected loss of the *Kamchatka* due to engine failure, just eight months after arrival, had hampered the colony for years. The ship had never been equipped or designed to found a new world, after all. Its crew and passengers had been woefully unprepared for life in the wilderness, even if it was a wilderness just like Earth.

Baylou said, "And the crop fungus, that doesn't help things. Or the locusts—"

"It'll all work out," Lisa said optimistically. "We've come this far, right?"

They passed a number of villagers, most of whom called out a hello and gave Myell sideways looks as they went about their morning chores. From the school-house came the sound of children's laughter, followed by a teacher's stern admonishment.

"This," Baylou said, coming to an abrupt stop, "is the most important place for a hundred miles. More work gets done here than at the town hall, and don't you let anyone tell you different."

Before them was a hole-in-the-wall building, not much bigger than a shack, with tables and chairs outside on the wooden deck, and a liquor bar with a lock on it. Baylou had a key.

"Hair of the dog?" Baylou asked, proffering a bottle.

Myell accepted a shot glass of something golden-brown that tasted not quite like whiskey. Lisa demurred. She'd sat down on one of the chairs, her bare knees exposed to the sun, and was watching pedestrians go on by.

"Miss this the most," Baylou said, indicating the glass. "Everything else, I can live without. But a good drink is hard to find in these parts."

Myell figured he had a few hours or so left. Not enough time to do much but get drunk, if he wanted. And to maybe make amends that wouldn't matter once his time here was up.

"I'd like to see Jodenny," he said.

Lisa sighed. "She said she's not up for company this morning."

"She didn't mean it," Baylou said. "Love of her life, come back from the dead? It's a girl's dream come true."

"I'm not sure you should go around saying 'love of her life,'" Lisa said cautiously.

Myell glanced up from his glass, slightly hurt by the remark.

Lisa spread her hands wide. "Not saying he's wrong, mind you. Just that, well, she did marry Sam eventually. And they had Teresa, and little Teren—"

The glass slipped from Myell's hands. "They did what?"

Baylou poured himself more of the not-quite whiskey and gulped it down.

Lisa's gaze was steady on Myell. "Teren was their son. My half brother. He died when he was little, of the flu. You didn't know?"

Mutely he shook his head.

"Broke them up with grief." Her expression was rueful. "Broke up their marriage, too. Neither one of them was the same afterward. So, yes, Dad, I think you were the love of her life. But maybe not the only one."

He wasn't sure he'd earned the name "Dad." All he did was float in and out of her life, twenty-four or so hours at a time, and she never remembered him. Myell tried to imagine Jodenny and Osherman having a son, raising him, and watching him die.

"I want to talk to her," he insisted.

Jodenny's house was back along the commons and not at all far from Lisa's. Two knocks on the unlocked door brought no answer. They stepped inside. Myell had to blink several times to adjust his eyes from the bright outside to the dim light of the living room. Without power, the overhead fans were all still. The air was hot and beginning to turn sour.

"You home, Mom?" Lisa called out.

Baylou said, "Come on out. We brought the dead man by."

"Last time I was here, you weren't so funny," Myell said.

Baylou smiled crookedly. "Jungle rot. Burrows into the brain."

The living room was sparser than Myell remembered. With each passing year Jodenny was shedding herself of material possessions until only the bare essentials remained: a sofa, a table and chair, a kitchen unit. If her grandchildren ever drew pictures for her, she was hiding them in a drawer somewhere. The walls were smooth and, in a way, soothing. The best feature, as always, was the small porch out back, and the large yard running downhill toward trees and the creek.

Jodenny was sitting out on that porch. She didn't look surprised to see any of them.

"I told you I didn't want company, Lisa," she said.

Myell spoke up. "I'm not company."

Baylou said, "Maybe some more beer would smooth over this happy reconciliation?"

Jodenny said, "Get out of my house, Baylou Owenstein. And you as well, daughter number one."

Baylou went off good-naturedly. Lisa gave them both a dubious look, but left without comment. Myell sat down in the rocking chair next to Jodenny's and they both looked at the sky and trees.

"Nice weather," she finally said.

Myell asked, "You want to talk about the weather?"

"Not much else to talk about. And apparently it won't matter what we say anyway. I won't remember."

"But I will," he said.

Jodenny slid him a glance. "So this is about you."

He stared at the trees.

She pressed on. "Not that I believe you, especially, but last night you said you've been here before. That you'll leave and come back, and we won't remember you've been here. That nothing you do ever makes a permanent change."

"That's right."

She rocked in silence for a moment, then said, "How do you know for sure? Maybe things do change, and we go off on some other timeline. You just don't get to visit there."

"We've had this conversation before," he replied. "Quantum physics and time-travel theory and branching timelines and everything. Schrödinger's cat. Asimov. Einstein. Branes and string theory. Theories, all of them, nothing concrete except what Homer—"

He cut himself off.

Jodenny cocked her head. "Who's Homer?"

"You never believe me when I tell you."

"Try me."

"He's our descendent from two thousand years in the future," Myell said. "He says that there's only one time-line that runs through eternity. No matter what eddy I visit—that's what he calls them, time eddies—well, wherever, whenever, I change things temporarily but not permanently. I could kill my grandfather, I could wipe out a planet, I could do anything at all. But when I leave, the eddy dissolves and the timeline reverts to its original course. Anything I've done is washed away. He says that only the gods can change history."

"That's crazy."

"I know."

Jodenny's chin jutted forward. "I'm not going to forget you came back. I'll write it down. Burn it in stone."

"We carved it into a tree trunk once," he replied. "Over there. That big oak. Your initials and mine, and the date, and a heart. In letters as big as your fist. And then you went off and married Sam anyway."

They gazed at the oak in silence. The bark was rough but unmarked. Insects buzzed in the grass and somewhere, out on the street, kids laughed and raced around. Morning recess at the school. His time was running out quickly.

"Maybe I didn't love Sam," she said. "Maybe I just thought I did."

"Don't lie to me, Kay."

Her eyes narrowed. The same old determination blazed out of them. "I won't apologize."

"I don't want you to." He leaned forward. "Our vows said until death we do part, and I died. On some giant rock called Burringurrah back on Earth. No one but you and Osherman seem to know how, exactly, and you never tell me. No matter how much I ask, you never tell me. For all I know, I slipped on a banana peel. But dead is dead, right? Buried up there on the hill, just a bunch of bones in the dirt."

"Now you're feeling sorry for yourself," she said.

His fingers clenched on the arms of the rocking chair. "That's not true."

"Being thrown around in time is better than being dead," she said bitterly. "You're strong and young and what more do you want?"

"You," Myell said.

Jodenny's expression turned sour. "Now who's lying?"

She rose and went inside the house. Myell let her go. He didn't know how to convince her that he loved her at any age, in any condition. But it didn't matter. Soon he'd be gone and the lives of everyone here would go on as they always had.

From inside the house came a soft thump as she knocked something over.

"Kay," he said, sighing, and went to see what she'd taken her anger out on this time.

Just three steps past the screen door, in the dimness of the house, he saw her lying on the floor in a crumpled heap.

"No, no," he muttered, hands cold, dropping to his knees so hard that bone cracked on wood. Myell turned her over. "Kay! Wake up!"

Her sightless eyes stared past him to the ceiling. Stroke, maybe. Aneurysm. Heart attack. He didn't know. She wasn't breathing. He laid her back gently, opened her mouth, and forced air in.

"You don't get to die yet," he told her in a fierce voice. "I'm not gone. It's Sam's birthday. You can't die, okay?"

From outside, someone screamed.

A kid's scream, high and terrified.

It took a second scream, maybe a third, for Myell to pull himself from Jodenny's body and step outside. He immediately saw Kyle and Twig standing in the middle of the town common, a soccer ball at their feet. Kyle was holding Twig protectively. Both were staring at a big gum tree just a few meters away. Other schoolchildren had run back to the school for cover, or were hiding behind trees or buildings. Myell didn't blame them.

Standing beside the gum tree was a Roon soldier.

It stood there like a statue, imposing and hostile in the sunlight. Unlike other Roon that Myell had seen, this one wore an ornate feather and steel headdress that added half a meter to its height. From its shoulders hung a black feather cloak. Around its feet was an ouroboros shaped like a silver lizard. In one hand it held a golden, oblong egg aimed right at Twig.

"Nobody move!" Sheriff Alice was standing on the porch of the cantina, a mazer rifle aimed at the alien. "I've got it."

The Roon turned its head toward Alice. She fired. The shot zapped harmlessly around its cloak and headdress, then dissipated like tiny bolts of lightning. Kyle and Twig tried to dash toward Myell, who was closest. The alien fired red-hot bolts over their heads and they threw themselves to the ground, shrieking.

"Stay where you are!" Lisa yelled from the other side of the commons. She sounded frantic. "Stay there!"

Twig was crying. Kyle was grimly silent, his hands clutched over his head.

The Roon kept the weapon trained on the children as it turned its head again. "Teren Myell," it said, loud enough for everyone to hear.

Murmurs in the crowd. "It speaks English!" someone said.

Myell was just as startled, but he tried to appear impassive. He took several careful steps forward. "Yes, I'm him."

"Teren Myell," the Roon said again. Around its feet, the silver ouroboros spun faster and faster. "Stop your quest for Kultana or be destroyed. Stop, and be rewarded with long life and wealth."

Sheriff Alice asked, "Kul what?"

From down in the grass, her face screwed up in fear, Twig asked, "Mom? I want Mom!"

Lisa tried to step forward, but Baylou had his hand firmly on her shoulder. Lisa called out, "It's okay, honey. Just stay there with Kyle."

The Roon ignored the family drama. "Do you agree?" it asked Myell.

Myell said, "Tell me who you are."

Its head tilted sideways. "The Flying Doctor. The one who will stop this. If you cease, they will not be destroyed. If you cease, they will continue. Stop your quest for Kultana."

The sun burned against Myell's skin. In the house behind him, Jodenny's corpse was already cooling. His head ached behind his eyes and the air around him grew thin, unsubstantial. For a moment he thought it was the weight of grief, but he knew better.

The blue ring was coming for him.

The Roon's stance shifted as it lowered its weapon. "Step here and join me."

Myell didn't move toward the silver ouroboros.

He was certain—or mostly certain—that events here didn't matter. The moment he left, the eddy would dissolve. Then again, Jodenny had never died before. Nor had a Roon showed up with its very own ring. Everything might have changed, or be changing as he stood in the sunlight. He couldn't be sure of anything anymore.

"Dad," Lisa said. "Please."

Still Myell hesitated.

"You refuse," the Roon said sharply.

It raised its egg-shaped weapon again.

Sheriff Alice yelled, "Kids, run!"

Cursing, Myell dashed forward, threw himself on top of Kyle and Twig, and shielded the children from the Roon weapon. Red bolts slammed into his back but he felt nothing, not even a sizzle. Instead there was only the familiar disorienting blur of the blue ring as it appeared in the airless space around him.

He had never been more grateful for its appearance. In a split second the ring would yank him from this eddy to somewhere else—to the future or past, to the dead and living, to another Jodenny who would scorn and reject him. Kyle and Twig and all the people here would remain. They would snap back to the lives they'd been leading without his interference. They would neither remember him nor mourn him.

The flash came, but Myell was only half right.

CHAPTER **FOUR**

Sub-lieutenant Jodenny Scott knew she was over-sleeping, but even on starships, Sunday mornings allowed for some indulgence. When her gib beeped for the third time, she shoved it under her pillow and rolled over. She was dreaming of a beach, a rolling blue ocean, and a handsome man rising out of the sea. Her fantasy was interrupted when the hatch to her cabin opened and her roommate spoke loudly.

"What are you doing, Jodenny?" Ensign Dyanne Owens asked.

"Sleeping. Go away."

"You plan on missing morning quarters?"

"No quarters on Sunday."

"Too bad this is Monday."

Jodenny forced her eyes open. "It is not!"

Dyanne sat in her chair and began tugging off her boots. She'd had the midwatch, and dark circles rimmed her eyes. "Okay, it's not. You're right and the rest of the ship's wrong."

Jodenny wasn't entirely convinced. The supply wardroom aboard the *Yangtze* was notorious for pranks. She retrieved her gib from under the pillow and demanded, "Kay! What day is it?"

Her agent responded, "Today is Monday, ma'am."

Jodenny wrestled free of her sheets and flung herself toward her locker. Long years of habit from the academy meant she had put out her uniform the night before. She tugged on her pants and boots, pinned her hair up with one swift move, and didn't bother rinsing the gummy feeling out of her mouth.

"Don't forget your gib," Dyanne said when Jodenny was halfway into the passageway.

She spun on her heel, grabbed the gib off her bunk, and sprinted down the passage. A small DNGO was cleaning the carpet, smack dab in her way. Jodenny squeezed past it. Another DNGO was washing down the bulkhead. She circled around that, too. A third DNGO was hovering near the overhead, cleaning a vent. This cleaning business was getting out of hand. Jodenny ducked under the robot and barreled into the lounge area, which was inexplicably filled with a dozen other officers all grinning at her.

"Surprise!" they shouted.

Her boss, Lieutenant Jem Ross, grinned widely. "Welcome to your promotion party."

"My—" Jodenny was speechless. Her face grew hot but she matched Jem's smile. "All this for little old me?"

"All this," Dyanne confirmed, coming up behind her and slapping her shoulder.

First came the very brief ceremony, in which Jem read aloud Jodenny's promotion to full lieutenant and pinned new insignia on her collar. After that Jodenny cut the cake, which was entirely too decadent for this early on a Sunday—yes, Sunday, not Monday—morning. That she'd fallen for their dastardly plan caused no end of merriment, from ensigns to commanders alike.

"You'll get yours," Jodenny told Dyanne. "Wait until it's your turn."

Jodenny was halfway through her slice of cake and eyeing another piece when her gib beeped and said, "Lieutenant Scott, you're needed in the Security Office."

She gave Jem a dirty look, but he raised his hands innocently. "No prank. It's probably AT Tossen again, drunk on duty. Your turn to deal with him."

"I'll be right back," she told everyone. "Don't eat all my cake."

Dyanne raised a glass of punch. "We'll be here when you get back."

She took a ladder down to D-deck, which was almost deserted this early in the morning. She thought terrible things about AT Tossen. He was more trouble than worth, always in some kind of mess or another. As an academy student she'd never realized how much time and effort went into personnel management. Why people couldn't just behave and do their jobs was a mystery to her.

The Security Office was a black-and-gray space dominated by a large counter and a sergeant wearing a scowl.

"Lieutenant Scott, reporting as ordered," she said.

"Take a seat, ma'am. The commander will be out in a minute."

Jodenny sat on a long gray bench. One minute turned into two and three and four as she sat with nothing interesting to do but stare at the deck, the counter, or the overhead. She checked her imail but didn't have the heart to start tackling the junior sailor evaluations piling up in her queue. Wistfully she thought of her promotion party carrying on without her, and resolved to make Tossen regret this morning for months to come.

She started to fidget, her stomach rumbled, and she longed for a big hot cup of anything filled with caffeine. Normally she drank only coffee but lately Jem had been drinking a special drink called horchata. Another ten minutes passed. Just as she was thinking about finding a vending machine, a hatch opened down the passageway and reprieve arrived in the shape of Commander Delaney, the Security Officer.

Delaney was a tall woman, big in the shoulders, and though they'd been at functions together Jodenny had never spoken to her one-on-one. She looked like she hadn't had any sleep at all. Tossen really must have gotten himself in trouble this time to require attention from Delaney herself.

"Lieutenant Scott, come on back," Delaney said.

They went down the passageway to a large conference room. Inside were two guards, a med tech, and some officers Jodenny didn't know. At the table were a teenage boy, a younger girl, and a man with his head pillowed on his left arm. No one looked very happy, but the girl and boy perked up instantly when they saw Jodenny.

"Nana!" The girl rose from her seat.

Jodenny recoiled. She inadvertently brushed up against a tall lieutenant commander.

He said, rather casually, "She called me Grandpa."

"Twig, sit." The man lifted his head and tugged the girl back into her chair. "She doesn't know you. Neither of them do."

"What kind of joke is this?" Jodenny demanded.

Commander Delaney shook her head. "Stowaways. With a most unusual story, though, including some rather tall tales about you and Lieutenant Commander Osherman here."

"We're not stowaways." The teenage boy stared defiantly at Jodenny. "I'm Kyle and this is Twig. You're our grandmother. This is Terry Myell. He's your husband, or at least he's going to be."

Osherman asked, "Then how am I your grandfather?"

Twig said, "You're going to be her husband, too."

Osherman made a faint noise of protest. Jodenny wanted to protest as well.

Delaney said, "According to Core, Sergeant Myell here is an active duty sailor stationed on the *Okeechobee*. But his dog tag lists his rank as a chief, with Lieutenant Commander Jodenny Scott as his legal spouse, and the most recent entries are dated three years from now."

"I've been trying to tell you. We're time travelers," Myell said wearily. He gave Jodenny the quickest of glances, as if it were painful to see her. "Any chance of getting some coffee?"

Myell had woken up just a few hours ago, relieved.

He was accustomed to waking up in unusual situations, often in darkness, far too often in some kind of danger. This new place was indeed dark, but also quiet and soothing. The air wasn't too warm or too cold. It smelled faintly like machinery. The background hum of a spaceship, perhaps. The floor beneath him felt like a metallic deck, and when he blinked his eyes open he saw conduits and ducts. Definitely a ship, then. He liked that. He might be able to blend in, steal some food, maybe grab a change of clothes.

He stood up, wincing at the ache in his back. Whatever the Roon had hit him with, it wasn't nice. As he straightened, he nearly hit his head. The overhead was low and busy with ducts.

Then he realized he wasn't alone, and bumped his head anyway.

"Where are we?" Kyle asked from where he was sitting against the bulkhead.

Twig, huddled beside him, was crying. "I want my mom."

"What are you two doing here?" Myell asked, sounding stupid even to himself.

Kyle pulled himself up. He was short enough that the pipes ran harmlessly over his head. "Are we on a ship?"

Neither of them had ever been on a spaceship, of course. They might have seen pictures or records, especially of the *Kamchatka*, but their experience was the forest and beach, and running barefoot through Providence.

"How did you get here?" he asked, still confused.

"There was a flash of light," Kyle said. "What did you do? Where's home?"

"I don't know." As soon as the words were out, Myell knew he had made a mistake. He was the adult here, a grandfather even if his first child hadn't been born yet. He had a responsibility to be confident and parental so the children wouldn't panic.

Too bad he was the one already panicking. Homer had never told him he could take anyone with him through the blue ouroboros. He had no idea how that worked. Or how to get them back where they belonged.

Twig hugged her knees close. "I want my mom."

"All right, look." Myell crouched down beside them. "We're on a Team Space ship. If we wait long enough, the blue ring will come and take us away. But you've got to stick by me, got it? All the time."

Kyle demanded, "What about the Roon? Is it here, too?"

"I don't think so," Myell said. "I never saw it before, and there's no reason to believe it can follow us. Anyone asks, you stay quiet. Leave it to me to handle."

Twig squinted at him. "Why?"

Kyle said, "How do we know you can handle it?"

"Because I've got a lot more experience than you," Myell said. "And if we are where I think we are, they're not going to believe you anyway. The people here don't know anything about the Roon yet."

And he gave them that little speech just in time, too, because five minutes later two security techs showed up, alerted by remote sensors to trespassers in the T6 cargo hold. Myell was dismayed to see *Yangtze* patches on their sleeves. The *Yangtze* was a doomed ship, fated to explode off Kookaburra. If the kids noticed the patches or recognized their significance, they didn't say. Myell tried to convince the guards that they were colonists who had gotten lost, but they didn't have any ship identification cards.

It also didn't help when one of the security techs ran his gib near Myell's collarbone and picked up on his dog tag.

"Says you're Chief Teren Myell of the Supply Corps," the tech said. He gave Myell's worn clothes another lookover. "You don't look like a chief."

Myell said, "I'm not. Your machine's wrong."

One of the techs turned to Kyle. "Is this really your father, kid?"

Myell hoped Kyle would be less than forthcoming, but Kyle said, "Actually, he's my sort of grandfather."

"Uncle," Myell corrected. "Uncle Terry, that's me."

The tech raised his eyebrow.

The techs decided to bring them back to Mainship to sort everything out. The five of them took the lift up to the access ring and crossed over to the Rocks. The long promenade of shops and restaurants was empty of people, and the sky on the overhead vid was just beginning to brighten with sunrise. They boarded the first car of an arriving tram and Kyle, obviously awestruck, pressed his forehead to the nearest window as they crossed the umbilical shaft to Mainship.

Twig wasn't as impressed. She was quiet and wide-eyed, and clung to Myell's side. He supposed getting caught by Security didn't really matter. The three of them would get fed and quartered until the ouroboros showed up. He thought he'd understood the rules of the ring, how it was determined to fling him around the universe willy-nilly and alone. Maybe he understood nothing at all.

"Is Lieutenant Scott on duty?" he asked one of the techs.

"Why do you ask?"

"She's my division officer. And my wife."

The first tech cracked a smile. "I think you're drunk, Chief."

"I wish," he said. "Could you call her, please? She needs to know."

And he needed to know she was alive.

But the tech didn't call Jodenny. Myell refrained from wrestling the gib out of his hands and doing it himself. There was time, he told himself, finding no amusement in the thought. The techs took them to the Security office and put them in a conference room. An ensign showed up to ask questions, followed by a lieutenant, followed eventually by Commander Delaney. Myell decided to be as honest as possible.

"We're from the future, we travel in time, this is my granddaughter Twig, this is my wife's grandson Kyle, can you call her? And Commander Sam Osherman, too. He's Kyle's grandfather."

Osherman arrived, looking impossibly young, followed soon by Jodenny, whose loveliness hit Myell in the gut all over again. Alive, young, disbelieving. Good for her. Skepticism was a healthy trait in a junior officer. He told them all that they wouldn't remember any of this later, and of course they didn't believe that, either.

"This isn't getting us anywhere," Commander Delaney finally said. "The children will be put in temporary foster care. Sergeant Myell, you're obviously AWOL from your current duty station. I don't know why you falsified the personal information on your dog tag, or what you hope to gain from this charade, but maybe a stay in the brig will convince you how serious this prank of yours is."

"The brig!" Myell said.

Twig latched on to Myell's arm. "No! We're not going anywhere."

Delaney said, calmly, "I'm afraid we don't have much choice. It'll take a while for us to analyze the DNA samples you provided. Do you have some other kind of proof to support your story, Sergeant?"

The bit about the samples was crap, of course. The results would be back almost immediately as long as they had the right equipment. Myell could tell them about the disaster down the road, the lives that would be destroyed when the *Yangtze* was lost, but that wasn't proof. He could tell them who would win the historic soccer match between Dunredding and Boomerang Moon, but that was another six months away. No one on this ship could verify the classified information he knew about the Wondjina Transportation System.

Aside from spilling intimate details about Jodenny, his only recourse was revealing information about someone else.

Myell said, "I'll talk to Commander Osherman. Just the two of us."

Delaney said, "Why?"

"Alone, please," Myell said.

Osherman nodded.

The kids stayed with Jodenny and the other officers while Myell and Osherman were led to a separate room. Myell was acutely aware of the overhead camera watching them.

He said, "If I were you, I'd ask them to stop recording."

"Why's that?" Osherman asked.

"Because I know your background, Commander. I've met you in the future on the *Aral Sea,* and I've met you even further in the future when you're marrying my wife, and I've met you when you're eighty years old and hate my guts. But right now, right here, I know all about your current duty assignment, and I don't mean the Data Department."

Osherman gave him a steady look. Myell didn't fidget or flinch. After a moment's consideration. Osherman left the room. While he was gone Myell rested his head on his arms again and counted to a hundred. The hum of the ship was strangely comforting, even if the whole vessel was doomed. Osherman returned a few minutes later and sat across from him.

"Go ahead, Sergeant," he said. "I'll give you five minutes."

"You'll give me more than that, sir. You work for the Inspector General office. You were stationed here undercover to investigate a smuggling ring, and that smuggling ring extends not only through the Supply and Data Department on this ship but on a dozen others."

Osherman's expression was inscrutable. "You don't say."

Myell kept going. "The point is that I *won't* say, not as long as you keep me out of the brig. I want temporary quarters with the kids. Keep us together, and you can ask all the questions you want."

"And you'll answer them?"

"I'll answer what I can," Myell said. "But I won't embarrass Jodenny."

"Tell me more about the smugglers."

"How do I know you won't throw me in the brig anyway?"

"Because you know me," Osherman said. "Or so you say."

"I knew you once," Myell replied. "We weren't exactly friends."

"I'm not worried about being your friend, Sergeant Myell."

On that, at least, they had something in common.

A half hour later, Myell was reunited with Kyle and Twig in temporary quarters on C-deck. The quarters weren't anything more than two cabins and a lounge, but it was better accommodations than the brig. Commander Delaney had restricted them there under guard, with techs stationed both inside and outside of the hatch.

They had twenty hours or so before the ouroboros arrived.

And maybe the Flying Doctor, too.

You believe this crazy story?" Jem asked.

Jodenny shrugged. They were in Jem's office in the Supply Flats, which were on minimal staffing because of Sunday schedule. Jodenny was standing at a window overlooking loading dock G. Down below, DNGOs loaded and unloaded smart crates for distribution throughout Mainship.

"I don't know," Jodenny said truthfully.

"So they're traveling in time, and we're just some temporary bubble that's going to pop when they leave. We're not even going to remember they've been here. Is that it?"

"So he claims."

"Very convenient. What did Medical say?"

"We're still waiting."

Jem kicked back in his chair. "It's not your everyday wild story. But if it's true, ask him where to invest money. What sports to bet on. You know, useful things."

"It doesn't make sense that he'd leave the *Okeechobee*

to go AWOL here," she said. "Besides which, they're four months behind us in the Alcheringa. How could he possibly have gotten onboard? And his dog tag? Why fake something like that?"

Jem picked up a genuine-leather, antique baseball from his desk. "Maybe he's just a stalker."

"You're not helping," she said.

"And you're getting too involved."

She turned from the window. "How can I not get involved if he's my future husband and those are my future grandkids?"

Jem tossed her the ball. "Just don't get all wrapped up in it. You always root for the underdog, which is great. But it's going to turn you prematurely gray, too. Instead of worrying about it, freshly minted lieutenant of mine, why don't you sit down and take a swing at these personnel evaluations? They're due tomorrow and we're only halfway through."

She tried to concentrate on the evaluations but in the quiet of the office she kept remembering the timbre of Myell's voice, and the look in his eyes when he gazed at her. When Medical called, it was almost a relief. Almost.

"You're sure?" she asked Dr. Coates twice.

"I'm forwarding the results to your queue, Lieutenant. You can see the sequence matches yourself."

Jodenny stared at the report for several long moments. Jem came to peer over her shoulder.

"Well, then," he said. "Congratulations. You're a grandma."

"I think I need a drink," she said.

"Just ignore it. Go back to your cabin, get some rest. We woke you up pretty early this morning. Come to dinner in the wardroom and I'll buy you a beer or two."

"Sure," she said, and closed down the DNA report.

She did go back to her cabin. Dyanne had gone off to get lunch, but Jodenny wasn't hungry. Instead she scrolled through her queue, made a halfhearted attempt on the evals for AT Harrison, who was a great performer, and AT Grant, smart but a troublemaker. After several minutes of rewriting the same paragraph over and over, she tried accessing Myell's performance records. She didn't have the clearance in Core.

With Osherman she had more luck.

"His public biography is on file in Core," Jodenny's agent replied, when queried. "Would you like me to display it?"

"Read it to me." She sat back on her bunk with her eyes closed as the computer recited Osherman's commissioning date, his ship assignments, his awards. His career so far was solid but unspectacular. Nothing she heard especially intrigued her. Like Jodenny, he was an academy graduate. Myell, on the other hand, would have started at the very bottom of the enlisted ranks and worked his way up. She pictured both of them in her mind. Osherman, tall and sandy-haired, dry and wry with his Kiwi accent. Myell, younger and more serious, with an intense gaze and something he was hiding. Time traveler.

Her future husbands, if Myell and the kids were to be believed.

Sitting in her cabin wasn't going to get her any more answers.

Up on C-deck, she found two security techs guarding the temporary quarters where Myell and the kids had been billeted. One of the techs checked her name against his access list and then let her in. Inside was a small lounge filled with comfortable furniture and a vidscreen. A kitchenette with a table and chairs was off to one side. A young tech was sprawled on the floor in front of the vid, teaching the kids how to play Izim.

"Is this how you stand watch?" Jodenny asked him sternly.

The tech stood hastily. "Sorry, ma'am!"

"At ease. Where's Sergeant Myell?"

Twig frowned. "He's a chief."

"Not yet, dummy," Kyle said.

"Stop calling me dummy!"

The security tech nodded toward one of the bedrooms. "He's back there, ma'am. With Commander Osherman, Commander Delaney, and some people from the Data Department. They're not supposed to be disturbed."

Twig climbed up on one of the sofas. She was amazingly skinny, all elbows and knees. "Are you staying for dinner? They're bringing chocolate ice cream. We never get to eat chocolate ice cream."

Jodenny lied instantly and without regret. "I have to stand watch."

"You could get out of it," Kyle said. "If you wanted to."

She didn't like the challenge in his eyes, or the way he saw through her. "There will be plenty of time to have dinner. We're two weeks from stopping at Kiwi."

Kyle's gaze slid back to Izim and he didn't bother to argue with her. Still perched on the back of the sofa, Twig said, "You look really young. How old are you?"

"Twenty-six. How old are you?"

"Ten. And he's thirteen, but he thinks he's so smart."

Kyle threw a pillow at her.

Twig ducked it and nearly toppled to the floor. Jodenny caught her arm and kept her upright.

"None of that." Jodenny cast a gaze at Myell's closed hatch and weighed the consequences of disturbing Commander Delaney. "Sit down properly and show me how you play this game."

She knew how to play Izim, of course, but it was mildly entertaining to watch Twig try to explain the various levels and puzzles to her. The security tech, Hadley, retreated to the main hatch to stand his guard. Kyle listened to Twig's explanations with growing exasperation and finally grabbed the pointer from her hands.

"You don't do it that way, stupid."

"Give it back! Nana, tell him to give it to me."

Jodenny blinked at the name. "I'm not your nana. Yet."

"You will be," Twig said. "When you're old."

"How old?"

Kyle's gaze was fixed on the screen. "Where we came from, you're seventy. Older than almost everyone else."

"Am I happy?"

Twig made a face. "Your back hurts, because you fell a few years ago. And your leg and hips hurt, because you broke them once. You never told us how. But you're gray and all wrinkled and you're grumpy a lot, but sometimes not so much."

Kyle remained silent on the matter, focused on the game.

Myell's hatch opened. Osherman, Commander Delaney, and two officers Jodenny didn't recognize emerged, all of them looking grim-faced. Osherman stayed behind as the others left.

"You saw the medical results?" he asked Jodenny.

She nodded.

"Bit awkward," Osherman said, running his fingers through his short hair. "You, me, and him."

"There is no me, you, and him," Jodenny said.

"You don't believe in time travel?"

"You do?"

He said, "I believe in genetics testing. Kyle has your DNA and mine. Twig carries DNA from both you and Sergeant Myell. That's mighty strange, don't you think?"

"No odder than a man claiming to be a time traveler." Jodenny glanced at the kids, but they appeared engrossed in the game. The sounds of explosions and gunfire rang out from the screen.

"He's fairly persuasive, Lieutenant. You should talk to him."

She took that as a dare. Myell's hatch was still open. He was sitting on the bed considering his own bare feet. He wriggled his toes and flexed his heels.

"Hello, Kay," he said, without much enthusiasm.

Jodenny leaned against the open hatchway in an attempt to look casual. "Why do you call me that? That's the name of my computer agent."

"I know. Did you come to hear stories about the future?"

"Maybe," she said.

He nodded toward an empty chair, but she didn't move. She said, "I received the medical reports."

Myell poured himself some water from a plastic pitcher. "So you know it's true. They're both your grandchildren, with different grandfathers. Myself and Commander Osherman."

"I still don't understand how."

"It's not that hard, is it, Lieutenant?"

She didn't like the sarcasm in his voice. Didn't like it one bit.

Jodenny said, "If I married an enlisted man, I'd be brought up on fraternization charges."

"There's ways around that."

"And we found them?"

Myell gave her a bland smile that meant nothing at all.

Jodenny folded her arms. "I hope this doesn't ruin the course of time, but I don't even like you."

"Doesn't matter." Myell reached for a pair of gray socks balled up on the deck. The boots beside them were freshly issued and spotlessly clean. "You know what I like best about Team Space? The socks. Excellent socks. You get them wet and they dry out. You rip them, and they mend back together. When your toes get cold they warm them up, and when your feet are hot they cool them off. My first day in boot camp, when I got my first pair, I knew I'd made the right decision."

"You're a man of simple pleasures. Obviously that's why I fall in love with you."

He pulled one of the excellent socks onto his left foot. "Who said anything about love? Maybe I just knock you up. Maybe we get married when we're drunk and you're going through a fit of rebelliousness. Maybe we get married just so you can screw me over for Sam. He's an officer, after all."

"And you're enlisted, so that's Commander Osherman to you."

The half-smile returned. "Commander Osherman. Yes, ma'am."

Jodenny wanted to take the remaining sock and shove it into his mouth. Good looks could only get this sailor so far, future husband or not. "Why are you here? Why are you traveling through time with grandchildren in tow? Some sort of strange vacation?"

"There's nothing relaxing about this." Myell pulled on his boots. "We were thrown here. I don't know how it works or how to control it. I don't know how to get them home, or if any of us can ever go home."

"Where's home to you?" she asked.

He shook his head.

She took a deep breath. "I don't believe your story, Sergeant. You appear to have convinced Commander Osherman, and who knows what Commander Delaney thinks. The tests say one thing but they can be wrong, or mixed up, or there could be some reasonable explanation other than time travel. This is my life we're talking about. My career. Which I don't intend on throwing away anytime soon."

His expression was shuttered. "Which is what you'd do, marrying me? Throw your life away?"

Jodenny spun away and left him with his socks.

CHAPTER **FIVE**

S o let me get this straight," Ensign Hawkins said, hoisting his beer. "You just put on your full lieutenant bars this morning and already you're a grandma? Fast work!"

The wardroom was busy and loud, and Jodenny regretted coming. Everyone appeared to have heard the tale of the time-traveling sergeant and the ridiculous claims about her future love life. Gossip had run rife through the department all day—nay, the entire ship, no doubt—and she was feeling like the butt of a particularly bad joke.

"Fraternization, too," said Lieutenant Holt, sitting on the stool at Jodenny's elbow. "Breaking ranks for love. That's our girl."

Another word or two and she was going to poke both of them in the eye. Dyanne rescued her before that could happen by taking her elbow and steering her toward a set of faux-leather chairs in the corner. In just a few minutes the hour would strike and they'd have to sit for dinner, but for now they had a moment of privacy.

"What are you doing here?" Dyanne asked.

Jodenny lifted her beer stein. "Getting sloshed."

"Your future husband is sitting in a cabin with your future grandchildren, and you're here? Aren't you at all curious?"

"It's a hoax!" Jodenny insisted. "Or another prank."

Dyanne gave her an impatient look. "A joke perpetuated by the Security Officer known so much for her sense of humor? By the doctors, who have nothing to do but yank your chain? Listen to yourself."

"No, you listen to yourself. There is no such thing as time travel. You were in the same academy physics classes I was. It's impossible."

"Impossible just means they haven't figured it out yet. What's really impossible is why you're here when you should be there. Don't you think they're scared? Don't you think they need you?"

Jodenny drank more beer and let her gaze roam over the familiar faces of her fellow officers as they chatted and joked. These men and women aboard the *Yangtze* were her true family. She didn't need any more than that. Didn't want it.

"I'll see them tomorrow," she told Dyanne.

"How do you know they'll even be here?"

Alarm spiked through her. "Why wouldn't they be?"

"Hello? Time travelers? Seems to me that if they can show up anytime they want, they could leave anytime as well."

The wardroom bell rang. People started toward their chairs at the long, formal table. Jodenny gazed at the bottom of her beer and then at Dyanne's earnest, eager face.

"If it were me," Dyanne said, "I'd go to him."

Jodenny replied, "I'm not you."

Dinner was excruciating.

The last thing Myell wanted was to share a meal with Osherman sitting across the table looking so young and vibrant while he himself felt scuffed and worn down, like the bottom of a boot. He'd almost retreated to his cabin, but he wasn't going to just stand by while this version of Sam Osherman made nice with the kids and tried to worm whatever information he could get out of them. Besides which, Myell was starving for a good hot meal.

The food sent up by the galley was tasty enough, and he shoveled into the ravioli and mushrooms and green beans while Twig and Kyle told stories about the future.

"—and so the ship gets thrown all this way across the galaxy and we're all stranded there, but this was before we were born," Twig said, summarizing the salient history of the *Kamchatka*.

Osherman nodded intently. "Because a snake came out of the sky, is that it?"

"Nobody really believes that," Kyle said, speaking for his generation. "It was the Roon."

"Oh, yes, the aliens," Osherman said, flicking his gaze toward Myell. "Who invaded Earth. Or will invade Earth, just a few years down the road."

Myell glared at the kids. He specifically remembered telling them not to talk about that.

"*Tried* to," Twig stressed. "When Grandpa here was killed on Burringurrah. But now he's back."

Myell deliberately reached for another dinner roll. Sure, he'd died on Burringurrah, but he still didn't know how exactly, or even why. He didn't feel dead. "Why don't you tell the commander about your schoolwork?"

Osherman refused to be sidetracked. "How is it you die, exactly, Sergeant?"

"Tragic spaceship accident," Myell said. "Flattened by a birdie."

He didn't mean to sound so flippant—or maybe he did. Because he'd been answering questions all day now, hundreds of them, for Osherman or Delaney or the men from the Data Department, and he was damned tired of it. He regretted being sarcastic and cruel to Jodenny but she'd come to him with more questions, always more questions, and none of them mattered because the answers would evaporate as soon as the ouroboros came to take them away.

He only hoped the Flying Doctor didn't show up instead.

"Flattened by a birdie," Osherman said. "That's a unique way to go, Sergeant."

"It doesn't matter how I die," he said flatly. "We all do, sooner or later. On this ship or the next ship or on Earth or on the other side of the galaxy, and there's nothing I can do to change it. What happens will happen. And people will die screaming, and the world will be smoke and ash, and what's the use, if it's already written in stone?"

The three of them stared at him as if he'd lost his mind.

He pushed away the plate and stood up. His feet carried him toward the hatch before he even knew he wanted to leave the suite. RT Hadley from Security held up a hand and said, "You're not authorized to go anywhere, Sergeant," and Myell almost punched him.

"Let me out," he told Hadley.

"I can't without authorization, Sarge."

"Out of my way," Myell warned. Because as friendly and helpful as Hadley had been, he was the one obstacle Myell could do something about.

The hatch opened and was blocked by Jodenny, who was wearing her dinner uniform. She looked surprised to see Myell standing there.

"What's going on?" she asked.

Osherman rose from the table. "Lieutenant Scott, you're just in time. Will you keep the children company? The sergeant and I were about to take a walk."

Jodenny looked uncertain. "A walk?"

Hadley said, "I'm not supposed to let him out, sir."

"It's all right. I'll authorize it. Commander Delaney won't mind."

Hadley started to object again, but Osherman was already steering Myell into the passageway.

Myell shrugged off the guiding hand and headed for the nearest ladder. The rungs were cool and sturdy under his fingers. He climbed down with no destination in mind. The galley on D-deck was busy with crowds, and he ducked away. The gym on E-deck was also teeming with sailors. Wasn't there any place on the entire damned ship where a man could be alone in his thoughts, and breathe without sucking in someone else's body odor, sweat, fear? He pushed open a hatch and stepped into the ship's library, which was a curved dark room with individual reading booths. A vidded expanse of stars stretched from the carpeted deck to domed overhead.

"What's wrong, Sergeant?" Osherman asked, following him inside.

"Chief," he corrected. "Or maybe not. It doesn't matter, does it?"

"Why don't you come sit down for a moment?"

"I'm not having a nervous breakdown," Myell said, though maybe he was. He paced toward the shelves and then away again, his hands fisted. Fight or flight. He told himself there was no reason to panic but reason couldn't belt back the hammering of his heart or the tightness in his lungs. "I'm not claustrophobic."

Osherman sat on a padded chair. "Wouldn't matter. There's nothing wrong with a healthy fear of enclosed spaces."

"You're just saying that."

"Let's just say I never plan to go spelunking. God's honest truth."

Myell scrubbed the side of his head. He needed a haircut. He needed a lot of things. He felt like he was going to vomit up those mushroom raviolis. "You lie all the time."

"Part of my job," Osherman said.

Myell pressed his face against the vid screen, glad for the coolness. He closed his eyes. "You won't remember any of this. The next time we meet, you'll have to be convinced all over again. All of you, convinced."

"Sounds wearisome."

"You have no idea."

"Well, then," Osherman said. "I know an excellent remedy. How about a beer or two?"

Myell opened his eyes. "Christ, yes."

"Come on. I know just the place."

It's bedtime," Jodenny announced.

Kyle said, "I don't want to."

Twig added, "We should wait up for them."

"Bed," Jodenny insisted. The two of them had dark circles under their eyes and had been yawning steadily for the last half hour. "Wash up, brush your teeth, and look in the closet for something to sleep in."

Kyle said, "You're bossy, just like she is."

"Bed," Jodenny repeated.

The kids' room had two single beds in it. Once cleaned up and changed into pajamas, Kyle jumped onto his mattress and began punching his pillow into submission. Twig wanted someone to tuck her in. Jodenny pulled back the covers, helped her get settled, and adjusted the blankets and sheets accordingly. She almost smoothed Twig's bangs back from her eyes, but settled instead for fluffing the pillow.

Twig yawned and said, "I want my mom. She's going to be worried."

"I'm sure she is," Jodenny said.

"You didn't have a mom."

Jodenny blinked. "Of course I did. She and my father died when I was very little."

From the other bed Kyle said, "You never talk about it. Where you grew up, or how."

"I don't?"

"You don't talk about much," Kyle replied. "You say the past is the past, and there's no use rehashing it."

Jodenny said, "Sometimes that's true."

She went back to the living area and tried to imagine herself at age seventy. The picture wouldn't come. After a few minutes of sitting on the comfortable sofa, she felt herself nodding off and curled around a large cushion. Her nap went undisturbed until Osherman and Myell stumbled in just before midnight.

Osherman burped loudly. "Sorry to wake you."

"Where have you two been?" she demanded.

"At the Pub with No Beer," Myell said, naming one of the crew pubs on F-deck.

They reeked of whiskey, and had the glassy-eyed stares of men on close terms with the bottoms of drinking glasses. Though she wasn't sure they'd used glasses and not just swigged out of the bottle. Osherman was walking especially stiffly, careful with every small movement. Myell was boneless and sloppy as he flopped down on the sofa beside her.

"We've been talking about you." He rested his head on a cushion and gave her a puppy-dog look. "But nothing bad."

Jodenny rose swiftly. "I'm so glad you had fun. I'm leaving now."

"Don't you want to know?" Myell asked.

Osherman, who was standing with one hand pressed to the bulkhead, said, "I'm going to break your heart, and then he's going to die on you, and then we're going to get married and have a daughter, and then our son's going to die. But we want to apologize."

"For the inconvenience," Myell added.

"You're both idiots," she said, and headed for the hatch.

"Jo, wait." Osherman caught her by the arm. "Say goodbye. He's going to be leaving soon."

Myell nodded earnestly, then burped.

"Leaving? Where's he going?"

"Blue ring," Myell said. "Very pretty. Comes to take me away. So I can save mankind."

He sounded earnest enough. For a lunatic.

"When is the blue ring coming?" Osherman asked.

Myell waved a hand. "Tomorrow. Say, noon? Noon would be good. I need to sleep in a little. Homer, make it so!"

Jodenny asked, "Who's Homer?"

Osherman shook his head.

She leaned closer. "Can you make it stop, Sergeant?"

"Nope." Myell slid sideways and burrowed into the sofa cushion. His eyes were sliding shut. "Don't know how."

"It's a very peculiar thing, this time travel," Osherman said.

Peering closely at him, she realized he was far less drunk than he appeared. Jodenny glanced back at Myell, who was snoring loudly. She said, "You got him drunk on purpose."

Osherman shrugged. "Got him to talk more."

"Anything worthwhile?"

"He loves you," Osherman replied. "Or he did, once. Before you started rejecting him at every turn."

"I've never even met him," Jodenny retorted.

"Do you remember Richi Miller's party? The Ithaca Café?"

The Ithaca Café on Porter Street had been a favorite of academy students for generations. Strong coffee, breakfast available at every hour, and when Jodenny had liberty there was always a friendly face or two to be found in the large vinyl booths. Richi was a bright guy, funny and stubborn, not the military type at all.

His father the general had pressured him into joining. For his birthday during their last year there had just been four or five of them from political science class, a few rounds of beer, a lot of peanuts and chips.

The most memorable part of the evening was when she and Richi slipped out to the alley for some kissing and groping, and returned flushed and smiling to their friends. If Myell was a time traveler, dropping in and out of her life without consequences, he could have been there at the party. Could have seen her with her hand cupping Richi Miller's firm backside, seen his hand fondling her breasts.

"This is all ridiculous," Jodenny said.

"If you don't believe him, why are you sticking around?" Osherman asked.

She glanced at the sofa but didn't answer.

"This blue ring of his," Osherman said. "He says it takes him around places, through space and time. He's trying to find something called Kultana. We looked it up while we were down in the pub. It's a male god from Aboriginal Australia, or sometimes a female god. From the Land of the Dead, or sometimes in charge of the rain. There's also a Kultana orchid, a village in India back on Earth, a Kultana museum on Mary River, and at least a dozen other possibilities. He says he knew all that, and none of them seem to fit the bill."

"So what's next?"

"If that ring shows up tomorrow, I intend to be here. Along with scientists and security guards and anyone else who might help us catch it."

"You want to catch it?"

"You don't?"

She thought that over. An intergalactic device that could transport someone across the galaxy and through time. The benefit of that to humanity could be enormous.

"Well," Jodenny said. "What kind of future wife would I be if I let you have all the fun?"

"Gampa," a voice said. "Wake up."

Myell rolled away into the warmth and softness of his blankets. He didn't want to talk to Homer. Didn't want to talk to anyone. His head hurt and his tongue felt thick, and he had the sneaking suspicion he was due a massive hangover if he actually dared to wake up.

"It's about the kids," Homer insisted.

He forced one eye open. The room was dark, but Homer was backlit by spectral blue light. Nice special effect, that. Homer was full of special effects

"What about them?" Myell croaked out.

"The ouroboros will be here soon. For you. Only for you. You can't take them with you."

Myell wished he had more whiskey. Or something smooth and warm to ease the grit in his mouth. "What the hell are you talking about?"

"The ouroboros is only for you," Homer insisted. "It's geared to your brainwaves, your body print. You damaged it by bringing the kids with you this last trip. It's like too many people clinging to one life preserver. You bring them again, and you all might drown."

Myell pulled himself up and sat against the bulkhead for support. He was still wearing the civilian clothes they'd given him, along with the excellent socks. His boots had disappeared, though. He squinted at Homer's bright light. "Did you say drown?"

Homer stepped back from the bed, bringing some of the light with him. He was dressed today all in red, with a silver cummerbund and large white sneakers. "I mean you can't do it. You'll get yourselves killed."

Myell pressed the palms of his hands to his eyes. "But I can't—I can't leave them here. They need their home. Their parents."

"They are at home. With their parents. The minute you left, the temporary eddy dissolved. Any changes you made dissolved with it."

"I don't think I've had enough alcohol to understand this conversation."

"Kyle and Twig are home in their beds right now, in Providence. The ones who are here are just remnants."

"And if I leave them here, they'll just—what? Cease to exist? Die?"

Homer sighed. "I don't make the rules of time travel, Gampa. I just report them. It's not dying if they're not supposed to be here at all."

"Sounds like dying to me," Myell insisted. "Besides, it wasn't my idea to bring them along anyway. There was a Roon. In Providence. Did you know about that? Is that in your historical records?"

"A Roon?" Homer squeaked out. "What do you mean?"

A knock on the hatch disturbed them. Myell stepped out of bed and slid his hand over the latch. Jodenny was outside, still in her uniform, looking tired.

"Is everything okay?" she asked, her voice low enough not to carry to the kids' room. "I heard you talking to someone."

Myell turned, but Homer was already gone.

"It was nothing," he said. "What time is it?"

"Almost oh-three-hundred."

Too early for the blue ring to show up, then. He still had a few hours. He turned into the cabin's small head and splashed cold water on his face. A merciful world would have provided some aspirin in the cabinet but the shelves were empty. Maybe someone thought he'd do something dangerous with it. But Sam Osherman was the dangerous one, him and that goddamned whiskey. He settled for swallowing cold water from his cupped hand. The sharpness made him cough, and he rubbed his chest.

He emerged from the head hoping that Jodenny had left, but she was sitting in the chair by the bed. She had turned the lights on, low.

"I'm really tired, Lieutenant," Myell said.

She didn't budge. "Who's Homer? You were talking to him. And you mentioned him earlier."

"I talk in my sleep. He's just someone I worked with once."

She didn't look like she believed him.

He tried to look innocent and sincere.

"Tell me about the academy," Jodenny finally said. "You've traveled in time and met me there?"

Myell sat on the edge of the mattress. He didn't know why he expected this Jodenny to be any less stubborn than the other ones. "It's not important."

"It's important to me."

He was careful with his words. "You were younger than now, but not by much. You were happy, I guess. You liked being in the academy. Liked the rules and camaraderie."

"That's not very specific."

He met her gaze squarely. "Your hair was short. Only came down to your shoulders. You were skinnier than you are now. Maybe a size smaller."

The tips of her ears turned red. "That's all?"

Myell coughed. "You kissed him."

Jodenny leaned back in her chair. Myell listened to the ever-present hum of the ship. His hangover was getting worse, not better. His head hurt with a steady throb and his chest was getting tighter. But it was the memory of her kissing Richi Miller in the alley that still stung, even though it had been several eddies since he'd seen it happen.

"You're jealous," she said.

He didn't deny it.

"Did you introduce yourself? Did we talk?"

"We talked." Another cough pushed out of his chest. "You weren't very—"

He stopped then, appalled, and rose off the bed. "It's coming. Get the kids."

"What's coming?" Jodenny stood as well. "It's three in the morning—"

Myell pushed past her to Twig and Kyle's room. The hatch slid open under his approach. "Kids, get up, wake up."

Jodenny, following, grasped his arm. "What's wrong?"

The lights flared up. Kyle grimaced and Twig said, "Nana?"

"It's all right." Jodenny scooped Twig up in her arms. "Nothing's going to happen."

Myell tugged Kyle from bed. "The ouroboros. It's coming for us. Hold on tight and don't let go, okay?"

"But I don't want to go," Twig said in Jodenny's arms. "I want to stay here!"

Osherman appeared at the hatch with a security tech behind him. "What's going on?"

"It's early," Myell's breath was a painful wheeze now. "It's coming right now. Twig, come here."

She buried her face in Jodenny's shoulder, her thin arms shaking. "No."

He tried to go to her, to wrench her away, but instead crashed to his knees on the carpet. Only Kyle's support under his arm kept him from collapsing altogether. The security tech was already calling for an emergency medical team. Jodenny had backed up against the bulkhead with Twig, and Osherman's hand was squeezing her shoulder.

"Please," Myell gasped. "She has to come with us."

Osherman had been staring at Myell. Slowly he said to Jodenny, "Give her to me."

Jodenny asked, "Sir?"

"Give her to me," Osherman said, and there was no mistaking it was an order. "Come here, Twig."

Reluctantly Jodenny handed over the little girl. Osherman smoothed back her hair with his hand and said, "He's your grandfather, right?"

She nodded.

"Then trust him. And trust me."

Osherman took three steps forward and thrust Twig into Myell's arms.

Jodenny cried, "No—" just as a blue light flashed, sparked, was gone.

CHAPTER **SIX**

Another Friday night, another romantic dinner. Jodenny hadn't been this happy in a long time. She and Sam Osherman made their way through the crowds as a comet blazed on the domed overhead of the Rocks. Passengers and crew alike dined at the sidewalk cafés, and danced at the nightclubs, and watched street performers. Teenagers flirted and children played tag and Jodenny slipped her hand into Osherman's. He smiled down on her.

"Drink or two?" he asked. "Dancing, or maybe an old-fashioned movie?"

"Let's just walk," she said. Duty and obligations and the constant pressure of shipboard life fell away. Outside the bulkheads, the great space river Alcheringa carried the *Yangtze* on its long journey through the Seven Sisters. Inside, Jodenny enjoyed the pull and push and vibrancy of the crowds.

A creek ran down the center of the promenade, flanked by winding stone paths. Koala bots frolicked in the gum and eucalyptus trees of the promenade. Lovers strolled there with heads bent low and eyes only for each other. Jodenny turned and kissed Osherman, and he gave her a wide smile.

"What was that for?" he asked.

"No special reason."

He kissed her back, right there under the trees and stars, and Jodenny could have stood there forever but for a girl's quick, high shout.

"Nana!"

She turned from Sam's lips to see a man, a boy, and a girl standing just a few meters away, gawking at her. The man wore wrinkled civilian clothes and had no shoes over his socks. The kids were in pajamas. The man had his hand on the girl's shoulder and appeared to be holding her back.

"Nana!" the girl said again.

"She doesn't remember," the man said. "Sorry, Lieutenant. Sir. She's a little mixed up."

Jodenny had never seen any of them before. A quick glance at Osherman confirmed that he, too, was confused.

"How do you know I'm a lieutenant?" she asked. Neither of them were wearing uniforms, after all. "Who are you?"

"Never mind," the man said. "We won't bother you anymore."

He tugged the children away. The girl left reluctantly, glancing backward over her shoulder.

"That was strange," Osherman said.

"They must have us confused with someone else," Jodenny said.

Every planet in the Seven Sisters boasted of pristine beaches and welcoming seas, but this stretch of golden sand on Kiwi was the best tropical shoreline Jodenny had ever visited. She bobbed up and down in the warm salty water with Osherman right beside her. Their masks and fins hung loosely on their arms, because kissing was much more fun than snorkeling.

"You should get out of the sun," Osherman murmured, his lips soft against hers. "You're getting a sunburn."

She hooked her arms around his neck. "I don't care."

He laughed and kissed her nose. "You say that now, but you'll be sorry later. Go on. I'll join you in a few minutes."

The private beach was mostly deserted on this midweek afternoon, with many of the resort's guests off at the pools or saunas, or getting massages, or eating in the fine restaurants. Jodenny didn't notice the man and two children standing on the shore until she waded into the shallows. They were dressed oddly for a day at the beach—heavy clothes, boots, and were those goggles on the girl's head?

"Good morning?" Jodenny asked, just to be polite, though she didn't like the way they were looking at her—with sadness, maybe, or perhaps it was resignation.

"We're really hungry," the girl said.

The boy pinched her arm. "She's not going to feed us, stupid."

Jodenny frowned at them. "Are you guests here?"

"No," the man said. "We're just passing through."

She continued past them, wondering if she should alert hotel security. Out in the waves, Osherman floated backward with his face turned to the sky. The strange man was steering the kids away from the resort and toward the trees. They'd find nothing in there but jungle, snakes, spiders, and monkeys.

She grabbed her tote bag and said, "Hey, wait up."

They waited until she caught up to them. Jodenny offered the bag. "Here. There's some sandwiches and water."

The man winced, but the boy grabbed the bag and held it tight.

"Thanks," the man said.

"Where are you going?" Jodenny asked.

The little girl said, "We keep jumping through time."

"Jo!" That was Osherman, striding out of the surf with water glittering on his torso. He gave the three strangers a thorough look. "What's going on?"

"Doesn't matter," the man said, and steered the kids toward the trees again.

Jodenny wanted to follow them, to talk some sense into the man. As the adult he shouldn't be dragging those children around with those heavy clothes on. But Osherman said, "Refugees, probably. I hear there's a bunch just moved into town. Come on, let's go inside before you get really sunburned."

Later, standing on the balcony of their room, she looked at the dark jungle under the nighttime sky.

"What are you doing?" Osherman asked, his hands sliding up around her waist. He smelled good, like dark spice. His lips brushed the back of her neck.

"Just thinking," she said. "I wonder who they were."

Out in the darkness, a blue light flashed.

Repeat after me," Captain Balandra said. "I, Jodenny Katherine Scott, do hereby take this man as my lawfully wedded husband . . ."

Jodenny's hands were sweaty on her bouquet, the lace collar of her dress made her neck itch, and the sun was slanting at an unfortunate angle through the trees over Providence. The summer day was achingly gorgeous, though, and all nervousness aside, she was happy to be standing in the middle of town with an appreciative audience and Sam Osherman at her side.

It had been ten years since their shipwreck on Providence. Ten years of Osherman gradually overcoming the trauma of his Roon captivity. His voice had come back after three years. He'd stopped prowling the town at night after four. By year six he'd proven himself to be a valued member of the community and by year eight, after he'd started dating one of the junior officers from the ship, Jodenny had realized just how much she and her daughter Lisa missed him from their lives.

And so here they were, standing under the sun, getting married. Osherman stood in his best pants and a white shirt that had been ironed. Lisa, her dark hair frizzy in the humidity, wore a green dress that she'd already managed to get dirty, and her bouquet of white lilies was already wilting. Jodenny thought her daughter had never looked more beautiful.

In fact, except for the shouting, it was all quite lovely.

"Let me go!" a boy was saying, indignantly twisting as Sheriff Mark Sweeney escorted him down the middle of the street. The kid was twelve or thirteen years old, tall, with sandy brown hair and a profile almost familiar to Jodenny.

Captain Balandra said, "What the—"

"Found this one hiding by the school," Mark reported, heedless of the fact that he was interrupting Jodenny's wedding. Or maybe not so heedless. He'd always had his own opinions about her love life.

"Who the hell are you?" asked Captain Balandra.

It was a great question. The kid hadn't come in on the *Kamchatka* with them. Jodenny knew every passenger, every member of the crew. He was also too old to have been born here on Providence. It wasn't as if strangers dropped by the planet every day, after all. And there was something disconcertingly familiar about him. Something in his eyes, something guarded and observant, and where had she seen that before?

"If you don't let me go you're going to be in big trouble!" the boy was saying. "He's going to come get me and he'll be mad!"

Mark kept his hand on the boy's arm. "Who's going to come get you?"

"Who are you?" Captain Balandra asked.

The boy was glaring at Jodenny as if she was the source of every sour thing in the universe. "You can't tell? Look at him and look at me."

Jodenny turned to Osherman, bewildered. And there she recognized the profile, the guarded eyes.

If Osherman recognized the similarities, he kept silent about them. Instead he said, "Why don't you tell us your name?"

"It doesn't matter," the boy said sullenly. "It never matters."

With that, the kid kicked Mark hard in the shin and dashed off toward the trees behind the town hall. He was young and spry and easily outpaced the colonists who gave chase.

Jodenny gave her bouquet to Lisa. "Hold this. And stay here."

"Where are you going?" Osherman asked.

"That kid," she said. "Come on!"

So they left their wedding and joined the pursuit. But it was a helpless cause. The kid seemed to know the woods pretty well. By nightfall, even though most of the colony had joined the effort, they had found nothing.

When they returned to town Alli Carter reported missing food from her kitchen, and Sydney Ford reported trousers and shirts were missing from her clothesline.

"He wasn't acting alone," Osherman said. "The kid's got companions. Or accomplices."

Jodenny would have answered, but deep in the woods a blue light flashed.

Myell was getting worse with each jump. He knew it. Each landing was followed by headaches and vomiting, and the ouroboros had begun to give off a high-pitched, off-kilter whine that ate at his eardrums. Luckily the kids weren't suffering the same symptoms, not yet. In each new eddy he needed their help to find shelter, rummage up food, lie to Jodenny, or otherwise survive until the ring whisked them away again.

It was risky to let them out of his sight for even a few minutes. The ring's arrival was erratic now, with his usual twenty-four-hour window now down to twenty, sometimes eighteen. It had been ten eddies since he'd taken Kyle and Twig from their home and the strain was showing in the dark circles under their eyes. They'd met ten different versions of the grandmother and had certainly experienced different parts of Jodenny's life; still, Myell was sure they regretted the entire trip.

Maybe Twig not so much—she woke up every day the same curious ten-year-old that he'd first met. But Kyle was increasingly gloomy and argumentative. Though he never said it in front of Twig, it was obvious he didn't believe Myell could get them home.

He wasn't sure he could get them home either. No amount of hoping, concentrating or praying to unseen gods could get the ouroboros to take him where he wanted to go. If there was a magic formula, it eluded his grasp.

Now, floating in darkness, he tried to remember where exactly he was—leaving an eddy? arriving in one? He couldn't hear the kids or any other sounds. When he cracked his eyes open he saw the white walls of a military infirmary. To the *Yangtze* again, then. He was tired of running into Jodenny as a junior officer but in some ways it was more comforting than the eddies where she was only a child, or those places she was an embittered old woman.

The funny thing about this infirmary was that there were no sounds other than his own breathing and the slap of his bare feet on the cold floor. He was dressed in a thin white gown, no privacy there. He went through the open hatch into the passage, which was empty of doctors, nurses, and techs. Even the admitting station was empty.

Then he saw the Flying Doctor.

The creature's head was turned Myell's way, its beady eyes alert, but it didn't move toward him. Its black feather cloak hung motionless in the still air. The head-dress was so high it nearly scraped against the overhead. Myell couldn't be sure the Roon was actually alive, and not a statue or hallucination.

"Go away," Myell said, a request that only sometimes worked with Homer.

The Roon lifted its head, turned to its right, and walked off silently. Goosebumps ran up and down Myell's arms. He didn't want to follow it, but he couldn't imagine leaving it to roam the ship among thousands of unsuspecting sailors and civilians.

Slowly, his limbs like ice, he walked after it.

The bulkheads around him billowed like white curtains in an unnatural wind. Myell noticed the absence of all smell—no antiseptic or blood, no medicine or perfume. There was a bitter taste in his mouth, as if he'd been chewing metal, with bits of aluminum still stuck between his teeth. His fingers were numb even though he flexed them, rubbed his knuckles. He was scared, oh yes, his bladder uncomfortably full, his pulse hammering, but he had started to recognize this as a nightmare, and nightmares couldn't truly hurt him.

A black hatch appeared in front of him. He opened it with a touch of his hand and walked into Garanwa's station, the nexus of the Wondjina Transportation System. The control room containing the rock hives and skin cloak was whole, intact, undamaged. No sign of the destruction he remembered. He rubbed at one arm, soothing the thickness of a scar on his dream body.

"What do you want?" he asked, unsure of who he was actually addressing.

Shadows moved against the skin cloak. The Flying Doctor turned toward him, backlit by circles and swirls and Aboriginal patterns.

"You inherited the helm. We saw, on the plains of Burringurrah. Now you seek to change Kultana, and we will stop you. Cease your quest."

This was a dream: the being couldn't hurt him. Probably. Maybe. He took a step forward, squaring his shoulders under the alien's relentless glare.

"What is Kultana? Where?" he asked. "Tell me."

Behind Myell, a voice whispered soft syllables. He couldn't quite make them out. When he glanced over his shoulder he thought he saw a woman, but then there was no one.

The Flying Doctor bared its teeth. Tall bastard, it was. Imposing and foul. "We know where you are now. We can follow you. Through the networks, through your dreams. If you abandon this quest, you will be rewarded."

The whisper grew louder, more urgent.

"I don't want a reward from you," Myell said.

Behind the alien, the skin cloak buckled and rippled as if alive and thrashing. The swirls across its surface darkened to red and burst into flame. Remembered pain rippled through him—skin blistering, smoke searing his lungs. This was where his journey had started, damn it. If the answers weren't here, they might not be anywhere. Already, though, the Flying Doctor was fading into blackness. Myell lurched forward and grabbed the thing with both hands.

"Tell me what Kultana is!" he shouted.

The Roon threw him backward. Waves of fire raced across the skin cloak. Myell landed hard, his legs and arms jerking against the rough unyielding ground. From somewhere high above came a waft of cold air, and a girl's frantic voice.

"It's okay," Twig was saying. "Please wake up, please, you can't keep sleeping."

He blinked his eyes open and saw Twig hovering over him. Behind her, the sky was gray and threatening with rain. With her help he sat up.

"Where's Kyle?" he asked.

Twig burst into tears.

"Where is he?" Myell demanded. "Where did he go?"

CHAPTER **SEVEN**

The baby kicked. Hard. Jodenny pushed her finger against her side and said, "Stop that. Mommy's trying to sleep."

Junior kicked again. The ocean continued to smash against the reef and roll into the lagoon, where it lapped up near her bare feet. Jodenny had put her beach towel down well above the high tide mark. It was amazing what the cargo holds of the *Kamchatka* had yielded up—she also had a garish pink beach bag, which was stocked with water and snacks for her and Junior as well as her gib, a flashlight and knife, and a romance paperback with a cracked spine and some missing pages.

Seagulls flapped overhead and continued northward. The breeze had kicked up during the afternoon and the sky was more gray than blue. She imagined another storm somewhere offshore, brewing up a potent mix of wind and rain. Jodenny hadn't gotten to the beach until nearly noon, and she was determined to relax there as long as possible. Anything to prolong returning to the village and the inevitable argument with people who thought they knew more than she did about her own body and limitations.

"I'm pregnant, not incapacitated," she'd said to Mark Sweeney. "Don't treat me like glass."

"You could slip," Captain Balandra warned.

"You could go into early labor," Ensign Collins said.

If she'd been in a more gracious mood she might have thanked them for their concern. Not many women in the colony had gotten pregnant yet. Everyone had a vested interest in helping her deliver a healthy baby. She was also a grieving widow, and everyone knew how often she trekked up the hill to where Myell's body lay rotting in a dark grave.

She'd let grief dictate her days and nights for almost seven months now, and had told herself she needed to move on. Let his memory rest, instead of pick at it like a wound that never had the chance to close up. The notion was sound. Laudable. Her future was here, not in the past. But when she woke up some mornings she found her face wet with tears and her hands scrunched under her chin, as if in prayer.

Mark Sweeney's last-ditch argument that morning had been "At least take Sam. He won't let anything happen to you."

Osherman would have come if she'd asked, but she didn't ask. He constantly acted anxious and jittery and on edge in ways that made it hard for many people to relax around him. He still couldn't talk, and Ensign

Collins couldn't tell if the problem was physical, psychological, or both. What no one saw was how far he'd come from the wreck of a man they'd found on Burringurrah—Osherman and Anna Gayle both, prisoners of the Roon, though one had clearly resisted with all his might and the other had thrown her lot in with the enemy.

Junior kicked again. Jodenny didn't like the kicking part of being pregnant. She didn't like her swollen ankles, either. Or the way her center of balance shifted daily, and how she had to trot off to the bathroom far too often, and how she felt hot all the time, no matter what the outside temperature was. But sitting in the shade was nice, and she'd decided a brief nap before the return trip was just the thing a tired expectant mom needed.

Her gib beeped.

"Just wanted to say hi." Louise Sharp's voice was as loud and cheery as ever. "Haven't heard from you lately."

Jodenny pulled her hat down lower on her head. "I'm sitting on the beach with a fruity tropical drink."

"Really? Damn nice, that must be. Any handsome hula boys for me?"

"No hula boys," Jodenny conceded.

"You're at Skipper's Point?"

"Near the lagoon."

"Come on down for dinner," Louise suggested. "We're having a fish fry. Again. Folks would love to see you."

Every night was fish night down at the Outpost. Though they'd negotiated their share of military rations from the *Kamchatka*'s stores, they saved it for special occasions and hard times. Their hunters weren't quite as good as the ones who'd stayed with Providence, and they hadn't had much luck with their crops, but no one was starving yet. Mostly they just complained about the menu. Complained and drank beer.

"I promised to be home by dinner," Jodenny said.

"Got you on a leash, do they?" Louise sounded amused.

Jodenny refrained from kicking sand on the gib. "I'll be on your doorstep by seven."

"We'll have a pajama party," Louise said.

She pinged Mark to let them know she'd be spending the night down at the Outpost. He didn't sound happy about it.

"Forecast has changed," he said. "We're due for some serious rain tonight."

"They have roofs down there, Mark. I'll call you in the morning."

After that she dozed off to the sounds of the surf, low and comforting. When she woke the sky had clouded over and the temperature had dropped. She hadn't meant to sleep so long. Her mind was still groggy as she packed up her things. Junior must have been napping along with her, but now he was awake and pushing his head against her bladder. For good measure, he threw in an extra kick or two.

"You better be one hell of a soccer player," she said.

She was on the path to the Outpost when she thought about their latrines, and how hard the beds were down there, and wouldn't it be nicer to be in her own bed. Standing in the middle of the coastal woods, one hand on her hat to keep it from blowing away, she considered how indecisive and muddy-headed pregnancy had made her. If she went down to the Outpost for a day or so, she'd get a much-needed break from all the do-gooders back home. If she went home, she'd have better creature comforts and wouldn't have to eat fish for dinner.

"Louise," she said, once she'd raised the other woman on her gib. "I'm taking a raincheck. I'll be down at the end of the week."

"You okay?"

"I want my own bathroom and bed," she said, and that brought a bark of short laughter.

"All right, missy with the full bladder. Come on down Friday. We'll have us some fish then."

Jodenny reversed course and headed back to Providence. Soon the hidden sun was setting, casting the woods in gloom, but she had her flashlight and knew the way, and had no concerns. The wild animals had learned to avoid the area and Mark Sweeney's great aim. The bugs came out but she had on her repellent, and though she had to stop again to piss in the bushes, she had more than enough water to carry her through another twenty minutes of walking.

Five minutes later, a man appeared in front of her on the path.

Appeared, just like magic. Popped out of nowhere. One moment she saw trees and the next minute she saw him, wearing a purple outfit that hadn't been in fashion for decades, if ever.

"Gamsa!" he said, grinning widely, throwing his arms open. "It's good to see you!"

Jodenny slid her hand into her pink beach bag and groped for her knife.

"Who are you?" she demanded. He certainly hadn't been aboard the *Kamchatka*. This planet lay millions of light-years from Earth and had no Spheres linking it to the Wondjina Transportation Network. Strangers were not only unheard of, they were *impossible*.

"I'm Homer," he said, friendly as could be. He was in his mid-twenties or so, with frizzy hair past his shoulders, dark brown eyes, and skin like milk chocolate. Though he was standing in place, he seemed ready to bounce on his toes, crack his knuckles, fidget like a teenager. He practically hummed with energy. "You're Jodenny. Jodenny Scott. My great-grandmother twenty times removed, or something. Gamsa!"

"Where did you come from?"

"The future," he said, flinging his arms open.

She didn't like the sound of that, but she didn't entirely discount the possibility. Her life had been strange enough these last few years.

"I could tell you things I couldn't possibly know," he said. "Like that time you were in the academy and you went to Richi Miller's birthday party and kissed him in the alley. Such passion, Gamsa! I didn't know you had it in you."

For a moment her memory failed her. The academy was so entirely long ago that it belonged to someone else's life. But there had been a cadet named Richi something-or-other, yes, and she had stepped out in the alley with him. She could feel her cheeks warm.

"I never told anyone about that," she said.

"I tell you, Gamsa, I'm traveling through time. I'm not the only one." Homer's expression and voice turned serious. "There are others. There's one other, most importantly, very vivid, you know? Someone who loves you very much and thinks he's lost you forever. Are you ready, Gamsa? Ready for him to come back into your life?"

Her heart thudded painfully against the inside of her chest. "You're lying."

Homer shook his head. "He's been through many

ordeals since you last saw him, and he's lost faith. You have to help him regain it. He needs that hope, more than even he knows, if he's going to do what he's going to do."

She had forgotten how to breathe, or so it seemed. Homer was talking about the impossible. Terry Myell was buried on a hill outside town, his corpse nothing more than rotted bones.

"Just a bit away this path turns down the hill. He's going to walk out of the woods down there and you have a choice," Homer continued. "You can treat him with suspicion and fear—the dead returned. You can be distant and cold. Hold him at arm's length. He's used to that. He'll expect it. He won't fight it, though it's killing him inch by inch. Or you can say to yourself, 'This is what I've been wanting. Answer to my prayers. The gods finally listened.' It's all your choice, Lieutenant Commander Scott. Gamsa."

He lapsed into silence.

Jodenny heard only the movement, soft and persistent, of the wind in the trees. She could no longer feel her fingers or toes.

"Show me," she said.

He went away," Twig said between her tears. "Hours ago, to get help, because you wouldn't wake up. But he hasn't come back and now it's getting dark."

Myell pulled himself upright. His legs were rubbery but they held his weight, and they damn well would until he found the kid. He tried to identify the forest around them. The air was cool, with a crescent moon sliding in and out from behind storm clouds that threatened to dump rain at any minute. The air smelled faintly salty. He clung to the slim, impossible hope that they had returned to Twig and Kyle's eddy in Providence.

"Homer!" he called. "Show yourself."

A flicker of light behind a bush, and there Homer stood. "I'm right here, Gampa. No need to shout."

"Where's Kyle?"

Homer's nose wrinkled in confusion. "Where'd you leave him?"

Twig and Kyle had met Homer a few times already, very briefly: Homer didn't seem very comfortable around kids, though, and rarely stayed to talk long. Twig didn't like Homer at all, and his arrival, on top of Kyle's disappearance, was maybe the reason she now burst into new tears.

"Please stop crying," Myell said, because he couldn't take that helpless sound on top of all the other things that had gone wrong recently. He pulled her close against his leg and rubbed her back. "He can't be far."

Homer pulled out a scanner and turned in a circle. "No sign of him, Gamps."

"Where are we?"

"Providence," Homer replied promptly. "Seven months or so after you died. Friday night. And your lovely pregnant bride is just up that hill over there. You should go see her."

Pregnant with Lisa, then. With Twig's mom. Myell pushed that thought away. "I have to find Kyle first. Keep scanning."

"Maybe she can help," Homer said. "Maybe she's seen him. She could find out. She has a radio to the settlement and to the Outpost."

Myell wasn't sure he could take another rejection

from Jodenny. The dull ache under his breastbone had grown worse every time she looked at him blankly or with disregard. Then again, Kyle was wandering out here in the woods somewhere, and if the ouroboros took Myell and Twig away before they were reunited, Kyle's life would vanish like a puff of smoke. Maybe Jodenny could be of help with that, at least.

"Which way?" Myell asked.

Homer pointed. And though he couldn't possibly be truly cold, he shivered and tugged up his collar. "Better hurry. Weather's going to turn worse before it gets better."

That, Myell could believe. "Come on," he said, and started walking with Twig pasted to his side. When Myell looked back, Homer had disappeared again.

Jodenny's feet started moving faster. She hurried down the open hillside as fast her pregnancy allowed.

"Hey, wait—" Homer said.

The grass was soft and spongy beneath her sandals. The wind kicked up and cold air wafted up Jodenny's sleeves to her still-damp bathing suit. She had the sudden fear Homer was a figment of her hormone-overwhelmed imagination, that she'd suddenly gone insane. Pregnancy psychosis.

At the bottom of the slope she stopped to frantically scan the trees. The silver-green grass rippled in the wind and the trees bowed left and right but there was no dead husband, miraculously returned.

No one walked out of the woods.

She wasn't sure what was worse—getting her hopes up and having them so cruelly crash down again, or the burning embarrassment that she'd believed it could be true. Homer appeared off to her side, staying at an arm's length away. Perhaps he was afraid she was going to punch him. His green velvet coat billowed in the breeze. Hadn't he just been wearing purple?

The important thing was Myell. Who was not here at all.

"Liar," she said.

"I don't lie," he insisted, and pointed to the trees behind her.

Jodenny almost didn't look. But there, stepping out of the trees. The man she'd loved and lost, with a child at his side.

CHAPTER **EIGHT**

They stood five meters apart, neither moving forward.

Myell looked terrible in the light from her flashlight. Hollow-cheeked, skinnier than usual, his hair longer than military regulations permitted. She didn't know what he thought of her, but couldn't imagine that her huge belly, beach-blown hair, and bloated features were very impressive.

"Nana," the girl said. "Kyle's lost."

Myell didn't say anything.

Jodenny forced herself forward on trembling legs. When she was close enough to touch him, she stopped. He was doing nothing, saying nothing, but in his eyes she saw wariness and resignation. As if he expected her to turn him aside, to deny him everything.

Jodenny reached out very slowly and cupped his face. He tried to flinch away but she held him firm and stared into his eyes. The cold hard knot in her chest didn't unwind, but it shifted fractionally. His skin was pale and soft, cool to her fingers. His lips, under her thumb, were warm.

"Hey," she said. "Aren't you dead?"

Around them, the wind stilled suddenly. The girl and Homer said nothing. The world had narrowed to only Jodenny and Myell, and her hand on his cheeks, and a crushing sensation so great that Jodenny thought she might collapse under its weight.

"You came back," she said.

His hands closed on hers and gently pried them away. He opened his mouth and she knew, with dreaded certainty, that he was about to say, "Not for long" or "I can't stay." If she heard those words surely she'd break apart. To block them she pressed her mouth against his and kissed him hard. Tears streamed out of her eyes. Grief fled, along with fear and uncertainty. He was here, he was here *now,* solid and unresisting as her hands swept down his shoulders to his waist.

He didn't move. He was a warm statue, still but for his breathing, no response under her lips and palms, under the press of her, the baby between them, while her tears dampened his skin.

His unresponsiveness made her draw back in slow horror. This man wasn't her husband after all. Or, if he was, he no longer loved her. How else to explain his passive resistance, his indifference? Jodenny stepped back with a sick churn in her belly. Myell caught her arm and then waist and pulled her to his chest.

"Kay," he said, with more grief than she expected. He buried his face against her neck and breathed deeply of her skin, and squeezed her so close they both could feel Junior kicking in protest or happiness.

* * *

Uncle Terry," the little girl said, tugging on Myell's arm. "We have to find Kyle. And it's raining."

Jodenny reluctantly let him go. Now that she was paying attention, she could feel the pelt of cool raindrops on her skin.

"This is Twig," Myell said, sounding embarrassed. "Your granddaughter."

"Oh." Jodenny looked at the little girl. She decided to reserve judgment on the "granddaughter" bit for later. "Hello. Who's Kyle?"

"Grandson," Homer said succinctly. Then he added more information. "*Lost* grandson."

Myell squinted at him. "You could make yourself useful for a change and go find him."

"Can't help you there, Gampa, but you three better take cover. Storm's here."

An impressive crack of lightning split down the sky, thunder close behind it. Twig flinched and Myell cast a worried look upward. "How far are we from town?"

"Too far," Jodenny said. "And too far from the Outpost. We'll have to take shelter somewhere else. There are caves—"

"We know," Twig interrupted. "We've been there lots of times."

Jodenny gave Myell a sharp look. "You've been here before?"

"Sort of. Long story. I'll tell you later, okay?"

No, it wasn't okay, because he'd been here before and never told her. Had never approached her, never made contact in any way, while she was grieving and carrying their child and trying to find a way to make a life without him.

"Time travel," Homer reminded her, with a cheeky grin. "His 'before' is still in your future, Gamsa. Caves sound good, though, right? You should get moving."

Myell reached for Jodenny's beach bag to carry it for her. She snagged her towel off the top and said, "Here, Twig, wrap yourself in this."

"I'm hungry," Twig said, sniffing back tears. "And what'll Kyle do in the rain? He'll get wet."

"He'll be fine," Myell promised. "Come on. Let's hurry."

Jodenny held Twig's hand as they ducked past tree branches. The woods opened up into another hillside, this one slippery with mud and wet grass. The rain slanted down harder, stinging her face. More lightning, more thunder, and she tried not think about what would happen if one of them was actually struck by a bolt. Myell led them down toward the river, which was a dark gushing torrent in her flashlight's glare. Jodenny looked for Homer, but he had disappeared.

"We lost your friend," Jodenny said.

"He's not my friend," Myell replied. "He'll be fine."

It was a drenching, quarter-mile trek along the muddy banks until they came to Balandra Bridge. The metal footbridge stretched across the narrowest part of the river to the rocky hill and caves on the other side. It was only ten meters long and had two sturdy handrails along its length. Engineer techs from the ship had made it with safety and durability in mind. The river was running high, but was well below the metal treads.

"Twig, you're going to have to go first," Myell said. "I'm right here behind you, okay? Jodenny, you stay here and I'll come back to help."

She almost argued with him, but he was already gone and helping Twig across. She started crossing by her own damn self, thank you very much. She kept her steps slow and sure, and held tight to the rain-slicked rails.

Myell reached the other side and started back.

"I told you to wait!" he said over the rain as he drew close.

"I can do it myself!" she shouted back.

Which was exactly when her right foot slipped out from under her. She lost both her balance and grip. Her right knee slammed into a support beam, her left leg slid over the water, and something twisted deep in her left hip.

She was dimly aware of Myell grabbing her under her arms but he seemed distant, dreamlike. Maybe she had also hit her head. Twig was saying, "Nana! Nana!," and Myell said, "Keep going. I've got her."

Jodenny couldn't see much in the darkness but the pain in her right knee and left hip were like burning bonfires, hot and red. She felt Myell lift her. She didn't envy him that, not considering how heavy and ungainly she'd gotten with the baby.

The baby. She couldn't feel it kicking or moving at all, and fear made her gasp out against Myell's neck.

"He's not moving," she said.

"Easy." His broad hand cupped the back of her head. "She's fine. You're both okay."

"She?" Jodenny asked.

"Sssh," he said, and then they were moving again through the darkness and rain. "Let me do all the work."

He sounded worried and that made her feel bad, because she hadn't wanted him to come all the way from the dead just to fret over her. Still, it was a relief to rest her head against his shoulder. She felt cherished and warm despite the pain in her knee and hip. Myell was murmuring again, soothing words that slowly took on a harder edge.

"It's okay, you're okay, but I need you to wake up now. Open your eyes, Jodenny."

She thought her eyes already were open. Jodenny forced the lids apart and instantly regretted it. Light stabbed at her from the flashlight. She, Myell, and Twig were crammed into some dark sloping enclosure that smelled like mud and old leaves, and the ground was hard beneath her. She was resting with her back against Myell, who was in turn wedged up against a stone wall with Twig at his side. Junior was quiet, but when she poked her side he kicked back.

"There's no room for a real fire," Myell said, apologetic. "But we've got a heat globe."

From one of his pockets he produced a crystal ball and set it down on the dirt. A moment later, the ball flared red and began emitting a comforting warmth. She had seen some of those before, though she couldn't remember where.

"Where did you get that?" Jodenny asked.

Myell's answer was indistinct.

"A what?" Jodenny asked.

"Gift shop," Myell said.

Twig said, "Kyle stole it. On Kiwi. Uncle Terry, I'm starving."

Jodenny had been to Kiwi before, with Osherman. She pushed aside the memory and said, "There are some apples in my beach bag."

Twig immediately began rummaging.

"How do you feel?" Myell asked.

"Confused," she said. "Where did you come from? Why does she call you her uncle?"

"Well," Myell said slowly, "we've sort of been coming from all over. There's a blue ouroboros. It drags us this way and that way, from the future to the past and back again."

She stared at him in disbelief.

He put his hand on her belly. "This is Lisa. She'll get married one day and Twig is hers."

"But—" Jodenny started, then stopped. She'd told Ensign Collins not to tell her the baby's gender. She said she wanted it to be a surprise. Yet she was sure it was a little boy.

"I want my mom," Twig said, around the bits of apple in her mouth. She wiped at her eyes with a dirty hand. "We haven't been home in weeks and weeks."

Jodenny said, "Come here, lie with me," until the girl nestled against her chest. Jodenny stroked Twig's hair, soothing out knots. "Is Kyle your brother?"

"Cousin," Myell said. "How's your leg? Did you break anything?"

"No, I'm fine," she said, which was mostly true. She still hurt from the fall but not too badly. The heat globe was warm and her clothes were beginning to dry out. Myell was a comfortable cushion beneath her.

Myell asked, "Are they going to come looking for you? From town?"

"They shouldn't," Jodenny said. "I'm supposed to be at the Outpost. Where's my gib?"

He held it up. "I think it broke when you fell on it."

So it had. Jodenny put it aside and instead traced the line of Myell's jaw with her fingers. So strong, always so strong for her. She moved closer to kiss him, awakening the fire in her knee and hip. The baby chose that moment to kick so hard that Twig jerked backward.

"I felt that!" Twig said.

"He kicks a lot at night," Jodenny said, gasping around the discomfort. "Or she, I guess. You're sure it's a girl?"

Myell kissed her forehead "A daughter. Lisa."

Twig said, "Mom's the town doctor. In the future."

Jodenny's goosebumps rose again. That the unborn daughter in her womb would one day have this daughter was an idea too bizarre to contemplate.

Myell shifted. "Kyle's still out there. I have to go look for him."

"No." Jodenny clutched his arm as fear flared in her, bright and cold. "You can't go."

Carefully he slid out from beneath her, though he couldn't really go far with his arm trapped under her fingers. He met her gaze squarely. "I have to. He's only thirteen years old. He could be hurt or stuck somewhere."

"And he has to be back before we leave," Twig said.

The fear inside Jodenny transmuted into a full-fledged panic. "Leave for where?"

"We're not going anywhere," Myell said firmly, with a pointed look at Twig. "Don't scare her."

"The ring comes and takes us away," Twig said. "Whether we want it to or not."

Jodenny said, "I'm coming with you," but when she tried to move her hip and knee both flared into hotness.

"Kay, listen to me." Myell crouched low. "I have to find Kyle. I'll be back as soon as I do. You and Twig will be fine here until I get back."

Twig shook her head vehemently. "No! I want you to stay."

"You're not going anywhere," Jodenny insisted.

Myell kissed her cheek, his breath hot. "I have to.

He's just a kid. I can't leave him out there. I'll be back right away, I promise."

Jodenny had never met Kyle. He was just an idea, an abstract grandson. And right now Myell was more important than he was, even if that made her the worst grandmother in the galaxy. She was sure her feelings showed on her face, because Myell cupped both cheeks and kissed her again. Hard and claiming, his lips tasting like salt.

"The sooner I go, the sooner I'll be back," Myell said. "I promise."

He was a damned liar, of that she was sure. He was going to walk out of the cave and out of her life again, and Jodenny couldn't do anything to stop him. She let go of his arm and wiped at her watery eyes.

"You better be," she said, her voice cracking.

Myell gave her a shaky smile, grabbed the flashlight, and stepped over Twig to exit into the rain.

Jodenny turned her attention to her granddaughter.

"Tell me about this ring," she said. "Tell me everything."

The torrential rain had eased to a steady cold drizzle. Myell didn't worry too much about it. Wet was wet and no amount of complaining would make it better. He eased himself carefully down the slope outside the river caves and started back across the bridge.

"Kyle!" he yelled out. "Answer me!"

If the kid was smart, he'd have found some kind of shelter for himself and holed up until the storm passed. The possibility existed that he'd hiked all the way to Providence in a quest to find help, though things hadn't gone well there in the last eddy they'd swung through.

It was hard to say what Kyle would do, however. He was stubborn to the point of muleheadedness, like his grandfather. Wouldn't accept a helping hand unless he was dying. Maybe not even then.

The dark trees whipped back and forth, and the wind drove water into Myell's eyes. He tried wiping them clear but rain filled them up just as fast again. His shoes squelched in the mud.

"Kyle!" he yelled again.

He made it over the hill and down again, following the river upstream through thick woods. Myell kept his arms wrapped over his chest and tried to think of warm memories, sun, deserts, barren hot wastelands, anything but this sodden forest and wretched storm. He slipped and went down hard, and rested for a moment in the cold mud with his face turned to the rain. He was drenched and uncomfortable but in a way the weather was better than explosions, than people dying or being disappointed in him.

A face appeared over him.

"What are you doing?" Kyle asked, scornfully.

"Nothing," Myell forced out. "Looking for you."

"I'm right here."

Myell hauled himself up and nearly banged up against Kyle's companion. Osherman, drenched as they were, his face startling white in a lightning strike. Osherman gazed at him without any sign of familiarity. Myell might as well have been a total stranger. True enough, they hadn't spent much time together on the *Aral Sea*. But they'd been trapped in the Wondjina network together for a short time, and the lack of recognition was unnerving.

"I got Grandpa," Kyle said. "So he could help. Where's Twig?"

"What did you tell him?" Myell asked.

"Everything. He believes me."

That was in doubt. Myell knew that this Osherman couldn't talk yet. It would be a long time before the effects of his Roon captivity wore off enough for him to start communicating. But he'd come with Kyle into the woods, so that was something.

"How did you convince him?" Myell asked.

"Birthmark. We've got the same one."

"What birthmark?"

"Wouldn't you like to know," Kyle said, and there was a definite sneer in his voice. "Where's Twig?"

"This way," Myell said.

On the muddy, wet hike back to the cave Myell imagined a dozen different ways Jodenny and Twig could have come to harm in the short time he'd been away. Maybe the water had dislodged mud and rocks, sending down a torrent to bury them alive. They'd be entombed in that hillside forever, like he was in his grave on a hill on the other side of the valley. Or maybe the fall had made Jodenny go into premature labor or start hemorrhaging, or done some other harm.

He hurried onward, careful to make sure Kyle was keeping up but less worried about Osherman. Occasional thunder shook the air and trees, but by the time they reached the caves the rain had thoroughly abated. Myell scrabbled up the hill, sure of the worst, but Jodenny and Twig were both sleeping peacefully.

"Thank you," Myell said aloud, and Jodenny opened her eyes.

"Hey," she said. "You okay?"

He couldn't help a crooked smile. "Fine. I brought company,"

Osherman and Kyle squeezed into the cave behind

Myell. Jodenny blinked at Osherman several times. "How'd you get here?"

"Kyle," Myell replied.

Osherman retreated as far as he could without actually leaving the cave. He slid down to a wary, hunched crouch. Kyle met Jodenny's gaze and said, "We brought stuff from your house. In case we couldn't get back in the storm."

Jodenny sat up. "You're Kyle?"

He nodded, hesitant.

"It's nice to meet you," Jodenny said, and to Myell she sounded sincere. "What stuff did you bring?"

Kyle distributed blankets, clothing, and food as if it were Christmas morning. Myell almost woke Twig, but decided to let her sleep a while longer. Osherman remained as far apart from them as the small space permitted. In the light of the heat globe, he and Kyle resembled father-son more than grandfather-grandson. They had the same narrow face and long nose, and chins that could take a solid punch. Myell could see Jodenny staring at them.

He opened up a tube of analgesic healing cream from the ship's infirmary and said, "How's your knee and hip? Some of this might help."

"A lot of that might help," Jodenny agreed. She wasn't deterred off the topic, though. "Twig said you two are cousins, Kyle. Who's your mom?"

Myell tried to shoot Kyle a warning look, but Kyle ignored him.

"My mom's named Teresa," he said. "She's your other daughter."

Jodenny caught Myell's fingers just as they started to spread the cream. "How can we have another child?"

"Not *his*," Kyle said. "Him. Grandpa Osherman."

Osherman, busy staring at Jodenny, didn't react at all. Myell felt a flush go through his face for no good reason at all. Jodenny smiled uncertainly, and cupped her belly as if to protect it.

"That's not possible," she finally said.

Myell smoothed the salve on her knee, trying to be careful with the swollen, tender skin. "It sort of is. In the future."

"You marry him later." Kyle shook out a blanket and wrapped himself up in it. "And my mom is Teresa, your daughter. And she marries my dad, and here I am, and then he showed up, and we've been jerked around in time ever since."

The "he" of Kyle's bitterness was Myell himself, who capped the analgesic and tucked it into his pocket. "That's about right. Look, it's late. We're all tired and with this weather, we're not going anywhere. Can we talk about everything in the morning?"

Jodenny gripped Myell's hand. "Twig says the ring comes for you every twenty-four hours, sometimes less. How do I know you'll still be here in the morning?"

He smoothed the hair from her forehead. "We're not going anywhere. I promise. Close your eyes, and I'll be here when you wake up."

She curled up against his side. Myell tried to tell himself that he hadn't just lied to her. Osherman stared at him, eyes burning and bright, from the other side of the cave. Outside, the rain picked up again and began battering against the hillside.

CHAPTER **NINE**

When Jodenny woke the next morning, she kept her eyes closed for several long moments. The warmness beneath her, the smell of river water, the shape of a man. Her husband, returned to her. But if she opened her eyes and saw someone else, that would be proof positive that she'd gone batshit crazy. And it wasn't as if the possibility were that remote—she'd felt crazy for months, crazy with grief and loneliness—but psychosis would be a whole new trick to add to her repertoire. If Myell wasn't the one she was lying against, she'd have to scream.

She cracked open one eye and saw her Terry. He was battered and thin, his hair dried in crazy directions, but he was there, tangible and irrefutable.

Jodenny reached up, planning to kiss him awake, but he jerked awake at that very moment, and his chin knocked into her forehead.

"Ouch," he said.

"Ow," she said.

After they sorted out that nothing was bleeding, they settled into a proper kiss. But then Myell, his hand against her belly, made a surprised sound.

"What's that?" he asked.

Jodenny said, "Junior's got hiccups."

His face broke open with wonder. "Does that happen a lot?"

"Enough. It's perfectly normal."

He patted Junior's bump with gentle fingers, then looked up for the kids.

And blanched.

"Where is everyone?" he demanded.

The other blankets were all empty. Jodenny's gib was gone as well. But the bag Myell had brought from her house was still there.

"They must be outside, checking on the weather," she said.

Myell eased out from under her and scooted toward the cave mouth. She wasn't worried about Osherman. He was far more stable than most people gave him credit for. Even her. Jodenny drank some water from her canteen, eased more healing cream on her knee and hip, and stiffly followed Myell into the brightness of day.

The weather was still wet, the sky filled with gray, fast-moving clouds. The wind swept branches back and forth vigorously enough to drop twigs and leaves on the forest floor. The river was running high under the footbridge, and the water churned a dark angry color. But there was no sign of Osherman or the kids, and Myell had a worried expression on his face.

"Where would they go?" he asked.

"Maybe they just took a walk to get some fresh air."

He valiantly stood guard while she relieved herself several meters from the cave mouth. After that she settled onto a large flat rock, glad for the fresh air.

"How's your knee and hip?" he asked.

She flexed her whole leg. "Not bad at all."

He nodded, distracted. Still worried about the kids. She asked, "Where did you get them?"

Myell gave her a puzzled look.

"In the future, sure. How far?" she asked.

"Forty years," he said.

Easy math, that, and the result made her wrinkle her nose. "I'm a little old lady?"

"Sure," he said, eyes on the valley.

Jodenny grabbed his hand and waited for him to look at her. Maybe talking about the future was the wrong conversation to have. He didn't seem comfortable about it. But she hadn't been comfortable either, these past months, grieving over his death. She thought of him cast back and forth through the decades, never able to stay in one place. Adrift and lost.

Goosebumps rose across her shoulders and climbed up her scalp. "You said you weren't leaving. But Twig says you can't control it. Tell me the truth."

Dismay crossed his face, quickly shuttered.

"You can't," she squeaked out. She stood up, both hands supporting her back. "You have to stay."

His shoulders tensed. He was looking down the valley still, unhappiness radiating out of him.

"Look me in the eye." She grasped his arm. "Tell me you're here for good. Because if you're not, if you think you're going anywhere, you better think again, mister. I'll tie you to a goddamned tree. I'll sit on you. Me and your baby here."

He turned from the valley to face her full on. His mouth was a downward slash and his hands were cold on her shoulders.

"I can't do anything about it," he admitted.

Jodenny felt numb through and through, so numb she wasn't even sure her legs were still supporting her. Junior twisted around inside her, the only sign her body was still working.

"I don't believe you," she said, and brushed his hands away.

Before she could even pick a good destination, she was heading down the slope to the footbridge. Home, she decided. Her little house and little bedroom, where she would lock the door forever. Because if there was a thing worse than being widowed it was having your husband come back from wherever he'd been, past or present or future be dammed, and announcing he wasn't staying.

"Jodenny!" he called out, following her. It wasn't as if she could set a land-speed record, not with her extra weight and the remaining twinge in her knee. But she stormed ahead of him anyway, the wet forest floor slippery beneath her sandals.

"Wait!" he said, very close behind her.

"No," she snapped. "I don't want to hear excuses. You can't control it? You find a way. You figure out how you're going to stay, because you're not going anywhere, and if you think you can just leave me here—"

Myell said, "You don't need me. You marry him. You marry Osherman."

She'd reached the footbridge, and her hand closed so tightly around the railing that her knuckles cracked. Jodenny stopped fleeing and turned. "I wouldn't."

He spread his hands wide. "You do. You're happy together. You make a life here without me."

Her heart skipped. "So this is revenge or something? You're not staying now because you've seen the future and I marry someone else?"

"Not seen it." His chin lifted, and a mulish look came into his eyes. "Been there. At your wedding. And later."

Jodenny abruptly had to sit. And for that there was either the muddy bank or the cold grates of the bridge, with the water rushing beneath. She sat on the grates with her back against a pole, breathing deeply through her nose.

"Easy," he said, touching her arm. He sat down beside her.

She swatted his hand away. "I won't. Now that you've told me. I'll never marry him, just to spite you."

"That's not how it works." He leaned his head against the railing, as if holding up his head was too much work anymore. His feet dangled over the rushing water. "You won't remember me after I'm gone. No matter what I do, nothing ever changes. This eddy—this moment of time—will just fix itself. Time heals all wounds, I guess."

"You don't know for sure," Jodenny said. "I mean, yes, from your perspective, maybe. But time could be changing in other places, or other ways. What's going to happen if you take Kyle and Twig home? Will they meet themselves?"

"I don't know if I can. It wasn't something I planned. Homer says they're just copies, that the real ones never left home. He says that I have to leave them behind, or we'll all end up drowning in space and time."

Jodenny's stomach twisted at the thought of that. "Could that be true?"

"I don't know. But if I leave them, that means they'll just evaporate when this eddy dissolves. Either way, I've doomed them."

Despite her earlier anger, she wanted to find a way to comfort him. To ease the tight lines between his eyes and somehow make everything all better. Instead she found herself saying, "So take them. And take me. I'm willing to risk the chance. Wherever we go next, we'll face it together. And we'll find a way to stop all this."

"He can't take you," said a voice from behind them. A Roon stood at the end of the bridge, a silver ouroboros spinning around its boots. "Go with him and your baby will die."

CHAPTER **TEN**

Jodenny surged to her feet. Myell rose just as fast beside her, shielding her as best he could. Though she was glad for Junior's sake, the gesture irritated her. She could take care of herself, thank you very much. Usually.

Then again, she had no weapons or means of defense.

Neither did Myell.

The Roon said, "I told you that the network was ours, Teren Myell. Every corner and every whirl. Take her with you and your child will die."

"It can talk," Jodenny murmured. None of the aliens she remembered from Burringurrah had been able to speak English.

"You lie," Myell said. "If you control the network, why haven't you stopped me? Why haven't you just killed me?"

It was silent for a moment. Jodenny wondered if it was surprised at Myell's impertinence. Thunder rolled through the sky as dark clouds moved in over the hill. Myell glanced upward, a small awareness flickering across his face.

"She protects you," it finally said. "She encourages you. But we have our own gods, and to you they'll show no mercy."

"Who protects me?" Myell asked. "Kultana?"

The silver ouroboros sped up.

"Step out of that," Myell dared it. "If you can."

The Roon made no move. "You persist," it said, "but

you will fail. Again and again you will fail. And we will meet again until you are nothing."

The ouroboros vanished, taking the Roon with it.

Myell let out a shaky breath and turned to hug Jodenny tightly. She found herself shaking—not in fear, but in anger. "Who the hell was that?" she asked.

"It calls itself the Flying Doctor. I'll tell you everything, but let's get out of here first."

They walked along the riverbank but kept the cave within sight. Myell kept a protective hold on Jodenny's elbow and supported her whenever the ground grew too slippery. She couldn't bear to look at him, and couldn't bear not to. Surely the Roon was a liar, but the thought of endangering Junior with a trip through the blue ring was a terrible pressure in her chest. She couldn't even consider the idea. But she also couldn't stand the idea of casting Myell back into the sea of time alone, with or without Twig or Kyle, on his mysterious heroic quest, while she would go on to find happiness with Osherman.

"Here's good enough," Jodenny said, once they found some flat rocks to sit on. "Everything, please."

He told her about waking on Garanwa's station, and traveling through the ring, and the first appearance of the Flying Doctor outside Lisa's house that night in Providence. "It was raining pretty hard," he said. "And the next day, when it showed up again, there was more thunder. Like now. I don't think it's all just a coincidence."

"You think Kultana is some kind of weather god?" she asked skeptically.

"There are some legends of Kultana as a goddess of rain, or a god from the Land of the Dead. Anything's possible."

"Do you believe that Roon? That if I go with you, Junior will be in danger?"

Myell gazed past her to the river. "It doesn't matter. We can't risk it."

"There has to be something we can do," Jodenny said. "There's still equipment on the *Kamchatka,* up in orbit. If we could somehow capture your blue ring, maybe keep you from leaving—"

"We've tried," he said. "Before. You and I, in the future. It doesn't work."

"This time could be different."

"It's never different. Homer says only the gods can change history."

She hated the bleakness in his voice. Wanted to reach over and shake him by the shoulders, jar that helplessness loose. "Then we'll just have to find some, won't we? But don't get any funny ideas. No more sacrifices, no more turning into a god yourself."

He stared at her.

"On Burringurrah," she said. "You died, and transformed. Sort of. Into Jungali, one of the Nogomain."

"That wasn't me," he said slowly. "Or, if it was me, someone changed history so that it never happened. I'm certainly not a god now."

"And you're not going to become one again," Jodenny vowed. "We'll just have to find Kultana, or someone else, to help us. Obviously the chances are pretty good, otherwise the Roon wouldn't be trying to stop you."

He didn't answer.

Twig's voice rang out over the hillside. "Uncle Terry!"

They turned their heads. The kids and Osherman had returned. Jodenny and Myell met them under a gum tree near the bridge. Twig's cheeks were bright, and Kyle seemed less grim than he had the night before. Osherman was uneasy, shuffling from foot to foot.

"Where have you been?" Myell asked.

"We went foraging," Twig said. "See? Nuts and these berries and this wild plum, but it's still kind of sour."

Kyle said, "I'm starving. Is there any real food left?"

Now that she thought of it, Jodenny was hungry too. Junior wanted his breakfast. *Her* breakfast, Jodenny reminded herself. Her daughter. She wasn't used to that idea after all these months of imagining the fetus as a boy. Myell fetched the heat globe from the cave and set it out by the river. He warmed up oatmeal for everyone and made coffee for the adults. Osherman declined to eat or drink, and sat near the bridge with his arms folded over his chest.

"How long are we going to be here?" Kyle asked Myell. "It's already been twelve hours."

Myell poked at his food with a spoon. "Maybe five more hours. Maybe four."

Twig tugged on Jodenny's sleeve. "You should come with us when we leave. You're the nicest you we've met so far."

"Oh, honey." She swallowed hard against the lump in her throat. "You're the nicest granddaughter I've ever met, too."

"That means no," Kyle told Twig. The bitterness was back in his voice. "And next time we come back, she won't remember you at all."

"Maybe." Jodenny reached for her bottle of water and took two careful sips. "Maybe not. Tell me, how did you all end up traveling together?"

"It was a Roon," Kyle said.

Osherman reacted instantly. He scrambled backward

in the leaves and mud, grabbed for a fallen branch, and rose up with the weapon as if the Roon were right there, ready to strike. Maybe in some warped corner of his mind there really was a Roon, a flashback of some kind, a delusion. Twig, who was nearest, ducked away toward Jodenny's arm. Kyle didn't move from his spot and Myell stood up with hands in a placating gesture.

"It's not here," Myell said. "You're safe right now."

The branch sliced through the air, right at Myell's head. He caught it and twisted it out of Osherman's hands. Osherman tackled him midwaist with a cry of terror. They both toppled down the riverbank toward the rushing water. Osherman was wild, striking and punching with no aim, kicking and biting with little accuracy. Myell, trying to subdue him, was ineffective against such frantic onslaught.

"Sam!" Jodenny yelled, following them. She tried not to slip or fall, one hand curved around Junior. Damn it that they didn't have a handy sedative. "Sam! Stop!"

"Grandpa!" Twig cried out, close behind Jodenny.

"I didn't know." Kyle's fists were clenched helplessly. "I didn't know I couldn't say it."

Osherman didn't hear them pleading with him to stop, or didn't understand the words, or didn't have the ability to control himself. Osherman and Myell rolled dangerously close to the water. The mud beneath them slid out, dumping both into the current. Myell was lucky enough to grab a tangle of weeds and roots that kept him from being sucked into the rush. Osherman flailed, was tugged under, and disappeared.

"Sam!" Jodenny yelled.

"Get him!" Twig said, dangerously close to the water's edge.

Kyle yelled, "I'll get a branch! Hold on!"

Jodenny didn't throw herself into water. She couldn't. Instead she grabbed for Myell and helped him back to sure footing. He was coughing up water and had livid scratches on his face, in no shape to go after a drowning man.

Kyle waded into the water. "I'll get him."

"No you don't," Jodenny said, and caught his arm.

"It doesn't matter," Myell choked out. "He'll be fine once we leave."

"You're not going anywhere." Jodenny tugged Kyle back to dry land and helped Myell up. "Twig, go get my beach bag."

"Where are we going?" Kyle asked.

"After him," Jodenny said.

Myell opened his mouth as if to argue, but coughed some more instead. Jodenny wasn't about to debate the matter, anyway. She said to Kyle, "Run ahead, call Sam's name, but don't get into the water yourself. You'll drown."

Kyle dashed ahead of them. Twig disappeared into the cave and came back with Jodenny's garish beach bag. They followed the river as it swung south, scouring the banks for any sign of Osherman. Jodenny sensed that Myell's heart wasn't in the endeavor, but he didn't complain out loud.

The bad weather cleared out and the morning grew increasingly hot as they hurried south. Sunlight through the trees made Jodenny's face heat up, or maybe that was the exertion. Junior set up a steady drumbeat of kicking inside her, *bam bam bam bam,* and she wondered if Twig's mom was some kind of martial artist. She tried imagining Osherman washed up in the mud, or clinging to a low-hanging branch, but all she saw was the deadly river. Her heart ached at the thought that he might be dead.

"What's the town like, forty years from now?" she asked, trying to distract herself.

"Not so bad."

"We never establish contact with anyone back home?"

"It's too far," he said.

She knew that. Had calculated the miles back to Earth a million times, and had lain out in her yard watching the stars in this new sky. "What about the *Kamchatka*?"

"Searched for an Alcheringa drop for months without finding any way home. They had to bring it down eventually, before it lost orbit completely. The engines failed under the stress of reentry. They lost it over the Southern Ocean."

He sounded like he was reciting lessons from a history book, but this was her future, hers and Junior's. She imagined how devastating the loss of the *Kamchatka* would be—all that recyclable material they hadn't yet stripped out, the power plants and mechanical parts, the computers.

"You don't have to sound so casual about it," she said.

He stopped walking. "I'm not. It's just—it's the way things are going to be. I've seen it."

She stopped him. Kissed him.

"We'll find a way out of this," she promised, though she had no idea how or why to follow through on it.

He kissed her back, and they resumed the search for Osherman.

Jodenny was trying to keep Twig close and make sure Kyle didn't get too far out of sight. In the process she didn't realize how far they'd come. When she saw a wooden platform in the trees above she stopped, surprised. The guard post was empty, which was alarming in and of itself.

"Kyle!" she shouted. "Come on back here!"

"But I see him, Nana!" Kyle called back. "He's here!"

By the time Jodenny caught up, Kyle and two other people were bent over Osherman's body on the east bank of the river. Large and ruddy Teddy Toledo was pounding helpfully on Osherman's back. Louise Sharp, her red hair pulled into a ponytail, was scooping mud out of Osherman's mouth with her two fingers.

"Swallowed half the river, he did," Louise said as Jodenny approached. "Finally got around to pushing him in, did you?"

"No," Jodenny said. "He fell."

"Not too graceful," Toledo said, and then caught sight of Myell. Toledo's mouth opened and stayed open, his teeth bright in the sunlight. "Ugh," he said, which was more articulate than Osherman, who began jerking and coughing up brown water.

Louise leaned back and blinked at Myell and the kids. "Hello. Where did you come from?"

"You're dead," Toledo said to Myell.

Myell sat down on the riverbank wearily. "Not yet."

Jodenny sat down beside him, all of her energy spent. She said, "Welcome to the Outpost."

Myell had been there before, of course. They all gave him crazy looks when he said so, but he just shrugged off their disbelief.

"About fifteen years from now, things will be going well," he said. "You'll have a good infrastructure, steady power, and enough food for everyone. But then there's a flu. Kills a lot of people. The survivors mostly disperse or go up to Providence, where they develop a vaccine in time to save everyone else."

They were sitting in the middle of the camp, surrounded by the small huts and most of the Outpost's adult population—the forty or so men and women who'd rejected living under military rule in Providence and opted for self-rule near the beach. The settlement had been slapped together using the same materials from the *Kamchatka* but had a more haphazard look, given that all the military officers, including the engineers, had stayed loyal to Captain Balandra.

"Bastards," Baylou Owenstein said. In this eddy, he was still young and strapping. Destined to survive. His husband beside him, Hullabaloo, would be one of the unlucky ones. Killed in the first wave of sickness, Myell knew. Feverish and delirious for days until the end. Baylou continued, "Bet they do it on purpose. Wait 'til we're sick and dying and then come up with a vaccine."

Louise Sharp, who would also be one of the unlucky ones, said, "Now that we know it's coming, we can prepare."

Myell rubbed his eyes and said nothing. Jodenny, who was sitting in a sturdy chair beside him, patted his knee.

"I tell you, it's creepy looking at you," Teddy Toledo said. "Leorah would have a good old fainting spell if she saw you."

Jodenny doubted that Leorah Farber had ever fainted in her life, but appreciated the sentiment. Farber was down the coast with three others from the camp, looking at a possible new site for relocation.

"I almost fainted, myself. You don't meet a resurrected dead man every day," Louise agreed, and passed Myell a beer.

The beer at the Outpost tasted like swill but it was alcoholic swill, and Myell appreciated that. He needed a wet throat to keep answering their questions about the future. To them it was all vitally important but to him it was just another exercise in futility, and a headache was beginning to blossom behind his eyes.

He supposed the ache in his skull was nothing compared to the pain in Osherman's. Osherman was sitting under a lean-to, a cold cloth pressed to the lump on the side of his head. Twig and Kyle were sitting with him, though the Outpost's nurse had declared him right as rain. A dunk in the river was nothing impressive around here. They didn't get truly worried unless someone lost a limb, and even that was treated as a mere inconvenience.

"So tell me, time-traveling man," one of the women asked. "Do I get married?"

"Do I have kids?" someone else asked.

"Listen to you all," Mrs. Zhang said. She was the oldest woman on the planet, ornery, and even the people who liked her were afraid of her sharp tongue. "Time traveler! What rubbish will you believe next?"

"He was dead," Louise pointed out. "And now he's not. What is he? A ghost? A robot?"

"He could be his own twin brother," someone said.

"Twin brother or not, you're at least staying for lunch," Louise proclaimed.

"That's not a good idea," Myell said. "There's a chance—a very slight chance—that a Roon might show up. It's been following me around."

Jodenny nodded. "I've seen it."

"Christ," Louise said.

Baylou reached for the knife at his waist. "Let me at the lizard."

Most of the crew and passengers off the *Kamchatka* had never met a real live Roon, but had instead watched on the vids as the aliens approached and reconnaissanced Earth. Myell guessed his other self—his twin brother, his doppelgänger, the version of him that had died, however he wanted to think of himself—had gotten up close and personal in a specifically fatal way, but this Jodenny hadn't given up all the details yet. Judging from the shuttered look on her face, she wasn't considering it a priority in their last few hours together in this eddy.

He remembered the Flying Doctor's threat about the baby, and felt a hot flush of shame that he wanted this Jodenny to come with him anyway.

It wasn't an option. Absolutely not. By the time the ouroboros came, he intended to be miles away from her. Him and the kids—

Myell turned. "Where'd they go?"

Jodenny followed his gaze. Kyle, Twig, and Osherman had disappeared from under the lean-to.

"Damn it," Myell stood up. "Anyone see where they went?"

"Up there," said a man sitting against a rain barrel. "Toward the waterfall."

With Jodenny beside him, Myell followed the curve of the camp to where a small river drained out of the dense eucalypt forest. A short, well-trodden path led to a waterfall only a few meters high. Most of the water frothed on flat rocks and rushed down to meet the ocean, but some of it pooled behind the waterfall in a area of slick damp rock and green ledges.

The kids were there, bathing away mud and grime, with Osherman keeping a close eye.

"You're not supposed to go anywhere without me!" Myell said sternly.

"We didn't go far," Kyle replied, unconcerned.

Twig splashed water their way. "Come on in! It's really nice."

Jodenny needed no further urging. She took off her T-shirt and shorts until only her bathing suit remained.

"We only have a few hours left," Myell protested.

She stepped gingerly into the water and gave him a wide smile. "More than time enough for a swim, sailor."

He peeled off his shirt and followed her in. The water was warmer than expected, fresh not salty, and he was glad to soak away the river silt that had been clinging to him all day. The bottom of the pool was slippery but not very deep. He dunked under, circled around to Jodenny, and surfaced with her arms linked around his neck. Her baby bump rested solid and warm against his stomach.

"I'm sorry," he said.

She kissed his forehead and his nose. Her voice was carefully neutral. "What for?"

"Everything."

"Everything's pretty big," she said, her mouth against his.

Twig called out, "Kissing!"

"That's gross," Kyle said.

Jodenny blushed. Myell turned his back to the kids and Osherman, who was watching with a flat blank look.

"You can't leave," Jodenny said.

He traced her lips with one finger. "If there was any way to stop it, I would. You know I would."

Her hands moved down his back and to his legs, determined to explore him. Myell nestled his head in the crook of her shoulder and let her have her way. She touched the burn marks and other scars left by his travels.

"Let's go lie in the shade," she said.

They climbed out. The kids seemed determined to stay in the water until they turned into fish. Myell led Jodenny to a stretch of grass under a rocky outcropping. She put her shirt back on and used her shorts as a pillow. He stretched out beside her and she nestled against him.

"Tell me all the places you've been," she murmured.

He considered the question. "I'd rather tell you where I'm going."

Jodenny's hand moved to lay flat on his heart, and he covered it with his fingers. Two blue-winged butterflies flitted past and rose up into the trees. In the water, the kids laughed and splashed each other under Osherman's supervision.

Myell said, "I'm going to see you when you're old and cranky but still have that spark in your eye. That never-give-up, get-the-job-done glint. I'm going to see you when you're running around the playground of the Simon Street orphanage—your hair in pigtails and scabs on your knees. There's some boy there that you always tease. You like to steal part of his lunch and make him come get it. I think you're sweet on him."

Her eyes were wide and dark. "Billy Lawrence."

"Billy Lawrence," Myell repeated. "And I'm going to see you at the academy, all prim and proper in your uniform, marching back and forth across the parade field

fifty times because you refused to rat out your roommate for pulling a prank on the company commander.
Later you go to a birthday party for Richi Miller and
make out with him in the alley. You come back all
smiles with your blouse buttoned wrong."

She used her free hand to cover her face, then peeked
between her fingers at him. "You see too much."

He kissed her softly. "I'm going to see you marry
Sam when he's whole and healthy again, and you're going to dance at your wedding with Lisa beside you. I'm
going to see your daughters when they're all grown up
and doing their best every day, because that's what you
teach them. To be strong and keep trying and never
look back."

Her eyes were watering now. His own eyes were
damp, but he wouldn't weep. Not in front of her.

"I'm going to see you stay here while I walk away
into the woods, because it's time for me to go now.
You're going to forget I was here, but you'll never forget I love you."

Tears spilled down her cheeks. Myell wanted to
spare her that, wanted to spare himself, but how could
he? Not with the ouroboros and the universe pitted
against them. He kissed her once more and then rose up,
determined to go.

"Come on, kids," he said. "Time to get out of the—"

All the air sucked out of his lungs.

The world tilted.

"Terry!" Jodenny reached for him, alarmed, and he
didn't have the breath to tell her to stay back.

Too soon. The ouroboros was hours too soon. Myell
shook off her arms and lurched away. The blue light
was filling his vision. She must have thought he was
choking, or having a fit, or maybe he'd swallowed his

tongue. The ground slid out beneath him despite his best efforts to stay upright. He tumbled into the pool just below the waterfall. On his way into the blue rushing water he saw Jodenny reach for him, and now here was Osherman making a grab, but the kids were too far away, too far—

"Kyle!" Myell managed. "Hurry!"

He saw Kyle hold tight to Twig and retreat. Shaking his head. Choosing this eddy and the chance of evaporation over anything Myell could offer him.

Too late now. The blue ring had arrived. It swept away Myell, Osherman, and Jodenny. And Junior, defenseless in Jodenny's womb.

CHAPTER **ELEVEN**

Sub-lieutenant Adryn Ling reached for her third coffee of the midwatch and grimaced at the bitter taste. She hated coffee but tea was even worse. At oh-four-thirty she'd drink raw sewage if it contained enough stimulants to keep her going for another four hours. Not that there was much chance of raw sewage on the flight deck of the UAC *Confident*. Just row after row of Eagle A7-40s ready to launch as needed to defeat the Roon.

"You're daydreaming again," said Chief Cappaletto, in his odd American accent. "Concentrate on the game."

"Sorry," she said. "I'm contemplating."

Silence for a long moment. Rows of chess pieces awaited her decision.

"We're off duty in three hours," Cappaletto said.

Adryn reached for her only remaining knight, moved

it forward carefully, and released her grip. Cappaletto grinned wolfishly and moved his queen in return. "Checkmate. Sunday rules."

The handsome chief, who was a few years older than her and considered quite the ladies' man among the Flight Department, tended to change the rules whenever he wanted to. No one else ever invoked Sunday rules, which required swapping the roles of the rooks and knights, or the Midwatch Option, which meant the bishop could clone himself. Still, their games killed the long stretch of time after midnight, when ship's dawn was only a dim prospect on the horizon.

"Mother said there'd be days like this," Cappaletto said, around a yawn.

"Days like what?"

"Stuck for hours on end with a beautiful woman and nary a bed in sight."

She grinned. "Are you hitting on me, Chief?"

"Never!" He held up his fingers boy-scout style. "My heart currently belongs to a beautiful young ensign in the Astronomy Department."

"I don't want to hear about you breaking regulations," Adryn said.

"Besides, if anything happened between us, your wife would probably drag me to the infirmary and castrate me. Without painkillers."

Adryn grinned. "She sure would."

An alarm began to trill on the control panel. Adryn swiveled for a quick glimpse through the observation window. The Eagles were all still, with no sign of movement. Just cold metal and engines down there, waiting to destroy or be destroyed.

"Alert in bay five," Cappaletto said. "One of the bots again, I bet. I'll get it."

Adryn rolled her chair back. "No, I'll get it. Need the exercise. Why don't you find a deck of cards while I'm gone and I'll kick your ass at poker?"

He grinned. "Why don't I break out a chess set with training wheels on it?"

She shot him a middle finger on her way down the ladder.

It took a full sixty seconds to hike across the deck to the flight bay in question. The air smelled like oil and fuel. The only sounds were the echo of her boots and the hum of the air-circulation system. She envied Laura, snug in their bed back in officer berthing. They'd been on opposite schedules for two months now. Adryn had taken an officer exchange slot with the Americanadian Forces precisely to be near her wife, but she was beginning to think she'd see her more if Laura came over to one of the big Team Space ships.

She was still brooding over the subject when she reached the bay and found three intruders in civilian clothes.

One of the strangers, a man, had pulled away to a corner bulkhead and was clawing at the metal with his fingernails. Another man, shirtless and sopping wet, was having some kind of convulsion or seizure on the deck. Beside him was an equally drenched pregnant woman in what looked like a bathing suit. She was crying and writhing and clutching her stomach. Adryn was afraid she was in the middle of delivering her baby, or maybe miscarrying it.

Adryn activated her SOEL. "Chief, get Security down here right away, fully armed. And a medical team."

"We need help," the woman said. "Please! We need doctors."

Adryn approached warily. None of them seemed armed, or dangerous in any way. "It's all right, help's coming. Are you in pain?"

"He said the baby wouldn't make it," the woman gasped. "Terry? Is he—help him!"

The man having seizures went abruptly still. Adryn carefully checked the pulse in his neck. When she caught sight of his features, her fingers went numb with surprise. She knew him. Hadn't seen him since she was a kid, but she'd grown up with the vids her parents had propped up on the mantelpieces and bookcases, and of course there were all the books, movies, and games that had been based on his life. The hero of Burringurrah. Right here on her flight deck.

Now that Adryn looked closely at the woman, she recognized her as well.

Bewildered, she asked, "Uncle Terry? Aunt Jodenny?"

The infirmary on the *Confident* was a long, low row of cubicles, closed rooms, electronic privacy screens, and uncomfortable furniture in the lounge. Adryn couldn't sit down for more than ten minutes at a time. She paced the lounge, pestered the nurses for information they didn't have, and chewed on her fingernails one by one. It was just past oh-six-hundred now but she didn't feel the urge for breakfast or even sleep. Instead she felt frazzled and empty and worried. She didn't think she'd be able to sleep even if someone tranquilized her.

She wasn't alone in the lounge. Lieutenant Commander Will Endicott from Security was there, conducting one conversation after another on his SOEL. She'd met him a few times, but didn't know much about him—tall, intense, nearly bald. A security guard was standing in the doorway, ready to be called upon. Myell was in a room down the passage, guarded by a petty officer who wouldn't let Adryn past the hatch.

Uncle Terry, missing fifteen years, arriving on her doorstep.

Now, when they needed him most.

She didn't know what to think about it.

Eventually a commander showed up, and like her he wore a Team Space uniform instead of an Americanadian one.

"Noel Haines," he said, shaking her hand. He had thin blond hair, a small forehead, and a crooked way of twisting his mouth that almost, but not quite, looked like a smile. "Let's go on down to the doctors' lounge and talk there."

She followed him reluctantly. By craning her head she could see the exam room where a cluster of doctors, including Adryn's wife, were working on Jodenny Scott. Laura had been called in because of her background in high-risk obstetrics. Laura had looked surprised to see Adryn in the lounge but there'd been no time to talk then, and there hadn't been any since.

The doctors' lounge was small and sparsely furnished, and smelled like old coffee. There was a real aquarium on the corner table. The water looked dirty and Adryn wasn't sure the two goldfish floating inside were even alive. Commander Haines sat down on an uncomfortable-looking green sofa and said, "Tell me why you think one of those men is your uncle."

Adryn ignored his gesture to sit beside him. She automatically clasped her hands behind her back. "I don't think it. I know it. He's my father's brother. She's his wife. I've grown up looking at their vids, wondering what happened to them after they disappeared."

"You only met Commander Scott once, when you were a child," Haines said. "She visited your family's farm."

That certainly wasn't in any records that Adryn knew about. Jodenny Scott's trip to the farm, all those years ago, had been a secret. Fraternization had been a big risk back then, as it still was.

Carefully she asked, "What department did you say you worked for, sir?"

Again, that twist of the mouth almost like a smile.

"Research and Development, Department Fifteen," he said.

She nodded. "Alcheringa geeks."

"That's what they call us," he agreed. "Commander Scott and Chief Myell have been missing for fifteen years. Now they show up during your watch. Any inkling why?"

"I don't think they planned it," Adryn said. One of the not-quite-dead fish in the tank swam toward the surface, looking maybe for food or rescue.

"Do you know who the third man is?"

"No. I didn't recognize him." She did know that Security had been forced to tranquilize him to get him out of the bay. He was somewhere nearby, probably strapped to a gurney.

Adryn wasn't surprised that the three of them were under heavy guard. Hero of Burringurrah or not, Myell and the other two had materialized out of nowhere onto a secure flight deck. Explanations would be demanded. She'd put a ping in to Legal Services over on the *Melbourne* but hadn't received a return call. The situation was going to be complicated by the fact that Myell and Jodenny were Team Space personnel, inactive roster of course, on the flagship of the Americanadian military forces, in a joint operation at war with the Roon.

Her head hurt just thinking about the possibilities.

She asked Haines, "Do *you* know who the third man is, Commander?"

"I have an idea, but his embedded dog tag is missing. It looks like it was dug out by a knife, years ago. There's a scar. But your aunt and uncle's tags are confirmed. Even the archaic chip model is authentic."

"What's going to happen to them?"

"Depends on where they've been and what they can tell us."

"They have rights," she said.

"They're also security risks," Haines said.

"How?"

"There are still parts of the Burringurrah mission that are classified," Haines said, which of course she already knew. "You don't have the necessary clearance. When and if it becomes necessary for you to need to know, Lieutenant, I'm sure you'll be briefed."

The fish in the tank were beseeching Adryn with their sad, bulging eyes. "What about Admiral Nam, sir? Has he been briefed?"

Haines's gaze narrowed. "I'm sure the news is working its way to all the fleet admirals."

Maybe he wasn't as smart as he thought he was.

"With all due respect," Adryn said, "the news better find him soon. I may not know the exact details of what my aunt and uncle were doing on their last duty assignment, but I know the admiral was involved. He told me so, the day I graduated from the academy. He also told me he holds himself personally responsible. I guarantee you that the minute he finds out, he's going to be on a birdie over here. And if he finds out they've been mistreated in any way, someone's going to pay for it. Sir."

A muscle twitched in Haines's check. "I'll consider your advice carefully, Lieutenant. You're dismissed."

Adryn returned to the lounge. Commander Endicott had stepped out somewhere. Ten minutes later he returned.

"You can see him," Endicott said. "Try to get as much out of him as you can. He's not very talkative."

Adryn went down to Myell's room and stepped inside. He was sitting on a stool as far as possible from the flat exam table. Someone had given him dry scrubs to wear but they were thin and not much protection against the cool air. His face was dry but his eyes were rimmed red.

"Damn it, Homer," he was saying. "Show yourself!"

She asked, "Who's Homer?"

His gaze swerved her way. "Do you know what's happening? To my wife?"

"I don't know." Adryn felt suddenly unsure, and cold despite her uniform sweater. "Can I get you something? Are you hungry?"

He shook his head. His gaze was on the bulkhead, where colorful medical posters outlined the symptoms of sexually transmitted diseases. "The kids. Were they with us? Two kids."

"I didn't see any kids. Just you, Commander Scott, and the other man. Do you know who I am?"

He blinked and focused on her for a moment. His voice didn't shift out of its flatness. "The nurse told me. Adryn Myell Ling. Last time I saw you, you were, what? Ten years old? You're all grown up."

Her turn to nod.

"I'm a pilot," she added, as if he couldn't decipher the insignia on her uniform. She mentally kicked herself. "You've been missing for fifteen years."

He rubbed his eyes with his knuckles. There were goosebumps on his forearms. Adryn opened the medical cabinet and searched through the shelves until she found a thin white blanket. She shook it out and put it around his shoulders. He held on to the edges with minimal effort.

"What ship is this?" he asked, and she had the distinct impression that his curiosity was a desperate last resort against something else.

"The *Confident*. It's ACF—Americanadian Forces. They don't dress for dinner and they don't have beer. Kind of uncivilized, if you ask me."

He nodded. Not really listening to her. Or listening harder to something she couldn't hear, something beyond their little room.

Adryn sat on the edge of the exam table and swung her feet against the base of it. "I guess there are more exciting ways to interrupt a midwatch but you've won the award for best so far. Dad's going to burst when he hears you're back. And Mom. And Jake, and TJ. Teren, Junior. He was born after you disappeared."

The hatch clicked open and Myell stood up so quickly the blanket fluttered to the floor. Dr. Cho entered, his large face shadowed with fatigue. Laura was with him, and she gave Adryn a very brief nod.

"Chief Myell," Cho said. "I'm taking care of your wife. She's doing fine now, as is the baby."

Myell gazed at him soundlessly, then started to topple over.

Adryn and Cho caught him before he could hit the

floor. He hadn't totally fainted away, but they manhandled him to the table and Laura got smelling salts out of the cabinet. One whiff made him shake his head and gasp sharply. Cho elevated the foot of the bed and took his pulse.

"There, now. Better?"

Myell asked, "Not damaged? Really?"

"She was in premature labor, but her water didn't break," Laura said. "We convinced her uterus to hang in there for a while longer. The baby has a good chance of survival if delivered right now, but the closer we get to full term the better off. All the fetal scans came back normal."

Myell covered his eyes with his left hand. Adryn patted his arm but didn't know what to say. Laura, ever practical, retrieved the fallen blanket and eased it over him. Cho scanned the vital-statistics display over the bed and asked, "How are you feeling? Light-headed, nauseous?"

"I'm fine. I want to see them."

"In a moment," Cho said. "Let's see your blood pressure come up."

"If you don't take me to my wife, I guarantee my blood pressure will come up, Doc."

Cho was not intimidated. But he helped Myell sit up, and a few moments later walked him down the hall with a security tech as escort. Adryn didn't go with them. She felt suddenly drained, and in need of a lie-down and blanket herself.

Laura cupped the back of her neck. "How are you doing?"

"I'm fine," Adryn said. "Just a little, you know, surprised. By the returning-from-the dead thing, or wherever they've been for fifteen years and not aged a single day."

"Your dad will be happy," Laura said.

Adryn supposed he would. She wondered how long it would take for the news to reach him in prison. She certainly wasn't going to be the one to break five years of silence and tell him.

"Let's go," Laura said. "I'll buy you some coffee and you can tell me all about your long-lost uncle."

Adryn steered her into the doctors' lounge and toward the dirty aquarium. "First we've got some goldfish to rescue."

Jodenny wasn't sure what drugs they'd given her but she felt perfectly relaxed and warm, and maybe a little hungry. She was in a private infirmary room, with pleasantly beeping machines monitoring her and Junior. The lights were down and a thoughtful nurse had put a pillow under her knees to ease the strain on her back. She was content to gaze at the swirly pattern on the overhead, circles and curls ever so entrancing, and when someone came through the door she dragged her attention away with great reluctance.

One look at Myell's face brought back all her fear and misery.

"Kay," he said, and then they were clutching each other so hard Jodenny thought she heard something crack in her shoulder. She didn't care. Myell was cold and trembling. He smelled like sweat. His voice stuttered against her neck with words she didn't understand. She rubbed his back and wet his shirt with her tears, and finally he eased her back against her pillows.

"You're okay?" he asked, brushing her hair back from her face. "Not in pain?"

"Not in pain, not in labor," she replied. "But that Roon said—"

"It was wrong," Myell said firmly. "Thank god."

Jodenny touched his forehead and kissed him. She never wanted to let him out of her sight again. She wished she were a witch, able to wield magic and reshape the universe.

Maybe if she kissed him hard enough she could bind him to her forever.

"Do you know where we are?" he asked, sitting as close to her as possible on the narrow mattress.

She hooked one of her bare legs over his, and tugged the blanket so that it was covering both of them. His arm went around her shoulders and she leaned into him with all her weight.

"ACF ship, fifteen years forward," he sounded very tired. "I don't know why. Every other time I've jumped, it's been to somewhere where you are. Every single time. But now you're with me and I don't know what happened to Kyle and Twig. If they're alive or if the eddy reset and wiped them away—"

She put her hand on his chest, feeling for the rhythm of his heartbeat. "Sssh. It's going to work out. We'll find them somehow. Have you seen Sam?"

"No. But I saw my niece," he said. "Adryn. You met her on Mary River, remember? She's a sub-lieutenant now."

Jodenny cast her memory back to a little girl playing baseball on Colby Myell's farm. "She became American?"

"No, Team Space. She's on foreign exchange, I think.

She might have tried to tell me. I wasn't listening very well. Her last name is Ling now."

"That's the doctor's name, too," Jodenny said.

He didn't answer. His breathing was regular but a little raspy. She hoped he wasn't coming down with a cold. Between dousings in the river and under the waterfall, maybe he'd swallowed too much water or had it go down the wrong way. She'd have to keep an eye on him. Junior kicked, as if echoing the sentiment, and Jodenny put both hands on her belly. It was as impossible as a dream, but here she was with her husband and unborn daughter, something she couldn't have imagined a day or two ago.

And Sam Osherman was here, too. She wasn't sure how that fit into the dream. They were far from Providence, not only in space but also in time. Kyle and Twig were stranded somewhere in space-time, or had ceased to exist altogether. And unless the parameters had changed, in less than a day the ouroboros would come to take Myell away again.

She supposed it was selfish, but she suddenly wished for another dose of the happy drugs.

Another hour passed. Jodenny dozed off and on. Myell snored against her shoulder. Dr. Ling and Dr. Cho returned together, checked the monitors, and then to Jodenny's relief and surprise said she could be discharged.

"No bed rest?" she asked. She had despaired at the prospect of spending the foreseeable future—which was not very foreseeable, granted—flat on her back with nothing to do but watch Myell save the universe, or do whatever it was he was supposed to be doing.

"Bed rest is good, but you're not limited to it," Cho

said. He adhered a thin sensor sheet to her belly to monitor Junior and gave her a prescription patch to deliver anticontraction medicine.

"And we'd like to download a Digital Duola into your head," Ling said.

Jodenny asked, "A what?"

Ling said, "It's an information database every pregnant woman gets these days. Full access to prenatal health guidelines, anatomical presentations, answers to common pregnancy questions. There are emergency instructions if you end up having to deliver the child yourself, and postdelivery information too. Usually both parents-to-be get it."

Jodenny looked to Myell, who was sitting on the bed looking rumpled and bleary-eyed. He asked, "You put it in our heads?"

"Not physically insert it, no," Ling said. "It's delivered via a retinal scan. All you have to do is look into this reader here. It only takes a few seconds."

"Technology these days." Myell slid off the bed, put his eyes to the small scanner, and shuffled his feet anxiously. "Is it going to hurt?"

Ling turned the reader off. "It's already done. The information will unpack itself over the next several hours."

Jodenny went next. She peered at a small blue light, blinked, and the procedure was over.

"If you're both not walking databases of pregnancy information by this time tomorrow, let me know and we'll try again," Ling said.

Myell and Jodenny were left in Adryn's care, with two guards posted in the corridor outside. Adryn had somehow rounded up uniforms for them to wear. Unsurprisingly, there was a shortage of Team Space maternity clothes, so Jodenny made do with a large green T-shirt and pair of trousers designed for an enormously large man. Myell was easier to outfit, although his shirt was too tight. Jodenny didn't tell him, but she liked him in tight shirts.

"I can ask the *Melbourne* to send over something better," Adryn said, eyeing the results once Jodenny was dressed. "A real uniform for you, Commander."

Jodenny pulled her hair back into a loose ponytail. "That's Aunt Jodenny to you."

Pink bloomed in Adryn's cheeks. "I didn't think you'd remember me."

"It wasn't that long ago as far as I'm concerned. You were, what? Ten years old? And you wanted to be a veterinarian. You're a long way from that."

"I like pets too much to kill the ones that need putting down," Adryn said. "I can't believe you just jumped through time. Where did you come from?"

Myell cleared his throat in a not-so-subtle way.

Jodenny said, "It's a long story."

"You're not going to tell me, is that it?" Adryn asked.

"Maybe later," Myell said. "Where to now?"

She didn't look happy with either of them, but answered nonetheless. "There's a team on its way from the *Melbourne*. That's the Team Space flagship. I'm supposed take you down to Security for debriefing."

"Are they going to turn us over to the *Melbourne*?" Myell asked.

"I don't know," Adryn admitted. "The commanding officer here, Captain McNaughton, isn't so keen in giving you up until everyone's sure how you got onboard. Team Space can't order him to give you up. No jurisdiction. And relations between Earth and Fortune are dicey enough as it is, you know? Friends, but not friends."

Jodenny would rather they were on a Team Space ship, surrounded by their own military. She said, "Before we go anywhere, I want to see Sam."

Adryn's face crinkled in confusion. "Who?"

"Commander Osherman. The man who was with us," Myell said.

"I'll have to check," Adryn said.

She stepped out to consult with someone. Jodenny grabbed Myell's hand and squeezed it tight. "What if they separate us? You can't leave without me."

He stroked her back. "I'm not going anywhere."

"That's what you said last time."

The hatch slid open a moment later. "This way," Adryn said. "Just a quick visit."

Jodenny and Myell followed Adryn down the passage to Osherman's room with two guards trailing behind. Dr. Cho was inside, making notes on a digital clipboard. Osherman was sound asleep, or maybe drugged. His wrists were in restraints and he looked very pale.

Jodenny's voice was faint in her own ears as she asked, "How's he doing?"

"Chief Myell said he was held captive by the Roon," Cho said.

She nodded. Myell, beside her, touched her elbow in support.

"He shows evidence of physical mistreatment—old ligament damage, skull trauma, formerly fractured bones. There's no sign of damage to his throat or vocal cords, but there's some unusual activity in the region of his brain that controls speech. We're running more tests. We'd like to get him talking. At least interacting with our mental health team."

Adryn said, "And if he was a prisoner of the Roon, we need to know what he knows."

"Why?" Myell asked.

Cho blinked at them. To Adryn he said, "They don't know?"

Jodenny felt goosebumps move down her spine. "Know what?"

"We're at war," Adryn said. "With the Roon. And in two days we're going to blast their armada out of the sky."

CHAPTER **TWELVE**

Ma'am," a chief said to Adryn when they stepped back into the passage. Myell hadn't seen him before. He was a tall, formidable Hispanic-looking man with olive skin and very muscled arms. "I'm Chief Ovadia. I'm here to bring them to Security."

Adryn said, "I'll come with you."

"That's not necessary," Ovadia said tightly.

"I insist, Chief."

Between Adryn, Ovadia, Jodenny, Myell, and two guards, the lift was crowded. Myell barely noticed. His palms itched with anxiety as they descended toward the Security Office.

War.

War with the Roon.

He had never been in a future eddy with the Roon in it. All his trips had been to various stages of Jodenny's life in the Seven Sisters or in Providence, which was cut off from the rest of mankind. The residents there wouldn't know if galactic war was being waged elsewhere in the galaxy. Their isolation had been their salvation.

He thought of Kyle and Twig, and nausea rose up his gullet.

As the lift descended, ship's bells rang oh-eight-hundred. Jodenny waited for them to pass and asked, "This war with the Roon. How long has it been going on?"

"Off and on, fifteen years," Adryn said. "Since the two of you, and the entire Roon army, disappeared from atop Burringurrah back on Earth."

Jodenny made a faint noise of surprise. "The army disappeared?"

"They've made a lot of movies about it," Adryn assured them.

Myell asked, "Where are we, exactly?"

Ovadia said, "Perhaps this discussion can wait."

"Their security clearances are a lot higher than ours, Chief." Adryn turned to Myell. "We're about four months out from Mary River. We've been tracking the Roon fleet for the last several years and plan to intercept them just past a small planetoid called PX2-843. According to our long-range sensors, they've got six carriers and maybe a dozen more support ships."

"And how many ships are in our fleet?" Jodenny asked.

She looked uncomfortable. "Fourteen."

Fourteen ACF and Team Space ships against six Roon carriers.

"But that's not nearly enough . . ." Jodenny said, and then fell silent.

When the lift doors opened they walked a short distance to the Security Office and were met by a Team

Space commander named Haines. He shook Myell's hand and then Jodenny's, but ignored Adryn and Ovadia.

"I'm with Research and Development," he said. "First off, welcome back. Second off, I need to sit down with each of you for a preliminary debriefing."

Myell wasn't surprised when Jodenny reached for his hand and grabbed it like a lifeline.

"Together," Jodenny said. "You can interview us together or not at all."

Haines's expression was perplexed. "I'm not sure that's feasible—"

Jodenny insisted, "Together. Don't upset me, Commander. I'm in a delicate condition, if you haven't noticed. And we don't have a lot of time left."

"Left before what?" Haines asked.

Myell's hand was beginning to ache under the pressure of Jodenny's grip. "Before the ouroboros comes to take me away again."

Jodenny looked unhappy at the word "me" but said nothing.

Haines pursed his lips, looking thoughtful, and then ushered them forward. Adryn was instructed to wait by the front desk. Jodenny and Myell were taken to a large conference room with an oval table in the middle of it. Bottles of water, a bowl of fruit, a tray of pastries, and a carafe of hot coffee had already been set up for them, giving the place an unexpectedly welcome air. Even the chairs were comfortable. Jodenny reassessed all she knew about Americans, took a pastry, and poured Myell a cup of coffee.

He was paler than she liked, and she knew why.

An entire Roon army was about to arrive on their doorstep.

The two guards remained outside the conference room, but Ovadia stood inside, by the hatch. Another commander, thin and wiry with dark red hair, entered the room. Haines introduced him.

"This is Commander Albright. He's in charge of ship's security. He's very interested in how you got onto the flight deck. How you got onto the ship, actually. You said it's an ouroboros?"

"That's not possible. The nearest Wondjina Sphere is back on Mary River," Albright said, taking a seat at the far end of the table.

"There isn't any footage to view from security cameras?" Myell asked.

"There was a glitch," Albright said, but he didn't elaborate.

Myell wrapped his hands around his coffee cup. "It was a Wondjina Transportation System ouroboros. My own personal albatross. It shows up and drags me off to somewhere else in the universe, other places and times. I can't stop it, and I can't control where I go."

Albright didn't look reassured. "Wondjina tokens can only travel between Spheres."

"Not this one," Jodenny said.

Haines made a notation on a clipboard. "How long have you been traveling in this ring, Chief Myell?"

"I don't know about days. Sixty-five jumps or so, give or take a few. It's hard to keep track. For ten or eleven trips, I had my grandchildren with me. On this last trip, I had just Commander Scott and Commander Osherman."

Neither of the men in front of him batted an eyelash at the mention of grandchildren. Instead Albright said, "Where did you come from most recently?"

Myell squeezed Jodenny's hand. She said, "The planet

where I've been living with the castaways from the TSS *Kamchatka*. We were flung through some kind of Alcheringa wormhole and landed there about six months ago."

Albright and Haines exchanged looks. Albright said, "The *Kamchatka* disappeared fifteen years ago."

"From your perspective," Myell said. "But you scanned us while we were in Medical so you know that we haven't aged since that time. The ouroboros is taking us through time as well as space."

Haines stood up. "I think we better pause for a moment. I need to ping some people."

He and Albright both left the conference room. Myell was happy just to sit with Jodenny and his coffee, though Ovadia's unflinching scrutiny was disconcerting. He bit into a pastry—cream cheese and strawberry, very nice—and asked Ovadia, "Want one? They're good."

"No," Ovadia said, not moving from the hatch.

Soon the conference room was full of more people, Americanadian and Team Space both. Some of them were scientists. The rest were from Security, Weapons, and Engineering. Myell lost track of the names. They wanted to know more about the blue ouroboros and how it worked without a Sphere.

"I don't know," Myell said. "It just does. It comes for me and takes me elsewhere, and dumps me for a while before it takes me away again. It's usually twenty-four hours or so, but it varies if someone made the last trip with me."

"Does it breach the hull?" a worried-looking officer asked.

Jodenny gave him a sharp look. "Did it breach it when we arrived?"

"You said it moves you through time and space both,"

Haines said. "Where have you been, Chief Myell, in all these trips you've taken?"

Myell closed his eyes for a moment. "Fortune, while Commander Scott was still in the academy. Then I saw her in the hospital on Kookaburra, after the *Yangtze* disaster. After that, I visited Providence when she was getting—well, about ten years had passed, which is still minus five from right now. I visited Kiwi and she was on a beach holiday. That happened a couple of times, actually. At least three times I saw her in the orphanage where she grew up, and there was another trip to the academy, and a couple more trips to the *Yangtze,* and Providence when she was seventy years old, and Providence just like you see her now. The rest is kind of blurry."

He opened his eyes to find them all staring at him.

Jodenny's expression, especially, was one of wonder.

"All those times?" she asked. "And I never remembered you?"

He shrugged. Behind him, the hatch slid open and someone moved into the corner of his vision. He concentrated only on Haines. "Neither will you nor anyone else on this ship. Once the blue ouroboros comes, it'll take me away—"

"It's not going to," Jodenny interrupted.

"—and none of you will remember a thing," Myell said. "Time will not be changed or altered. Nothing I do makes a difference."

Jodenny leaned forward, both her hands resting on Junior's bump. "You have to deflect it, Commander Haines. You have to make sure that token doesn't take him away."

"They can't," Myell told her. He tried to sound patient, not helpless, though the idea of leaving her again made his stomach knot up. "Not a ring like this. They don't have the technology."

"You're wrong," said the man at the edge of Myell's vision. "Our technology's changed a lot since you were last around. No one's going anywhere."

Myell turned. The last fifteen years hadn't been kind to Byron Nam. His hair was gray, his waist had thickened, and the worry lines in his forehead looked deep and permanent. His admiral's uniform bore an impressive row of battle medals and his right hand was a silver prosthetic.

"We'll stop it," Nam said confidently. "Welcome home, Chief."

Jodenny had to go to the bathroom, but she wasn't about to excuse herself. Nam had ordered everyone out of the conference room except the three of them. He was sitting across from them now, his collar loosened and his hands, real and prosthetic, folded on the table.

"You died," he said to Myell. "On Burringurrah. After you and I trekked half a continent to get there."

Myell said, "The last thing I remember is being on Garanwa's station. It was all hot and burning."

Jodenny rubbed his arm more for her own comfort than his.

Nam leaned back in his chair. "You saved us from the station as it was being destroyed and transported us to the *Kamchatka*. Later, we ended up on a lifeboat that crashed into Australia. You and I went to Burringurrah, where you were killed by the Roon and turned into a god."

"I'll take your word for it." Myell squeezed Jodenny's hand under the table. "And hers."

Nam said, "As a god, you dissolved the entire Roon fleet and army. They vanished into thin air. Gone. Entirely. Along with Dr. Gayle, who appeared to be helping them. The Earth was saved. Mind you, the only surviving witnesses were myself, Commander Scott here, and Commander Osherman, plus a slightly crazy whirlybird pilot, and the three of you disappeared seconds later. Some people have had a hard time swallowing the turned-into-a-god part, but you can't argue with good results."

Myell didn't look happy. Jodenny rubbed his arm a little harder. It hadn't escaped her notice that he hadn't mentioned a thing about Homer or the Flying Doctor to anyone. She could understand why. It was hard enough for anyone here to believe they were time travelers, never mind that they were being visited by a menacing Roon and a graduate student from the future.

"Sir, have you ever heard of Kultana?" she asked.

Under the table, Myell's hand jerked.

"Kultana," Nam said. "Not offhand. Why?"

"I heard it somewhere," Myell said. "Thought it might be important."

Nam squeezed the bridge of his nose. "I'll tell you what's important. Every ship that Team Space and the ACF can dredge up is in this fleet, en route to intercept a Roon armada headed for Earth. Their weapons are better than ours. Their defense systems are better than ours. We've run into them, time and time again, out in the Wondjina Transportation System. Every time we try to establish a new colony, they destroy it. Every time we try diplomacy, they slaughter the diplomats. If Mary River falls, they'll gain access to the Big Alcheringa and all the Seven Sisters. They won't rest until they hunt down and destroy every one of us."

Jodenny could anticipate what he was going to say next, and she didn't appreciate it at all.

"So do you think you could turn into a god again?" Nam asked. "We need the help."

Myell stared at him.

Jodenny smothered a burp. She'd had one too many pastries. And she really had to pee. But if Nam thought he was going to talk her husband into sacrificing himself again, he was about to discover the wrath of a pregnant wife.

"First things first," she said. "Stop the blue ring from taking him away. Then we can talk about saving the whole of mankind."

CHAPTER THIRTEEN

The *Confident* didn't have a lot of open workspace other than the flight deck, which wasn't feasible given the proximity of the Roon armada. A group of scientists from the *Melbourne* instead converted a botanical bay into their laboratory but removed only half the plants. Myell was sitting on a stool between a row of bamboo plants and potted ferns, answering questions from a dozen different scientists as they placed monitor pads on his skin. Jodenny sat nearby, her feet up. The botanical bay was hot and humid, and she felt like a bloated whale.

"Can I get you anything?" Adryn asked.

A pillow would have been nice, because she was so damn tired she could have fallen asleep standing up. But she said, "No. I'm fine."

Adryn sat down on a stool. Chief Ovadia, constant

bodyguard or just plain guard, continued to stand by the bulkhead and watched everyone as they passed. Commander Haines was in the corner, making a call on his gib.

A grim-looking scientist with green eyes and bearded chin came over to Jodenny and offered his hand. "Commander. I'm Stefan Beranski. I'm in charge of stopping that ouroboros."

"Can you really stop it?" Jodenny asked.

"Absolutely." Beranski handed her a gib that was running different illustrations across its screen. "We've learned a lot about the Wondjina Transportation System over the years. How it works, how it's powered, how the tokens travel through the Universal Bulk to get here."

Jodenny frowned. "The what?"

"The big cheese," Beranski said. "You know. Everything. The world around us? A three-dimensional chunk of something a lot bigger."

She raised her eyebrows. Myell looked blank.

Beranski kept talking. "I can give you a digital primer, if you'd like. The important thing is that we know how to capture an incoming token, and even more importantly, how to deflect one. We've had to, to keep the Roon from using the network to invade us."

Jodenny marveled at what a difference fifteen years could make. "Have you mapped the entire system? The crew and passengers of the *Kamchatka* are stranded on a planet called Providence. We never found any Spheres, but maybe they were hidden. They could really use a rescue about now."

Beranski gave a guilty look to Haines as the commander came their way.

Haines said, "Answer the commander, Stefan."

"We had to stop mapping the system years ago," Beranski said. "Stop exploring. The Roon were everywhere we went. They're much more adept at the technology than we are."

Jodenny thought back to Garanwa's station. "They seized the helm? The hub?"

"We don't know," Haines said. "We've never found the station that you, Admiral Nam, and the others abandoned under duress. If we possessed it, we might be able to find and invade their world."

There wasn't much accusation in his voice, but Jodenny heard it nonetheless. She tried not to lose her temper. "If we'd stayed there, you might have kept the hub but lost Earth to the Roon."

Ovadia looked suddenly interested in what Haines was saying.

Haines lifted his chin. "No one's saying that would be preferable, no. But it was an option."

Jodenny turned back to Beranski. "So you're going to deflect the blue token? You think you can?"

"Oh, yes," Beranski said. "It's very simple. It'll continue on without him just fine."

Myell, who'd been listening, asked, "Will it continue onward and then loop back again? That's what rings do, right? Go around and around."

Beranski rubbed his chin. "We can keep you surrounded by protective shields for as long as necessary."

"For the rest of his life?" Adryn asked, and Jodenny was glad she wasn't the only one to see the problem with this.

"Er, maybe. We usually run the deflectors in our Spheres on a constant basis, so the Roon can't slip in. I can make a portable one that Chief Myell can wear. That might work."

Jodenny was sure the idea had flaws, depending on

how much power a deflector shield required and how cumbersome the equipment might be. She was distracted from answering by a particularly heavy set of kicks from Junior, who was apparently practicing his— her, she reminded herself—soccer skills today.

Beranski turned back to Myell. "Chief, you said this blue ouroboros is shaped like a man?"

Myell nodded. "Holding his own feet. The first one we ever used was shaped like a snake. And then there was one shaped like a crocodile."

"It's kind of fascinating how the incarnations change—" Beranski started, but a look from Haines quelled him. "Right. So do you hear a horn when it's incoming, or some other sound?"

"I don't hear anything. But all of a sudden the air goes away, like I'm standing in a venting airlock."

Jodenny hadn't known that. Myell didn't seem upset about it, but if someone took her air away, she'd have been perturbed. "I didn't experience that."

Beranski was smiling. "This is fabulous data. Mind you, we've never had a case of an ouroboros traveling on its own, linked to a person. But I'm sure we can deflect it anyway. We just have to run some experiments, try a few scenarios—"

Jodenny didn't feel reassured. "Dr. Beranski, if the ring is on a twenty-four-hour schedule, it'll be here around oh-four-hundred. That's fifteen hours from now."

"Fifteen hours," Beranski repeated. "Oh. No problem."

Myell looked less confident than ever.

More of Beranski's team arrived with equipment in tow. Jodenny tried to keep an eye on things but she was way too comfortable in her chair, and exhausted, too, and it was possible she dozed off because the next thing she knew, a handsome chief from Adryn's department was bringing in an oversized tray loaded with hot sandwiches, fresh salads, and chocolate cake.

"This is Chief Tom Cappaletto," Adryn said. "Thorn in my side."

"That's me." Cappaletto put the tray down and offered his hand. "Nice to meet you, Commander Scott."

She had never felt less like a military officer, but Jodenny appreciated the courtesy. She grabbed half the food and asked Cappaletto to take the rest of the tray to Myell, who was trapped in a circle of equipment answering questions. For conversation, she asked Adryn, "So how are your mom and dad?"

"Mom's great. She's teaching at the university on Warramala."

"And your dad?"

Adryn chewed on a pickle. "They're not together anymore."

That statement brought Jodenny's head up from her cake, which she'd decided to eat first. "What happened?"

"Drifted apart." Adryn reached for another pickle. "Different ideas, different goals. You know how it goes. People change."

The chocolate frosting in Jodenny's stomach curdled. She didn't think Myell would take the news well. "Was it a difficult breakup?"

"I wasn't there for that part," Adryn said. "I was at the academy by then. Mom sent imails and Dad—well, he was off with his new crowd. Didn't hear much from him."

"I'm sorry."

"Nobody's fault," Adryn said with a shrug.

They talked about Adryn's experiences as a pilot

serving in Team Space and on foreign exchange, and how she'd met and fallen in love with Dr. Laura Ling.

"We were married six months after our first date," Adryn said. "I changed my name to hers so it was easier for me to get a foreign exchange billet. Plus, the Ling family name goes pretty far in ACF. They're all over the place. Captains, doctors, a few admirals even."

Jodenny was watching Myell, who had taken only one bite of a sandwich before putting it down. "Isn't it risky for both of you to be here, facing the Roon?"

"Neither of us would have it any other way," Adryn said firmly.

A few minutes later Commander Haines returned from Security with a list of questions for Jodenny. She didn't like the man, but it wasn't the worst interview Jodenny had ever undergone. For nearly an hour she talked about Garanwa's station, the *Kamchatka,* and Providence. She gave Haines the coordinates of the planet, as best the onboard computers could ever figure it. She insisted that Team Space or the ACF send a ship to rescue them.

Haines looked doubtful. "How? It's too far."

Adryn said, "If we could steal the Roon interstellar engine technology, we could get to them in a few years."

"Or if we figure out a way to control your husband's personal token ring," Haines said.

"To do that you'd have to grab it," Jodenny said. "Not just deflect it."

Haines's gaze shifted sideways.

"No." Jodenny struggled out of her chair. She called over to the scientists. "Dr. Beranski! What are you going to do with the blue token?"

"Commander, calm down," Haines said.

"Aunt Jodenny, maybe you should sit," Adryn said.

"I'm not an invalid," she snapped at them both.

Myell stood up from his stool and caught her by the arms. "What's the matter?"

"He's not going to send the token away," Jodenny accused. "They're going to try and catch it. That's what destroyed the *Yangtze*."

Haines said, "Maybe we should take a break. Rethink and regroup."

"Maybe you should stop lying to us," she snapped.

Myell said, "I think a break is a good idea. Is there somewhere we can rest for a few minutes?"

"I don't want to rest," Jodenny said, but apparently today was the day that no one listened to her, because soon Ovadia was escorting them up to the cabin Adryn and Laura Ling shared in officer country. Another armed guard trailed behind them. Jodenny hated the idea of being watched as if they were prisoners or threats, but she kept that to herself. Things were stressful enough already.

"They want us back in an hour," Ovadia said. "Let me know if you need anything."

The cabin was small but had homey touches, including Laura's medical diplomas and a blue quilt on the bed built for two. Jodenny was in no mood to appreciate the accommodations.

"We can't trust any of them," she said. "You can't believe anything they say."

Myell sat on the edge of his bed and pulled off his boots. He wriggled his feet and examined his socks. "Even Admiral Nam?"

"Even him," Jodenny said. "*Especially* him. Remember how you met?"

"Come on. Lie down for a few minutes. You've got to be as tired as I am."

She considered denying it, but it was nicer to stretch out on the soft mattress. Myell reclined beside her, his gaze on the overhead. The look on his face meant he was beating himself up over something.

"You can't blame yourself for Kyle and Twig," she said, a lump in her throat. "For all we know, they're fine where we left them. Louise and the others, they'll take care of them."

His voice was bleak. "Or the eddy dissolved and they ceased to exist."

"Which means the originals are still alive back in their own time period. So it's still okay, right?"

Myell took her hands. "If you're right and someone or something changed history at Garanwa's station, sent me off in the blue ring, then I'm just a copy of the original dying Terry Myell. I turned around and pulled you out of Providence. Do you feel like a copy? Is the baby unreal? Am I?"

She stared at the bulkhead. If she was a copy of the original Jodenny Scott, it didn't matter one bit. She still felt like herself, and thought like herself, and was going to fight like hell to keep him and her baby both.

"I don't think you can trust Homer, and you certainly can't trust that Roon," she said. "But one of them wants you to find Kultana and the other wants to stop you. So that's what we have to concentrate on. I asked Adryn to run a computer check but there's nothing on the list that you haven't already told me about."

"What I don't understand is why here," he said. "Why now. Every other trip I've made has been about you. Of all the places the ouroboros could have taken us, why to a place neither of us has ever been? Is it because the Roon are coming?"

Jodenny kicked off her boots and wriggled her feet.

"I don't know. But maybe the answer will come to you if you rub my feet."

He cocked his head. "You think that's possible?"

"Absolutely."

He found some hand lotion in Adryn's locker. The first press of his thumbs against her archways had Jodenny groaning in pleasure. Warm flushes traveled up her legs to her groin. She watched him with half-lidded eyes, breathing deeply.

"Take off your shirt," she said.

Myell quirked a smile. "What for?"

"It's wrinkled," she said. "I want to iron it."

He peeled it off and tossed it into the corner. He was thinner than she liked to see him, but the shape of his shoulders hadn't changed, nor the brown little points of his nipples. He bent closer to her ankles, his hands warm and careful and strong. His wedding ring was warm against her skin.

"You're not going anywhere," she told him. "You know that?"

The smile faded away. "I don't want to."

"Things are different this time," she said. "I'm here. You don't have to go around the universe looking for one who'll keep you. I'm keeping you."

Something shadowed flitted across his face, quickly gone, but she knew him. "Come here," she said.

"I'm not done."

"Here," she insisted, and he crawled across the pillows. She turned on her side and ran her hands down his chest to his waist.

It was Myell's turn to groan. "You're going to ruin these trousers."

"Then why don't you get out of them?" she said.

Once he was stripped bare, she forbade him to do

anything but lie on the mattresses and enjoy himself. He watched her face, his lips parted and his breathing fast.

"I want to touch you," he said.

Jodenny let her hair fall across his chest. "Nope. I'm in charge. You stay right where you are."

His head fell back.

She wished they had more than an hour.

She wished they could lock themselves in Adryn's cabin forever.

CHAPTER **FOURTEEN**

Adryn said, "I strongly object to this plan, Admiral."

Before Nam could answer, Captain McNaughton said, "And I strongly object to not doing everything we can to defeat the Roon, Lieutenant Ling."

The briefing room was full of the *Confident*'s senior staff as well as Admiral Nam and his aides. The captains of the fourteen ships were tied in via vid, and some had sent representatives in person. Adryn was the youngest officer present. She was tempted to feel intimidated and outranked, but this was her family they were talking about.

"If I may repeat myself." Dr. Beranski coughed into his hand. "We have no evidence the accident which befell the *Yangtze* will repeat itself here. We're not in the Alcheringa or near a drop point. The token ring that brought them here didn't cause any problems. I'm positive we can deflect the next one with no trouble at all from anywhere on this ship."

"Deflecting it is not enough," McNaughton said. "We need to catch it."

Beranski scratched his chin. "Capturing a normal ring is no problem. We can do that with our eyes closed. A ring that can move in the Universal Bulk through enormous amounts of space and time—well, that's an animal of a different color."

Commander Haines said, "We don't have objective proof that it really moves through time."

Adryn said, "What do you think, they're lying?"

Dr. Cho spoke up from his corner. "Chronologically speaking, neither of them has aged in fifteen years. Every test confirms it. You can't refute science."

Admiral Su lifted his gaze from his gib. He was the senior admiral of the fleet, outranking both Nam and McNaughton. Adryn had the distinct impression that Su didn't like Myell, even though he hadn't met him. Or maybe Su didn't like anyone. Couldn't afford to like anyone, not with thousands of sailors serving his command and facing death by the Roon.

"Deflection isn't enough. You've got to capture it. But not while he's aboard this ship," he said. "Captain McNaughton, ready a birdie that can carry Myell, Dr. Beranski, and all the equipment needed. Recruit a pilot who doesn't mind the fact this might be a one-way trip."

Adryn said, "I'll do it, sir."

"I think you're too involved," Haines said.

Su said, "Let her. I want that birdie away with a safe window—no waiting until the last minute. Until then, I want every single shred of information you can get out of those two. Anything that can help."

Adryn met Admiral Nam's gaze, hoping her concern showed through. It wasn't as if her uncle and aunt were the enemy, after all. Su's order sounded like a dictate to treat them without care to their rights or achievements, and what kind of way was that to reward the heroes of Burringurrah? Nam didn't give away anything in his expression, but then again, he rarely did.

"Sir," Nam said. "If Myell doesn't disappear with the ouroboros, we're going to need his continuing cooperation. And his goodwill."

Admiral Tyler, on the vid, made a faint noise of disapproval. "Because he can talk to the gods, is that it?"

Captain McNaughton sniffed. "I heard he was a god himself."

Adryn opened her mouth to speak, but Nam beat her to it. "If there's anyone else around who can make the entire Roon army vanish, I'd like to meet them."

"No one's sure exactly why they disappeared from Earth," Admiral Tyler said.

"I'm sure," Nam said.

McNaughton glowered. Su raised a placating hand and said, "Commander Scott and Chief Myell are decorated heroes. No one's questioning that. But we don't know for sure where they've been or what they've been doing all this time."

Fifteen years by their calendar, Adryn thought. Six months by Jodenny's. Only a month or two by Myell's. Time travel made her brain itch.

"What's the status of Commander Osherman?" Admiral Su asked.

"He's awake, but not responding," Dr Cho said.

"Is he ever going to be useful?"

"With treatment, I hope so."

The meeting broke up shortly afterward. Adryn knew she would have to get to the flight deck to supervise the birdie, but she had to break the news to Laura first. She found her down in the infirmary, catnapping on a sofa in the doctors' lounge. The clean aquarium looked like it was flourishing.

Adryn brushed back Laura's bangs and kissed her on the temple. "Wake up, sleepyhead."

"Hmm?" Laura blinked up at her. "Hi there."

"Hi, yourself." Adryn pulled up a chair and straddled it. "Sorry to wake you."

"It's not as comfortable as our bed, but someone gave our cabin away," Laura grumbled good-naturedly. She sat up. "What's going on?"

"I have to fly a mission. Birdie run, nothing hard."

Laura knuckled sleep from her eyes. "What else? You've got that look on your face."

"What look?"

"Spill it," Laura ordered. A yawn made her eyes water. "Boy, do I need a good night's rest."

Adryn put her hands on Laura's knees. "Uncle Terry. They're not sure he'll be safe when the blue ouroboros comes, so they want me to fly him outside of ship's range. Make sure it all goes well."

It took Laura a moment to see through that. When she did, her eyes widened in horror. "They're assigning you to a suicide run?"

"No!" Adryn tightened her grip, ran her thumbs along the inside of Laura's knees. "It's not like that. Nothing's going to happen. Just a bunch of overprotective nansy-pansy worriers, that's all. He got here just fine, right?"

Laura was staring at her. "What about Commander Scott?"

"They're not going to let her go," Adryn said. "She has to stay here."

"I don't like it." Laura leaned forward and took Adryn's hands in hers. Their wedding rings clinked together.

"Get someone else. You're family. You shouldn't be involved."

"Someone has to do it. Besides, there's no danger. We're going to go out, spin around, and be back in time for supper."

Laura said nothing.

Adryn kissed her. "It's going to be fine." She was just glad that she wasn't the one who got to give the news to Jodenny Scott.

What did you just say?" Jodenny asked.

Myell sympathized. Not with Jodenny, but with Haines, who had to withstand her withering gaze.

The break in Adryn's cabin had stretched to two hours, a courtesy Jodenny found suspicious. Then Haines had appeared at the hatch with this news.

"I can't believe any of you people," she continued.

"The decision was made over my head," Haines said. "The admirals don't think it's safe to try and do this onboard. A birdie seems like the best alternative."

Jodenny said, "But you're only going to deflect it."

"Yes," Haines said.

She turned to Myell. "And you agree with this?"

"It might be safer," he said.

"In the middle of space," Jodenny said. "Nowhere near any doctors or emergency equipment. The damned thing isn't even due for hours!"

Haines said, "The twenty-four-hour clock is shorter when people have traveled through the ouroboros with him. He's said so."

"It's true," Myell said.

Jodenny gave him a narrow look. He knew he wasn't helping things. The time for tact had passed, though.

Aside from a few hours in the infirmary and a post-coital doze, he hadn't had much sleep lately. He was tired and nervous and sure that above all, he wanted Jodenny and Junior safe.

"We won't be far," he said.

"You could get killed."

"Which is why you're staying here."

She gave him a look that clearly said he was an idiot. "Not the point."

"Yes, it's exactly the point," he said.

She turned her back on him, furious. Haines lingered in the passage, not looking directly at them. Chief Ovadia, who'd been standing watch, answered a call on his SOEL and said, "They're ready for you."

"Give us a minute," Myell said, and pulled Jodenny back away from the hatch.

"I just—" he started, then silenced himself. Words weren't going to solve this. He grasped her arm, turned her around, ignored the glare in her eyes, and crushed his lips against her mouth. Without syllables he said *You're mine, I'll be back, and I'm sorry.*

He broke off. She was silent, unforgiving. Myell got two steps away before she said, "Oh, no, you don't—" and pulled him back for another kiss.

"You have to come back to me," she whispered, her mouth against his.

"I will," he promised.

The birdie was a standard Team Space model, with two seats in the cockpit and a seating capacity of forty passengers. Most of the passenger seats were being removed to make room for Beranski's equipment. Myell tried not to shiver in the coldness of the flight deck while he watched the preparations, which were dragging on longer than expected.

"She'll soon be ready," a voice said behind him. "Should be quite a trip, right?"

Myell turned to see Cappaletto in his flight suit. "Did you volunteer for this or get drafted?"

Cappaletto grinned. "Wouldn't miss it. History in the making, right? I can tell my kids one day I got to ferry around the Hero of Burringurrah himself."

Myell was appalled. "That's not a real nickname, is it?"

"Oh, sure," Cappaletto said. "Saved the Earth, all that? Killed by the Roon the night they dug up Big Daddy on Burringurrah Mountain. Plateau. Whatever you call it."

The shuttle bay was crowded with too many people for more casual conversation. Adryn and Cappaletto had to do their preflight checks, and the flight crew was busy reconfiguring the shuttle for the deflection equipment. The equipment took longer to load than expected. When it finally came time to board for flight, Myell looked up at the observation deck and saw Jodenny at the plastiglass window. Even from a distance he could tell how unhappy she was.

He raised his hand. Whether Homer was right about the eddies or not, if he failed and was taken away by the ouroboros, he'd never see this version of her again. If he tried to take her with him, he endangered her life and Junior's to an unbearable degree.

She raised her hand and then used it to cover her mouth.

He turned to the ship, unhappiness digging into his chest like a knife.

Beranski was apparently coming along for the ride.

With all of the extra equipment, quarters were very cramped. Launch went smoothly, though, and almost immediately Adryn started steering them away from the fleet.

"So how will we know when the token ring thing is inbound?" she asked.

Myell replied, "I'll look like I can't breathe."

Cappaletto winced. "Sounds painful."

Beranski said, "We're going to capture this thing for you, Chief. No more problems after that."

"Then you can make the whole Roon armada disappear, like you did before," Cappaletto said. "They'll make all new vids and songs about you. My kid brother plays Burringurrah Quest all the time. Loves to blast the Roon out of the sky."

Myell didn't believe him. "They didn't really make computer games out of classified military operations, did they?"

"Not much of it is still classified," Adryn said.

On his flight board, a sensor beeped. Cappaletto flipped a switch and it silenced. "The Roon digging out the Big Daddy power source from the Burringurrah plateau. You, the commander, and the admiral all defeated them—no one's sure how, depends on how much religious stuff you can stomach—and you got yourself killed in the process. You're looking pretty normal for a dead man, Chief. Or a god. Or a dead god. Whatever."

"Not everyone believes that you turned into an ancient Australian god," Adryn put in. "Right, Doc?"

Beranski grimaced. "I was born and raised in the Russian Orthodox Church, Lieutenant Ling. Australian gods aren't my specialty. There could be many reasons why the Roon army retreated. Certainly I don't believe that Dr. Gayle aided and assisted the Roon."

Myell squinted at Beranski. "We've met before, haven't we?"

"Very briefly. I was one of her assistants, back when she was recruiting you and Commander Scott for the rescue mission to save her husband's team."

Myell considered that. Adryn and Cappaletto obviously didn't know this part of the story and were listening attentively.

"She was there? At Burringurrah?" Myell asked.

"She was one of their prisoners. Forced to do what they wanted her to do. I'm sure Commander Osherman will confirm that when he's able to speak again."

Myell would have to ask Jodenny about Gayle. He asked, "The First Egg. Big Daddy, you called it. It's still there? On Burringurrah?"

"Under the plateau," Beranski said, though clearly reluctant to change the topic. "Every now and then people on Earth think about digging it up, and Team Space persuades them not to. We believe it powers the entire Wondjina network. And obviously the Roon want it. So it's better off right where it is."

Myell said, "I imagine Team Space kicks in some financial incentives to keep Earth's governments from digging it up."

Cappaletto grinned and jerked his head toward the *Confident*. "Brand new ship, Chief."

"We've reached a safe distance," Adryn announced. "I switched on the autopilot. Nothing to do now but wait."

The onboard equipment hummed and beeped. No one spoke until Myell asked, "Is everyone going to stare at me until the ring comes?"

"The price of fame," Cappaletto said. "Hero of Burringurrah and all."

"I wish you'd stop calling me that."

Cappaletto grinned. "Sure. Besides, once this is all done with, they'll be calling you the Hero of Kultana instead."

Goosebumps rippled up his arms and down Myell's spine.

Surely he hadn't heard that right.

"What?" he asked.

"Kultana," Cappaletto said. "Right over there."

He nodded on the scanner to the icy planetoid on display. Vaguely Myell remembered Adryn mentioning it before. The one tiny barrier between the human fleet and the Roon.

Adryn said, dismissively, "PX2-843. That's its official name. Just a chunk of frozen methane floating around in the middle of nowhere."

"On the old astronomy charts, they used to call it Kultana," Cappaletto said. "That's what Ensign Voight told me. They changed it way back when, though. Made every name more boring."

With a quirked eyebrow Adryn asked, "Who's Ensign Voight?"

"Astronomy Department," Cappaletto said. "Nice girl. Likes old maps."

"Kultana," Myell murmured, and now he knew why the blue ring had brought him and Jodenny here. "Can we get closer? Can we——"

All his air ran out.

Jodenny had been listening to the conversation aboard the shuttle. She could watch it, too, courtesy of the vids playing overhead in the flight deck observation room, but it was easier to keep her eyes on the bulkhead and listen to Myell instead of see him so far away.

They still had no good idea when the ouroboros would show up. Her heartburn was back and her poor overtaxed bladder was beginning to kick up again. But she was too tired to get up, even if the chairs in Flight Ops were all uncomfortable.

She listened as they discussed Burringurrah. Dr. Beranski's defense of Anna Gayle was admirable if misguided. The woman had been heartily supporting the Roon while Osherman, who'd resisted, had knelt on the ground all beaten and worn. She tried to imagine the First Egg sinking back into the mountaintop, where it remained a source of political wrangling.

Admiral Nam arrived in the control room. "How are they doing?"

The flight control officer, a blonde with very short hair, said, "Holding steady ten thousand kilometers to port."

Jodenny said to Nam, "I'm surprised you went along with this, sir."

He didn't back down from her cold anger. "I don't mind losing some battles if it helps us win a war, Commander."

"You think one ouroboros can do that?"

"I'm willing to try. Are you?"

She turned back to the screen just in time to see panic cross Myell's face as he tried to suck in air. Jodenny had seen the same expression when he stumbled away from her at the waterfall.

"The ring!" she said. "It's coming!"

They must have heard her on the birdie, because Beranski sprang toward his equipment. Blue light flooded through the compartment and the small ship suddenly rocked, forcing Adryn and Cappaletto to fight the controls. Myell sat, seemingly paralyzed in his seat, tugging at his neck as if an invisible rope had been looped around it.

"Your equipment's not working!" Adryn shouted at Beranski.

"It should be!" Beranski shouted back.

The birdie shuddered under another onslaught of blue light. Myell wasn't panicking, but it was clear he couldn't breathe. Alarms were going off in the birdie, sharp and urgent. On an overvid, Jodenny could see that the ship was diverting off its holding pattern.

Haines demanded, "What's going on out there?"

"We've almost got it," Beranski reported.

"You don't have anything," Jodenny said sharply. "Look at Terry!"

A deep humming noise rolled through the speakers, and then the vids went dark.

"Lieutenant Ling, report!" the duty officer said.

Darkness on the vid. The humming noise shifted tones and became a screech. The duty officer was talking to a second birdie that was shadowing them and Nam was demanding that Adryn answer. Jodenny's heartburn rose up her throat with the sour taste of bile, and cold sweat broke across her neck. He couldn't be dead. Couldn't be, couldn't be, couldn't be—

Adryn's voice cut through the hum on the speakers. "We're here," she reported. "We're alive."

"Terry," Jodenny said. "Talk to me."

Silence on the audio. The video remained dark.

"We've got the ring," Cappaletto reported. "But Chief Myell's not breathing."

CHAPTER **FIFTEEN**

Myell was floating in a sea of murky green light, his arms and limbs akimbo. He wasn't sure if he was alive but he sure hoped he wasn't dead. Death in this endless sea of blue wouldn't be a kind fate at all.

"Fate," a voice sneered. "What do you know of fate?"

He turned in a green hallway lit by a single garish lightbulb. There stood the Flying Doctor, his cloak of black feathers fluttering in a nonexistent breeze.

"This is Kultana," Myell said. "This is where you didn't want me to come."

"You see it but you don't understand it," the Flying Doctor said. "Typical of your kind. You are no threat at all."

Very clearly, a woman's voice said: "Inscribe."

Myell turned to see who she was, but the green light of the hallway collapsed into utter darkness. He coughed, thrashed, and opened his eyes to find himself on the deck of the birdie, with Chief Cappaletto's hands on his chest. Cappaletto was breathing hard and had a worried look on his face. Myell realized he'd been performing resuscitation on him.

"He's awake," Cappaletto announced.

"Uncle Terry?" That was Adryn, chewing on her bottom lip in worry.

Jodenny's voice nearby asked, "Terry?"

He coughed some more and rubbed his throat. "I'm here. Why is everything blue?"

Cappaletto nodded toward the back of the birdie.

The blue ouroboros spun slowly, humming. Beranski smiled triumphantly. "I caught the fucker."

* * *

Captain McNaughton disagreed entirely with the proposal to bring the captured token ring back to the *Confident*. Admiral Nam said he understood and that was fine, but the *Melbourne* had no such qualms and would be happy to claim the ouroboros as Team Space property. Admiral Su surely weighed in on the matter at some point, but Jodenny wasn't privy to that part of the conversation. More debate followed, perhaps more negotiations and payoffs, and in the end Adryn Ling piloted the birdie to the *Confident*'s auxiliary docking bay, where it could do the least damage if the hull was breached or compromised in any way.

Chief Ovadia kept Jodenny out of the docking bay control room.

"Orders, ma'am," he said. "You can wait over here, in the pilots' ready room."

Jodenny considered arguing with him, but Junior was kicking and her energy was draining away. Besides, Ovadia didn't look like he would be an easy sucker for disobeying orders. Or for tears, which she could maybe deploy at a strategic point later.

The ready room was small and sparse, but there was a sofa. She didn't sit down. Instead she paced until the hatch opened and Myell returned to her. She flung her arms around him.

"It's fine," he said, holding her tight. "They got the ring."

"I don't care about that," she said, her eyes wet against his shirt.

"Did you hear what Cappaletto said about that planetoid?"

"No. What?"

He rubbed her back and eased her to the sofa, where she sat against him. She had never felt so exhausted in her entire life. It was entirely possible she might fall asleep against him.

"What about the planetoid?" she asked.

Myell shrugged beneath her. "Humanity's last stand. PX-whatever. Stupid name for it."

That sounded like a non sequitur, or would have if her brain wasn't so foggy and slow. She was content to simply listen to the steady beat of his heart. Behind them, the hatch opened. Jodenny didn't bother opening her eyes. Myell's voice rumbled in her ear as he said, "She needs to rest."

Jodenny forced her eyes open. "You, too. But what about the ring?"

"The bastard's not going anywhere," Myell said. "Dr. Beranski swears it."

It took some pointed discussion to get their own quarters, instead of displacing Adryn and Laura again. Spaceships in wartime didn't usually deploy with empty accommodations for the convenience of time travelers. Finally a senior officer volunteered to move, and they were quartered in a cabin with a bed wide enough for two, if they spooned together side by side. Jodenny splashed water on her face, threw her uniform into the corner, and crawled under the sheets. Myell picked up her trousers and shirt, hung them in the locker next to his own, and slid up beside her.

"Long day, honey?" she asked, and was asleep before he could answer.

When she woke it was oh-nine-hundred and she was alone. She couldn't believe she'd slept so long. Myell had left a tray of muffins, juice, and fruit on the desk with a handwritten note beside it. The note was nice enough—"Love you, eat well"—but he shouldn't have left the cabin without her. She took a sixty-second shower, dressed and pinned up her hair, and opened the hatch to ask Ovadia where her damned husband was.

Not Ovadia outside: instead, the guard was a squir-relly looking young man with curly red hair.

"He's up in a briefing, ma'am," the guard said. "I'm to escort you to Medical when you're ready."

"I feel fine," she protested.

"Those are my orders, Commander."

Jodenny grabbed a muffin and followed him, dis-gruntled, to the lift.

The *Confident* was busier today than it had been in the middle of the night, and she found herself the object of scrutiny by passing members of the mostly male crew. She realized it was Junior they were probably intrigued by, and not her prenatal Raphaelite beauty. At the infirmary, Laura Ling met her and scanned her belly.

"How are you doing today?" Ling asked.

"Fine," Jodenny said, puzzled. "Why am I here?"

Her mouth a tight line, Ling nodded toward Sam Osherman's room. "He's awake and agitated. I think he'd be happy to see you."

Jodenny thought there was more to Ling's frown than Osherman's well-being. "Is something wrong?"

The doctor folded her arms. "Not with him."

"With you," Jodenny said. "Or is this about Adryn?"

"She does what she needs to do, her duty," Laura said. She leaned against the bulkhead and looked down at the deck. "But there's no reason her life should be endangered just because she's Chief Myell's family. I resent the fact she was pulled into that dangerous duty yesterday just because she's his niece."

Jodenny was confused. "She was?"

"It's unfair. If it continues, I'll complain through my chain of command."

"I see." Jodenny scratched an itch on the back of her neck. "Okay. I'd do the same thing."

Ling nodded. She brushed past the guard outside Osherman's room and led Jodenny inside.

Osherman was awake, sitting up, his wrists in restraints. He was glaring at the bulkhead as if it were personally responsible for his plight. His gaze turned to her, and there was no easing of the anger.

"Hey," Jodenny said, not as strongly as she wanted to. "You feel better?"

He yanked on the restraints. He looked tight and sinewy and lucid, which was preferable to him being withdrawn and nonresponsive. She'd seen him both ways since Burringurrah, and many other variations as well.

"It's not up to me," she said.

He looked away.

She added, "But I'll see what I can do. Do you know where we are?"

He gave her nothing at all.

Jodenny turned to go, the best response whenever he was like this, and was startled when he thumped his feet on the bed to get her attention.

"What?" she asked.

His face twisted up in frustration.

"We're on an ACF ship," she told him. "Americans and Canadians, mostly. Some Team Space. There was an ouroboros that brought us here. You, me, and Terry."

His fingers splayed wide, resisting the restraints. Jodenny touched his closest hand, trying to calm him. "You're safe here. Maybe they can even help you."

Scorn in his expression. Sometimes he was bitter, sometimes lost, sometimes so angry that people in

Providence became concerned. She never thought herself in danger, but she sometimes worried he might hurt himself.

Jodenny debated whether or not to tell him they had moved forward in time, but she saw no reason to really withhold the information. So she told him, watching him closely to see if he understood. He looked skeptical.

"When you're up and around," she promised. "You'll see."

A knock on the hatch, and it opened under the hand of the curly-haired guard. "Commander? They're wondering if you want to join the briefing now."

She realized she was still holding Osherman's hand, and hastily released his fingers. "Sure. I'll be back later, Sam. Promise."

The briefing room was a theater-seating chamber up on Deck Two. The rows of seats were crowded with senior officers and scientists. Adryn, Cappaletto, and Ovadia were all there, wedged into an aisle. Beranski was giving a multimedia presentation at the front. A live feed of the trapped blue ouroboros was displayed on an enormous screen. It cast light down on Myell, who was sitting near the front between Haines and Nam.

Haines gave up his seat for her, but only so he could chase off a lieutenant and take his seat instead. Jodenny eased down onto the cushioned chair gratefully. Myell gave her a kiss on the cheek in blatant violation of the regulations against public displays of affection. But there was something distant in his eyes, something she didn't like at all. She suspected he was upset about something and trying not to show it. Maybe Beranski, at the front podium, had delivered news he didn't like. Maybe he was thinking about Kyle and Twig again.

Beranski was saying, ". . . and I don't see any reason why we can't hold it indefinitely, but the trick is trying to figure out what path it follows through the Universal Bulk. There are no glyphs or symbols on it. No way of telling what loop it's following."

"It's not following a loop," Myell said, loud enough for only Jodenny to hear.

"We need to be able to use it," Captain McNaughton said to Beranski. "We need the tactical advantage."

Jodenny squeezed Myell's hand.

A commander from the Science Corps got up to take the podium from Beranski. "I'm Commander Perry, Research and Development. We've charted its course through time and space based on everything Sergeant—er, Chief—Myell told us. Here-now is its current point of existence. And his. Then-there is wherever it goes, whether backward or forward. Because space is curved, we think there's only a limited area for where a user can go with it. Think of two ice cream cones, joined at the smallest tip. That's right now, right here. Chief Myell is the point between them."

"Why does it take him into the past and future randomly?" Admiral Nam said.

Perry said, "It's not random. There are rules. For instance, he never lands anywhere where there's a chance of running into himself. Something or someone is controlling it."

Myell said, "Well, I'm not," and this time he spoke loud enough for everyone to hear. "Maybe the gods are."

Murmurs in the room. Jodenny watched Captain McNaughton lean close to Admiral Su and say something in a low voice. Beside her, Haines asked, "Does he really believe that?"

She and Myell had talked about it, long ago—whether

the Wondjina gods such as the Rainbow Serpent were really deities, or aliens with incredibly advanced technology. She didn't know the answer then and she didn't know it now. Most of her life she'd been undecided about religion, and before Myell there'd never been any reason for her to believe in any given faith over the other.

Jodenny said, "You'll have to ask him."

Nam spoke up. "He says nothing ever changes. Is that possible?"

Perry's gaze went to Myell. "From his perspective, yes. If there's any such thing as an outside observer, maybe not. To the people whose lives he changed and the historical events he might have altered—I don't know. They might be able to tell us, if only we found some way to communicate with them."

Jodenny hoped Myell took that to mean that the copies of Kyle and Twig were still alive in the eddy where they'd left them. She still couldn't read the expression on his face, though.

"This is the first time we have a token ring that works outside the network," Admiral Su said. "Commander Haines, your people are supposed to be the experts at Wondjina technology. The Roon are going to be in range in less than twenty-four hours. Make that ring work for us, so when those sons of bitches show up, we'll have something in our corner."

"Token rings aren't weapons," Jodenny said to Nam as the meeting broke up.

"They are now," Nam said.

She joined Myell, who had gone to the podium to corral Commander Perry and was saying, "Tell me about the cones again, sir."

Perry grabbed a pen and his SOEL. He drew what

looked like an ice cream cone, then drew a reverse cone below it. "Your window of travel. From the here-now going backward until your date of birth, forward until the day you die. You can only travel through time periods in which you're alive."

"But I'm already dead," Myell said. "Killed on top of Burringurrah and buried on Providence."

Perry used his pen to scratch the side of his head. "Not from my perspective. From where I stand, you disappeared from Burringurrah with Commander Scott and Commander Nam. I don't know what happened to you after that, but clearly you're alive now."

"He died and I buried him," Jodenny insisted.

Myell squeezed her hand. "And I've seen the grave."

Perry sighed. "I don't know. Maybe the gods did send you back as some kind of clone. Maybe time has been changed without you being aware of it. It's possible that this isn't your original timeline at all, just one that's a few inches off. Have you ever seen yourself die? Been there at the moment you fall?"

"No," Myell said. "But I never visit anyplace where I could run into myself."

Haines appeared at Jodenny's elbow. "We need you down in the docking bay, Chief."

Myell gave Perry's drawing one last look, clearly unwilling to go. "If I leave here tomorrow, will you continue on in your timeline and remember my visit? Or will it all be wiped away?"

"I'd hope that I remember," Perry said. "But you would never be able to confirm it."

Haines, clearly impatient, said, "Chief Myell, we need to go."

Cappaletto and Ovadia had made their way through the crowd down to the podium and had overheard

Haines. Cappaletto said, "We'll take him down, Commander. Grab some coffee in the chief's mess on the way down. Can't be a chief on this ship and never stop by the goat locker."

Haines looked exasperated.

Jodenny said, "Only if I can get some coffee, too."

"Absolutely," Cappaletto said.

Haines said, "They need him now."

Ovadia folded his arms over his chest. His muscles bulged under his short-sleeved khaki shirt. "We'll only be a few minutes, sir."

Nam called Haines over. Haines went reluctantly. As soon as he was gone, Cappaletto said, "Let's go."

The two chiefs headed for the hatch. Jodenny touched Myell's arm, urging him to follow. They'd only gone a few steps when Perry said, "Chief Myell."

"Yes?"

"We don't know our unconscious minds," Perry said. "But surely it's no coincidence that you keep following Commander Scott in time. Why every jump directs the ouroboros to her."

"Until this one," Jodenny pointed out.

Perry glanced back down at his ice cream cone drawing.

In the passage outside the briefing room they ran into Adryn, who agreed to come with them down to the chiefs' mess on Deck 4. Cappaletto murmured something to Adryn that made her face furrow. They were barely off the lift before she pulled Jodenny aside.

"I need your advice," she said. "Can we talk? I promise, I'll get you some coffee."

Ovadia, Myell, and Cappaletto were still heading for the chiefs' mess. Jodenny looked longingly after the men. "Does it have to be now?"

"We don't exactly have a luxury of spare time," Adryn said.

"I suppose not."

Myell looked back, quizzical. Jodenny said, "We'll catch up." She let Adryn steer her into a small snack lounge filled with vending machines. Adryn ordered up two cups of coffee and they settled on hard black benches.

"It's family stuff." Adryn ran her finger along the rim of her cup. "About my dad, and where he is. I don't know if Uncle Terry wants to know it, or needs to know it, or if he'll just be distracted by it. You know, the divorce and all. Or have you already told him?"

Jodenny poured sugar into her coffee, twice as much as she'd used prior to the pregnancy. "Like you said, we haven't had a lot of spare time."

"I don't want him to be caught off guard if he finds out," Adryn said.

"Thank you. I appreciate that." Jodenny sipped at the coffee but it was too hot, so she inhaled the aroma instead. "I saw Laura down in medical. She's upset about yesterday's mission."

Adryn frowned. "What about it?"

"That it was dangerous, and apparently you got assigned to it because you're family."

"But that—" Adryn stopped herself from completing the sentence. "I never told her it was dangerous."

"A ship this size, I bet it's hard to keep secrets."

"I didn't get the job because I was anybody's niece," Adryn said. "I volunteered for it."

Jodenny tasted the coffee. She needed more sugar. "I think you should tell her."

Adryn grimaced. "I think that'll get me into even

more trouble. Did I tell you we've only been married six months?"

Jodenny raised her coffee cup in salutation. "Congratulations. It only gets harder, trust me. Now, why don't you tell me why we're really here?"

Adryn put on an innocent expression. "I don't know what you mean."

"You and me, right here. Don't get me wrong. Family talk is important. But I suspect you were more interested in splitting Terry and I up than anything else. Is this a guy thing?"

A quick smile. "No," Adryn said. "It's a chief thing. They wanted to talk to him in private."

"Hmm," Jodenny said, and drank the rest of her coffee.

The chiefs' mess was a large compartment filled with comfortable furniture, a table for eating and playing cards, large-screen entertainment devices, and vids of members past and present. It smelled like old sweat, dirty socks, and a whiff of forbidden tobacco. It was also crowded with chiefs, at least a dozen of them, men and women standing around in uniform as if attending a disciplinary hearing.

Myell figured he was in serious trouble the moment he walked in. Cappaletto and Ovadia effectively blocked any retreat, leaving him in front of the square-jawed beanpole shape of the *Confident*'s master chief.

"Chief Myell, I'm Master Chief Halvert. You've been summoned on down here because I've been talking to Master Chief Talic, over on the *Melbourne*. He says he served with you at your last command. He claims you never went through a proper chief's initiation before you disappeared on your last mission, and that's a bit of a concern."

A few of the chiefs nodded. Most were giving Myell a thorough lookover. He remembered Talic well, the son of a bitch.

Halvert's gaze was unforgiving. "We understand what he's talking about. Becoming a chief means more than just putting on a different uniform and making more money. We've got the same kind of tradition in our military, so I understand where he's coming from. You want the respect of the crew on this ship, you've got to have the respect of this chiefs' mess first. You understand what I'm saying?"

The broad American accent wasn't too hard to decipher, and Myell understood all the words. Jodenny, when she found out, was going to be pissed. But he was willing to stand his ground, at least on a minute-by-minute basis.

In as neutral a tone as he could manage, he replied, "Yes, Master Chief."

"Well, then." Halvert turned to Cappaletto. "You've got the charges there, Chief?"

"You bet." Cappaletto reached into his pocket and pulled out a thin roll of paper. He unrolled it. "The Kangaroo Court of Neptune the Sea King is hereby called to order. To wit, to writ and to all ye present, defendant Teren Myell of the malarkey-filled Team Space is accused of the following. Number one, he saved the lives of his shipmates and colleagues on the TSS *Aral Sea*. Number two, he made the bastard Roon disappear from the entire planet Earth. Number three, any Team Space pissant whiner who wants to disrespect the Hero of

Burringurrah isn't worth crossing the street to spit on even if he was on fire."

"Who's got the anchor?" Cappaletto asked.

Ovadia pulled a box out of his pocket and handed it over.

"Go ahead, Tom," Halvert said to Cappaletto.

The anchor was small and gold. Cappaletto pinned it onto Myell's right collar flap and gave him a solid whump on the upper arm.

"Congratulations, Chief," he said. "You earned it."

The rest of the chiefs came around to congratulate him as well, each with a nice punch to the arm, and Myell didn't mind the pain at all even though he'd have bruises come morning. Someone broke out champagne and there was a cake, too, bearing Myell's name and the logo of the ACF.

"Can't stay long," Ovadia reminded everyone.

Master Chief Halvert said, "Don't be a worrywart, Noberto."

Myell hated to leave his own party but he did have a job to do, so after fifteen minutes of coffee and cake he, Ovadia, and Cappaletto squeezed out the hatch. Jodenny and Adryn were waiting for them. Myell handed her a plate of cake.

"Where'd you get that?" she asked, noticing the anchor.

He kissed her. "Present from the chiefs' mess."

They all went down to the ready room off the auxiliary deck. After several minutes of waiting around, one of Beranski's men came to get them. The blue ring was humming and turning slowly half a meter above the deck. Sensors, scanners, and force shield equipment surrounded it from every angle. Security guards stood on watch, armed and ready. Beranski looked like he hadn't slept at all.

"It's incredibly cool," Beranski said. "They're going to shit themselves in jealousy back on Fortune."

"If we ever get back to Fortune," one of Beranski's aides said gloomily.

Jodenny was holding on to Myell's arm as if she feared he'd get too close to it and vanish. Myell patted her fingers. He had no intention of getting near the thing. Just looking at it made his skin itch.

"What now?" Myell asked. "Am I supposed to try controlling it with my mind?"

"Can you?" Beranski asked, intrigued.

"No," Myell said.

"Would you tell me if you could?"

Myell raised an eyebrow.

Beranski spread his hands. "Admiral Su says you never wanted the responsibility of controlling the system. That you turned it down."

"True enough," Myell said. "But I'm not going to lie about it. If I could control it, I probably wouldn't be here in the first place."

Denials and protestations aside, Myell spent the rest of the day with Beranski as the team ran tests and scans on the blue ouroboros. Again and again he answered questions he'd already answered—where he'd been, when, under what circumstances, how long each trip had lasted. Jodenny stayed close by, obviously bored, but every time he suggested she go back to their cabin and sleep, she gave him the evil eye.

Instead she amused herself by borrowing Chief Ovadia's SOEL and watching library vids about the Hero of Burringurrah, and the Roon invasion of Earth, and the Big Daddy Sphere, also known as the First Egg.

Some of the vids were documentaries, and others pure fiction, and still others pure fiction done very badly with actors who looked nothing like Jodenny or Myell.

"Do you know how many things they've gotten wrong?" Jodenny asked.

Myell had come to her chair for a short break from the questions and tests. He put a hand on her belly to feel Junior and said, "How could I? I wasn't there."

"I can guarantee you there were no spectacular explosions or beautiful native women on your trip across the outback." She gave him a speculative look. "I don't understand why you're here. Not that I'm complaining. But you *died*."

"Turned into a god," Myell said.

She nodded.

He sat down on the small stool beside her. "Anna Gayle. She was there?"

Jodenny nodded.

"One of their prisoners?"

"Maybe at first," she said, begrudgingly. "But not by the time I saw her. She was helping them."

He scratched his chin. "Could be that she had no choice."

"Everyone has choices," Jodenny said. "Sam didn't help them. He was barely alive. Even when he got his physical health back, he couldn't talk, couldn't sit still, prowled the woods, woke up screaming at night— you've seen him."

"I know," Myell said. "You save him, though. Eventually. In the future that I've seen."

She lifted her chin. "You've seen wrong, though. If there's any saving to be done, he'll do it himself. He's one of the strongest people I know."

Captain McNaughton came by, though he mostly

ignored Myell and Jodenny. He quizzed Beranski on their progress, inspected the ring from afar, and stalked off again. Admiral Nam had apparently shuttled back to the *Melbourne* but would be back in a few hours. Adryn had gone off duty and had said something about working out some misunderstanding with her wife. Myell, who was still marveling that Adryn wasn't a little kid anymore, hadn't realized she was married to another woman.

"Does that bother you?" Jodenny asked.

"Blows my mind," he admitted. "Not the marriage thing. That she's even old enough to be in the military."

"I wonder if the wedding announcement was in the news." Sitting there in the middle of the hangar, Jodenny did a search and came up with a clipping from the news archive. She read it and frowned.

Myell asked "What?" and leaned over her shoulder to read it. "Mr. and Mrs. Conrad Ling and Mrs. Dottie Myell announce the marriage of their daughters," Myell read. "Why isn't Colby mentioned too?"

Jodenny didn't feel comfortable telling him about the divorce. "Maybe he opposed the marriage."

Myell scratched his chin. "I don't see why."

"We can ask Adryn later," Jodenny said.

Around sixteen hundred hours, just as she was getting hungry and tired and bone-dead exhausted again, Commander Haines came by for a status check and announced, by the way, that he and Jodenny were invited to the ship's wardroom for dinner. There were only twenty-two officers in the wardroom aside from the pilots, who dined separately. Dinner was at eighteen hundred hours.

Jodenny was completely sure she would rather eat in

with Myell in their cabin. Her preference must have shone in her face.

"It would be prudent to make nice with the captain," Haines said. "This is the last formal dinner before we're in Roon range tomorrow."

"I want to bring my husband," she said.

He frowned. "Chiefs aren't allowed in the wardroom."

"Hero of Burringurrah," Jodenny reminded him. "I'm pretty sure you can swing a special invitation."

Haines swallowed a reply and went off. Soon an airman relayed the message that Myell was also invited to dinner in the officers' wardroom. Myell took the news with a grimace. At seventeen hundred Beranski called for a dinner break, and they went back up to their cabin. The security escort that had followed them around until then was gone. Nearly dying in pursuit of the blue ring must have convinced someone important that Jodenny and Myell weren't a threat after all.

Once in the cabin, Myell stretched out on the bed and kicked off his boots. "You go dine with the nice officers. I'll nap."

"You're coming," Jodenny said. "I need backup."

"You don't have to go, either."

"Help me figure out what to wear," she insisted.

She didn't have a formal uniform to wear and fretted over that. On Team Space ships, officers always dressed for dinner. She polished up her insignia and pinned her hair up as tightly as she could. Then her scalp began to ache, and had to put her hair down again.

Myell watched with amusement and made no attempt to help.

"Don't make me hurt you," she said.

He dragged himself into the shower unit. The steam

rolled out, soapy-smelling and hot, and Jodenny contemplated slipping inside with him. She peeked through the shower door. Even with the burn marks on him, even that small thick one on his thigh, he was as handsome as she'd ever seen him. Her ardor was diminished by a comparison of her size to the width of the unit. She might be able to wedge herself in there, but they'd both get stuck and require extraction by the ship's engineers.

"What's that frown for?" Myell asked when he emerged. A towel was wrapped around his waist, and beads of water dotted his chest.

"I swore I would never do this," Jodenny sniffled.

"Do what?"

"I'm fat and I'm ugly," she said.

Myell pulled her close and squeezed her shoulders. "You're pregnant and you're beautiful."

"My ankles are swollen like grapefruit."

"There's an entire fleet of aliens on their way to destroy us. They don't care about your ankles."

Jodenny tweaked his nose. "That's supposed to cheer me up?"

"That's supposed to put things into perspective." His lips were soft on her forehead. "Do you want me to try and free the blue ring? Make it take us away from here?"

She had been thinking about it, though she wouldn't admit it. All her reasons against it rose to her tongue. "You can't. We can't. Leave Adryn and Chief Cappaletto and anyone's who been good to us? They'd have to face the Roon without us."

"This battle has already happened. I've been to the future forty years after the *Kamchatka* was stranded there. That's twenty-five years from this moment now. You're seventy years old and I'm still dead. I don't know what happened in this corner of the galaxy but by that then-now, as Commander Perry calls it, this is all over."

"Time travel makes my nose bleed," she said. "I refuse to believe things can't change. Ignore what Perry said. Ignore Homer. We'll figure this out. We'll find out what Kultana is, and how you can get there."

He paused. His warm hands went still against her back.

"What is it?" she asked.

"Nothing. I'd rather not talk about Homer when I'm half naked and holding you in my arms."

She wouldn't be distracted. "We have to stand with everyone here. Here and now. For better and for worse."

Myell answered with a kiss.

CHAPTER SIXTEEN

At seventeen-forty-five Commander Endicott came by. He assured them it didn't matter if they didn't have formal uniforms, because the *Confident*'s crew didn't dress for dinner. Jodenny was only slightly relieved. She felt it incumbent as a representative from Team Space to at least set the standard.

"Don't worry," Endicott said. "People want to meet the Hero of Burringurrah no matter what he's wearing."

Jodenny's lips pursed. To Myell she said, "Maybe you should go on and I'll just stay here."

Endicott coughed. "I mean, they want to meet both of you."

The *Confident*'s wardroom was a long, low compartment with dark blue walls and oil paintings of bygone sailing ships. A blue-gray rug stretched across the deck, and the furniture was made of heavy, bulky faux wood. A long bar lined one of the bulkheads. Most of the officers were male. They offered friendly handshakes to both Jodenny and Myell upon introduction.

"Good to have you," said a lieutenant commander from Engineering.

"Biggest surprise since the cook served fresh turkey at Thanksgiving," said a lieutenant from Supply.

A commander from Navigation said, "You're a damned sight prettier than most of our visiting officers."

Jodenny didn't appreciate that last remark, but she let the comment go in favor of finding a chair to sit in. Myell went to the bar to get her a glass of lemonade. He looked uncomfortable and wasn't talking much. She almost regretted bringing him along, but was utterly glad he wasn't out of her sight getting in trouble somewhere.

"Chief Myell," said a young ensign. "Is it true? Everything that happened in the vids?"

Jodenny gazed at his round cheeks and dewy skin. So young. So unprepared.

"Probably not," Myell said.

They were introduced to several more officers, and though once upon a time she might have remembered most of them, baby brain made it hard for her to hold to any specifics.

A lieutenant said to Myell, "So tell us, Chief. Are those Roon bastards as ugly as they say?"

"Uglier," Myell said. "And they smell bad, too."

Smiles all around. Confidence, boisterousness. Jodenny was going to be ill. None of them understood what they were getting into. She knew firsthand the stench of the Roon army, the stink of them so vivid in her memories she could smell it now, in the wardroom.

The young ensign said, "Dumb assholes, aren't they?"

Myell looked surprised. "Not at all. They're smart, fast, stronger than we are. If nothing else, they have interstellar engines that can carry them across the galaxy. And control of the Wondjina network."

"We've got the new Apollo missile system," Haines said. Jodenny hadn't noticed him at the fringe of the crowd. He added, "Better than ever. It'll take care of them."

"You don't know that," Myell said.

Several officers turned his way. Jodenny felt a headache trying to squeeze into the space between her eyes. The friendly conviviality of the wardroom was shifting into something hostile not toward the Roon but toward Myell himself. For daring to speak the truth, or how he saw it. It was a trait she admired, though there was such a thing as *timing*, wasn't there?

The arrival of Captain McNaughton, tense and unhappy as usual, brought the wardroom to its feet. He was flanked by his equally grim-looking senior staff, none of whom looked particularly happy Jodenny and Myell had joined them. Then again, their attention was probably focused on the upcoming battle, and they had a much more realistic idea of the odds than Haines or any of the junior crew.

"Ladies and gentlemen," McNaughton said.

"You're just in time, Captain," Haines said. "Chief Myell is telling us how superior the Roon armada is."

McNaughton gazed at Myell, who met his eyes without flinching.

"Is that so?" McNaughton asked.

"They were ahead of us fifteen years ago, and they've had all this time to get even better," Myell said.

McNaughton said, "But we have you, Chief. Made

the whole Roon army up and disappear, didn't you? That's the story. You're the hero."

The wardroom had gone quiet around them.

"There's probably only one way to survive this encounter," Myell said. "You won't do it, and I doubt it would work, but it beats wholesale slaughter."

Jodenny knew what was coming.

McNaughton didn't, or didn't care. "And what's that?"

"Surrender," Myell said.

A murmur through the room. Disagreement. More hostility. Jodenny wanted to strangle him. He had deliberately picked this fight. Had known what he was doing the minute he stepped into the room.

Myell put his drink down and gave Jodenny an apologetic nod. "Excuse me, Commander Scott," he said. "I'll be in the chiefs' mess."

Contrary to whatever Jodenny believed, Myell hadn't intended to turn the whole wardroom against him. But he couldn't just stand there and encourage them toward their own destruction, either. There were too many young foolish people on this ship. Too many old ones, too. He himself felt incredibly old, as if all the years he'd visited had suddenly accumulated and were pressing down on his shoulders.

He didn't go to the chiefs' mess. Instead he wound up in the infirmary, which was dark and soothing this time of the evening. The doctor on duty, a young ensign named Connelly, asked if he needed medical attention. He replied that he was only there to visit Osherman.

"He's sleeping," Dr. Connelly confided. "It was a

hard afternoon. Dr. Cho discovered a neural plug. Very small, very discreet, some kind of Roon technology. It might eventually dissolve on its own given enough time, but he tried a few things today and they'll try some more tomorrow if it hasn't worked."

"If it dissolves, he'll be able to talk?"

"He'll be able to talk and maybe more. We think the plug affects not only speech, but other areas of the brain, too. It might cause hallucinations, depression, anxiety."

All the years Sam Osherman had suffered—would suffer—and people assumed it was the Roon captivity that had done it to him. Myell felt sick knowing that it was something else entirely.

"Thanks, Doc," he said.

He didn't want to wake Osherman and so he retreated, heading back toward his and Jodenny's cabin. He was halfway to the nearest lift when Homer appeared out of nowhere, as crazily dressed as ever in pinks and yellows.

"Gampa!" he said. "I've got to talk to you."

"Maybe I'm not interested," Myell said, and continued past him to the lift.

Homer followed him inside. "It's very important. You've got to get out of here, and fast. The Roon are on their way and they're in a bad mood."

Myell said "Deck Four" to the lift control and added, to Homer, "I thought you weren't supposed to share information about the future. Doesn't it ruin your research?"

"My research will be fine," Homer said earnestly. "The important thing is that you get out using the ring."

"Why?" Myell affected boredom. "This is it. Kultana, right? I made it."

Homer rocked back and forth on his heels. "It's not the same! It's more than just a place, Gampa. You have to come the right way or it won't work."

"Full stop," Myell said to the lift.

The small car glided to a halt. The beige walls glowed with soft light and the controls hummed, waiting for further instruction.

Myell turned to Homer. "You come in and out of my life whenever you want, never giving a damn about when I really need you. I'm not sure anything you tell me is ever the truth, and even if it is, I think you're keeping some of it for yourself. If you want my help, you've got to tell me everything. That starts right now."

Homer's face crinkled up in a grimace. "I would if I could, Gampa."

Myell told the lift to resume its journey.

"Honest!" Homer said. "Please listen to me."

"Why haven't you asked me about the Flying Doctor?" Myell asked.

Carefully Homer said, "I don't know what you mean."

"I told you I was being visited, and you were surprised. Didn't know everything after all. But since then, you haven't asked me a single question about that. Isn't it important for your so-called research?"

Homer waved a hand. "I don't need to know, Gampa. I went and looked it up. That Roon is just a fluke. He's inconsequential. Ignore him and he'll go away."

"Funny. That doesn't work with you."

"I'm not kidding!" Homer blurted out, almost a shout. "You have to leave before the Roon armada gets here. Your mission is too important. Mankind is too important."

Myell gave him a level look. Evaluating. Judging.

"What about Jodenny and the baby?" he asked.

"You saw what happened last time," Homer said quietly. "You want to risk that again?"

The lift slid to a stop and the doors opened. Homer vanished. Myell clenched his hands in frustration. He hadn't expected much in the way of information, and what he'd gotten was disheartening. The armada was coming, this wasn't the right Kultana, and Jodenny and the baby were in jeopardy no matter what.

You see it but you don't understand it, the Flying Doctor had said.

Maybe he just had to see things for himself.

He went to find Cappaletto.

Jodenny declined an escort back to her cabin after dinner. She could find it just fine, she told Commander Endicott.

"It's my honor," he said. "Really."

"If you insist," she replied, and let him walk her through the *Confident*'s quiet passageways.

"I hope Chief Myell's not too upset," he said.

"Chief Myell will be fine," she assured him. It had taken all she had not to follow him, but she thought he needed some time alone. "I shouldn't have pressured him into coming. I was surprised that Lieutenant Ling didn't come."

"It's a little difficult for her," Endicott said. "With her father and all. Captain McNaughton holds it against her."

Jodenny gave him a puzzled look.

"You didn't know?" He frowned. "Sorry."

"Know what?"

"Adryn's father is in jail, convicted of being an agent for the Colonial Forces Project."

"She didn't mention it," Jodenny said. Maybe because admitting your father was a terrorist wasn't easy, or even advisable.

"Captain McNaughton, he means well. Hates the CFP, but most people do, right? He'll do anything to defeat the Roon. Do you really think—I mean, do we have a chance?"

She thought carefully about her answer. "There's always a chance."

It was a relief to leave him at the hatch, a relief to not carry hope for him. Jodenny didn't turn up the lights. Instead she sat on the edge of the bed in the darkness, with only the small light in the head for illumination. She listened to the hum of the *Confident*'s engines and thought about all the sailors onboard, and how they were spending what was probably the last twelve hours of their lives. Making love, fighting, gambling, drinking. She pressed her hand against Junior's bump and wondered how she was going to save little Lisa, how she could possibly protect her. The outside and inside world shaded into one, filling her with regret and anger that everything had come to this one battle, the impossible showdown with the Roon.

The hatch beeped. She opened it to see Haines outside.

"Your husband," he said, furious. "Where is he going?"

Jodenny blinked at him. "What are you talking about?"

"He just hijacked a Team Space birdie." Haines nodded to the two security guards behind him. "Put her under arrest."

* * *

Let me get this straight," Cappaletto had said, a short time earlier. "You want me to steal a shuttle and fly you over to a chunk of lifeless ice because some guy from the future told you to save mankind at Kultana, and you're taking him seriously?"

Myell nodded. They were alone in the cramped quarters that Cappaletto shared with Ovadia, who was nowhere in sight. Myell was grateful for that. He didn't know how Ovadia felt about helping out the Hero of Burringurrah, and didn't really have time to find out.

"What about Commander Scott?" Cappaletto asked.

Myell was trying not to think about Jodenny. "I can't put her and the baby in more jeopardy. I won't. This probably won't end well."

Cappaletto rose off his bunk. "I'd planned to spend the next few hours getting drunk and making illicit love to Ensign Voight before we all die in a fiery battle tomorrow. I'm sure she'll understand if I send my regrets."

The *Confident* hadn't been built with secret passages, but there were shortcuts through Flight Ops that Cappaletto navigated with ease. They cut through the pilots' ready room without being seen and came out at the starboard end of the flight bay behind a line of Eagles. The bay was heavily guarded, which was no surprise, but Cappaletto pointed out a Team Space passenger birdie parked in the less secure end.

"Some bigwig must have used it to come to dinner," Cappaletto said. "That's our best bet. She's got the range and the speed, and can go cammie."

"Cammie?"

"Invisible to ACF sensors. Little bit of technology

Team Space picked up and didn't share with us until we twisted their arms. Our sensors aren't compatible."

"How are we going to get over there without alerting Security?"

"See those cameras up there? They've got a blind spot. It's how you and your friends got onboard and no one saw how. Stay on this side of the launch line and we'll be fine."

It took thirty seconds to traverse the bay. Myell was sure that at any minute an alarm was going to start shrieking over his head. Cappaletto seemed to be having a fine time of it, skulking along until they reached the birdie and he palmed open the hatch.

Nam was onboard, settled into the pilot's chair. He didn't look surprised to see them at all.

"I thought you might show up," Nam said. "Chief Cappaletto, you're dismissed."

Cappaletto slid his hands into his pockets. Casual and firm.

"Begging your pardon, Admiral," Cappaletto said. "But I wouldn't miss this even if you doubled my salary."

Nam stared at him hard. Cappaletto didn't flinch. With the barest of nods, Nam motioned toward the copilot's chair.

"I figured you'd want to talk to the Roon yourself," Nam said to Myell as Cappaletto went through the launch sequence. "Good to see old age hasn't addled my brain."

Nam wasn't that old, but he'd gotten it wrong. "I don't want to talk to the Roon," Myell said. "I want to visit Kultana."

"You want to visit a lifeless, airless planetoid?" Nam asked.

Myell nodded.

Cappaletto added, helpfully, "Because it's his destiny to save mankind."

Nam stared at them both. Myell was acutely aware of movement on the flight deck. Nam was their only hope of getting off the ship and anywhere near Kultana, and he didn't look convinced.

"You followed me once," Myell said. "To Burringurrah. I don't remember why or how. But you had faith then. I'm asking for it again."

Slowly Nam said, "It's a damn good thing I don't have anything better to do."

Cappaletto added, "That's what I said, sir."

It was no problem for Nam to get permission to launch. Takeoff was smoother than Myell expected. He undid his safety belt and joined them behind the controls. The Americanadian and Team Space fleet was all around them, evening traffic darting between the ships, running lights blinking everywhere. Myell clutched the back of Nam's seat as they passed the underbellies of carriers and transports. Fourteen ships, armed and ready to fire. Thousands of people ready to risk their lives. They all measured nothing against the Roon.

"This might be a one way trip," Myell said, trying very hard not to think about Jodenny and the baby.

"Better to go out in a blaze of heroic stupidity than a slow death doing nothing," Cappaletto said cheerfully.

They broke free of the fleet and headed into open space. Kultana appeared ahead, as lifeless a chunk of ice as Myell had been told.

"Cammie's on," Cappaletto reported. "Team Space can see us, but my people can't."

"Can anyone stop us?" Myell asked.

"I've disabled the remote functions, so they can't control our flight. But they can always blow us out of the sky."

Nam said, "Probably not going to, though. Unless Captain McNaughton convinces Admiral Taylor that you're some kind of Roon spy out to deliver the goods to your lizard masters."

Myell was appalled. "McNaughton thinks that?"

"It's one of the theories," Nam said.

And he'd left Jodenny back there. Myell hadn't been letting himself think of her, her fury, or the odds he'd see her in this eddy again. He wasn't willing to watch her die, though. To stand by and do nothing.

"Tell me more about your so-called mission to save mankind," Nam said. "Especially why you didn't mention it before."

"I didn't think you'd believe me," Myell admitted.

The comm clicked on. Captain McNaughton's image flickered on the main screen. "This is the *Confident*. State your course and heading."

"So much for a stealthy trip," Cappaletto muttered.

Nam flicked on their radio. McNaughton was visibly surprised by Nam's appearance but he recovered quickly. Starship captains usually did.

"Admiral Nam," McNaughton said. "What's going on out there?"

"Chief Myell wanted to see the planetoid," Nam replied, as if it was a perfectly normal request. "I decided to oblige him. I have Admiral Su's permission."

That was news to Myell. He wondered if it was really true. If anything, it was a delaying tactic while the ACF tried to get information out of Team Space.

A click, a pause, on the other end. Then Jodenny's voice came clear through the cockpit.

"What do you think you can accomplish, Terry?" she asked.

Her voice was remarkably steady. More steady than his would have been, if their situations had been reversed.

"I don't know," he said. "But this planetoid's original name was Kultana. Anything's better than what's going to happen if I don't at least try. I'm sorry I couldn't bring you with me. You're safer back there."

"I'm not on the *Confident*," Jodenny said. "I'm in the shuttle behind you."

Cappaletto hit a control. The overhead display showed an ACF shuttle intercepting their course. Another vid flickered and rolled on, depicting Jodenny in the ship with Commander Haines and a pilot Myell didn't recognize. Security techs sat in the seats behind them.

"Go back, Kay," Myell said.

"It's not exactly up to me," she replied.

Myell cursed Haines under his breath.

"They put a tracker in you," Jodenny said. Her expression was furious. "And in me. When you left the ship, it went off."

"That's enough, Commander," Haines said. "Why Kultana, Chief Myell? Who's out there?"

Cappaletto said, "Big hunk of ice, dead ahead. Any place special you want to visit? North Pole, South Pole, equator?"

Myell turned his attention to the scanners. The planetoid had a methane atmosphere and frozen methane surface, with no signs of life or civilization. Even if they landed and started strolling around in spacesuits, there was no place to go and nothing to see.

It would be awfully nice if Homer showed up and explained everything. Right about now. Right now.

Nam said, "You really don't have a plan, do you?"

"I've got something on the sensors," Cappaletto said. "Coming over the horizon. Dark side, out of Fleet range."

Myell leaned closer to the controls. He tried not to think about Jodenny or Junior, or Adryn and Osherman back on the *Confident,* or any of the thousands of ACF and Team Space sailors whose lives might hinge on what he was able to do here.

"What is it?" he asked.

Nam recognized it first. "Son of a bitch," he said.

An enormous Roon carrier, bulbous and grotesque, rose up from behind Kultana's backside. Myell did a double check. The main alien fleet was still far off on the scanners, on schedule to arrive tomorrow. Either this was an advance scout of some kind—

Another carrier rose up behind the first one.

"Ambush," Cappaletto said. "Jesus Christ. They must have been out here for months, just waiting for us."

The vid connection to Jodenny's shuttle and Mc-Naughton on the bridge both went dark. Instead the visage of a Roon rolled into view. A Roon that Myell recognized instantly from its silver headdress. The Flying Doctor.

And beside him, beautiful and terrible in her own feather cloak, stood the traitorous Anna Gayle.

"Chief Myell," the Flying Doctor said. "The end meets us both."

Cappaletto said, "We are so dead."

The Roon carrier opened fire.

CHAPTER **SEVENTEEN**

J odenny!" someone was saying, sternly. "Wake up."
She opened two blurry eyes, saw whitewashed walls and antique furniture, and promptly closed her lids again. Something soft and lumpy was beneath her, some kind of bed that smelled like lemons. A pillow had been wedged beneath her head. Her body was heavy and full of pins and needles, as if she'd been sleeping for a long time. Her belly felt dull and weighted down with lead.

Fear had her bolting upright, or at least trying to.

"Easy!" Osherman caught her by the shoulders. "It's okay."

She slapped at his hands but didn't dislodge them. He forced her down and she acquiesced, for the time being, only because her head pounded terribly and all the strength had run out of her body. The world swam with unbearable heat.

He said, "The baby's fine. You hear me? She's okay. So are you."

Slowly her vision focused on Osherman. He was dressed in a formal white shirt and dark pants, and there was a strange caterpillar of a mustache sitting on his upper lip. Of all things, a mustache. The bed she was on had tall wooden posters at each corner, and the room had two square windows brilliant with sunshine.

"You talked." Her voice came out rusty and she coughed. "Sam, you talked."

He nodded. He looked thinner and older than she thought he should, and his face was sunburned.

Suspicion made her look down at her own clothes.

She was dressed in a ridiculously long white nightshirt that belonged to someone twice her size. Junior's bump was a solid presence underneath, and she rubbed her belly with both hands. Junior kicked out a hello and then kicked again, for good measure.

"Where are we?" Jodenny demanded.

Osherman scratched his neck. "Not where we were."

"Terry?"

"Not here."

"Where is he?" She started to swing her legs out of bed, but Osherman wouldn't move out of her way. "Get off. Where is he?"

"You have to calm down," he said. "He's not here."

"Where's here?"

"Sydney, New South Wales," he said.

She stared at him. "Sydney. As in Earth?"

"And it's the year 1855," Osherman added. "January. Summertime in this part of the world. And damn hot."

She didn't believe any of it. "How did we get here?"

"What do you remember?"

Bile rose up in her throat. The next thing she knew, she was vomiting into a ceramic pot that Osherman held for her. When she finally sagged back against the pillows, he held a wet cloth to her forehead.

"You've been sick," he said. "But you're getting better."

Slowly her senses came back to her. She remembered the Roon ambush at Kultana and seeing the carrier open fire—first at the Fleet, then at Myell's fragile little shuttle. She had screamed at that. In the terrifying moments afterward she seen the *Confident* on fire, the *Melbourne* splitting amidships. Then nothing.

Myell wasn't dead. Couldn't be dead. Not now, not

then. She squinted at the room and at the open windows, took a deep breath. The sky outside was blue, and the air was sweltering.

"You're talking," she repeated, as if he didn't realize how momentous that was.

"I've had practice." He stood up and paced to the window. His leather shoes made the wooden floorboards squeak. "I've been here about eight months. Homer brought me here. I was in the infirmary on the *Confident* when he showed up and introduced himself. He said he was taking me away 'for safekeeping.' Next thing I knew, we were here. I haven't seen him since, not until yesterday, when he brought you."

"But we were on the *Confident* just a little while ago."

"It's been eight months for me," he said. "Alone here, with no idea what happened to you or anyone else."

Jodenny eased back on the pillows. They smelled strange, and she suspected they were stuffed with real feathers. She tried to imagine how lonely he must have been, how isolated, but her brain was still busy with denial. "Whose house is this?"

"Lady Elizabeth Scott."

"Say that again."

He peered out the windows at the street. "Lady Elizabeth Scott. Your great-great-great-something-grandmother, according to Homer. She's out shopping with her friends right now, but you'll meet her later. She doesn't know you're her whatever-granddaughter, of course. She thinks you're my wife. Are you hungry?"

Jodenny stared at him.

The tips of his ears blushed.

"This is the nineteenth century," he said defensively.

"We're in the respectable house of an English noble-woman. I couldn't very well tell her you're a lieutenant in Team Space."

"Lieutenant commander," Jodenny said. Might as well set the record straight.

He grimaced.

She studied the room further. "Homer didn't say anything about Terry?"

"No. I swear. Where did you last see him?"

"He was in a birdie," she said. "The Roon attacked."

Silence for a moment. Osherman said, "Well, then. How about something to eat?"

"Sure." Jodenny heard the brittleness in her own voice but couldn't stop it. "We're hundreds of years in the past and I'm starving. Coffee and pancakes?"

"I can do tea and biscuits. Maybe some eggs."

He went out the door, down a hall, then down some stairs. She heard the solid *thump-thump* of his retreat. Left alone, she swung her feet to the floor, tested her weight, and looked for a bathroom. She spied only a blue-and-white chamber pot.

"Homer, I'm going to kill you," she said.

She waddled into the hallway, which was wallpa-pered with a pink-and-gray floral motif. Sunlight poured through a lace-curtained window. Three ajar doors led into dim bedrooms but no rooms with indoor plumb-ing. From downstairs she heard murmuring voices and the sound of water being poured. Standing on the land-ing above the stairs, clad only in the nightshirt with her bare feet on a handmade rug, she felt like an eaves-dropper on a conversation she couldn't quite hear.

Sydney, 1855.

By the time Osherman returned, Jodenny had used the pot and was studying the cobblestoned street below.

The houses along the narrow, sloping street were small mansions of sandstone brick and wood, congruent with the era. There were no power or telephone lines, or signs of any modern technology. The smell of sewage was strong in the air, and some kind of meat was burning nearby. How did people live like this? She was afraid to find out.

"The sky's blue," she said, gloomily. The skies over Earth were no longer that color, not since the Debasement. "And it smells foul."

"You get used to it." He put a breakfast tray down on a side table. "Come eat."

She wasn't very hungry, but Junior needed fuel to grow. Some warm porridge tasted better than she thought it would, and there was toast with jam on it, and some kind of protein strip.

"Bacon," he said.

Jodenny paused. "Pig bacon?"

He nodded.

She put it aside. The tea was lukewarm, which was a blessing. She didn't need hot liquids. Outside, the sound of hoofs clip-clopped on stone and a man shouted out something in a language she didn't understand.

"Australia," she said.

He nodded again. "About seventy years since the first convicts were transported here from England. About fifteen years since they stopped sending them to Sydney. Five years since they struck gold in the mountains. It's the frontier, Jodenny. Edge of a whole nation beginning to rise up."

She thought he was being very careful with her, as if she would fall to pieces with one inopportune word. It annoyed her to be treated like spun glass. But she wasn't so annoyed that she was going to call him on it.

It was too much of a relief to hear him talking, and she was still trying to ignore the very real possibility that Myell was dead.

"Homer said he could only appear to his direct ancestors," she said. "But you talked to him? You saw him?"

"Yes. Doesn't mean he's honest or reliable. Do you want to come downstairs? See what it's like here in 1855?"

"No."

He looked surprised. "Why not?"

Jodenny cupped her belly. "Cholera. Tuberculosis. Lockjaw. God knows what else is out there. Doesn't smell like they've got much for sewers and I bet the medical care is just as shitty, pun intended. You think I'm going out there with Junior? I'm staying right here."

Osherman blinked. "Your immunizations are all up to date. We've got each other, and we've each had medical training."

"Do you have any penicillin on you? Any antibiotics? A bone-knitter, any kind of scanner whatsoever? Pregnant women can get eclampsia, Sam. My blood pressure could soar through the roof and I could have a stroke. I could get gestational diabetes. Or a fistula. Do you know what a fistula is? When a woman is in labor too long, her bladder—"

He held up a hand to forestall her. "You can't stay in this house forever, Jodenny. The world is dangerous but it's our world now."

"It's not mine." She cupped Junior. "Terry's alive somewhere. If Homer saved us, he could have saved him. Or maybe the blue ouroboros did—it was on the *Confident,* and she was hit first. It could have broken free. But no matter where he is, what he's doing, he's not going to leave me here. He'll find both of us, rescue us."

Osherman stroked his mustache. "You really think so?"

"Yes. Maybe tomorrow, maybe next month, maybe a year from now, but he'll come. You know he will."

He said nothing.

She lifted the hem of her nightshift. "But in the meantime, you could at least find me something better to wear."

After all, nineteenth-century recluse or not, she wasn't going to spend every day waiting for Myell in her underwear.

The dress was a catastrophe of lace and silk, with narrow sleeves and a tight-fitting bodice that wasn't going to fit around Jodenny's pregnancy-enhanced breasts. She wasn't even going to address the corset and petticoats under the full skirt.

"Maybe you should talk to the girls," Osherman said, fleeing her dismay.

The "girls" were the two housekeepers of the residence. They were both tall and skinny, with dark hair, missing teeth, and freckled faces worn down from hard work. Lilly was the older sister, perhaps Jodenny's own age or so. Sarah, whose nose had been broken sometime in the past and was now unfortunately crooked, was barely out of her teens. Both had thick accents that Jodenny found hard to understand—old English, maybe, or whatever passed for the local dialect in a city jammed full of immigrants from across the world who'd come in search of mountain gold.

She supposed she was in turn hard for them to understand, but she was very clear about the dress.

"What do pregnant women wear around here?" she demanded. "Surely not corsets and hoops!"

Lilly gave her a curious look. "What's do they wear back where you come from, ma'am?"

Sarah added, "The Captain, he said you'd had a knock on the head and might be a bit confused."

"The Captain?" Jodenny asked. "Who's the Captain?"

Lilly looked aghast. "You poor thing!"

Sarah wiped her hand across her crooked nose. "You don't remember your own husband! Here he's been, sitting by your beside so worried and weeping."

Jodenny gazed down at her wedding ring. Myell's ring. "What's he a captain of?"

"The army, of course," Lilly said. "Retired early from service to the Queen. Very brave man, he is. Now in the trade business."

Osherman had obviously been busy spinning tall tales. Jodenny was afraid to ask anything more. Let them believe he was a general, for all she cared.

"Let's pretend I remember nothing about modern fashion," she said, almost choking on the word *modern*. "If you were me, what would you be wearing?"

"If I were a fine lady," Lilly mused, "I'd have some of that nice blue cotton from Mr. Johnson's shop on George Street."

"I'd have a new summer hat and some white gloves," Sarah said wistfully.

"And shoes with pointy toes," Lilly added.

Jodenny sighed. It was going to be a long century.

The two sisters went off to brainstorm alternative clothing arrangements and came back a half hour later with a voluminous blue dress with ample room in the bodice and more than enough room for Junior. They pinned alterations in place, took the dress away for some first aid with needle and thread, and returned an hour later for a second fitting.

"Much better," Lilly said, as Jodenny considered herself in a hand mirror. A Team Space uniform it was not.

Sarah beamed. "And hardly at all out of date. I think Her Ladyship will be happy."

"Is this one of her dresses?" Jodenny asked.

"Was," Lilly said. "It was supposed to go to the charity for the old transport girls."

"The what?"

"Oh, you really did get a conk on the head," Sarah said.

Lilly said, as if talking to a child, "You know, transport. From England. The convicts. They used to send them by the shipload."

Jodenny had been born and raised on Fortune. Australia's history was a dim, distant chapter in a book she hadn't opened in years. She knew that England had spent several decades shipping off its convicts and other unwanted denizens to Australia, but surely that was over by now?

"Are you convicts?" she asked.

"Of course not!" Lilly said.

"England doesn't send them to New South Wales anymore," Sarah said. "Just out West. Lilly and I and our eight sisters, we were all born here."

Jodenny exclaimed, "Eight!"

Sarah added, "They didn't all live. My dad, he was free first. He got mum at the Female Factory in Parramatta."

Jodenny tried to convince herself that Sarah had not

just used the words *female* and *factory* in the same sentence, but horror must have shown on her face.

"That's enough," Lilly said pointedly. She snatched up her sewing basket. "We've lunch to go make for Lady Scott, if that's all you'll be needing."

Lilly swept off. Sarah curtsied and followed hastily. Jodenny wanted to call out an apology but the enormity of the situation—and the dress, which was heavier than expected—made her flop down in a side chair and cover her face with both hands.

She was a trained military officer—or had been, once—but now she was something else entirely. A castaway, maybe. A prisoner. A pregnant woman whose real husband was missing and whose fake husband was, until recent memory, a psychologically unbalanced mute severely traumatized by his captivity with the Roon.

A knock on the door brought her around to face Osherman.

"Nice dress," he said.

She snorted. "You want to wear it?"

"I'm satisfied with what I've got," he said. "Come downstairs? I'll show you the house."

Jodenny hesitated.

"You won't get leprosy going downstairs," he promised.

Reluctantly she followed him. She was no expert on Victorian architecture but the house was nicely done, with three bedrooms for the residents and a tiny one for the housekeepers. Everything smelled like wax and wood smoke and perfume. The kitchen had an enormous hearth, and the table in the dining room was a carved slab of mahogany imported from England along with most of the other furnishings. The hardwood floors were spotlessly clean. All of the wood in the staircase, wainscoting, and doorways had been carved by hand.

In the front parlor hung a large oil painting of Lord Scott, he of the stern countenance and steely eyes. His domain included an upright piano, Oriental rugs and small sofas, pastoral landscapes of the English countryside, and white curtains that billowed in the harbor breeze.

"Admiral Lord Scott," Osherman said. "Dead twenty years ago in England. The week after the funeral, Lady Scott packed up her things and sailed here to start all over again. Left all her children and grandchildren behind, how's that for unsentimental?"

Jodenny stared at the Admiral's formidable nose and weathered face. He didn't look friendly. Then again, approachability wasn't a characteristic highly prized in British sea captains. She studied the lace curtains on the windows, the thin books of poetry on a side table, and the small clock ticking on the mantelpiece. The nineteenth century was quieter than a spaceship.

"She met me when I was at my worst, just after Homer left me here. Took me in," Osherman said. "In addition to stray Team Space officers, she also takes in cats and dogs."

Jodenny laughed at that, but only a little. Her heart was too full of other feelings to let amusement creep in. She sat down in a chair that afforded a view of the sunlit street.

"I can't be trapped here," she said. "I can't, Sam. I can't sit here without knowing what's happened to him. He could be out there, hurt. Alone. Needing help."

Osherman said, "Or he could be dead."

"Shut the fuck up," she said, and it was the first time she'd ever said anything like that to him.

He moved to her chair and crouched down. His hands grabbed her fists. "Listen to me. He could be dead, Jodenny. At Kultana. He could be trapped in the future. He could be stuck traveling in that ouroboros, never finding a home. You don't know. I don't know. We might never know."

She bowed into herself, grief like a heavy anchor.

"But I'm here," he said. "I'm here, and I'm not going anywhere. Let me help you."

Jodenny didn't answer—couldn't answer, not with so many words locked up in her throat.

The front door opened with a jangle, and a brown-haired woman in finery and jewels bustled in with a tall Aboriginal servant in tow. "Well, now!" she called out. "I'm home! I'm home and I've brought wonderful things for all of us! Where is everyone?"

She stopped in the parlor doorway to gaze at them in frank surprise. "My dearest Mrs. Osherman, why are you weeping?"

CHAPTER **EIGHTEEN**

Jodenny rose out of her chair and wiped at her face. She was absolutely not crying, no matter what anyone said.

"Lady Scott," she said formally. "Thank you for your hospitality."

Lady Scott peered at her with watery blue eyes. Her face was deeply lined and her hair stark white. She was as tall as Jodenny, but much larger in the bosom. Her jaunty hat sported a peacock feather, her leather shoes had golden buckles on them, and there were enough frills and lace in her voluminous dress to make curtains for the entire house.

"My dearest Mrs. Osherman," Lady Scott said. "You are welcome here in my home for as long as you'd like. The Captain told me how arduous the journey was for you, so heavy with child. It's a miracle you arrived in Australia unscathed. I trust that Lilly and Sarah have been seeing to your needs? What a fine dress you have!"

Jodenny smoothed down a sleeve. "It was yours."

Lady Scott beamed. "Excellent choice, then. You haven't met Tulip. Tulip, this is Mrs. Osherman."

The Aboriginal stepped forward. His clothes were common but sturdy, and he wore no shoes. He was forty years old, maybe, his hair gray at the edges. One eye was clear and focused but the other was damaged and milky. He had an armful of bags and packages that were no doubt the fruits of Lady Scott's shopping.

"Missus," he said, with a nod.

Jodenny replied, "Pleased to meet you."

Lady Scott clapped her hands. "I'm famished, aren't you? We must have dinner. And wine! We must have wine!"

She swept herself off with Tulip in tow and barked out orders for Lilly and Sarah. Within minutes Jodenny was sitting down beside Osherman at the dining room table, where a meal of cooked chicken had been set out along with cheese, potatoes, and fresh hot bread. There was wine and milk to drink, and Jodenny couldn't decide which was worse for Junior—alcohol or god knew what bacteria in the milk.

"Maybe just hot tea for you," Osherman said.

Lady Scott was a chatterbox; she rambled on about the weather, the market, her visit with her banker, her visit with the doctor, and did she mention the gossip about the governor, and had she told them the charming story about the shoemaker's son? Osherman indulged the old woman with conversation while Jodenny ate around the dead animal on her plate and swallowed all of her tea. She couldn't believe this woman was her grandmother however many generations back; Homer had said it, but Homer couldn't be trusted.

"Dear girl, don't you like the chicken?" Lady Scott asked.

Jodenny squared her shoulders. "I'm a vegetarian, ma'am."

"Vegetarian!" Lady Scott frowned. "I've heard of that. Strange beliefs about food and health, those vegetarians."

"Actually, where I come from"— Jodenny started, and then felt the nudge of Osherman's foot against her shin. She ended with—"people have all sorts of ideas about food."

"You have the strangest accent," Lady Scott mused. "The captain here says you're from the American colonies. How is it, living in Boston?"

Jodenny was trying to think of a suitable response when Osherman said, "My wife's parents took her all over the world, ma'am. She has an accent reflecting global travel."

"Very global," Jodenny agreed.

Lady Scott lifted her glass of wine. "To global travel! It broadens the mind and empties the purse. Though for some I suspect it empties the mind as well. When you see too many marvelous things you grow jaded and cynical, don't you think?"

"Josephine is neither cynical nor jaded," Osherman said, patting Jodenny's hand.

She wasn't sure exactly when she had become *Josephine,* but for appearance's sake she squeezed his hand back. Hard. "My husband speaks too well of me. He has no idea how cynical my heart has grown."

Lady Scott smiled at her. "Cynicism becomes you, child. I was afraid you were a mere wallflower. This city needs more female leadership. More feminine grit and backbone. You must come with us next week to the governor's luncheon. He's sailing back to England soon, and this is his big farewell. I shall introduce you to the finest of society."

"I couldn't," Jodenny said immediately. She put one hand on Junior's bump. "My condition."

"Don't be silly," Osherman said. "The fresh air and good company will do you good."

Lady Scott said, "Exactly!"

Jodenny kicked Osherman and gave Lady Scott her most sincere look. "I grow anxious in crowds."

"I do, too," Lady Scott confided. "But the rooms at Government House are very large."

Jodenny let the argument lapse. Surely, by next week, Myell would have already found some way to come for her, or Homer would have returned, or maybe she could just fake an illness. She could see that Osherman was going to be a significant problem. He was used to this place—perhaps he even liked it—but she had no intention of making this century her home.

Then again, she didn't suppose Osherman had money to support them, and Jodenny certainly had no income. The prospect of losing Lady Scott's hospitality wasn't a pleasant one. Not without a credit chit to put them up in a hotel or some wild fortune to see them into their own house.

Not that she needed a house.

Myell would come for her.

Lady Scott wasn't unpleasant company, but she talked so much and so eagerly that Jodenny wondered if she'd run off all her friends and neighbors with the chatter. Granted, Jodenny had sat through many interminable meetings and some truly awful wardroom dinners, but this time the food was an additional horror. Her ears ached and her stomach roiled at the sight of the chicken, and without any warning at all Osherman was saying, "I think perhaps some rest is in order. Josephine, you don't look well."

"I feel fine," she protested, but that wasn't true. She was dizzy on the stairs and it was a relief when he got her to her room and the bed.

She stared up at the slowly rotating ceiling and said, "What's wrong with me?"

"That dress, the food, and traveling through centuries of time," Osherman said. "I slept a lot my first few days here."

Jodenny wanted to know more about that, but her eyelids closed on their own. She told her subconscious to conjure up Myell. Surely in dreams they could be connected. But her vision remained dark and dreamless, as if he'd never even existed.

True to Osherman's word, Jodenny spent much of the next few days sleeping. The most comfortable position was on her side, with a pillow wedged between her knees and another to keep her and Junior from rolling backward. Otherwise Junior's weight and position made her back ache and her breathing grow short. The heat was relentless, but Osherman kept the curtains drawn and had a hand fan to move the air around. He was very attentive, bringing her food and drink whenever she was awake. But lethargy was her most constant companion, dragging her under for hours on end to nightmares about burning ships and Roon carriers. It wasn't until the third morning that she woke up feeling as if she'd passed the worst of it.

She blinked her eyes in the predawn light and wondered why someone was snoring down near the floor. Jodenny peeked over the bed and saw Osherman stretched out on a blanket and pillow. When he was awake, she asked him about that.

"Well," he said, looking embarrassed, "this was my room before you showed up. There aren't any other spares. And everyone knows we're man and wife."

"How long are you planning to sleep down there?"

He ducked his head and didn't answer.

"We can share this bed," Jodenny said. "Unless you're afraid I might roll over and squash you."

"You're comfortable with that?"

Myell wouldn't have been. Archly she said, "I'm comfortable as long as you stay on your side of the mattress, Commander."

He offered her a rare, small smile.

Junior, meanwhile, was using all of Jodenny's sleep time to grow at some mutant super-speedy exponential rate. Jodenny was getting so large, and so ungainly, that surely labor was about to descend upon her at any moment. Luckily she had the Digital Duola in her head. Every day she consulted her brain for what to do if the baby was breech, if the bleeding couldn't be stopped, if the afterbirth didn't come out. She felt fairly sure she could handle any problems, with Osherman's help.

Somewhat sure.

Confident. That was the word, bitter on her tongue.

She learned the routine of the house—breakfast, dinner, afternoon tea, and a light supper after dark. The girls went out every morning to do the shopping for the day. Lady Scott's social and civic obligations had her out of the house much of the time. She also had a suitor, a history professor named Wallace who kept a house just down the street. Osherman spent most of his days out as well, on business or visiting "friends," and from the latter he often returned with glassy eyes and his clothes smelling like tobacco and cologne. She wondered if he had a girlfriend somewhere in the city that he didn't want to tell her about, or a men's club where he was playing poker and drinking beer.

"Sometimes I make some money at cards," he admitted. "Mostly it's business—meeting the right people, making the right deals. Sometimes I just listen to people. Jodenny, we're travelers in an entirely different century. Aren't you interested in what they think? What they're going to do?"

"Not especially." She was sitting in the largest chair of the parlor with her hands laced over Junior, her swollen feet propped up on a stool. Her back ached and her lower legs had been cramping all day. Piano music from a neighbor's house drifted on the breeze. Jodenny didn't recognize the melody but the notes were slow and melancholy. If she listened too hard she might start thinking about Myell, and then she'd start crying again.

His mouth twisted. "I don't think that's true. I think you do care. No matter where you go and what you do, it's your nature to care."

"I won't be here long enough to make friends, Sam. And you know that when we go, they'll never even remember we were here. This world will evaporate. There's no use growing attached to any of them."

It might be too late for him, having already spent eight months in this eddy. He was bound to have formed friendships and favorites. But their century awaited them like clouds on the horizon: Team Space, the Roon, Myell. Especially Myell.

To distract herself from the hollow loneliness in her chest she tried helping Lilly and Sarah with the housework. They were aghast at the very idea. While they were outside pinning up wet laundry she snuck into the kitchen and was happy to discover it wasn't crawling with maggots or bugs or other obviously unsanitary creatures. Still, there wasn't any ice in summertime to keep things cold and electrical refrigerators had yet to make their debut. The food they ate every day was fresh but spoiled easily, so she resolved to eat only food that had been thoroughly boiled.

"Your wife has a strange preoccupation with food," she heard Lady Scott tell Osherman in amusement.

Osherman said, "She's had some unpleasant experiences."

That was a lie. But she'd worked in Food Service divisions aboard spaceships and knew that salmonella, E. coli, and other microscopic dangers lurked in raw or contaminated food. It was bad enough that she could smell sewage in the air, both day and night. The stink of it sank into her clothes and hair and she had to douse herself with some of Lady Scott's perfume to keep her nose from turning up. Worse, perhaps, were the armies of flies, lice, nits, bedbugs, ticks, and rats crawling the streets and walls and air, all carrying bacteria and viruses, with nary an antibiotic or disinfectant in sight.

"The bugs, they do bite," Lilly said, unnecessarily, as she made Jodenny's bed up one morning. "We boil the sheets once a week and that kills the little beasties.

Tulip, now, he's got himself a paste that he uses to keep the flies away. Lady Scott uses it, too."

Tulip, when cornered in the little yard behind the house, couldn't tell her much about what was in the brown salve that he carried in a glass jar, other than he got it from his brother whenever he went to visit his people. Jodenny took a sniff and felt her eyes water. She wasn't sure she wanted to spread something that powerful on her skin, where it could be absorbed into her bloodstream and then into Junior.

"Thanks anyway," Jodenny said, handing back the jar. The day was hot but the yard was shadowed. Some flowers were wilting in a raised garden and there were rain buckets for water, but few other amenities. "Lilly says you sleep out here?"

"On the grass," he said. "Better than some stuffy-up house."

"Have you worked for Lady Scott long?"

"Twenty years, missus." He was seated on a stool, mending a bucket that Sarah had accidentally put a hole through. He didn't say if they'd been happy years or sad ones, or if he liked being in Lady Scott's employment, or if he'd rather be out in the bush somewhere. Osherman had told Jodenny that sometimes he disappeared for weeks or months on end, on walkabout, later showing up on the doorstep as casually as if he'd never left. His tribe was called the Eola. Like most Aboriginal Australians, they weren't faring well under British rule. The convict ships had brought disease, pestilence, and the dangers of alcohol. The government treated them with disdain. Their culture, history, and way of life hadn't been completely destroyed, but they had centuries of hardship still ahead of them.

Jodenny wanted to tell Tulip all was not lost—the

Alcheringa itself would be discovered by an indigenous astronaut, and in her time the injustices of the past would have been mostly righted. But she had no idea of how to broach such a conversation, or if it would bring comfort to him, or if he'd just think she was crazy.

"Missus?" he asked, because apparently she'd been standing there and staring at him for several moments.

"Nothing." She took the jar back from him. "I think I will try a little after all. Thank you."

Osherman didn't seem bothered by the heat, the smell, or the flies, but he patiently listened to her complaints about bugs, bacteria, germs, and viruses crawling over everything.

"We've got plenty of vinegar," Osherman said. He was sitting in her room. "It's a natural disinfectant. And alcohol. Plenty of that, too. This isn't the stone ages, Jodenny. There are doctors and medicines—morphine, laudanum, chloroform, lots of things."

"Painkillers. Not antibiotics. I have no idea how you can stay calm with all these diseases running around," Jodenny said.

Osherman said, "I stay calm because freaking out is not going to help."

"I'm not freaking out."

"So does that mean you're coming with us to Government House tomorrow? The farewell lunch for the governor?"

"Absolutely not," she said.

Lady Scott, however, was not to be deterred. That evening she swept into Jodenny's room with a new yellow dress over her arm, extolled the virtues of Sir Fitz-Roy, the governor, and promised that the event wouldn't last very long at all. Best of all, it would do good for Osherman to be seen in public with his wife.

"No one believes he's married," Lady Scott said. "It'll do all the desperate women good to see the real live Mrs. Osherman. They'll stop pestering him so."

"Pestering him how?" Jodenny asked curiously.

"In the way desperate women will, my dear. You know what a handsome and intelligent man he is. Yours must be a very happy marriage."

"Many beautiful, intelligent people are unhappily married."

Lady Scott fingered the yellow dress, which she'd laid out on Jodenny's bed. "Of course you're right. But the way he looks at you! The devotion he shows. Surely you've noticed. That man would throw himself off a cliff if you asked him to."

Jodenny didn't like that one bit.

"It could mean very much to his career if you go," Lady Scott said.

"What career, ma'am?"

"The import business, of course. He's trying to establish himself as a broker. You need connections for that. If his lovely wife were to smile at the right people, to take tea with their wives, then surely more doors would open in his favor. Would you really disappoint him by sending him off with only silly old me for company?"

Jodenny put on the damned dress and let Sarah pin up her hair. The pins hurt and the curls look ridiculous, but the end result was someone who looked like a Victorian lady, or at least like someone masquerading as one. Lady Scott insisted on lending her some jewelry to wear, including earrings and a thin string of pearls that felt cool against her skin. Jodenny was too bulky to lace her shoes properly and so Sarah helped her with that, and then a bell was jangling from their coach in the street below.

Osherman had been waiting nervously in the parlor. He was resplendent in a crisp summer coat and matching trousers, hat, and tie. His hair had been slicked back and his sideburns recently trimmed. Quite the gentleman of the age, even if he wasn't of this age at all.

"You look lovely," he told Jodenny.

"I look like a beached whale," she said.

He winced.

Jodenny regretted her asperity. "What I meant to say was 'thank you.'"

The ride in the carriage was worse than she'd feared—all that jostling and rocking back and forth, and the heat was horrible, and the streets were full of pedestrians, carts, Aboriginals, immigrants, sailors, and stray dogs, lots of stray dogs. Jodenny saw dirt-poor women with babies on both hips, and malnourished children darting through traffic. The squalor of it all made her ashamed in her fine dress. The stench of it had her sniffing through a handkerchief doused in perfume. Osherman had mused that her pregnancy made her more susceptible to smells but she told him that, on the contrary, his olfactory senses had obviously been burned out by prolonged exposure to Sydney's sewers.

"I can still smell the roses," he'd said dryly.

That was the old Osherman, one she hadn't seen in a long, long time. Since before the destruction of the *Yangtze*, when they were lovers and he was using her to get information about the Supply Department—no, she told herself, she'd forgiven him for that on Providence, during the nights he'd lain shaking and terrified on their sofa as his Roon captivity played out in night terrors. He'd paid for his sins and paid more than he owed.

The trip to Government House was soon over. Their carriage joined a line of coaches curving up the driveway to what looked like a stone castle hauled over from England and reassembled stone by stone. The Gothic stonework and crenellated towers reminded her of old romantic vids replete with dashing heroes, beautiful damsels in distress, and disputes resolved by sword-fights. The finest citizens of Sydney disembarked their carriages or arrived by foot with parasols to protect the women from the hot summer sun. Footmen in finery stood at the ready, and somewhere nearby a string quartet was playing classical music.

Jodenny accepted Osherman's help stepping down. The salty breeze was steady and refreshing, the lawn wide and luscious, and she could see the beginnings of an ornate garden filled with shrubs and trees. Suddenly she didn't regret coming.

"I told you it wouldn't be so bad," Osherman said.

Just a few steps inside the house, and Jodenny was changing her mind again. The ballroom was lovely—hand-carved wooden panels, high ceilings, beautiful paintings. The state apartments were closed but the dining room was open, with its ornate chandeliers and high windows full of light. The thick stonework kept the interior cool and there were sideboards full of fruits, desserts, and little appetizers. All in all, it was the finest Sydney had to offer.

And all those citizens who also considered themselves the finest had turned out for the occasion. Too many of them, Jodenny decided. Hundreds of people had jammed their way inside, the women in their fancy gowns, the men in their tailored coats. Conversation and laughter bounced off the walls and contributed to a loud, confusing din. Lady Scott immediately disappeared into the fray, her face and voice a blur. Jodenny was afraid to move through the crowd—if not for her own sake, then for Junior's.

"Captain!" a boisterous man said, gripping Osherman's hand. "So good to see you."

A woman in a tight blue dress eyed Jodenny over the tip of her Oriental hand fan. "We thought you might not come."

"I wouldn't miss it," Osherman said. "May I introduce my wife, Josephine?"

He made the introductions but Jodenny immediately forgot the other couple's names. She forgot the next set of introductions as well, and the ones after that. The part of her that had once been able to memorize dozens of invoices and hundreds of names had evaporated like smoke into the blue Australian sky. She blamed Junior for stealing away her brain cells but she supposed she wasn't very motivated, either. All these people in their fine clothes, ignoring the poverty and problems of the colony outside Government House's fine doors. They weren't here to make Australia a better place for women or Aboriginals or immigrants. They were here for their own selfish interests, and the interests of commerce.

"Did you hear me?" Osherman asked.

Jodenny blinked at him. "What?"

He steered her to a small corner alcove by the staircase. "Stay here," he said. "I'll get us something to drink. And there are some people you should meet."

He moved off into the crowds. Jodenny lasted all of two minutes, feeling huge and ridiculous and out-of-place, before she had to go out for fresh air. A pair of open side doors led her to a small water garden with an exquisite view of Sydney Harbor. Men and women glided by, arm in arm, smiling with their nineteenth-century dirty teeth and sweat-stained clothes. Jodenny headed for a marble bench and sat heavily, gripped the stone beneath her to keep steady.

"Madam Scott?" a concerned voice asked. "Are you all right?"

Jodenny looked up into a stranger's face. "Osherman," she said immediately. "That's my name."

"My apologies." The man tipped his hat. "I saw you arrive with Lady Scott and assumed you were her daughter, visiting from England."

"No." Jodenny said. "And you are?"

Again, a deferential tip. "Benjamin Cohen, Esquire, at your service."

He was about forty years old, maybe forty-five. He wore a dapper suit and hat and looked as uncomfortable in the heat as she was. He signaled a servant and sent the man to fetch fresh juice. Jodenny was grateful for the kind gesture. She kept herself talking and focused on him. "Are you a native of Sydney, Mr. Cohen?"

"Of London," he said. "May I sit?"

"Of course."

He sat with her on the bench and gazed across the lawn at the harbor. "I've been here thirty years, more or less. Long before this house was even built. The city's changing faster than old men like me can keep track of it."

"I'm sure men of all ages say that," Jodenny replied. She felt steadier now that she was sitting down. "Progress never stops."

"Sometimes it does," he said. "The local tribes, for instance. We usurped their entire way of life by sending our convicts here. Destroyed it, for all intents and purposes."

"Are you a lawyer for native rights?"

He blinked at her. "A what?"

Jodenny supposed that was a concept yet to make its debut. "You could represent them in court."

Cohen made a harrumphing noise in the back of his throat. "You strike me as a lady of radical thought, Mrs. Osherman. How stand you in disposition to the Queen?"

She sensed she might get herself in trouble. Australia belonged to England and Victoria was the sovereign. "I've never met her, Mr. Cohen. She has my loyalty, of course."

The words were thick on her tongue. Team Space had her loyalty, but it was an organization hundreds of years away. Fortune held her loyalty, but she had her doubts about ever seeing her home planet again. Most of Fortune's colonists had come from Australia and the Pacific Rim and so she supposed she owed something to this century, to these people, but did it mean bowing before a monarch? She didn't even know what rights she had as a citizen here.

"Long live the Queen," Cohen murmured.

The servant returned with some apple juice for Jodenny. She inspected it for impurities and winced at the idea of how many germs might be crawling across the glass, but was too thirsty to turn it down. She was about to ask Cohen more about law and justice in Sydney when a middle-aged blond woman in a stunning green dress interrupted them.

"Benjamin, are you bothering Mrs. Osherman?" she asked, smiling warmly.

Cohen rose to his feet. "Lady Darling," he said, in a tone that wasn't quite cordial.

"You can prattle on, you know," Lady Darling said. "You wouldn't want to abuse Mrs. Osherman's kindness by boring her, would you?"

Jodenny's impression of Cohen was distinctly opposite. She thought he wasn't much for prattling on at all.
She wondered what history the two of them had, what
quarrel or fundamental disagreement.

Cohen had flushed in the cheeks but was standing his
ground. "I thought you were in Katoomba, my lady."

"The farm and village grow tiresome when so many
exciting things are happening here," Lady Darling
said. "Won't you find me a glass of wine? My throat is
parched."

Cohen backed away with a small bow and hurried
into the house.

Lady Darling sat beside Jodenny on the bench. She
really was a striking woman, all of her teeth intact, her
complexion healthy and undamaged by sun. The jewels
around her neck sparkled in the sunlight—blue and
green on silver filaments, with similar rings on her fingers. She gave Junior's bump an appraising glance, but
Jodenny couldn't decipher if that was envy or disgust
in her gaze.

"We shouldn't speak long," Lady Darling said, lifting her eyes. She leaned forward in earnest. "Too many
prying ears and eyes. But you must understand. We have
a mutual friend."

"We do?"

"He calls himself Homer."

The glass in Jodenny's hand nearly slipped from her
grasp. "You know Homer?"

"Yes, I know him," Lady Darling said. "And he's told
me such wonderful tales of his travels. Into the future,
Mrs. Osherman. The future you yourself come from."

The glass of apple juice tipped, spilling the brownish
liquid across the grass.

Lady Darling rose to her feet. She pressed a calling

card into Jodenny's hand. "You must understand there are some things Captain Osherman doesn't want you to know. He'll be very cross if he finds out I've told you, and he'll forbid you to come see me. But you must. I'm staying at the Hotel Victoria on College Street, near the museum. Find me tomorrow, and I'll tell you everything."

"What about Terry Myell?" Jodenny demanded. "Did Homer tell you anything about him?"

"Find me," Darling said, and walked away.

CHAPTER NINETEEN

Jodenny pushed her way through the crowds at Government House, determined to find Lady Darling again. Here was a link back to the future other than just Sam. Here was someone who might know what Homer had done with Myell.

Lady Darling, however, had disappeared. There was no sign of her in the dining room or hallways, or on the grand stairs, or anywhere that Jodenny could see. The well-dressed, loud crowds of resplendent men and women swirled around her, opening and blocking doorways, moving back and forth in the increasingly warm air with their loud voices and strange accents. Jodenny was hot and flustered and getting dizzy again. But still she kept looking.

"Josephine," Osherman said, grasping her by the elbow. She hadn't even seen him approaching in the hallway. His face was a mixture of concern and annoyance as he said, "Where have you been? I've been looking for you everywhere."

She blinked at him and tried to come up with a convincing lie. Her capacity to obfuscate had vanished in the heat.

"I got lost," she said. "I couldn't find you."

Osherman said, "You look terrible. Come on, sit down."

He escorted her to a velvet settee in a small room lined with bookshelves and leather volumes. Jodenny sat and tried to compose herself. The room wasn't empty; two men in fine summer coats were conferring by the window.

"Your Excellency," Osherman said, with a bow. "Forgive the intrusion. My wife needs to rest."

The governor of Australia, Sir Charles FitzRoy, nodded graciously. "Of course. Captain Osherman, is it? Lady Scott has spoken highly of you."

"She flatters me," Osherman said.

FitzRoy took Jodenny's hand. "Mrs. Osherman. I hate to leave Australia with loveliness such as yours newly arrived on shore."

Jodenny wasn't in the mood for flattery, and she didn't care who FitzRoy was. She needed to find Darling and shake the truth out of her. But years of ingrained respect for authority kept her from shaking off FitzRoy's hand. She offered the only smile she could manage, under the circumstances.

"Your Excellency," she said. "I'm sorry to hear of your departure."

"England calls." He tilted his head at her. "Forgive me. You remind me very much of my Mary."

"My lord?"

Sadness darkened his face. "It was a tragic accident that took her from me."

She didn't need to hear about any tragedies. She was

close enough to tears of frustration as it was. Luckily a secretary came to the door in search of Governor Fitz-Roy, and he left to attend to some pressing business. Osherman watched him go and turned a grateful look to Jodenny.

"You did great," he said.

Jodenny wanted to hit him. "Take me home."

"I can't," he said. "It's Lady Scott's carriage and she's not ready."

"Tell her I want to go home," she insisted. "You can send the carriage back later."

She would have set off on foot, crossed the wilds of unknown Sydney on her own, but she didn't know the city's geography and she didn't think she'd get far anyway. At that moment she resented Junior for everything—the weight, the dizziness, no stamina, swollen ankles, the constant pressure on her bladder. She was tired of being kicked from the inside. Tired of missing Myell. Tired of the heat and the flies and the stink, and tired of being tired.

She sat there, hating everything, but hatred was no good. Hatred didn't solve anything, nor did acting like a spoiled child. Jodenny wiped her face and sat up straight until Osherman returned. On the ride back to Lady Scott's house she was silent, mulling over Darling's words. She knew Osherman was worried about her, but she wasn't about to reassure him if it was true that he knew more than he was letting on. It wouldn't be the first time he'd deceived her, but it was damn well going to be the last.

Back at the house, Lilly and Sarah helped Jodenny to bed and fussed over her with wet cloths until she sent them away in irritation. Fatigued, she dozed off and on until darkness, and then roused herself enough to go downstairs. Osherman had gone out without leaving word when he'd be back, but Lady Scott was enjoying a cold snack by candelabra in the dining room. The older woman's hair was down, her dressing gown billowing and flowing around her.

"My dear girl, are you better?" Lady Scott asked. "Sit and eat something."

Jodenny sat down carefully, hating how the chair groaned under her weight. "I feel much better now. I'm sorry I had to leave early."

Lady Scott smeared soft cheese on a cracker. "I remember what it's like to be with child. Never again, I swore. Each and every time. And then the Admiral would have his wicked way with me, and there we were. Parents again."

Jodenny reached for a cracker of her own. "I think this will be my only one."

"The Captain doesn't want as many as he can get?"

"He might," Jodenny allowed.

Lady Scott gave a quite unladylike snort. "A woman who knows her own mind. You are a rare creature. Don't let them convince you otherwise."

"I suspect we are both rare creatures," Jodenny said. "May I ask how it is that you came to help my husband so? I know he came to Sydney without many friends or resources."

"You'd be surprised how many people wash up on these shores needing help," Lady Scott said, reaching for more cheese. Candlelight flickered across her face. "He was robbed, you know. Frightful business. Those people down on the Rocks, I suspect. Hooligans, thieves, murderers all. But Lady Darling, she found him. Rescued him from a terrible fate."

Jodenny's hand dug against her thigh. Carefully she said, "Lady Darling found him?"

"Remarkable woman, you know. We had a Governor Darling here, back before I arrived. Distant relations, I gather. Of course, she travels so much among her businesses and homes that it was impossible to take him in. Knowing my kind heart, she asked me to shelter him for a time."

Osherman had lied. He'd said Homer had brought him here. Why lie about that? Jodenny said, "There's kindness, and there's generosity. Not only did you take him in, but you helped him get on his feet and have spoken up for him with the governor."

Silence for a moment, while Lady Scott examined her cracker with detachment. Eventually she said, "Women of my age, Mrs. Osherman, find little hope of suitable companionship in New South Wales. Tea parties. Luncheons. Dinner parties, occasionally. Old men want young, pretty girls for their wives. Those who profess interest in me are more likely to be passionate about my jewels and fortune than anything I say, do, or am."

"But what about Professor Wallace?" Jodenny asked.

"Dear Joseph has many admirable qualities, but a romantic appreciation of women is not among them," Lady Scott said. "If I did your husband any kindness, it was motivated entirely by a foolish old woman's self-interest."

"I thank you anyway."

Lady Scott rose and gave Jodenny a kind smile. "You're a lucky woman. If I were you, I'd count my blessings every day."

Jodenny sat at the table for several more minutes, listening to the quiet night. Junior's fist punching her ribs persuaded her to head back to her room and get some rest. She had her foot on the first step when she heard low worried voices from the kitchen. Sarah and Lilly were there, hovering over a girl sitting in a chair. Candles sputtered on the tabletop.

"What's wrong?" Jodenny asked from the doorway.

Sarah jumped. Lilly said, "Sorry, ma'am. No need to bother you."

The visitor was only a teenager, and she wore servant's clothes. She was several months pregnant and very haggard, with dark circles under her eyes and high cheekbones made stark by malnourishment.

"Is she ill?" Jodenny asked.

"Just tired," the girl said.

"This is our youngest sister, Helen," Sarah said. "She works for the Frasers."

Lilly patted Helen's shoulder. "It's normal to be tired. It'll pass."

Jodenny sat down next to Helen. Carefully she felt the girl's wrist with the tips of her fingertips. "Have you always been tired, or is it something new?"

"Just this last week, ma'am," Helen said.

"Do you sleep?"

"Every night, like the dead."

Sarah crossed herself and Lilly said, "Heaven forbid."

Helen's pulse was fast and weak. Jodenny consulted the Digital Duola. Without lab results she couldn't be sure, but one diagnosis jumped out at her.

"You need iron," she told Helen. "Your body's spending all its resource on the baby, draining you."

"What's she going to do with an iron beam?" Sarah asked.

Jodenny said, "It's a vitamin. Something you get when you eat the right food. Eggs and liver, green vegetables, yams—the more you eat of that, the better you'll feel."

Helen wiped a tear from her eye. "So I'm not dying?"

"You're not dying," Jodenny said.

"Food like that's not cheap to come by," Lilly pointed out tightly.

Jodenny didn't have her purse with her, and she didn't have any shillings or pounds anyway. Osherman had all the money. She was irritated with Lilly for bringing up the subject, but poverty and the scarce resources of Sydney couldn't be ignored.

Sarah stroked Helen's hair. "We'll get it for her, ma'am. Thank you for advising us. They've got good doctors back in England and America, yes? Not like the butchers here."

Jodenny went to her room and climbed gratefully into bed. Sleep came hard. Lying on the lumpy bed, the pillows flat and feathery, she stared out the open window into the nighttime sky and thought about governors and servant girls, midwives and babies. She had to find Lady Darling again and learn more about Homer. At some point she must have slept, because the sky was light and Osherman's side of the mattress was still empty, but she felt exhausted all the same.

Sarah brought morning tea and news of Osherman.

"He slept on the sofa downstairs, ma'am. It looks like he's been in an awful fight! His eye's all bloody and there's a bruise on his chin."

Jodenny pulled on her dressing robe. "I'll go talk to him."

"Thanks again for your help last night," Sarah said. "Helen, she's the youngest. We love her dearly."

"I can tell," Jodenny said. "Are you going to market this morning? I want to come."

"You're sure, ma'am? It's not quite right for a lady like yourself—"

"Don't leave without me."

Jodenny went to see Osherman, who was nursing a cup of tea at the dining room table. He smelled like whiskey and tobacco smoke, and his gaze was unhappy.

"Don't tell me," he said. "I know I was an idiot."

Jodenny remained standing in the doorway. The morning light was strong through the windows and already the weather was broiling hot. "Where did you go?"

"Saloon," he said.

"Why?"

He shook his head.

She was angry with him, and suspicious, and all sorts of feelings she couldn't quite put a finger on. It had occurred to her that maybe he thought he was protecting her in some way—that he'd lied about Darling and Homer because her safety and well-being were still important to him.

"I'm going out with Sarah today," she announced. "To the market. It's about time I get out and around, as you've said. And soon I'll be too big to walk anywhere. I need money."

Osherman reached into his pocket and handed her a small sack of coins. He pressed the steaming cup of tea against his swollen left cheek. "You really think that's wise?"

"You don't?"

He sighed. "I think you'll do whatever you mean to do, Commander, whether I agree or not."

"At least you've learned that lesson," she said, and left him to his tea.

* * *

They set out in the early morning on foot, Sarah carrying a basket, Jodenny armed with a parasol against the sun. She was carrying her own canteen of boiled water and had stripped out the heaviest of her undergarments. She figured that the fine citizens of Sydney had no need to know what was going on under her skirts and propriety was best reserved for women who gave a damn.

Junior seemed happy enough with the activity. Jodenny had more tolerance for the interior kicking and squirming today than on other days and so she simply poked back occasionally as Sarah led them past the small mansion houses on Lower Fort Street toward the market shops downtown. Though it was barely eight a.m. everyone in town seemed up and about already, maybe trying to get things done before the later heat. Dogs and dirty children ran loose in the streets, full of noise and energy, while housekeepers and servants haggled with shopkeepers. Carriages, wagons, horses, and pedestrian traffic made Jodenny walk close to the stone and wooden buildings that rose up on either side of the street.

"Is this a lot like London, ma'am?" Sarah asked. "I hear London's very fancy. Much bigger, much fancier."

"Yes, it's much bigger," Jodenny said, though she had little idea what Victorian London looked like. She watched a horse slurp from a wooden trough while flies buzzed around its tail. "Your parents came from London?"

"My dad was from Ireland and my mum from Liverpool," Sarah said. "My mum, she said that Sydney then was nothing but shacks and cesspools. Nothing would grow right and all the animals would up and die. She was set down to Parramatta with the rest of the women on her ship and that's where my dad met her while he was looking for a wife."

"They were happily married?"

"Not so much," Sarah said. "Not like you and the Captain, ma'am."

A mangy horse and a long wagon were stuck in the middle of the street while two beefy men unloaded its cargo. Jodenny felt bad for the horse. As the years marched on, beasts of labor would be replaced by street-cars, automobiles, flits. Gas lamps would be erected, followed by lights powered by electricity or fuel cells. The buildings around her would fall into decay and be leveled for the next wave of shops, banks, businesses. Some would be saved for posterity but most would be ground to dust. Civilization would steamroll through here the way it did every other corner of the Earth, leading to the Debasement and the settlement of the stars, and Jodenny's own birth on Fortune just a few centuries away. But if Jodenny didn't find a way back to the future this here-and-now would become Junior's world.

Sarah was still talking. "My dad, he wasn't a bad man. Just liked to drink a bit. He helped build the Rum Hospital. All those stones! And he worked on the roof, too."

"I hear there's a museum," Jodenny said.

Sarah's nose wrinkled. "Big stone building, over by Hyde Park. They don't let people in it except on special occasions."

"Maybe we could walk that way."

"I need to get today's chicken," Sarah said doubt-fully. "Lilly won't be happy if I don't get the best of the offerings. And we need eggs. And some brown sugar, some apples—"

Jodenny squeezed Sarah's arm. "Of course you do. And food for your sister, remember? Full of iron. Here's some money. I want you to take it and spend it on her. While you're busy with that I'm going to do some shopping and sightseeing of my own. I'll meet you back at Lady Scott's house."

"You don't want to be walking alone in your condition," Sarah protested. "You could turn your ankle or trip, ma'am."

"I'll be perfectly fine. I promise."

Sarah looked doubtful but the shillings Jodenny pressed into her palm were obviously too tempting to ignore. Jodenny set off on her own toward Hyde Park. It was both a relief and a worry to be surrounded by strangers in this half-civilized wilderness. A relief not to have anyone hovering over her, but worrisome that she didn't have a gib or a comm-bee or any way of reaching Osherman if she or Junior suddenly needed help. Her life as a Supply Officer in Team Space was more remote than it had ever been—a dream she half-remembered, as if someone else had lived through it to end up here.

But the wedding ring on her finger and the baby in her womb were more than enough proof that she had been that person, and was still Terry Myell's wife wherever he was in time and space.

The streets of Sydney unfolded around her. She'd become acclimated to the stink of it all, more or less, but the variety of people amazed her—sailors and laborers, Aboriginals and colonists, all of them wearing faces stamped by weather, illness, malnutrition, misadventure. On spaceships the population tended toward homogenous beauty. Everyone had access to vitamins and skin repair creams and cosmetic improvements, and hardly anyone was fool enough to turn raw skin to the sun. Even back on Providence, the crew and passengers of the *Kamchatka* had more soaps, gels, and dental resources than these people in this era ever would. And so she was surrounded by the toothless, the wrinkled, and the prematurely aged, or men missing their eyes or hands, and women without hair. Even the young were afflicted with acne or pox marks, and some were so painfully skinny that she was sure the idea of three square meals a day was as foreign to them as their strange accents were to her.

Yet they were alive and vibrant, these strangers walking upright in the pages of history, and Jodenny understood for a moment why Osherman had come to embrace them as his own. For as long as this eddy lasted, they were more real and more important to him than sailors yet to be born on planets yet to be discovered. He had been imprisoned by the Roon and stranded on Providence, but here he could walk free and talk to people and be not a damaged military man but instead a man with opportunities ever unfolding.

Jodenny was so busy studying faces and listening to the crowd that she almost walked past the Australian Museum. It was a solid, stately affair built of sandstone with two Greek columns flanking the front entrance. Farther down the street was the Hotel Victoria, a small exquisite building with a reception lounge decorated with marble, dark wood, and velvet-padded furniture. The interior was cool, dim, and muffled compared with the hot dustiness outside, and Jodenny was pleased that the clerk said Lady Darling was indeed in and receiving visitors.

"I'll send word of your arrival," he said.

Jodenny sat herself down in a chair and waited. She tried imagining what connection Lady Darling had with Homer, but her imagination failed her. Fifteen minutes passed before a woman in a white dress fetched Jodenny from the lobby and escorted her upstairs to a receiving parlor. The furniture there was even more luxurious, all dark and heavy wood carved by artisans. A tray of tea, tiny sandwiches, and fresh fruit had already been set out on a sideboard.

"Her Ladyship will be with you in a moment," the woman said before disappearing behind a set of pocket doors.

The hotel was quiet around Jodenny but for the sounds of street traffic through the open window. She studied the artwork on the walls and mantelpiece. The paintings were all of Sydney in its infancy, or British ships meeting indigenous people in canoes, or lush tropical landscapes that looked nothing like the Australia that Jodenny had seen so far. They were full of color and detail and had obviously been done by a deft hand. She herself had no skill at artwork; she wondered if Junior might be a latent artist or musician, in addition to her obvious gymnastic skills.

The pocket doors opened behind Jodenny. Lady Darling asked, "Do you like the paintings?"

"Very much," Jodenny said. "Did you do them yourself?"

Lady Darling smiled. She was dressed in a blue dress that was much more casual than the gown she'd worn at Government House, and her long hair was loose down her back. "You flatter me. The artist's name is Conrad Martens. It used to be that you could commission his work rather inexpensively, but those years are over.

Hundreds of years from now, those pieces will be in museums."

Jodenny wasn't sure if Lady Darling's words were meant to be a prediction or if Homer had told her about the artist's future work. Before she could ask, Lady Darling motioned for her to sit and poured tea for both of them.

"Does Sam know you came?" Lady Darling asked.

"No."

"He wouldn't be happy." Lady Darling poured milk into her tea. "He thinks the less you know, the better."

Jodenny sniffed the fragrant tea. Lady Darling's earlier smile had revealed straight white teeth that were a rarity in Sydney. Her skin was clear and luminous, and what little makeup she wore accentuated her good health. Perhaps it hadn't been such a good idea to trust her. Maybe Jodenny should have given Osherman a chance to explain his relationship with her, or at least left word of where she was going today.

No one knew she was here, after all. No one knew where to look for her if she didn't return.

"You look alarmed," Lady Darling remarked.

Jodenny kept her voice steady. "I think I've been misled."

"He means well."

"Not only by him," Jodenny replied.

A door closed somewhere with a soft click. A mantelpiece clock ticked past the hour and kept counting. Lady Darling put down her teacup and gazed at Jodenny with something soft in her eyes. Regret or resignation.

"You've seen through me, Commander," she said. "Before I was Lady Darling, I was Ensign Cassandra Darling of Team Space. And before I came here, I died in the arms of your husband, Chief Myell."

CHAPTER **TWENTY**

One minute Myell was engulfed in the red-hot terror of the Roon ambush at Kultana. The next, he was waking in a soft bed under a yellow bedspread. The room was full of recycled furniture, and the smell of bad coffee hung in the air.

He lurched to his feet and blacked out. The next time he opened his eyes, his adult daughter Lisa was bent over him.

"Careful," she said. "You hit your head when you fainted. How do you feel?"

Behind him stood Jodenny, crooked and wrinkled and suspicious.

Neither of them remembered him being there before, of course. Twig poked her head in later out of curiosity and it was clear she didn't remember him either.

He stayed in bed until the blue ring finally came and took him away.

On the *Yangtze* they threw him in the brig, which was fine with him. No one could explain the embedded dog tag that said he was a chief or that Jodenny Scott was his wife. She came to visit, but he couldn't look at her face or listen to her voice. Grief for the real Jodenny—for his Jodenny, seven months pregnant and happy to see him—kept him huddled in the corner, every breath like inhaling broken glass.

On Fortune he avoided the academy, the Ithaca Café, and anyplace he might run into Jodenny. Instead he picked a fight in a bar and got tossed in jail. That was fine, too. Pain in his jaw and around his swelling right eye kept him distracted. He was throwing up into a urinal when the blue ring came for him.

On the planet Kiwi he saw Jodenny and Osherman laughing and loving each other in the clear blue ocean. He thought about drowning himself, but the idea of them pulling him out of the surf for mouth-to-mouth resuscitation was too depressing to contemplate.

Back to the *Yangtze* he went, and nothing ever changed. The ring took him to Jodenny and tore him away, took and tore, with no sign of Homer and no hope of rescue.

Then he got mugged on Fortune, and everything changed.

The thief wasn't anyone he knew or had ever met before. He appeared in the back alley of the pub where Myell was puking up a day's worth of beer.

"Give me your yuros," he said, brandishing a sharp knife.

Myell heaved up more beer.

"Don't have any," he said.

For that he got a sharp crack on the head with the knife's hilt. Sprawled on the ground, senses reeling, Myell felt the man rummage through his empty pockets and then wrench his wedding ring off his hand.

"No," he said. "Not the ring—"

Feebly he tried to rise up to his knees, to give chase, but his head swam and he sank back into the muck of the alley.

Staring up at the sky, thoroughly disgusted with himself, he cursed himself. And Homer, wherever the little bastard had gotten to. Kultana. The orchid, the village in India, the god or goddess of Aboriginal Australia. Surely it was an honor to be chosen to save all mankind but was it too fucking much to ask for a little help and guidance now and then?

He was still thinking of Kultana when the ring came for him.

He didn't remember the trip. When he woke, he saw gray metal bulkheads and dim emergency lighting. The place smelled stale and the cold air raised goosebumps on his skin. He had the distinct impression of weight bearing down on him from all sides—thick, immutable weight that blocked all light and sound and that counted centuries like he counted minutes. This small room resembled nothing but a large metal tomb. Only the trickle of air through a low vent and the hum of the doors opening indicated otherwise.

One moment he was alone, and in the next two teenagers in military uniforms were aiming mazers down at his chest.

"Who are you?" asked the taller of the two. She was blond and gaunt and maybe eighteen or nineteen years old. Ensign bars glinted on her collar but that was ridiculous. Team Space didn't commission officers that young.

The younger teen was maybe fifteen or sixteen, wearing a sergeant's insignia and a scowl. He prodded Myell with his boot. "What's your name?"

He turned his head. What was this place? Nowhere he had ever been before. But Jodenny had to be around here somewhere—

The sergeant teen kicked him in the shin.

Myell jerked in pain on the cold metal deck.

"What was that for?" he demanded.

"Answer the question," the sergeant said, his face red.

Myell clutched his leg. The hot pain was subsiding, though not fast enough. "Who are you?"

"Kick him again, Speed," the ensign said.

Myell caught Speed's foot and brought him crashing downward. A mazer shot from the ensign zapped into him, ending the conversation.

When he woke the next time he was in another small room, also dim and cool, and he was strapped down to a medical table at the wrists and ankles. Panic surged through him. He cranked up his head and saw that his boots and clothes were intact. "Hey!" he yelled, his voice hoarse. "Let me go!"

No one answered. The room was empty but for the table, old medical equipment and useless supplies spilling out of dusty, half-opened crates. Myell banged his head back against the table and pulled at his wrists. The restraints held. The absence of his wedding ring felt like a missing tooth in his jaw. He kicked out both legs, hard, and that was more rewarding. Something creaked underneath him, and he realized if he pulled and kicked enough he might be able to crash the table, disentangle himself, fashion a weapon, and sneak off through this complex or ship or whatever it was until he found out where and when he was.

The prospect was mildly entertaining, but it was easier to just stare at the ceiling and ignore the thirst in his throat and wait for the blue ring. Frankly, he didn't have the energy to do much more. The energy or the interest.

The hatch opened. He pretended to be asleep.

"I know you're awake," the ensign said, her voice clear and hard. "If you want, I can yank a power cable out of the wall and stick it up your nose until you cooperate."

"Jesus," he said, and squinted up at her. "What kind of person are you?"

"The kind of person who's in charge around here. How did you get in?"

"You won't believe me," he said.

"Quit stalling."

"I'm not stalling." Myell pulled futilely at the restraints. "Where's Lieutenant Scott? Lieutenant Jodenny Scott?"

"Never heard of her," the ensign said.

That was impossible. He'd never been in an eddy without her. But that was a problem he could deal with later.

He said, "Read my dog tag. I'm military, just like you. Team Space."

She gave his civilian clothes a skeptical look. He couldn't remember how many eddies ago he'd lost the uniform that Adryn Ling had given him on the *Confident,* but he supposed he didn't look much like a Team Space sailor. Or maybe in this eddy, sailors died off once they were done with puberty.

"How'd you get here?" she said. "Beam down here from some spaceship in orbit?"

He was startled by the idea he was in a time and place when teleportation technology actually worked. Then he figured she was being sarcastic. She was good at being sarcastic.

"Cassandra!" Speed came skidding into the room. "The scanners!"

She said, "*Ensign Darling,* remember?"

His face twisted up as he remembered military protocol. "Ensign Darling, ma'am. The scanners lit up like Christmas Day. There's Roon in the tunnels! On their way here!"

"Fuck it all," Darling said. She and the sergeant dashed off without bothering to untie him.

Myell swore and started rocking the table back and forth.

The restraint around his left ankle gave way first, which let him kick at the restraint around his right ankle, and when both were free he swung his legs to the floor and rammed the table into the bulkhead. The noise was loud, too loud, but no one came to investigate. Finally the supports snapped and he was able to free his wrists. He was looking for something to use as a club or a knife when the dim lighting flickered and died, plunging everything into darkness.

"Goddammit," he said to himself, but not very loudly.

A battery-operated light switched on in the passageway outside the room. Myell crept toward it, listening hard for weapons fire. He was half tempted to find a deep dark hole and wait out the arrival of the blue ring, but what if this was the one damn time the ouroboros didn't come for him? He'd never been in this eddy before. The rules might be all different.

He might actually die and stay dead this time.

The passage led to a lift whose doors were frozen open and with a floor littered by debris.

Near the lift was a ladder through the deck and overhead. Voices drifted down from somewhere up above, and another light shone from two or three decks overhead. Myell investigated the rest of the passage, which led to three locked doors and the room where he'd been prisoner.

He returned to the ladder and considered going downward, but the pool of darkness there was complete.

Up, then, quietly, one hand over the other, his knee throbbing from Speed's kick. The next deck proved to be as empty as the one he'd left behind, but opened up more questions. In the absence of any engine noise and in light of their comments he concluded this was an underground military complex, not a spaceship, but the absence of an adult staff worried him. The equipment and space indicated that once the place had been home to more than just a skeleton crew, or had been planned for full staffing. Now it was just a shell.

And the Roon were on their way.

He climbed up one more level. The passage there led to what was some kind of makeshift control room. In the dim red light Myell could make out five kids. The main power was still out but they were monitoring cell-powered scanners and casting anxious looks toward a large hatch. The sergeant had said tunnels; Myell guessed that the labyrinth lay beyond that plated door.

Ensign Darling was the only one standing and glaring at the hatch as if her resolve alone would keep it sealed. Speed was crouched under a console, fixing something. Three other children in ragtag clothes and dirty faces were huddled against the bulkhead. The two youngest were crying.

"Bell, Ammy, stop that," Darling ordered.

One of the equipment scanners was giving off a low beep slowly increasing in tempo. A proximity alarm, Myell figured. His hands felt itchy without a weapon to hold. He might have been trained as a supply tech, but he was more than willing to shoot at any Roon that came through the door.

"Shouldn't we fall back?" he asked.

His voice made the children jerk in alarm. Darling swung her mazer on him but didn't fire. He wondered if the thing was even charged.

"Shut up," she said. "Falling back is the last thing we're going to do."

"Who is he, Cassandra?" asked the boy sitting with Ammy and Bell. He was maybe ten years old or so, and incredibly filthy. None of them looked like they'd seen a bath in a long time.

Speed crawled out from under his console. "Ignore him, Nelson. He's nothing."

Myell didn't make any sudden moves. "How many Roon?"

"Hundreds," Darling said.

"You can't evacuate?"

Incredibly, she almost smiled. "There's nowhere to go under a million tons of mountain."

That partially answered one of his questions. The beeping on the proximity alarm grew closer. Nelson pressed his fist against his teeth. The two little girls wept. Speed scooped up one of them and hugged her tight.

"It'll soon be over, Bell," he said.

Whoever these kids were, they had little illusion about what was going to happen in the next few minutes.

"Where exactly are we?" Myell asked.

"Why don't you know?" Darling asked.

"Because I'm not from here," he said. "The last time I saw the Roon was at the battle of Kultana."

"Kultana!" Nelson said, past his fist.

"Shut up," Darling told her. The gaze she turned on Myell was cold and hard. "You're lying."

Nelson said, "My dad died at Kultana. When I was a baby."

Myell didn't have time to do the math before the scanner began to whine a steady annoying alarm. Something solid slammed into the other side of the hatch. The vibration rattled Myell's teeth and made the littlest ones shriek. A circle of red appeared in the metal.

"They're burning their way in?" Myell demanded. "Why?"

Darling didn't deign to answer. Instead she slapped her hand down on the console in front of her and thumbed a series of switches jury-rigged to wires stretched across the floor and into a junction box.

"Speed, now!" she said.

Speed threw a lever.

A soft walloping sound drifting up the ladder behind Myell. As far as explosions went, it wasn't much at all. But more explosions ripped out after it, a series of louder blasts that rushed up shafts and tore down bulkheads and collapsed overheads, letting tons of rock crash through old barriers. Myell understood then the cables he'd seen in the passages. Remote-controlled explosives. This children's army's plan to fight off the Roon had nothing to do with fighting and everything to do with self-destruction.

The deck heaved wildly under Myell's feet and tossed him backward. He landed hard; pain flashed across his shoulders and ribs. The rippling explosions kept slamming through the air. The darkness was full of dust and the smell of burnt chemicals. He couldn't breathe through the debris, couldn't think through the chaos and panic, but after a while he realized the noise had stopped and the wet, limp bundle across his legs was someone's body.

He reached down, groping. The girl against him let out a gasp that sounded like she was drowning. Myell lifted her body and brought her close. There was no light, and no sound but their own panicked breathing and her spitting out blood.

"It worked," Ensign Darling said, when she could.

"Why?" he asked. He couldn't quite hear out of one ear, and his whole body felt like it had been pummeled by sledgehammers. "Why destroy everything?"

She was quiet so long he feared she'd fallen unconscious. But then she said, "So they couldn't get it."

"Get what?"

Her head was heavy against his shoulder. The wetness pooling on his shirt was her blood, and his slippery fingers could neither find the source nor stanch it.

"They can't have it," she whispered.

"Have what, Ensign?"

She died without telling him.

CHAPTER **TWENTY-ONE**

Jodenny's tea had gone cold in the cup, but she was thirsty and drank it anyway. Her fingers shook against the delicate china.

"I don't understand," she said. "This was what—twenty years ago?"

Darling's gaze was steady. "You flatter me, Commander. Thirty. I was seventeen at the time. Oldest of us all, and the leader by default. It's not a position I would have chosen on my own. But the rebel army in our area had been decimated, and I was the only one left to lead them."

"I don't understand how you're here if you died. Did Terry resuscitate you?"

"No." Darling reached toward the tea tray. "I died, in that—what does he call them? Eddy. I died in that eddy. So did the rest of my crew. We'd rigged the caves to blow in case the Roon came knocking. We all knew we wouldn't survive."

Confusion twisted through Jodenny and must have shown in her face.

"I wasn't there," Darling said. "This me, that is. I'm not the one who died in Chief Myell's arms. He told me about it later, though. When he came back the next time and convinced us there was another way. But I fear I'm getting ahead of myself. Ask me where he went when the blue ring came for him in that rubble."

Jodenny obeyed. "Where did he go?"

"To the Roon," Darling said. And this time her fingers were the ones shaking against her cup. "Your husband traveled to the heart of the Roon empire to face down the one they call the Flying Doctor. And that whore, the traitor Anna Gayle."

Myell remembered this: Darling limp in his arms, the heat and dust of the collapsed complex, the slow suffocation and icy terror of being entombed.

Worse were the digging noises around him. Metal against rock. Intermittent but undeniable.

The Roon, digging their way in.

This new place? Wasn't much different.

Pitch-black. Deep, rumbling sounds of machinery made the rough ground vibrate beneath him. But this place was colder, wetter, and he could hear voices both distant and indecipherable. The ring had again brought him somewhere he'd never been before. It was nowhere he wanted to stay, but his body didn't have the strength to move. He couldn't even find the strength to say his own name. Then a foot stepped down on his leg and Myell let out a yelp of pain.

"Jesus!" a man said from almost on top of him. "What the hell?"

Light flared, and Myell tried to turn away. Rough hands probed at him.

"Lemme alone," he mumbled.

"Human," a woman said. "Lots of blood."

Myell insisted, "Not mine," because it was true. Most of it was Ensign Darling's. The stink of it and his own waste made him want to vomit. But the man and woman above him, their blurry faces indistinct, weren't that clean or sweet-smelling themselves.

"What's your name?" the woman asked. "Who did this to you?"

An obnoxiously loud buzzing sound filled the air. "No time," the man said. He slid his hands under Myell's shoulders. "Look, pal, you've got to get up and get moving, or they'll leave you down here all night. You'll never survive the farols."

He didn't care. The ring would come for him, as it always did, and this nightmarish place would be another memory.

"He's going to slow us down, Chief," the woman said. "If we miss that last lift, we're no better off ourselves."

"He's fine." The man dragged Myell upward. "Get on your feet. You don't want to die down here, not like this."

Myell would have happily disagreed with him, but his feet were already moving. He understood that these strangers were risking themselves for him and their lives weren't his to throw away. Still, he resented them for pushing him forward, steering him in this cave or tunnel or whatever, making him struggle alongside them. When absolutely none of it fucking mattered at all.

"Tom," the woman said. "They're going to notice the blood."

"They don't care."

"But they'll still notice."

The man cursed, stopped. The next thing Myell knew, his shirt was being ripped off and discarded. He shivered in the cold air. They started moving again, which struck him as funny. Blood got people's attention around here, but being shirtless didn't?

A moment later the darkness opened into a large, dimly lit cavern forty or fifty meters high. Hundreds of people were moving quietly forward. Myell's vision cleared enough that he could see fashion was not a priority; the men and women around him were filthy, their clothes sometimes nothing more than rags, and even without a shirt on he was better off than half of them. The strangest thing, though, was that his eyes obviously weren't working right—it looked like some of the people had elongated faces, or faces with fur, or bodies with extra limbs, or other tricks that his brain couldn't process.

The woman had said, "Human," as if there were other options.

Myell recoiled from the sight and the stench of the human and alien crowd. The man holding him by the arms didn't let his grasp slip, however. "Don't stop now," he warned, steering him forward. "Remember the Monitors."

The woman accompanying them gave Myell a brief glance. Her hair was longer than it had been on the *Confident* and there was a livid scar down the right side of her face, but he recognized her nonetheless.

"Adryn," he said, louder than intended.

"Inside voices, as Mother would say," the man said.

He was bearded and thin, but there was a cheerfulness about him that not even this filthy, smelly place had managed to dampen. He was steering them, slowly but surely, toward one of three enormous metal lifts embedded in the stonework ahead. A tall, spindly silver robot stood at the entrance of each lift, looking like nothing more than long strips of steel welded into a tripod.

"You're Tom Cappaletto," Myell murmured.

Adryn's dirty fingers dug in his forearm. "Who are you?"

He couldn't bear to explain it. Couldn't. Around him were the human survivors of the *Confident* and the rest of the fleet at Kultana and the alien survivors of—of what? Other battles with the Roon, maybe. Prisoners of war. Captives from worlds he'd never even dreamed of, from somewhere beyond the Seven Sister planets that the Wondjina had built as mankind's cradle.

His knees threatened to give out again but Cappaletto and Adryn got him past a grilled gate and into one of the enormous elevator cars. Bodies pressed up against him from all sides until Myell felt pinned in place. He couldn't have collapsed even if he'd wanted to. The creature to his left had red scales and a snout that made a faint whistle whenever he/she/it breathed. The creature on his other side was short and thick with brown, leathery skin stretched over a watermelon-sized skull. Though there were brief snippets of sounds as the lift rose upward—disgruntlement, a complaint or two, someone weeping—the ascent was mostly quiet, and tense, and surreal enough that Myell was half convinced he was having a nightmare.

When the lift opened the crowd surged forward into more caverns. These were warmer than the ones below, with lower rock ceilings and occasional bright alcoves that let off yellow illumination. Silver Monitors similar to the ones below stood watch at various intervals, overseeing several hundred more workers—some curled up on the ground, others sitting and eating out of bowls, others limp and perhaps dead on short gray pallets. The humans clustered in their own groups, and the aliens likewise.

Cappaletto and Adryn knew their way around. They took him to a smaller rock chamber filled with humans resting on crudely constructed cots and bunks. Adryn watched without comment as Cappaletto sat Myell down on one cot and passed him a small canteen of water. After that he loaned him a short-sleeved shirt that wasn't clean, but wasn't covered with blood, either.

"What's your name?" Cappaletto asked. "What ship were you on?"

Myell couldn't answer.

Adryn said, "He's not our responsibility, Tom. He'll find his own people."

"I keep telling you, Lieutenant," Cappaletto said. "They're all our people."

She looked away in obvious disagreement.

Myell might have slept. He didn't remember lying down on Cappaletto's thin blanket, but for a time his vision and hearing faded, and when he opened his eyes Adryn was gone. Cappaletto was sitting on the cot just an arm's length away. The light was dim but he was writing something on a piece of wrinkled paper.

It took a moment for Myell to wet his lips enough to speak.

"How long have you been here?" he asked.

Cappaletto's pencil, which was worn down to a short nub, paused against the paper. "Hard to tell. No natural light, no way of keeping time. Two years, I think. Maybe longer."

Two years. Jesus. Myell thought he might go insane if he were stuck here for anything longer than the time it took for the blue ring to return.

"What about you? You've got that newbie look. Just got in?"

Myell pulled himself up. "Yeah."

"Then how'd you know my name?"

"We met before. A long time ago. You were on the *Confident*. Do you remember Chief Myell? Lieutenant Commander Jodenny Scott?"

Cappaletto shook his head.

"Admiral Nam?" Myell persisted. "Commander Haines?

"Never met any admirals on the *Confident*. There's none here, anyway. Haines is still around, though it won't do you much good to talk to him."

"Why not?"

Cappaletto answered, "He can't talk. They do that to people sometimes. The Roon. If you cause trouble or try to tamper with the Monitors. Take you away, bring you back looking like shit, can't talk."

Myell tried not to think of Osherman. "When I met you, you were working with Lieutenant Ling. She was on loan there from Team Space. She was married."

"Yeah." Cappaletto shoved the pencil and paper into a pocket. "Dr. Ling didn't survive the attack. I saw the body. Wasn't pretty. My lieutenant, she was a lot broken up over it. Still is."

The words were flat, no signs of grief, but Myell didn't believe Cappaletto was over the loss, either. Most of his sailors and friends were dead, news of mankind lost to him, and he was stuck in this godforsaken place where he'd probably die. Myell wanted to offer condolences but it was a tragedy too enormous for words to smooth over in any way. And he had his own deaths to grieve. The next time he visited Providence, Jodenny would be there—old Jodenny or younger Jodenny, Jodenny getting married, Jodenny giving birth to Lisa. But the copy he had taken with him to the *Confident*? Had died in pain and terror before the eddy reset. Or had vanished completely, unmourned by anyone but him.

"So who are you?" Cappaletto asked. "Team Space, by your accent. Civilian? Military?"

Myell's gaze traveled over the prisoners in their cots. Thin, dirty, and malnourished, doomed to live the rest of their lives surrounded by rock and their own waste. He hadn't expected the Roon to take prisoners but maybe nobody had.

"Civilian," Myell said. "Last name's Kay."

"Kay, it is." Cappaletto shook his hand. It was a funny gesture, given the circumstances. Sad, actually. Whatever civility existed down here was of their own making, under tragic circumstances.

"Come on," Cappaletto added, rising. "If we're lucky, we might be able to get some food."

Myell's brain wasn't much for the idea of food but his stomach grumbled anyway. Cappaletto navigated through the cavern with practiced ease, moving past dozens and dozens of cots on the way to the low opening that led into another chamber, and another after that. Some areas were quiet and others louder, in a pattern Myell couldn't quite figure out. They passed a makeshift human infirmary, and then a gaming area where a dozen short aliens were playing dice. One chamber with curtains reeked of excrement and another was some kind of nursery, with alien toddlers playing tag under the weary eyes of their scaly mothers.

He saw no human babies or infants at all.

"How many people are down here?" Myell asked.

"Oh, good question. My captain, he tried to do a census when we first got here. About three hundred of us survived Kultana. Then Mary River fell, that brought a lot of people in. We've never really been able to get a head count on the Albasta—those are the aliens with the red scales—or the Indil, they've got the furry faces. Call it two thousand or so in this mine? Who knows how many other mines there are. Where did they get you?"

"Doesn't matter, does it? We're all here now."

Cappaletto clapped him on the arm. "Truer words were never spoken, Kay."

The food hall, such as it was, consisted of four large metal chutes snaking down through the rock ceiling into dispensing nozzles. More Monitors kept watch on the crowds. Some workers were tasked with washing out and reissuing shallow wooden bowls. Cappaletto dug into his pocket, brought out a folded-up cloth, and extracted two jewel-like ruby rocks to exchange for a bowl.

Myell had no rocks to trade.

"My treat," Cappaletto said, handing over another rock. "You can pay me back later."

"Is that what you dig for, down below?" Myell asked.

"We call them rubies, but they're not." Cappaletto led the way to another long line that gradually shuffled forward to one of the nozzles. "Some people think they help power the Roon ships. They collect most of what we dig out of the rock and let us keep a few for food each shift. Sometimes you can buy blankets, or clothing, or whatever else the Roon deign to bring down here. Keep them on you too long, though, you get skin lesions. Then pus, then gangrene, then you lose the limb."

"They're radioactive?"

"They're something," Cappaletto said.

Their turn at the nozzle came. Thick gruel slopped down into their bowls. Sniffing at the brown stuff made Myell wrinkle his nose, but it was the sight of something moving in it, sluggish and thick, that made his stomach twist.

"Some days you get the good gruel, some days you get the bad gruel," Cappaletto said philosophically. "Today's our lucky day."

A furry alien over two meters tall growled at them from his spot in line. The teeth he bared were slimy and sharp.

"We're moving," Cappaletto said. "No problem."

"Do you understand what they say?" Myell asked as they found a place to sit against the stone wall.

"Not a word." Cappaletto ate steadily, without seeming to mind the taste or the contents of what was in the gruel.

Two years of that food, Myell thought. Two fucking years.

"You get used to it," Cappaletto added, as if reading Myell's mind. His gaze was on his bowl. "The food, the filth, not being able to communicate with the aliens, half the time not being able to communicate with your own people. The lieutenant and I used to think alike, had the same goals. Not so much anymore. Everyone just does whatever it takes until we get out of here."

Myell asked, "You think rescue is coming?"

"I think you never know what's going to happen until

you wake up and face the day." Cappaletto shrugged. "Everyone else thinks I'm a hopeless optimist."

"Are you?"

"Nah. I just don't know how else to keep living." Unexpectedly Cappaletto grinned. "My day would be much improved if you told me Team Space and the ACF are out there kicking Roon ass. Even if it's not the truth. Especially if it's not the truth, you know?"

Myell heard the heartbreak now. Heard it and understood it.

"The last place I was, a bunch of teenagers managed to bury half a Roon army under a mountain," he said truthfully.

Cappaletto searched his expression, looking for sincerity. He must have found it, because his smile grew wider. "See? Lucky day indeed."

Near the food hall was a place to bathe, though only in handfuls of cold water dispensed with more nozzles. There wasn't nearly enough water to get clean, but Myell made the attempt anyway.

"I miss showers," Cappaletto said wistfully. "Nice hot baths. A whirlpool. Swimming pools. You don't know how spoiled you are until everything gets ripped out from under you, you know?"

"I know."

When they were done they made their way back through the warrens. Myell kept close watch on the Monitors. They didn't move or make noise in any way. Their only signs of life were the silver beams of light that swept out of their torsos and through the caverns every few minutes, scanning the environment. They didn't even respond when some of the furry aliens deposited red rocks in piles at their feet.

"We think the Albasta worship them as gods," Cappaletto said. "They say prayers to them. Leave them presents. Sometimes leave a dead infant, though I don't know if they were dead at birth or sacrificed to the cause."

Myell swallowed hard. "Do the Monitors ever respond?"

"Not to human prayers. But you can go talk to them all you like, if it'll make you feel better. You're sure you don't have any people at all here?"

"No."

"And you're going to remain remarkably close-mouthed about how and when you got here?"

Myell said, "If there's time, I'll tell you later."

Sleeping arrangements in the workers' chambers were matters of species, military status, and rank. Cappaletto and Adryn bunked down in an area reserved for Team Space and ACF officers and senior enlisted. Adryn didn't look pleased when Cappaletto tried to give the empty cot beside him to Myell.

"That's Commander Endicott's," she said.

Cappaletto gave her a patient look.

"He's coming back," she added, biting her lower lip. "It's only been a few days."

"Didn't make the lift," Cappaletto told Myell. "You've always got to make the lift. Those farols come in when the outside world gets dark. Nasty things, like dogs but three times bigger. They won't leave much behind, if anything. Sometimes a bone or two. Sometimes teeth."

"The Roon don't care about losing people down there?" Myell asked.

"The Roon don't care if we get eaten or eat each other," Cappaletto said. "They don't even know us by name. There's no roll call, no tracking, no rosters. Only the Monitors to make sure we don't try to hijack the lifts or damage their equipment, and to send in other machines that haul out the dead. We work as much as we want to earn our rubies and food; the only rule is survival."

Myell was flummoxed. "There are no records of who's down here?"

Cappaletto shook his head. "But we try to keep their names in our heads. On pieces of paper, when there is any. If we don't remember, who will? People who die, people who disappear, people who get taken . . ."

He trailed off.

Myell said, "Taken."

Cappaletto's expression darkened. "The Roon come down every now and then and haul people away. Not often. Mostly we never see them again. The ones who come back—well, they don't live very long, usually. Or they can't talk. But those who do, they tell stories about a woman. Some horrible woman. Used to be human. Now—not so much."

Myell's throat tightened. "She have a name?"

"Gayle," Cappaletto said.

"Anna Gayle?"

"Maybe. Can't say for sure."

Adryn sighed impatiently. "We've only got a few hours until the next shift begins and I, for one, am going to work it. You two want to gab, gab somewhere else. Otherwise it's bedtime. And Commander Endicott's coming back for his cot, so find your own place and people, Mr. Kay."

Cappaletto objected. "Lieutenant—"

"No," Myell said. "It's okay. I'll just stretch out here on the ground."

Adryn made a harrumphing noise and curled up with a thin blanket over her shoulders. Cappaletto tossed his blanket down to Myell.

Cappaletto said, "Ground can be pretty hard. Try to get as much rest as you can."

Rest was a nice idea, but instead Myell was thinking about Anna Gayle. Here. Now. He tried to figure out if he could save Cappaletto and Adryn when the ouroboros returned, how he could convince them to hold tight in the flash of light. Despite Cappaletto's optimism, Myell doubted rescue was ever coming from Team Space or the ACF. If he didn't take them with him, he was consigning them to a slow and steady death.

If he did take them with him, they might end up someplace worse. Someplace where they'd soon be dead anyway. Kyle and Twig? Evaporated or trapped when he'd left them in the eddy at the Outpost. Jodenny? The original lived on, but the copy he'd ripped from Providence had either evaporated or died in the Roon ambush at Kultana. And for what? For no good reason at all.

He swiped angrily at his eyes just as someone stepped over him and peered down anxiously.

"Gampa!" Homer said. "Finally. I've been looking all over the galaxy for you. What are you doing on the floor?"

CHAPTER TWENTY-TWO

Myell bolted upright. "Where the hell have you been?"

Adryn asked, "What?" She obviously couldn't see Homer.

Neither could Cappaletto, who said, "Huh?"

"Nothing." Myell untangled himself from the blanket, stood up, and gave Homer a pointed look. "I need to go walk around."

Homer, who was dressed today in purple trousers and a flowery shirt, spread his arms wide. "It's not my fault. You know how hard you are to find now that you've figured out how to direct yourself?"

Myell wasn't going to get into a conversation with an invisible visitor, not in front of Cappaletto and Adryn. He moved off between the cots with the blanket wrapped over his shoulders. Homer followed, as he expected. Talking and talking, which Myell also expected.

"I know you think I'm not much help," Homer said. "But I tried to warn you! You wouldn't listen. Everything I do is for a good reason, Gampa. A million of them. And so it would really help if you gave me the benefit of the doubt once in a while, okay?"

There was little privacy anywhere to be found, but Myell settled on a narrow alcove. He spun on Homer and tried to wrap his hands around his neck. His fingers passed through Homer's flickering image without any hindrance at all.

"Not really here, remember?" Homer waggled his eyebrows. "Student. Concerned observer."

"I want the goddamned truth," Myell said. "For once in your miserable life. What do you mean now that I know how to direct it? I've never known how!"

Homer laughed. Actually laughed, the little bastard. Though it sounded more hysterical than amused.

"You don't know?" Homer's gaze went upward as he struggled for composure. "I didn't see that coming, not at all. Here I thought you'd figured it out."

Myell wanted to kill him all the more. "Tell me."

"Don't you think I want to? All I want is for you to succeed. To get to Kultana."

"I was there," Myell said savagely. "Jodenny died."

Homer said, "No. She didn't."

Myell tried to strangle him again. His hands passed through nothingness. He demanded, "What do you mean, no?"

"I saved her. Her and Sam. You didn't make it easy for me, Gampa. I had to sneak around, couldn't do it in front of my advisers. You know those academic types. I was almost too late. But I got them out and to a safe place."

"What safe place?"

Homer looked past Myell's shoulder. "They're coming. Gotta go. Get back to Kultana, Gampa! The right way!"

And then he vanished.

Myell slapped his hand against the rock face where Homer had been standing. His fingers stung at the sharp bite of stone but he didn't care. Damn it all. Jodenny's copy couldn't be alive. But if she were? Waiting for him somewhere, she and Junior both, who knew where.

He wanted to kill Homer.

Myell turned and found Adryn standing an arm's length away, staring at him.

"I recognize you now," she said. "You're Uncle Terry."

Fatigue sluiced through him, turning his legs to jelly. "No. Your uncle died on Burringurrah a long time ago."

Her expression didn't shift. "You were talking about Jodenny. I remember her from the time you both visited our farm."

Myell sat down on the hard ground. "The only Jodenny that I know was stranded on a planet called Providence. She's still there."

"Why are you lying to me?"

He shook his head. He pulled his knees up and rested his head on them, trying to think through Homer's game. It wasn't as if the blue ring followed his orders. Dozens of times he'd tried to verbally or mentally direct it to specific times and places. Sure, he'd been thinking of the Roon this last trip, and the ring had brought him here. But the trip before that, he'd been thinking of Kultana and the ring had brought him to Darling.

All of the eddies he'd ever visited either revolved around Jodenny or somehow involved the Roon. The armada, the invasion of the mountain, these mines.

At least two of those places had Anna Gayle in common, and he wasn't willing to discount her presence at the mountain.

Myell put his head back, banging it slightly against the wall. "The Monitors," he asked Adryn, his mouth dry. "Do they understand human speech? Can they be used to communicate with the Roon?"

Her mouth twisted in disgust. "They don't want to be communicated with. You can talk to them until you're blue in the face if you want. They won't send down more food, any medicine, and doctors. No amount of begging or pleading work."

"I don't want them to send anything down," Myell said. "I want them to take me up."

Adryn said, "You're crazy."

"And I want you and Chief Cappaletto to come with me," he added.

It took some time for Myell to convince Adryn and Cappaletto that he was not, in fact, insane. It helped that he remembered many of the details of his trip aboard the *Confident* and things he couldn't possibly know otherwise, including specifics about Adryn's wife and their cabin, and the decorations in the chiefs' mess.

"A time-traveling supply chief," Cappaletto muttered. He was sitting on his cot, his elbows folded on his knees. "Stranger things have happened, I suppose."

Adryn said, "You can't possibly think your life will get better if you make yourself and your situation known to the Roon."

"The Roon already know," Myell said. "Or at least one of them does, I think."

Adryn shook her head, her mouth a thin line.

"I'm game," Cappaletto said.

"To throw your life away, Tom?" she asked.

"It's not much of a life right now," Cappaletto said. "And if it's one step, or a bunch of steps, toward bringing the Roon down? I'm game to try. Lead on."

Myell took in a steadying breath. Now that he was really contemplating doing it, he wasn't sure he had the nerve. "All we need is the nearest Monitor."

Cappaletto stood. Adryn remained sitting.

"I'm not ready to give up," she said. "Whatever happens is fine for you, Uncle Terry. If they kill you or keep you alive, you get to keep traveling. But who knows what happens to us? You say the timeline reverts, but how do you know from our point of view? Tom could get killed and stay dead. Or he could stay alive, tortured by the Roon because of this fool plan of yours. Whatever copy goes gallivanting off with you will never know."

Cappaletto said, "I'm willing to take that chance, Lieutenant. Good scenarios or bad."

"I'm not," Adryn said.

The shift bell rang. Weary members of several species stumbled to their feet and walked toward the lifts.

"Please," Myell said.

She shook her head.

Cappaletto steered Myell down a narrow passage to a small, sloped cavern not much bigger than a birdie. The place smelled worse than anywhere else, despite the large ventilation grille ten meters overhead. The Monitor at the back of the cave was surrounded by what looked like small bones and dried, leathery flesh.

"When we first got here, there were a bunch of little aliens that looked kind of like upright iguanas," Cappaletto said. "They used to shed their tails and leave them here, sort of a tribute. They all died off in the end."

Myell looked up at the ventilation grille. "Anyone ever try to climb up that?"

A snort was his answer. "Sure. People have tried. There are plenty easier ones to get to than that one. The Monitors shoot them down."

"I won't make any sudden moves," Myell said.

He approached the Monitor carefully and slowly. The silver beam that had been sweeping the overhead and cavern came to focus on him exclusively. A cold sensation, like the touch of an ice cube, spiked on his forehead. Myell ignored it. Cappaletto, beside him, didn't move at all.

"My name is Robert Gayle," he said. He'd debated which name to use. Better this lie. Better the memory of a man that Myell had never met, but who'd once been important to Gayle. He continued, "I need to talk to Dr. Anna Gayle. She's my wife."

The Monitor did nothing.

Myell said it again. "My name is Robert Gayle. We need to talk to Dr. Anna Gayle. She's my wife."

"We don't know that the Roon speak English, or anything like it," Cappaletto murmured.

"One of them does."

So he repeated it again: who he was, what he needed. And again. Once a minute for the next several minutes, and for the next several more. Cappaletto stood silently beside him throughout it. Myell thought about the enormous leap of faith Cappaletto was making by being there with him in this small foul prison of rock and rotted flesh. He repeated his statement again, and then once more, and until his voice started to crack.

Cappaletto handed him the small canteen. Myell took two gulps and wiped his lips with the back of his hand.

"My name is Robert Gayle—" he started again.

The rock wall behind the Monitor started to move.

"Bingo," Cappaletto said.

Two Roon emerged from the passage in the rock. They were as large and menacing as Myell had ever seen them, and the weapons they held did nothing to diminish the impression. Myell resisted the impulse to step backward. He raised his hands in surrender, and Cappaletto did, too.

"I hope you know what you're doing," Cappaletto said, and for the first time there was a tremor in his voice.

Myell looked over his shoulder, hoping Adryn had changed her mind and joined them, but the cavern was empty.

The hidden space behind the Monitor was a small elevator. It was big enough for two humans and two Roon, but just barely. The walls were smooth gray metal with no sign of a control panel. When the car picked up speed Myell looked in vain for something to hold on to. The dizzying, lurching feeling of swift ascent made him close his eyes. He had no idea of how fast they were traveling but had the impression they were barreling upward in a way that couldn't end well; they were either going to slam to a bone-crunching stop or continue onward and upward until he blacked out—

Something popped, like a cork from a bottle of champagne. Cappaletto, who obviously didn't have his eyes closed, said, "Jesus. Look at that."

Myell blinked at the gray sky surrounding them. The car's walls had turned translucent. Below them, rapidly receding, was a barren landscape of rocks, crags, and craters that looked as inhospitable to human life as Earth's moon. Smoke plumed out of fissures and large, motionless drills stood in decay and ruins on the tips of mountains.

"You can't tell," Cappaletto said. "Thousands of people down there, and you can't even tell."

Myell forced his gaze upward and regretted it. An enormous city of metal and rock was floating in the sky overhead them, attended to by hosts of flying aircraft. It was larger than any Team Space freighter Myell had ever served on. It spoke to a technology so far in advance of humanity's achievements that defeat was inevitable. Team Space didn't have cities that flew, or elevators that doubled as aircraft. The sight of so much metal and engineering and sheer power made Myell want to go back down into the mines and curl up in hiding rather than face whatever was waiting for him above.

He told himself that nothing they did in the city would matter. The blue ring would come for him no matter what. But he'd dragged Cappaletto into this mess and for that he was sorry.

Cappaletto didn't look like he had any regrets, though. He looked scared, and impressed, but not as if he wished Myell had never passed through his life.

"That's something I never expected to see in my whole life," he said, his forehead pressed to the translucent wall.

They slowed as they got closer to the city. A port opened and the little car sailed into it gracefully. The walls turned gray and opaque again. The doors opened to a long dark passageway with white markings on the walls and deck. They reminded Myell of the Aboriginal cave markings he and Gayle had observed so long ago. Art of some kind, or maybe history lessons, or regulations on how to treat human prisoners; maybe the markings were security notices or safety manuals or the history of the Roon empire, laid out for all to see.

Cappaletto, though, wasn't looking at the markings. His head was tilted upward. "Look at that," he said hoarsely.

Myell tilted his gaze.

And gasped.

A river of beautiful blue-green water rippled over

their heads, flowing gracefully down the passage ceiling in total defiance of gravity. A faint mist drifted downward, fresh and dewy against Myell's skin. *Water, water, everywhere and not a drop to drink,* he thought. He wanted to laugh at it, but a prod in the back from one of their Roon escorts moved him forward.

With the markings beneath their feet and river over their heads, they were forced to whatever fate awaited them.

There was no opportunity for Myell or Cappaletto to try and seize their weapons to turn the situation around; that had never been the plan, in any case. They passed no one, saw no one. Myell thought that was deliberate. He had the idea this part of the floating city was remote and not used often, though he didn't see any dust or other signs of neglect.

He was still shirtless, though he had shoes on and trousers still rimmed with Darling's blood. He felt grimy and insignificant. Cappaletto looked filthy, his uniform in rags, but his head was high.

"Lieutenant Ling should have seen this," Cappaletto said. "I just hope they don't throw us out a window when they're done."

That was an unhelpful image. Myell shunted it aside immediately. The passage ended in a set of doors that swung inward at their approach and he steeled himself, mustering the last shreds of whatever courage he still had left.

Inside was a long chamber of wood and stone that reminded Myell of a sacred temple. The floor was covered with the same white symbols and figures as he'd seen in the passageway, and gentle folds of curtains hung along the walls and overhead—blue and green fabric shot through with gold streaks, lightweight and shifting.

The effect was beautiful, the entire room a peaceful oasis, except for dozens of tall narrow golden cages that lined alcoves in the bulkhead. They were tall enough for a man Myell's height and some of the bodies pressed inside them might indeed have once been men. Or maybe aliens. The decayed state of the bodies made it hard to tell. There was no smell but for a soft, citrusy sort of scent. But some of the corpses were streaked with blood that still glistened, and some of them appeared to be moving because of the colonies of maggots swelling and boiling under split-open skin.

Cappaletto made a sound that might have been a stifled retch.

He was probably regretting everything now.

Myell wrenched his gaze away and saw more cages ahead—dozens on each side of the room, some stacked on one another, others swaying from chains. Some of these were empty. Others were filled with captive birds that fluttered and chirped against the bars, or little monkeys with blue eyes and red fur, or sea-lion-sized creatures that had grown so large the metal bars cut into their flesh. In the center of them all was a large stone dais holding up a silver throne. Here was the heart of the menagerie: the blackened vile heart.

On the throne sat a figure wearing a red feathered cloak and a headdress reaching for the sky. Beneath the cloak were high black boots, shiny enough to reflect a vision of the chamber. Who knew the Roon were so fashion-conscious?

Then again, Anna Gayle had always prided herself on her appearance.

The Roon guards who'd brought them here forced Myell and Cappaletto to their knees before the throne. For a moment Myell heard only the pounding of his own heart, which was so powerful and so frantic that surely everyone else could hear it, too. The deck was hard on his knees, and when the Roon knocked him forward he realized he was supposed to prostrate himself with both hands stretched toward the altar and his nose to his own knees.

A thwack sounded to Myell's left. Cappaletto gave off a soft grunt and then was silent.

Quiet again, except for the scrape of footsteps on the dais. He didn't dare look up. The footsteps grew closer, paused. The sound was soft and slight, like flesh falling in strips from bone.

A short chirping sound from the altar made the Roon guards retreat from the room. The doors closed behind them. Myell wasn't sure how long he was supposed to stay prostrated, but he didn't think it wise to move yet.

More rustling, as the headdress and robe fell away. "You can sit up now," Anna Gayle said, the syllables and words rusty.

Myell eased himself back on his haunches. Gayle stood nude above him, her body not quite human anymore. The shape was familiar—shoulders and arms, breasts and hips and legs—but her skin was roughened and scaly, and her legs and arms were thin as sticks. Her long blond hair was dark and stringy, patchy in places. Her skull had sores on it. Her eyes had darkened to gray ovals rimmed in black. Once she had been beautiful, but that was before her capture and subsequent aiding of the Roon.

He looked away, unable to bear her terrible gaze.

"I have no vanity," she said. "Stare all you want."

Cappaletto said, "No disrespect, ma'am, but what happened to you?"

Gayle made a hacking sound that might have been laughter. "I'm exactly who I always was. But neither of you are my Robert."

She swung her feet down off the dais, dropped to the deck beside them, and then went down on all fours. Myell was so startled that he backed away and fell sideways. Gayle bent low to Myell's leg and sniffed it. Her tongue darted out past blackened teeth to taste a patch of his leg where his trousers had ridden up past his socks.

"You don't taste like him either," she said.

Cappaletto said, "This how you imagined your reunion, Chief?"

"No." Myell backed away some more. "Dr. Gayle, do you remember who I am?"

Gayle arched her back. "No. I don't even remember who I am. I'm told that once I was Anna. But I failed him once too often. Now I am the Queen's plaything. Do you know what that means?"

Sharp pain unfolded in his chest as he realized just how much of a mistake he'd made. Still, maybe if he stalled for time, a brilliant new plan would make itself known.

"Tell me," he said.

She stood up so swiftly that something cracked in her back. Gayle climbed back up on her dais. Her hands clawed out for her feather cloak and pulled it close.

"You're not my Robert," she said. "Liars, both of you."

Myell rose. "Wait. I want to talk about Robert. What you remember about him. Your family, your studies back on Fortune—"

Gayle sniffed. Her gaze had gone elsewhere, focused on something outside of the room. "I'm weary of games. You're not my Robert and there is no Fortune. It was destroyed, along with the rest of mankind's cradle. Don't you know that? Silly men. Silly, stupid men. You've destroyed yourselves."

"Now might be a good time to run," Cappaletto said. Myell nodded.

They got as far as the door before it opened to allow more Roon in. Myell's arms were seized in a grip he had no hope of breaking. Cappaletto was also subdued.

"Put them in their cages," Gayle said.

CHAPTER **TWENTY-THREE**

A knock on the door interrupted Darling's story.
"Excuse me," Darling said, and rose and crossed the room gracefully.

Jodenny, sitting with one hand curled against her chest, forced her fingers to unfold. They had gone numb without her even realizing it. She was also having trouble breathing. The very idea of her husband caged up by Anna Gayle was enough to make her light-headed with fury. She told herself that Darling had heard the story from either Myell or Cappaletto and so one of them, if not both, had survived. But logic was no comfort.

The visitor at the door was the hotel clerk, who delivered a folded-up card. Darling read it with an absent smile, sent the clerk away, and returned to her seat on the velvet sofa.

She blanched when she looked at Jodenny's face.

"I'm sorry," Darling said. "I've upset you."

"I'm okay," Jodenny replied, which was a lie of the highest order. "You have to keep going."

"I think you'd feel better if we took a rest—"

Any break now, and Jodenny would leap over the coffee table and kill Darling where she sat.

"Tell me," she said.

Darling poured herself more tea. "I'm not sure of all of it, mind you. I don't think they were imprisoned long, but I can't be sure. Your husband realized very quickly that Anna Gayle was insane. Years of captivity and cooperating with the Roon had done that to her."

Not for the first time, Jodenny thought Darling might be toying with her. "Tell me."

Darling lifted her teacup.

The cage pressed in on Myell from all sides. He couldn't turn around because of the metal bars against his bare body. He couldn't raise his arms or scratch the maddening itch on his nose. Everything around him was blurry and disconnected; he suspected he'd been drugged. He couldn't actually remember being put into the cage, though the reality of it around his body was undeniable. The only part he could really move was his head, and if he craned far enough to the left he could see Cappaletto in his own cage. There was no way to reach across and grasp his hand. No way to take him away when the ring came.

"I'm sorry," Myell said, low, not eager to attract Gayle's attention.

Cappaletto's eyes were closed. He shrugged. "It was worth a shot. Maybe it'll work better the next time you pass through."

Something hummed at the top of Myell's cage. He tilted his head back as far as he could and caught a glimpse of silver light concentrated directly above his skull.

"You can't escape," Gayle said from nearby shadows. "Already the ring has come, and come, and come. Knocking on the door. Turned away."

Of course the Roon would know how to deflect an incoming ouroboros. Myell was a fool for thinking otherwise. He leaned his forehead against his bars. The cage was hanging from a single cable, and the sway of it made his stomach feel squirrelly. But motion was better than stillness. Proof of life. He flexed his fingers and tried shifting his arms, but they were pinned tight against his sides.

"Son of a bitch," he said.

The chirping of birds grew louder as Gayle moved through her pets. The birds did not sound especially happy. Gayle was humming and singing, in notes that were so off-key Myell's ears began to ache.

"Anna," he called out. "This isn't right. This isn't you."

More singing. Some old Australian folk tune. Not "Waltzing Matilda." The name of it danced around his brain, elusive. He'd ask Cappaletto but Cappaletto was American, and what good was that?

Gayle moved into the edges of his vision. Her feather cape rustled against her legs. The bird feed in her leathered palm was black and gristly. The chamber had grown dark above them, though Myell hadn't noticed it happening. He thought time was slipping from his perception.

"There's a rover," she said. "Wild rover. Gets the

gold he's looking for and goes home. Do you know the song?"

Myell said, "No."

Cappaletto said, hoarsely, "How crazy is she?"

Gayle held her hand up to a group of small yellow birds. She stroked one that came to feed, then circled its neck with her fingers as if to snap it clean.

"Dr. Gayle," Myell said. "You can come with us. Escape."

Her chin lifted suddenly. The bird squawked frantically against her fingers, aware of its jeopardy.

"I'm not the Flying Doctor," she said. "I'm just the doctor who flew to the stars."

The monkeys in their cages began screeching. Myell lifted his head and saw a Roon striding across the enormous chamber toward them. The headdress was instantly familiar, though the uniform had changed to a simple tunic that revealed the Flying Doctor's powerful, scaly legs and arms. Its tail dragged on the deck. The eyes were bright with awareness but the creature reeked of something rotten—something foul and unwanted, sour to the core, that hung around it as it came to a stop just a meter away.

Gayle made a whimpering sound and fell to her knees.

The Flying Doctor ignored her.

It peered at Myell with its head cocked in consideration. Made a hissing and clicking noise and bared its teeth. All Roon were strong, but this one looked powerful enough to part the cage bars as easily as Myell could push aside a curtain.

"Now you can kill me," Myell murmured.

"Your gods don't protect you here," the alien agreed.

It stepped closer, dragging its gaze from Myell's bare feet up to his face. "Many times I offered you conditions. Terms of negotiation. You could have had everything."

Cappaletto gave a snort of laughter. "I'll take everything. No problem."

Myell alternated between admiration for the other man's gumption and the urgent wish he would shut up.

The Flying Doctor showed no interest in Cappaletto. Instead he said, "You were Jungali. Chosen by the gods. Now sent on a foolish errand. Did they think we would be unaware? That we wouldn't stop you?"

Gayle peered up at them through her stringy hair.

"There's nothing you can offer now," the Flying Doctor said. "Your life is forfeit."

So it appeared. There was no Jungali here. Myell possessed nothing but his body and some clothing that included a pair of excellent socks. Even his wedding ring was gone.

The wedding ring.

Gayle's focus went to Myell, then dropped to the floor.

His *inscribed* wedding ring.

Homer had presumed he knew how to control the ring now. Obviously observing something in Myell's travels that Myell himself had not seen.

Carefully Myell said to the Flying Doctor, "That's not true. I have something you want and you know it."

Silence for a moment. The birds and monkeys and other animals had all gone quiet. Gayle's head was bowed again. Cappaletto was watching carefully, but with no discernible expression. The vast hall paused as if in the middle of some intricately choreographed dance, and Myell hadn't even realized he was one of the dancers.

"Negotiate," the Flying Doctor said.

A thin fountain of confidence welled up in him, tiny but nourishing. "You control the Wondjina network. You control that silver ouroboros you used to follow me around without having to use Spheres. But you can't step outside it. Wherever and whenever you go, you're tied to it."

The Roon was listening.

"I can give you the blue one," Myell said. "I can teach you how to use it."

Cappaletto said, "Son of a bitch."

Myell deliberately ignored him.

"You don't how to control it," the Flying Doctor said. "Such a human thing, to be so blind."

"I know how to control it." Myell pressed on. "I will give it as a gift. But not to you."

The Flying Doctor bared its razor-sharp teeth. Fetid air swelled past them, filled with rot.

"I'll give it to your boss," Myell proposed.

Blurriness again.

Myell was still trapped in one of the swaying upright cages. He knew that much. Cappaletto had stopped talking some time ago and wouldn't respond to Myell's questions. The vast chamber had gone dark and the river across the overhead was red with blood.

He heard a murmur. Gayle, near his feet. Her face down and her spine bent in supplication. He couldn't see her lips moving but the words carried softly.

"Inscribe," she was saying. "The ouroboros is yours."

"Did you start me on this trip?" he asked. "Were you the one who came to me?"

A slight shake of her head. Her face was down, her expression hidden. "Someone else. But we witnessed."

Because only the gods could change history, he reminded himself.

"You have to let us go, Anna," he said.

If possible, she pressed herself even closer to the floor.

Across the chamber, a hundred synchronized drums beat out a one-two-three beat and went silent. Myell twisted and tried to see, but all was darkness there.

"Please," he said. "You can come with us."

Again she shook her head. He tried to imagine how terrified she was, how much in danger, but it was hard to think through his own fear and desperation. Before he could find any more arguments she crawled off into the shadows. Birds squawked in alarm but more thumps on the drums—one-two-three-four—silenced them.

Something small glinted on the floor, exactly where Anna had left it. A tiny sharp knife.

Out of reach. Utterly useless.

He tried anyway. Bent his knees against the bars, squeezed his fingers through, groped blindly. The tips of his fingers were far enough away that they might as well have been on the other side of the chamber.

A moment later, the silver light over Myell's head went out and the cage door swung open.

It happened too fast for him to catch himself. Instead he tumbled out clumsily and heavily, bones like lead. Only a last-minute instinctive turn of his head kept him from smashing his face on the floor. The shock of impact rattled through him as thick as a shock wave. His hands and arms shook as he forced himself to his knees and groped for the knife.

Cappaletto was still imprisoned in his cage. His eyes were mere slits, but the pupils were tracking Myell.

"You can't," Cappaletto said hoarsely. "Don't give them the ring."

"I'm not going to," Myell said.

Instead he took the knife in his hand and pressed the tip against his arm. His fingers were shaking so hard he dropped it. Already the ring was making its way toward him, pushing away his air. He had only seconds until it flashed. He groped for the knife, grabbed it. Dragged the tip through flesh to make large awkward letters. A short word, the only one he had time for.

"What the hell?" Cappaletto demanded.

Tiny beads of blood rose up like tears. Across the chamber, mammoth doors began to swing open. A retinue was arriving. The drums began beating in a steady thunder that sent all the animals squawking and swinging wildly.

Cappaletto lifted his head. "You're too late—"

The letters finished, Myell hurled himself forward and grabbed Cappaletto's cage.

CHAPTER **TWENTY-FOUR**

All the tea was gone. Somewhere a church bell was ringing, loud and insistent. The good people of colonial Sydney passed outside Darling's windows by foot and on horse and by carriage, and strolled through Hyde Park, and went about their morning business. Jodenny thought everything in this room was a dream, and the world beyond an illusion. All she could focus on was Myell and Gayle's chamber of horrors.

A knock on the study door made Darling say, "Just one moment, Maude." To Jodenny she added, "She'll be nagging me about my lunch appointment. It's a business meeting that can't be avoided."

The idea that Darling might soon abandon the story for some meeting made Jodenny's stomach churn. She tried to speak, couldn't get the words out, tried again. "They escaped?"

"Of course."

Jodenny gripped the armchair tightly. "But what happened next?"

"I'm not sure," Darling said. "The blue ring took them, yes. Eventually it took them back to my base. Obviously my crew and I treated them with distrust, and had no memory of any previous visit. Then Chief Myell told us his story and convinced us to come with him or die at the hands of the Roon. He and Chief Cappaletto brought us here, saving our lives."

"He's here?" Jodenny demanded.

Another knock.

"One moment, Maude!" Darling said, louder than before. "No, Commander. He's not here. Not now. Remember, this was thirty years ago from my perspective. I haven't seen either of them since. Four of us from the future settled here and have done reasonably well with our lives. But when I met Sam, I recognized his name. And, of course, yours. Chief Myell spoke highly and well of you."

A third knock, and then the side door opened. Maude said, "Madam, you must not be tardy."

Lady Darling stood up with a cross expression. "Yes, Maude. I know. The entire industry of charity in New South Wales will grind to a halt if I'm late." To Jodenny she added, "It's for the hospital. They have no nurses here, no comprehensive system of care. We're trying to change that. Won't you come back and see me tomorrow morning? We can further this discussion."

Still dazed from course of the conversation, Jodenny stood up. Her balance felt off, though her feet were flat on the floor. Junior, who'd been quiet for most of the morning, shifted around and poked Jodenny's kidneys with a foot or a fist.

"I'll be happy to," Jodenny said, but only got as far as the door before a question made her turn back. "Why doesn't he want me to know?"

Lady Darling had turned her attention to a sheaf of papers that Maude had brought in. "Hmm?"

"Sam. Why didn't he want me to learn this from you?"

A pause. Lady Darling glanced back down at the papers. The church bells had stopped, but Jodenny's ears were ringing.

"He doesn't want you to think about Chief Myell," Lady Darling finally said. "His heart is large, but not large enough for all three of you."

Jodenny made her way back through the hotel's corridors to the lobby and the hot, dusty street outside. She didn't remember much of the walk back to Lower Fort Street, or even how long it took her. The city swirled around her with noise and color and sewage, the dogs and goats wandering freely, the ex-convicts and immigrants all building up and out, transforming the harsh land into civilization. She saw bloody carcasses hanging in the windows of the butcher shops, dark mottled meat covered with flies. She passed urchins sitting on doorsteps or playing in the streets, with their thin faces and crooked teeth and threadbare clothes. By the time she saw Lady Scott's house in front of her, she had sweated through her dress, and blisters covered her heels. Lilly met her at the door, all concerned.

"We thought you were lost, ma'am!" she said. "The Captain and Tulip, they're out looking for you. Sarah said you were going to see the sights but that was hours and hours ago!"

"I'm fine," Jodenny said. Just looking at the steep staircase made her dizzy, though, so she sat on the sofa in the front parlor. The urge to lie down struck her as an extremely good idea, and the next thing she knew, Lilly was putting a cold wet cloth on her forehead and saying, "Sarah, go find the Captain."

"No," Jodenny murmured. The very last person she wanted to see was Osherman. Yet the next time she opened her eyes he was there, leaning over the sofa with his fingers taking her pulse.

"Stop it," she sat, batting him away.

Osherman didn't move. "Stay still. You fainted."

"I did not," she said.

Still, she didn't have the strength to sit up or push him away. Jodenny lay quietly for a few more minutes while Lilly fetched more cold cloths. Someone had undone the collars of her dress, which was a nice gesture. Her feet were up on a pillow and Sarah was fanning her with a large hand fan.

"All right, enough fussing," she finally growled. "I just walked too far, that's all."

"Where did you go?" Osherman asked.

Jodenny sat up, waving off their helping hands. "The museum. The park. Nowhere special. It was good exercise."

Osherman frowned. "It was too much exercise."

"I'll decide what's too much exercise," she retorted.

"Didn't you take a parasol?"

Jodenny blinked at her hands. "I must have dropped it."

"Dropped it," Osherman repeated. He shook his head. "Let's get you upstairs. You can rest more comfortably there."

It was true that she felt more comfortable once she'd shed the dress, and it was easy to slip off to sleep once the curtains had been drawn against the bright sun. Still, the room was hot and she missed air-conditioning with every ounce of her being. When she woke from the nap it was night, and Osherman was reading in the corner chair by the light of a lantern.

"She lied," Jodenny said.

"Hmm?" Osherman put his book aside and stretched his arms in front of him. He looked tired. "Who lied?"

Jodenny rubbed her eyes with her hand. "No one. I was dreaming."

"About who?"

She didn't answer. There was no easy way to tell him that Darling had been in her dream, and in fact no compelling reason to tell him at all. She sat up, happy to discover that her head didn't spin.

"You really overexerted yourself today," Osherman said. "You do that, and you could endanger the baby."

Perhaps he didn't mean to sound so condescending, but Jodenny certainly interpreted it that way. "Thanks for the medical advice, but she's not your baby."

That last part slipped out before she could stop herself. Osherman blinked, surprised. He leaned forward with his elbows on his knees.

"I know she's not," he said. "I'm not trying to take Chief Myell's place."

"You couldn't."

"I know," he insisted.

Jodenny groped for the glass of water someone had left on the bedside table. The water tasted lukewarm but soothed her dry throat.

"I can't take his place," Osherman repeated, "but I can try to repay the debt, Jodenny. He gave me my life back. The least I can do is look after his wife and child."

"How did he save your life?" she demanded.

Abruptly he turned his attention to his shoes, and made to undo the laces. His fingers were long and strong, but now they were shaking.

"He yanked me out of Providence," Osherman replied. "If he'd left me there, I'd still be the gibbering town idiot. The one everyone was afraid of, the one who couldn't be trusted around sharp knives or small children. The monster."

Jodenny put the water glass down so abruptly that it clanged against the wooden tabletop. "You were not the town idiot."

"For months and months I was the fool." His voice was low and angry. "You think I didn't know how people talked, what they said about me? Dangerous. Psychotic."

"They were wrong."

"They weren't wrong. I was dangerous. Because of the fucking Roon. You were the only thing—the only solitary damned thing—keeping me sane. And then Chief Myell showed up. Next thing I know I'm in the infirmary on the *Confident* and they cured me. The miracles of modern medicine. So who do I have to thank for that?"

"You don't sound particularly grateful," she observed.

He wrenched off his left shoe and set to work savagely unlacing the other one. "Your husband. That's who. Who, if I'd listened to the first time around, would have saved me from the damned Roon in the first place. Go through the Child Sphere, he said. Both of you did. You begged me come with you. And I was so smart, I said no. I was going to get home on my own."

The leather laces in his hands broke off. He threw them into the corner and pulled off his shoe, only to throw the shoe after the laces.

Jodenny decided silence was the best option.

Osherman gazed after the shoe bleakly. "Now I'm here. Stranded in medieval Australia. You're pregnant and who's going to take care of you, if I don't? Like I should have from the beginning, on the *Yangtze,* and spared you all of this."

From out in the hall there was the sound of someone coming up the stairs. The footsteps continued past Jodenny's room to Lady Scott's room. Jodenny listened for the snick of the bedroom door closing, unwilling to have this conversation when there might be eavesdroppers.

Jodenny said, carefully, "I'm not your responsibility, Sam. And no matter how much you regret it, you can't change the past."

"No, I can't." Osherman rubbed his eyes with the palms of his hands. "I can't. Can't change how you feel about him or about me. But I know that in our original timeline we married and had our own children, and I think it can happen here, too. If you let it. I want you to marry me, for real. Here and now. You loved me once and you could love me again."

The bed didn't feel strong enough to support her. Jodenny imagined it splintering out from under her, and the floor breaking as well, and then the foundation of the continent itself.

"He's not dead," she said. "I know he's not."

She knew it even without Darling's story; she knew it in her heart, and in the beat of Junior's heart as well.

Osherman gave her a bleak look. "How long do we have to be stranded here for you to accept that he's not coming back?"

Jodenny twisted her wedding ring.

"Until my dying breath," she said.

Any hopes she had of returning to Lady Darling's hotel the next day were dashed by Osherman, Lilly, Sarah, and Lady Scott, all of them determined to hover over Jodenny until she squeezed Junior out in sheer exasperation.

"I'm fine!" she told them

None of them believed her.

"Best that you rest in bed all day," Lady Scott said. "Did wonders for me during my childbearing years. I added it up. I spent over three years in bed while in your condition!"

"But I want to walk around," Jodenny protested.

Osherman said, "You can walk anywhere you want, as long as one of us is with you. What if you faint in the street?"

Jodenny seethed, but she didn't see any clever way around their helpfulness and truth be told, her back and legs did ache. But she was desperate to see Lady Darling and hear more about Myell, as well as dig for more inconsistencies.

It was obvious, in retrospect, that Darling had been vague in some areas and downright deceptive in others. The question was why, and what secrets she was holding back.

"I'm at least going downstairs," Jodenny insisted. "It's cooler down there, and I can sit by the parlor windows."

The breeze through the front was thin, but much better than no breeze at all. The morning paper had come in. The pages were full of announcements and classifieds, notices from ship's captains, tales of crime or social news. Junior was kicking up a storm and breakfast was giving her heartburn. She wanted to take Lady Scott's advice and go back to bed, but pride kept her on the sofa. Osherman was writing out notes on a desk, something for his shipping business. When he was done he called on Tulip to deliver a batch of them to the post office.

"Can't," Tulip said, worrying his hat between his fingers.

Sarah, who was dusting Admiral Scott's portrait, offered more of an explanation. "They don't let Aboriginals into the post office, sir."

"I'm sorry to hear that," Osherman said. He looked as if he wanted to say more but was holding himself back.

Jodenny said, "Go take them yourself. I'll be fine here."

"I don't trust you to stay put," he said.

She sent him a scowl that would have made her sailors scurry for cover, if she were still a division officer.

Hastily he said, "I'll be back soon."

Jodenny did not take his absence as an opportunity to go off to Lady Darling's hotel, but she did pen a hasty note and asked Tulip to deliver it. It took him an hour to go there and return, but at least he did it before Osherman made it back to the house.

"The clerk said Lady Darling had to go away," Tulip told Jodenny. "Very quick, this morning."

Dismayed, Jodenny asked, "Where did she go?"

"Maybe Melbourne, he said. Wasn't sure."

Melbourne was hundreds of miles away. Devastated, Jodenny slowly paced around the room. Her back hurt from Junior's weight but sitting was proving to be just as uncomfortable these days. She needed to talk to Darling, needed to know more. About why she'd lied, for instance. Myell and Cappaletto couldn't have come to 1855 by the blue ring. It was before Myell's date of birth by hundreds of years, and the cone of space-time that Perry had drawn on the *Confident* didn't allow for that.

Either Perry was wrong, or Darling had come to Australia's past by some other means.

Maybe she'd gone not to Melbourne but back into the future.

Jodenny's worried thoughts were interrupted by Sarah, who'd been in the kitchen fixing supper. Now she was standing in the doorway with an unhappy frown and her hands knotted together. "I hate to bother you, ma'am . . ."

"Yes?"

"It's Molly. One of my other sisters. Maybe you could help her?"

Jodenny followed Sarah to the kitchen, where a red-headed girl was sitting on the floor with her legs drawn up and spread wide. Molly was younger than Sarah, with a strong family resemblance in the nose and jaw-line. Molly was also extremely pregnant, with both hands clenched around her tummy and air bellowing in and out of her lungs.

"Stop pushing," Lilly was ordering, from between Molly's knees. "It's not time!"

"The midwife's drunk," Sarah explained. "She had nowhere else to go."

Lilly surrendered a brief glance toward Jodenny. "I don't need any fancy help. I helped bring you into this world, Sarah-girl, and aside from dropping you on your head, look how you turned out." Turning back to Molly she said, "Just push when I tell you to and not just because you want to."

Another contraction gripped Molly. Sarah clamped her hand over her mouth to stifle the scream. "Not yet," Lilly warned. When the spasm passed, Molly panted and gasped for air.

"Let's get her to your room," Jodenny suggested.

The airless room behind the kitchen was barely big enough for Lilly and Sarah's single beds, but Molly was happy to be off the floor and said so. Sarah lit a lantern, then bathed her sister's head with a cold cloth. When another contraction hit, Lilly shook her head.

"That baby just doesn't want to come out," Lilly said.

Jodenny checked with the Digital Duola. "Maybe her cervix isn't fully dilated."

"Her what?" Sarah asked.

Damn this era, and the prurients who kept women ignorant of their own body parts. Jodenny said, "If she rests on her hands and knees, that'll take the pressure of the baby off. The swelling will go down and her opening might get wider."

"I'll do anything if it'll help," Molly panted.

Jodenny guided her up on her hands and knees with her head down and her butt sticking up in the air. "It's indecent," Lilly said, with a sniff, but she didn't stop it.

The Digital Duola instructed Jodenny on how to do a vaginal exam but she held off, afraid of spooking the girl more.

"Now what?" Sarah asked, her voice a whisper.

Jodenny said, "We wait. Boil some water, won't you? We need clean cloths, too."

Sarah looked at Lilly, who nodded in agreement.

They didn't wait long. Within an hour the cervix had opened, Molly was unable to stop pushing, and the baby's head was crowning. Jodenny let Lilly take over for that part. "You're doing fine," Lilly said, as the tiny head emerged facing sideways. Lilly glanced up at Jodenny, fear in her eyes. Sideways wasn't a good position at all. The next few contractions didn't push the baby out any further, and his skin began to turn blue.

Jodenny forced herself to sound calm. "His shoulders are stuck."

"I'll pull him out by the head," Lilly said.

"No, wait." Jodenny bent low. "See if you can get your finger up there and find his arm. If you get the arm out, the rest may follow. But you need to wash your hands first. Sarah, here, hold the head up."

While Lilly washed up, Molly sobbed and sweated and swore in fear. Jodenny looked her straight in the eyes and addressed her like any young sailor. "Listen to me. The baby's stuck. It happens all the time. But we're going to get him out, okay?"

Molly nodded.

Five minutes later, her baby was born. Alive and kicking. Jodenny sagged back on the other bed, her hands leaving prints on her dress. She felt exhausted, and this wasn't even her delivery. And as far as deliveries went, it hadn't even been a bad one. A hundred different things could have gone wrong. Without medicine, equipment, or any kind of decent hospital, Molly and the child could have both died.

"What should I call him, miss?" Molly asked. "You pick. You saved him."

"I couldn't," Jodenny said.

"Please. For good luck."

"Terry," she said. "Call him Terry."

CHAPTER **TWENTY-FIVE**

Myell blinked his eyes open to find himself covered with a bright yellow bedspread. He bolted upright so fast the room spun out from underneath him, and the next time he woke, his daughter Lisa was peering down at him in concern.

"That was a nasty dizzy spell, wasn't it?" she said. "Feeling a bit better?"

"There was someone with me," Myell said. "Right? Someone else?"

"Two of you," Lisa confirmed. "Showed up here stark naked and bleeding. You don't get that around here every day."

"Cappaletto?"

"That's him," she said. "Quite a fellow."

Myell sank back into the mattress in relief.

Lisa said, "I know who you are, and maybe you know who I am. You've obviously been through hell but there's nothing wrong with you a nice stretch of bed rest wouldn't cure. Still, I want to ask. Why did you scratch the name 'Kay' into your arm?"

"I promise I'll tell you everything later," he said. "Where's Cappaletto now?"

"He's off with the sheriff and my mother and the town council, telling them about the Roon."

The meeting, as such, was taking place under the metal roof of the town pub. A dozen people were drinking beer as Cappaletto regaled them with stories of the Roon mines and their escape from the Flying Doctor. By the time Myell reached them, his head pounding and borrowed clothes hastily thrown on, Cappaletto had almost finished the tale.

"There he is," Cappaletto said, raising his mug. "The man who took on the Roon and lived to tell the tale."

Baylou Owenstein said, "Man of the hour! Even if you are, you know, dead."

"Especially since you're dead," seventy-year-old Jodenny said, giving him a suspicious look.

Teresa Romero, her feet propped up and hands laced across her small pregnant belly, said, "He doesn't look very dead to me, Mom."

Myell took a cold mug and downed some of the beer. Everyone looked at him as if expecting him to speak, but when he opened his mouth a burp startled him and his audience both.

"Good one," Baylou said.

Someone offered him a stool. Myell sat. He felt refreshingly light, surprisingly at ease. "What did you tell them?" he asked Cappaletto.

Cappaletto passed his mug to get refilled. He was pale in the sunlight, thin from his captivity, but still cheerful. "Everything, of course."

Everything turned out to be the awful mines, yes, and the Flying Doctor and Anna Gayle for sure, though only Jodenny cared about Gayle. Cappaletto had also touched on the sad tale of the Roon ambush at Kultana, and the legends about Burringurrah and the *Kamchatka* from his perspective in the timeline.

"What you're talking about all happened twenty-five years or so ago," Jodenny said, her gaze going briefly to the clouds. "Are you saying all of mankind has fallen under the Roon? That there's nothing left?"

The mood around the table shifted, darkened.

"I don't know," Myell admitted. "It's possible."

"Possible, my ass," Cappaletto said. "I'm sure we've kicked their asses by now."

Silence as they grimly considered the possibilities.

Baylou raised a toast. "Here's to kicking their asses!"

The beer ran freely all night long, and Myell didn't remember much about stumbling off to bed at Lisa's house. Cappaletto, who was bedding down at Sheriff Alice's house, had disappeared an hour earlier. At breakfast, nursing his hangover, Myell was startled when Lisa casually said, "We're having trouble deciding who you're going to take with you."

Myell's water glass paused halfway to his lips. "Sorry?"

"Who you're going to take," Baylou repeated. He was sitting with his tree bark coffee, which Myell knew better than to taste. "With you. When the ring comes."

"I think Mom would like to go," Lisa said. "She and Sam. I mean, it's not the fairest thing that they've been stuck here all these years and won't ever get to see the rest of the universe. But they're also a bit old. Might slow you down."

Myell very carefully spread some butter on a roll. It tasted like cardboard in his mouth. "You understand that it doesn't really change anything? If I took you,

Lisa, you'd still be here. It's just another copy of you that would be floating around time and space."

"I know." Lisa cut an apple into slices and popped a slice into her mouth. "But it's something, right? A way of living on. And maybe there's a way to send back help anyway."

Baylou said, "I think you should take me. I'm not much use to anyone here, after all! No one would miss me."

"That's the point," Myell said, but it was useless; they either didn't want to understand what the blue ring would do, or didn't care anyway. Cappaletto's honesty and witty tales had hurt the situation all around.

"We'll figure it out," Lisa said. She looked at the clock. "Round noon, right? That's when it's coming for you?"

"It'll come for both me and Chief Cappaletto," Myell said. "Where is he?"

"Oh, you'll see him," Baylou said.

"I'd like to see him now."

"Around noon," Lisa repeated. Not for the first time he saw Jodenny in her, and under other circumstances might have been pleased.

"Noon," he said. Sure.

Lisa patted his hand. "Maybe you should go back to bed for a while. Rest up. We'll sort this out and come get you."

It was almost nine o'clock. Myell couldn't be sure how short this eddy would be with Cappaletto's weight changing the window, but he wasn't about to wait around and find out. He retired to the guest room, climbed out the window, and made his way to Sheriff Alice's house. He didn't have the time or inclination for anything but the direct approach, so he knocked on the door. Alice answered.

"What are you doing here so early?" she asked.

He punched her in the face. He wasn't used to punching women in the face and hurt his knuckles doing it. Cappaletto, who was half undressed, caught Alice before she could crash to the floor. He laid her out carefully on the sofa.

"Why'd you do that?" Cappaletto demanded.

"Because we have to get out of here."

"You couldn't just lock her in the closet?"

Myell threw him a shirt. "Put your clothes on. We've got to go."

He took Cappaletto into the jungle. They heard search parties a while later, but Myell knew the land and figured they wouldn't search as far as Balandra Bridge. They hunkered down in the cave by the river where Myell, Jodenny, and the kids had once camped out. Cappaletto looked unimpressed with the accommodations but took an interest when Myell produced the small kitchen knife he'd stolen from Lisa's house.

"You're not going to hurt me, are you?" Cappaletto asked. "I didn't know what they were planning."

"It's not for you," Myell assured him. "I'm not even sure I need it."

"What do you mean?"

"Every Wondjina ring I've ever seen has glyphs inside to guide it. The blue ring? Nothing. It needs some kind of guidance. First it was following my wedding ring inscription. After it was stolen, it started following my thoughts. Thinking about Kultana took me one place, and thinking about the Roon took me to you and Adryn in the mines."

"If all you have to do is think real hard, why did you carve the name 'Kay' on your arm?"

"In case I wasn't conscious when the ring came," he said. "Kay is Jodenny's nickname."

Cappaletto sat back, satisfied. "Where to now?"

He thought about that for a while, then scratched the *Yangtze*'s name into his arm. Then he carved a date.

Nice place," Cappaletto said, as they strolled down the promenade on the *Yangtze*. "Pity it's going to blow up in a few months."

"At least the date worked," Myell said. He had a pounding headache, and the smell of food from the cafés they passed wasn't helping at all. Without yuros or debit cards, they had no way of purchasing even the cheapest painkiller.

Cappaletto grabbed some French fries from a neglected plate and shoved them into his mouth. He was still gaunt and pale from the mines, though he didn't complain about fatigue or hunger. Myell figured he wasn't the complaining type. Cappaletto said, "Good job. Though maybe you could just draw on yourself with ink instead of blood? That cutting thing is kind of gross."

One of the shops they passed sold stationery and writing instruments. Cappaletto, clever with his fingers, took Myell down an aisle and stole a few pens. "Because it won't do to have just one and lose it," he said. On their way out they passed Jodenny and Sam Osherman, the two of them looking ridiculously infatuated with each other. Myell kept walking.

He penned the name of the *Confident,* and picked a week before the ambush at Kultana. Instead they wound up on Fortune with the *Confident* in docking orbit high above. The ACF and Team Space fleet was just beginning to assemble for the long haul to meet the Roon armada. Myell figured his destination hadn't worked because there already was a Tom Cappaletto on the *Confident,* and he couldn't bring another one into the eddy.

Cappaletto, who'd kindly mugged a businessman for some yuros, smiled broadly at the waitress who brought them fish and chips. They were sitting in a darkened pub at noontime with the bright daylight kept at bay by screened windows. Cappaletto hadn't been planet-side before, and was pleased by the beer he'd sampled so far.

He said, "As much as I appreciate this tour of history, Terry—and I do appreciate it, mind you you can't keep dragging me around with you, right? The trips are getting shorter and you're getting sicker each time we land."

Myell knew that was true. He also knew, based on his experience with Kyle and Twig, that he could keep going for several more jumps. He explained that to Cappaletto, who said, "Still, don't you want to have some kind of plan or other?"

"I have a plan," Myell reached for his own beer. "Find my wife and baby. The ones Homer said he saved."

"Oh, yes, Homer," Cappaletto said. "Your invisible friend from the future who hasn't shown up since I've known you."

"I don't trust him," Myell said.

The waitress brought them more beer. Outside, the sun moved across the sky and shadows grew longer in the street. On the overvids, Dunredding won a soccer game against Carver North. Myell kept his eyes on the shadows, watching for any sign of the Flying Doctor.

He wasn't naive enough to think the Roon had abandoned its mission.

Cappaletto said, "Trust him or not, he's got the answers you need. You want to find your wife and kid, he's the place to start."

The pub doors opened, letting in an afternoon crowd of business folk. Myell said, "You don't have to keep coming along if you don't want to. You can walk out that door. You've done enough."

Cappaletto thought about it for a while. "You leave, this place might evaporate. That's what you think happens, right? The whatever, the eddy, washes away."

"Maybe. I don't think I'll ever know for sure."

They finished their beer. The soccer game played out. The men and women at the bar, so uniform in their business attire, began to drink themselves silly.

"I'll take my chances with you," Cappaletto said.

Myell started writing on his arm. "Next stop, Homer."

CHAPTER **TWENTY-SIX**

The blue ocean heaved and rolled for as far as the eye could see, or at least as far as Myell dared look. His stomach made a sick twist just breathing in the fresh salty air. Cappaletto was standing on the edge of the cliff looking down, because he was a crazy American. The sun was blistering hot and the People gathered around Myell kept touching him, as if for good luck.

"You jumped off this?" Cappaletto asked.

"Long story," Myell said. "I need some help here."

Cappaletto helped shoo off the crowd to make room

for Shark Tooth, leader of these Aboriginal Australians. Shark Tooth was considerably older and grayer than Myell remembered him. By his best guess, they had landed maybe twenty years after Myell's last visit. The village hadn't grown much since then, but it was busy in the afternoon sun. Shark Tooth was so happy to see Myell that he almost hugged the air right out of him.

"Nice to see you, too," Myell said.

The villagers set about preparing a feast, which Myell appreciated but really didn't look forward to. His stomach had settled a little but his headache was back, and he felt achy all over as if coming down with the flu.

"Homer," he said to Shark Tooth. "We're looking for a man who calls himself Homer."

Shark Tooth spread his arms wide. "Homer!"

"We're looking for him," Myell said.

Cappaletto said, "Maybe that's the name of the village. Homerville. Homer City."

Which was possible, if not plausible. When Myell, Nam, Gayle, and a bunch of marines had come through the first time, in search of Gayle's husband and his team, they'd been a bit too busy to learn the name of the place.

"So now what?" Cappaletto asked. "We drink bad wine and make nice with the native women until the ring shows up again?"

Myell dared a look toward the open ocean. "There's a Wondjina Sphere on one of the islands along this coast. And a group of women far more familiar with the Wondjina gods than I am. Maybe they can help."

Cappaletto eyed the horizon. "Island, eh? We'd better find us a boat."

The People weren't too happy about it, but finally

Myell got Shark Tooth to walk them down a path from the cliff to the sea. Shark Tooth was much more unhappy when Myell proposed, through gestures, the idea that he and Cappaletto were going to take one of the tribe's long narrow canoes out for an excursion. Shark Tooth made his displeasure known by sitting in the boat with both arms across his chest.

"I guess you can come with us," Myell said.

Cappaletto paddled, because Myell was too busy clutching the sides of the canoe for dear life to be of much use. Funny how his fear of the ocean never really had gone away, death or godhood notwithstanding. Shark Tooth apparently didn't think much of Cappaletto's rowing, because he finally grabbed one of the long thin paddles and took over the job himself.

"Does he know where we're going?" Cappaletto asked, shading his eyes against the sun.

Myell blew out a breath, hoping to calm his queasiness. "I don't even know where we're going. But the women are out here somewhere."

Shark Tooth finally beached them on a stretch of sand and scrub that looked vaguely familiar. Myell's watery legs supported him long enough to get him up to the high tide mark, where he sat with complete relief. Shark Tooth and Cappaletto dragged the canoe up into the sand and Shark Tooth went off into a long incomprehensible story in his own tongue, waving his hand to illustrate.

"Beats me," Cappaletto said.

Myell got himself upright. "I don't know. Let's find the village. It's here somewhere."

They headed off into the jungle along a path grown over with grass. Myell told himself the women and children used another path now, had abandoned this one for some reason, but he couldn't rid himself of a growing apprehension. After several minutes of swatting at flies and pushing vines out of their way, they came to the painted Child Sphere he remembered from a long night of drinking and dancing and divine preparation.

The Sphere was broken. Half of its topmost part had been crushed in as if by a giant thumb. The bridges and tree houses that Myell remembered hung in ruins from the trees like banners from that long-ago party. Some dead trees bore scorch marks along the length of their trunks, and there were no sounds of birds, insects, or other animal life in what had once been the main clearing. Even the grass was dead. The place smelled like burned flesh, and things that had rotted into the dirt.

Cappaletto said nothing, which Myell was grateful for. Shark Tooth turned in a circle three times and stomped down his foot, as if warding off evil spirits.

"Not what I expected," Myell managed.

"Looks like an army tore through," Cappaletto said.

If there'd been any survivors, they were long gone. If Shark Tooth knew the story, the language barrier kept him from sharing it. The nausea that had been his companion during the canoe trip rose up again, and maybe Cappaletto read it in his face.

"There's nothing here, Terry," he said. "Let's go back."

Shark Tooth led the way back to the beach, where he and Cappaletto set to work hauling the canoe back into the water and Myell, standing near the grass and rocks, sought to steady himself. The wind over the water made a lonely sound. Birds that had been scarce inland—gulls and cormorants, and egrets, too—whirled through the sky. Myell tried not to think it was his fault that ruin had come to Ishikawa and her friends, but the suspicion remained.

He stared down at his arm, at the word *Homer* now faded into skin. A rustling in the grass made him turn to see an enormous crocodile racing toward him, its claws kicking up sand, its razor-sharp jaws opened so wide he could see down the beast's gullet.

"Stop!" Myell yelled, as if crocodiles took orders—as if this crocodile did, because he recognized the markings. Cappaletto and Shark Tooth yelled something that he couldn't quite make out in his panic. "No, wait—"

The crocodile barreled forward, grabbed him with its jaws, and dragged him into the ocean.

You're a fool," Free-not-chained said, for not the first time in the dark seaweed-smelling sea cave she called home. "A fool to come back here, as if you could change things now!"

She was in her human form—slight and long-haired, her skin a fine mesh of tiny scales. He wasn't sure if he preferred her as a human or as a crocodile. She'd saved his life at least twice during his last stay on the planet, for which he was indebted. But he didn't trust her much.

He sat back on a wet rock and rubbed his head. "Change what things?"

"Your son," she retorted.

Myell almost slid off the rock.

"My what?"

She paced the cave angrily. One end of it tapered into the sea. The other end, perhaps ten meters distant, twisted off into caves under the reef. Myell's chest and back ached from where her teeth had dragged him along. If she were a real crocodile, or at least the kind known on Earth and the Seven Sisters, he'd be dead by now. Her teeth, however, hadn't even broken his skin.

Free-not-chained folded down to the floor, changed into crocodile form, and slithered out of the cave.

He followed, of course. There was nothing to do but follow. Through the narrow, sloping caves with water puddled on the floor, past open pools full of fish, along passages barely wide enough for him to pass without scraping himself raw. The only light came from glowing sea moss on the cave walls. The steady slosh of the sea around them made him nervous. High tide could sweep in and drown him, or maybe a tsunami would roll in. It would be just his luck to die in a tsunami.

"Why did you bring me here if you don't want to talk to me?" he called out. "And what son?"

He squeezed out of a passage into a square chamber that was too low for him to stand without banging his head. The light here was bluish green, and most of the floor was a pool of calm seawater. Free-not-chained, human again, sat on a flat rock in the middle of the pool with a pouty expression on her face. With her was an enormous white seal. The seal lifted its head, stared at Myell, and then transformed into a large, bearded man with water glistening on his naked chest and legs.

"They call me Sea Unchanging," the man said. He gazed steadily at Myell while stroking Free-not-chained's back. "I'm her husband. I told her to bring you here and apologize."

"I won't," Free-not-chained said.

The seal man threaded his fingers through her long hair and tugged firmly.

"I wanted a child," she protested. "There's nothing wrong with that!"

"You wanted a god," Sea Unchanging replied, sounding annoyed. "You took this human's seed and it grew rotten."

Myell sat on the ground. He thought about putting his feet in the water, but didn't know what was swimming down there in the murky depths.

"Tell me about him," he said.

Free-not-chained wrinkled her nose.

Sea Unchanging waited, his hand still entwined in her hair.

"He's half man, half god, half of me," Free-not-chained conceded. Myell didn't bother to correct her fractions. She continued, "One of his names is Wind-not-sea. He was a good boy. Strong enough to kill sharks, smart enough to outwit the whales. We sang our stories to him and taught him how to swim the stars."

Myell thought she was speaking metaphorically, but Sea Unchanging said, "You taught him to swim too far. To Earth. To Burringurrah."

"Wait," Myell said. "How did he get to Burringurrah?"

"Through the oceans," Sea Unchanging said. "Over the land. Planet to planet."

Myell wished Jodenny were here. Because surely she wouldn't believe some crazy tales of crocodiles swimming their way across the universe. She was the voice of skepticism and reason. But Myell himself? Didn't have enough energy to doubt. He could clearly picture saltwater crocodiles diving into the deep blue of one ocean and surfacing in another. The freshwater ones, too, crawling into a muddy watering hole on Earth and emerging on Fortune or Baiame or anywhere else they choose. Free-not-chained had dragged him down to this sea cave without injury or drowning and so he imagined she could drag him across the universe if she wanted, her teeth locked into his flesh and bone.

Sea Unchanging said, "At Burringurrah, Wind-not-sea made himself a boomerang of rock. Bad magic. And you let him bring it back here."

"I didn't know!" Free-not-chained protested.

Myell asked, slowly, "What did he do with this boomerang?"

Free-not-chained slid out away from her husband into the saltwater pool. She disappeared beneath the surface. He saw a flash of skin, the kick of her foot. When she surfaced near him she had a silver fish in her teeth. It thrashed for air as she dropped it onto the rock near Myell's feet.

"The old human witches, they taught him how to call his father," Free-not-chained said. "He said, 'Jungali, Jungali, Jungali,' and was lifted up into what you call the Dreamtime. It's not a place you can swim to. It's not a place you can sing to. But there they were. Wind-not-sea said, 'I'm a god like you' and Jungali said, 'You're a god the way a fish is a whale,' which Wind-not-sea didn't like at all."

From the rock in the pool, Sea Unchanging said, "Tell him what he did with the boomerang."

"My story!" Free-not-chained shouted back. She was hanging off the edge of the pool, her feet kicking lazily behind her. The silver fish had gone still with one eye glaring dourly at Myell.

"What did he do?" Myell asked.

Free-not-chained closed her eyes. "He threw it at them. Angered them. And for his hubris and arrogance, they punished him."

And maybe it was more than just his imagination at work here, but Myell could see the scene unfolding in front of his eyes. Night on the island of women. Wind-not-sea, his face in shadows, calling on the ancient gods as part of his birthright. The Dreamtime unfolding: sinuous and long and like honey on the tongue, beneath the feet. A quarrel. Fury and punishment.

"What did the gods do to him?" Myell asked.

"They chained him to a chunk of driftwood and threw the wood into the sea," Free-not-chained said. "Where even now he drifts, lost. Only his human father can help him. Only his father can intercede with the gods to free him from his punishment."

Myell squeezed the bridge of his nose. "I have no influence with the gods. I have nothing to do with them anymore. I died on Burringurrah, but someone came to Garanwa's station and changed time. Don't you understand? I'm as adrift as Wind-not-sea."

"Untrue," said Sea Unchanging, who had abandoned the rock and was now bobbing in the water next to his wife. "You were cast off not adrift but with a purpose: save your people."

"Humanity has already fallen," Myell said. "I can't change that."

Free-not-chained said, scornfully, "See? He's learned nothing."

Sea Unchanging swam to the edge of the pool, picked up the dead silver fish, and pressed it into Myell's hands. "Take your son to the gods of the Dreamtime.

Petition them to forgive Wind-not-sea and save your people. With the proper sacrifice, all will be well again."

The fish was slimy in his hands. Myell skipped past the word *sacrifice* because nothing good had come of that the last time around. Instead he said, "I don't even know how to find Wind-not-sea."

"You'll find him again," Sea Unchanging promised. His eyes were warm with the compassion that Free-not-chained lacked. "You've already met him. He uses a human name now."

Myell didn't have to think hard to come up with the answer.

"Homer," he muttered.

"Homer," said Sea Unchanging.

Cappaletto and Shark Tooth were sitting on the beach when Free-not-chained surrendered Myell from the surf. Dusk had come on, with a smattering of stars across the rose-blue sky. They dragged him out of the waves and laid him down into the sand while he caught his breath and spat out salt water.

"What the hell happened?" Cappaletto said.

Myell told him the bare bones of it.

"So some crocodile and her husband a seal want you to save your only son, who pissed off the gods?" Cappaletto said.

More salt water rose in the back of Myell's throat. He was never going to get the taste off his tongue. "Basically, yes."

"He's not some university student from the future?"

"Apparently not."

Shark Tooth's head swiveled back and forth, watching them speak.

"And he's trapped somehow, but he can appear all over time and space?"

"That's what they said."

"Huh." Cappaletto threw some twigs into the fire. "You're going to write 'Australian Aboriginal Dreamtime' on your arm?"

"Not that easy." Myell scratched sand off his legs. His clothes were wet and his skin itched. The smell of dead fish was stuck in his nose. "According to Sea Unchanging, we can get to Homer through a Painted Sphere. Like the one on this island, but one that hasn't been broken. And we need witches or shamans to call the gods to us. Whatever witches or shamans we can find."

Shark Tooth fed more twigs into the small fire. Cappaletto opened his mouth to ask the obvious question, but Myell already had the answer.

"Yes," he said. "I know. Team Space has never surveyed a Painted Sphere. Only regular Father, Mother, and Child Spheres. But Sea Unchanging told me where to find another. Turns out, I know the place. A bunch of kids died to protect it."

Carefully he inked another name on his arm.

"Who's that?" Cappaletto asked.

"Ensign Darling," he replied.

CHAPTER **TWENTY-SEVEN**

After delivering Molly's baby, Jodenny found herself enormously popular with the impoverished pregnant women of Sydney— or at least with the servants who heard of the eccentric American at Lady Scott's house who could diagnose ailments and deliver infants.

"But I'm not American," Jodenny said.

Her medical patients usually arrived on the kitchen doorstep early in the morning, on their way to or from market—thin, emaciated girls expecting their first babies, worn-out women who'd birthed and lost children already, tired women who were already supporting children and grandchildren. Most of them were rugged enough to have survived Sydney's harsh environment so far, and most were resigned to the pain and danger of labor—some flat-out told Jodenny they expected to die giving birth, and at least one told Jodenny she was looking forward to dying.

"Anything to get this beast out of me," said one girl, Nancy, as she poked at her stomach.

Jodenny asked, "You don't want the baby?"

Nancy frowned glumly. "Tried throwing myself down some stairs, that didn't work. Tried drinking some poison. Just gave me a headache."

Jodenny hadn't thought much about colonial Australia in terms of birth control or abortion, though the situation became more clear with every new patient. The women who came to see her had no access to reliable family planning, and no options for unwanted pregnancies. Another mouth to feed was no welcome news in most of the families, assuming there was a family—many of the women had only casual relationships with the sailors, diggers, or other laborers who'd impregnated them. Some were victims of rape, with little hope of justice from the colonial legal system. Nancy wasn't the only one who'd tried to end her fetus's life.

"What'll become of the child?" Jodenny asked Lilly, after Nancy was gone.

Lilly was carefully polishing some silver. "Orphans' home, likely. Front step of the church, maybe. Down to the state home in Parramatta. Or it won't live long past birth. They die in their cradles, either on their own or because someone helps them."

The women came to Jodenny with symptoms of anemia, malnutrition, constipation, hemorrhoids, and sexually transmitted diseases. They reported migraines, leg cramps, back pain, and painful varicose veins. Jodenny insisted on washing her hands so much that Sarah and Lilly thought she was crazy. They wouldn't believe her stories about little tiny germs no one could see but did start keeping hot soapy water always available. Jodenny taught them what she knew from the Digital Duola, even though they both claimed to be stupid and not worth teaching.

"Never went to school," Sarah confided. "We can't read or write or anything, ma'am."

"You can learn it in your head," Jodenny said. "And teach others."

Osherman was not delighted by her new vocation and fretted over Jodenny picking up a disease or two. "You don't even have sterile gloves," he said.

"Don't I know it. But what do you want me to do? Abandon them?"

He was quiet for a moment. "No. You would never do that."

Jodenny resumed drinking her morning tea.

"Come out with me to the lighthouse," he said. "It'll do you good. Fresh air and sunshine."

She was tired all the time now, but Jodenny agreed that it might do her good to get out of the house. The Macquarie Lighthouse was an impressive sandstone tower near the entrance to Sydney Harbor. It overlooked the cliffs near South Head and though the trip was long, the magnificent view and ocean winds were worth the effort. Here was the edge of the continent, where million-year-old rock met the clashing sea far below. A three-masted ship was slowly making its way into the harbor bearing food or silk or immigrants looking for new lives. The ship was still too far away for Jodenny to see anyone standing on the decks, but she had the urge to wave her hand at them—a welcome, or maybe a warning. It was hard to say.

She settled into the shade of a fig tree near the tower while Osherman made a trip up the stairs with the lighthouse keeper, a friend of Lady Scott's named Joseph Siddons. Lady Scott had already been up to see the oil lamps and metal reflectors. She was more than happy to stay with Jodenny and watch the ocean waves.

"It's said that a man can see his whole future from here," Lady Scott mused. "What do you see, Josephine?"

Jodenny wanted to see Myell walk across the grass. She wanted to throw her considerable bulk into his arms and knock him down and kiss him to pieces. She wanted to see the look of wonder on his face when he felt Junior kick or hiccup. Instead she saw Osherman returning from the lighthouse tower. His expression was relaxed and happy, and his face was tanned under the clear relentless sky.

Lady Scott, following her gaze, smiled knowingly. "He's a fine gentleman."

"He is," Jodenny agreed faintly.

She knew then, sitting in the shade, what she had to do. When Osherman reached them, smiling and satisfied, she asked him to take her for a stroll along the cliff line and they excused themselves from Lady Scott's company.

"I want you to do me a favor," Jodenny said as they walked along. She kept her voice calm and her gaze on the horizon. "You're going to say no, but it's only fair. It's something I should have done weeks ago."

"What's that?" he asked.

She decided she had to be looking at him to say the words. Jodenny stopped, took his hands, and fixed her attention on his face. She still didn't like his mustache much but he was handsome, no doubt about that, and he'd come a long way since their first days together. She supposed they both had.

"I want you to divorce me," she said.

The happiness on his face abruptly vanished.

"Don't be silly," he said flatly.

"It's not fair," she said. "I haven't been fair, that is. I haven't been very good to you lately. Everything that happened before this, though? It's gone. The *Yangtze* and living on Providence and all of it. What we were together is gone. We're something else now, but we're not lovers, and we won't be. I've been clinging to you, counting on you as a backup, but you deserve a true love of your own. Someone who's not me."

His gaze shifted from her face to the ocean. He took a deep breath but didn't say anything.

Jodenny cupped his face and made him turn back to her.

"I've been selfish and afraid for myself and for Junior," she admitted. "But I can stand on my own two feet. I need to stand, Sam. And I need you to be happy in your own right. Can you do that for me?"

His voice was shaky. "You don't know what you're asking."

"I think I do," she said.

The ride back to Lady Scott's house was made in silence and contemplation. Osherman would look at nothing but the view out the jostling window. Lady Scott snoozed, her head tipping against Jodenny's shoulder, and that was fine. Jodenny herself felt exhausted. When they reached Lower Fort Street, Professor Wallace hurried from his house to meet them.

"There's been terrible news," he told them breathlessly. "Tragic!"

Lady Scott allowed Tulip to help her down to the ground. "What happened?"

"They found Lady Darling murdered! Past Parramatta, on the way to Katoomba."

Jodenny couldn't help a little startled noise. Dead. Murdered. And all her secrets, gone with her.

Osherman, quick and angry, demanded, "Murdered? By who?"

Wallace's expression was stricken. "No one knows. The body was discovered half buried in the woods by a farmer out walking with his dogs. The corpse was in a sorry state. They identified her by her clothing and a ring the robbers overlooked."

Osherman stepped from the carriage and stalked inside the house. Jodenny tried to maneuver herself out and down, but Junior's bump made balancing difficult.

She was grateful for Tulip's helping hand and told him so.

"You're welcome, missus," he said, ducking his head.

She had the strangest feeling, then, that she'd known him at some other time outside of this tidy house. Not quite déjà vu, but something close. Jodenny bit her lower lip, thinking hard, but Tulip moved to help with the horses, and the feeling vanished.

Lady Scott and Professor Wallace continued to commiserate about the murder. Jodenny went in search of Osherman, who was in the dining room pouring himself some whiskey from a decanter. He downed three gulps, steadied himself, and splashed some more into the glass. His hat had been carelessly tossed on the table and he'd ripped open the collar of his shirt.

"Sam, tell me," Jodenny said.

He glared at her. "Tell you what?"

Though she too felt unsteady with shock, Jodenny followed her instincts. "Who she was to you. Why you're so distraught."

"I don't get distraught," he said, but that was patently untrue. He wiped his hand across his eyes. "It doesn't matter."

"Did you love her?"

Osherman turned away from her. Jodenny wanted to step forward and put her hand on his shoulder, but she didn't think he wanted that. He had always had more pride than was good for him. It was a pride that had been badly battered these last years, but had finally regained some footing here in Australia.

Either Lilly or Sarah had partially closed the curtains against the blazing afternoon sun. The stripes of light fell over Osherman like long streaks of paint.

Lady Scott and Professor Wallace murmured outside, the words indistinguishable.

"We were involved," Osherman finally said. "Before you came. And that's all I can say about it. Excuse me."

He left her standing alone in the dining room— alone but for a new idea about why Darling's helpfulness had seemed subtly laced with resentment. She wondered how far their romance had advanced before Jodenny's arrival had disrupted it. Maybe they'd been engaged. Maybe Darling had been hoping for a ring or a promise from a man who understood what it was like to be trapped in an age that was not her own.

Osherman went out for the rest of the day, and returned stinking drunk long after midnight. Lady Darling's murder was reported in the *Sydney Morning Herald* the next morning, with sensationalistic headlines. Murder was not uncommon in the colony but it didn't usually occur to women of high society. It was through the article that Jodenny learned that another body had been located along with Darling's. Her paid assistant. Both women were presumed to have been killed on the road by thieves. Their private coach driver was being sought for questioning.

The funeral was held the next day at St. Mary's Cathedral on Church Hill. On the way Lady Scott delivered a history lesson about Irish convicts and hidden sacraments, most of which Jodenny missed because she was too busy trying not to throw up. Her acclimatization to carriage travel had disappeared. Perhaps it was because Osherman was miserable company—withdrawn, haggard—or because the morning was abysmally hot. The breeze smelled like the slaughterhouses and flies were out everywhere.

"Why did people have to hide being Catholic?" she asked, to keep the conversation going.

"The government was Church of England, of course. Most of the Irish convicts were Catholic and obviously, that meant Catholics were troublemakers. The only services you could attend were Protestant." Lady Scott looked ill at the prospect, or maybe the carriage ride was nauseating her as well. "You actually had to go, or be flogged for being absent."

The cathedral was a large Gothic building built entirely of local stone. The mourners were arriving by foot, carriage, and horseback, decked out in their finest clothes and carrying on them the dust and sweat of the day. The dim interior was much cooler than the day outside, even with all the bodies crowding inside. It was long and narrow, running east to west, with small clerestory windows, a high arched ceiling, and an enormous stained glass window fronting the street. Lady Scott's stature got them to a row of hard pews cushioned by thin pillows, and Jodenny was happy to sit. Catholicism was mostly unknown to her. She didn't know the differences between one saint and another, or one Bible and the next, and the few Catholics she'd met in Team Space weren't especially illuminating on the matter.

"The organ came from London," Lady Scott murmured.

It played loud enough to be heard back in London as well. Jodenny fought the urge to hold her hands over her ears as a thin, bald organist worked the stops and pedals. She could still hear the echo in her head as the congregation rose for the arrival of Bishop Polding in his fine robes and very tall hat. When he began the service she thought maybe she was mishearing him, because not a single word made sense.

"Latin," Osherman murmured.

"I knew that," Jodenny whispered back.

It seemed to her that a bishop shouldn't be doing the Mass himself, but maybe the junior priest was sick or Darling's wealth earning her special note. Polding was sweating copiously under his layers of clothes. She was sweating, too, in a dress that ballooned around her like a camping tent. She hoped Myell, wherever he was, appreciated just how much she was going through in this semitropical limbo, and abruptly missed him so much that her eyes began to tear up.

She didn't want to weep in the middle of these strangers, in this strange and awkward land, so she concentrated on the unfamiliar Latin words and the response of the congregation when called upon. She assured Junior there would be no Catholicism in their future. Then again, she couldn't predict anything about their future at all. In her best wild hopes it would involve Terry Myell at her side, and a healthy Junior in her arms, and beyond that she could make no presumptions on the universe. None at all, not sitting there in her enormous dress in this Gothic cathedral with the heat and light of colonial Australia outside the windows.

She lost track of the Mass. She might have even dozed off once or twice. Certainly she wasn't the only one, because Bishop Polding's no doubt fine qualities did not, it seem, include succinctness. More than one elderly man and woman across the aisle nodded off during an exceptionally long passage. At one point the congregation stood and began to line up at the altar for communion, and Jodenny felt her dress and throat tighten so constrictively that she feared fainting. Even though they hadn't reached the part of the ceremony

that would commemorate Darling, she tugged on Osherman's sleeve.

"I have to go outside," she told him.

He immediately ushered her to the side aisle. She took
one look at the distance to the front door and gauged it
at a thousand steps, maybe a million. Osherman must
have realized she wouldn't make it, and steered her instead into an alcove and out into the sunshine. She felt
as if she were falling, spiraling into darkness, so maybe
she did faint after all. The next thing she knew, she was
sitting on a bench in a garden adjacent to the cathedral.
Osherman fanned her with his sleeve.

"Better now?" he asked.

"A little," she said. "I hate this."

"I know. Stay here, I'll go get some water."

She was sitting upright, fanning herself, when a concerned man's voice said, "Mrs. Osherman?"

Jodenny blinked up at the man. He looked vaguely
familiar, but his name eluded her.

"Benjamin Cohen," he supplied. "We met at Government House."

The same day she'd met Darling. Jodenny tried to look
more alert and not like a miserable pregnant woman.
"I remember."

"Is there anything I can get for you?" he asked.

"No. My husband will be back in a minute or two.
Do you want to sit?"

Cohen awkwardly sat on the far end of the bench.
"Such a terrible shame about Lady Darling. There have
always been robbers on the roads outside the city but
this kind of violence, this mayhem—it makes me think
the colony's no safer today than it was thirty years ago.
A trip to Katoomba should be as safe as a walk down
King Street."

"Was she a good friend of yours?" Jodenny asked.

"The most valued kind of friend. One who knows you from the heart inside out, and still accepts your weaknesses and foibles. The kind you might not speak to for years and years, and then the day you cross paths again, it's as if the conversation never had a pause. Do you have a friend like that, Mrs. Osherman?"

From inside the church came the murmur of the faithful.

"Not here," she answered.

Cohen smiled sadly. "I understand. When we first got here, it was a terrible adjustment. Learning the local dialects, customs, how to hide ourselves, protect ourselves. Some of us didn't make it. Cassandra never gave up, though. Surrender was not in her vocabulary."

Jodenny blamed the heat for the slowness of her thoughts. But she eventually collected enough of them to piece the story together.

"You were one of the children," she said. "You're from the future."

He replied, "My nickname then was Speed. I know that Cassandra told you part of the story, but I suspect she didn't tell you all. How we came here through the Painted Child. Where the Child is And what happened to Chief Myell."

Which was exactly when Osherman returned and found them.

CHAPTER TWENTY-EIGHT

Well, you see, I'm Chief Cappaletto and that's Chief Myell. He's the Hero of Burringurrah. Haven't you heard of him?"

Cappaletto had to do some fast talking under the aim of Ensign Darling's mazer. Myell would have interjected a word or two but he was sprawled on the floor, retching. He didn't know how many more trips he could make with Cappaletto's weight; the screech of the ouroboros was still ringing in his ears, and the migraine was so bad that the passageway flickered in his vision.

"Honest truth," Cappaletto was saying. "We're time travelers. The Roon army's going to be here in a few hours to destroy the Painted Child you're hiding somewhere in this mountain. But we've got a better plan."

Myell heard mazer fire. Cappaletto slumped to the floor.

"Search that one for weapons, Speed," Darling ordered. She crouched over Myell. "Now, you. Tell the truth. And I don't want to hear anything about time travel."

He took a steadying breath past the pain. "Your name is Cassandra Darling. You're in charge here because you're the oldest and no one else is suited for the job. There's Speed, Bell, Nelson, and the other girl—another little girl. I don't remember her name."

Darling stared at him, giving him nothing in her expression.

"The Roon army is on its way. They want the Painted Child. But you're going to blow the base up rather than let them get it, and everyone here's going to die. But if you let me help you, you can escape and still keep the Roon from getting what they want."

Silence. She squinted at him, tilted her head. "Okay, Future-man. You know everything? What's my middle name?"

"I have no idea."

"Fair enough. I don't have one. Come on. Sit up. No funny stuff."

He didn't think he was going to be able to stay up-right, not with the passage lurching wildly around him, but Darling sent Speed for a medical kit and, once in hand, gave Myell a painkiller. She handed him a canteen as well.

The water was flat and stale-tasting, but he was glad for it. Myell said, "So it's true? You've got a Painted Child somewhere on this base."

Darling sat down across from him in the middle of the dusty passage. Cappaletto was still mostly uncon-scious, but he was beginning to stir.

"Speed, go keep watch with the others," she ordered.

The boy looked rebellious. "Why?"

"Because I said so!"

He moved off, sulking. Darling said to Myell, "Tell me everything. As fast as you can, if it's true what you say about the Roon coming. Are you really the Hero of Burringurrah?"

"So they say," Myell replied.

"Jungali."

He gave a start at the name. "It's a long story."

"You better start talking."

So he told her as much as he could, as quickly as he could, as persuasively as he could. It wasn't easy. The migraine was fading but leaving him muddy-headed.

Many of the details of his travels were confusing despite the fact he'd lived through them. Darling was a tough audience, neither encouraging nor questioning him, until the end.

"So you think this Painted Child will let you save mankind," she said.

"Something like that."

"And if I take you to it, and the Roon get it, nothing matters because this has all already happened?"

Myell nodded.

"Protecting that Sphere is the only thing my dad ever made me promise to do," Darling said. She chewed on a dirty fingernail. "Don't let them get it, he said. Me and my mother both. Before they died in the bombs."

"Why didn't he destroy it himself?"

Darling rubbed her eyes. "Hope that it might work one day. That we could escape, when the day came. But that day's today, Chief Myell, and until you showed up, I didn't see much hope."

"Let me try to save you," he said.

Cappaletto groaned from the floor. Myell had to help him sit upright. Darling watched them with her mazer ready to fire again.

"We don't have much time," Myell said. "Last time, there were only a few hours or so between the time I woke up to the time the Roon came knocking. It's best that you gather up your team, Ensign."

She didn't move. "Here's the thing, Chief. Even if I take you down there, there's no guarantee we can get to it. The caves flooded a few years back, water everywhere. The Painted Child might be completely submerged by now. And even if we get there, it won't work. Captain Doubleday broke it."

The last pain of the migraine spiked behind Myell's eyes. "Who?"

"Captain Homer Doubleday," Darling said. "He showed up here, told my parents he was on a top-secret mission. He had a man named Sam with him. They used the Painted Child and we didn't see him again for a few years. Then he came back with a pregnant woman. Same kind of mission. My mom didn't believe him either time, but my dad did. He told us that the Roon were coming, that Earth was in jeopardy, but that a man named Jungali would save us all. After he was gone, the Painted Child never worked again."

"I don't understand," Cappaletto said. "He broke it?"

Myell got to his feet. The complexities of time travel made his head hurt. That Homer had come here years apart with Osherman and Jodenny confused him. Years apart? Though he'd rescued them both from Kultana before the Roon decimated the Fleet? Maybe Homer wasn't as good at time travel as he professed to be. Maybe he wasn't in control of his travels as much as he claimed.

"There's no time left," he told them. "Whatever he did to it, we'll undo. Either piss or get off the pot, Ensign. We've got to go."

Darling didn't move for a long moment. Then she stood, dusted off her pants, and clicked on her comm-set. "Speed, get everyone down here. We're going to the caves. Bring the controller."

Cappaletto asked, "Controller? For what?"

"In case I have to blow the place up after all."

She didn't believe Myell, obviously. Or didn't believe him enough. He was simply happy that she was willing to take them down to the Painted Child. Key to the

Dreamtime or not, it had suddenly, unexpectedly become the only clue pointing to Jodenny and Junior's location. Homer, that bastard. Whatever his intentions, he'd sent Jodenny and Osherman through the Child's ring on a one-way trip and doomed everyone on this base by blocking off their one avenue of escape.

The rest of Darling's crew joined them—Ammy with her missing teeth, Nelson with his filthy hands and face, and Speed with his thinly veiled suspicion. The youngest girl, Bell, was in Speed's arms. She cringed at the sight of two strange men.

"It's all right," Darling said. "That one there is Jungali."

"No he's not," Speed said.

Nelson squinted hard. "Doesn't look like a Jungali."

"He is," Darling said, with confidence. "Everyone follow me."

They all started down the ladder. Some of the rungs were broken or missing, though the children didn't seem to mind as much as Myell did. The lower decks were dark and moldy as they stepped downward, heavy with the emptiness of abandoned spaces—of plans that had gone nowhere, of people who had put forth their energy and hopes and were now nothing more than rotting bones.

"My mother was the base commander," Darling said as they climbed. "My father was in charge of Wondjina Transportation System research. They'd found the Painted Child here in the mountain and built the base around it, top secret, hush-hush."

"I never heard anything about it," Cappaletto said.

"Like I said, hush-hush. The whole world knew about the First Egg buried in Burringurrah, after all. This one, Australia wanted for itself. Besides, even before Captain Doubleday, it wasn't very reliable. Some days it worked like they wanted and some days it didn't work at all."

They reached the lowest deck in the complex. Myell was dismayed at the brackish water that pooled under his boots. Cappaletto asked, "Where exactly are we?"

"Jenolan Caves."

"Where's that?" Myell asked.

"Blue Mountains," Darling said. "About a hundred and seventy kilometers outside Sydney, if you take the roads. Less as the bird flies."

The hatch at the end of the farthest passage could be unlocked only by an alarm code Darling tapped into a keypad. The large metal slab groaned but didn't open.

"Stuff rots out," Darling said. "Speed?"

He put Bell down, ripped open a side panel, and fiddled inside. A moment later, the slab opened into darkness. Cool, humid air breezed past them. Stepping forward, Darling threw a switch that lit up a string of weak yellow lights embedded into the cave walls. The metal deck sloped downward into more water.

"Is it safe down there?" Cappaletto asked.

"Not really," Darling said.

An ominous clang sounded out several decks above them. Darling glanced upward apprehensively. Bell made a whimpering sound and Speed patted her back awkwardly. Myell, who had no intention of letting the Roon get hold of the children, gathered them up and ushered them down the passage.

The water was colder than he expected, and deeper, too. One minute Myell was shin-deep and then next he was soaked to his thighs. The deck became uneven as it descended, treacherous with hidden debris and slippery with some kind of lake slime.

"It's a little late to ask," he said, "but is there a map to this place? A wall diagram?"

Darling forged ahead of the group. "No."

"He's scared," Speed said, with obvious scorn.

Nelson wiped his hand across his mouth. "I'm scared, too."

"Don't worry," Darling replied. "It's not far."

The caves were limestone; the deeper they went, the more deposits Myell saw hanging from the ceiling like icicles or popping out of the water like jagged icebergs. Pretty formations. Dangerous, too. Catwalks and scaffolding had been erected to navigate the twisting passages, but some had fallen aside and others were completely washed away.

"Nice caves," Cappaletto grumbled. "You should sell tickets."

"Older than the dinosaurs, my mom said," Darling said over her shoulder.

As the water grew deeper and the footing more chancy, the two smallest children started having trouble. Cappaletto scooped up Bell and planted her against his hip. Speed glared at him, but he was submerged to his thin chest and couldn't help. Myell carried Ammy, who buried her snotty nose against his neck.

"Down here!" Darling called, from somewhere in the darkness up ahead.

Myell followed carefully, imagining a dozen different ways this was going to end badly. He heard Darling throw another switch. A power transformer snapped somewhere and an ugly buzz filled the air. No electricity surged through the water, which was a relief. The lights went out, though, which was a less fortunate development.

Darling's voice drifted through the darkness. "Damn it."

Cappaletto, sounding braver than Myell felt, asked, "Need some help?"

"Nope."

Bell said, "It's too dark!"

Speed said, "I told you it was the other onc. Let me have a go."

"Shut up," Darling said. Another switch clicked. Then another. The lights flickered and stayed on, and then a warm white glow filled the passage just around the bend ahead.

"Ha!" Darling said triumphantly.

Speed said, "That was just good luck."

"I'm cold," Ammy said, from the crook of Myell's arm.

Myell movcd forward, Ammy still clinging to him, and then stopped short at the sight in front of him.

The Painted Child was the most beautiful Sphere he had ever seen. The colors on it—aquamarine, coral, red like rubies—glowed beneath twin ceiling-mounted spotlights. Scaffolding that had been mounted along its far side was now half collapsed, and was hanging off like a floppy metal arm. There was no sign of damage to the Child, which gave Myell hope.

But most of the Sphere was submerged in the middle of this underground lake of limestone columns, and there was no sign of the Child's arched entrance.

Cappaletto let out a low whistle.

"That's what you wanted to see," Darling said. She hauled herself up on a rickety formation of broken cat-walks and sat on a sloped patch of grating while Speed and Nelson climbed over her. She kicked her feet into the water and threw Myell a challenging look. "Still think you can make it work?"

"Yes," he said. He hoped he sounded confident.

Cappaletto hooked one arm around the catwalk and hung off it with Bell still tight in his arms. "Where exactly does it go?"

"Right here," Darling said. "More or less."

Myell said, "I don't understand."

"It's not the where, it's the when," Darling replied. "This here's a Wondjina Sphere that transports you into the past. If the Roon get it, they'll be able to go into Australia's history and kill everyone and everything. See? That's why we have to destroy it."

Myell's hip was beginning to hurt under Ammy's weight. His legs were cold, and he was desperately keeping an ear out for any sign the Roon were on their way.

"You did destroy it," he told Darling. "In the permanent timeline. Now it's time to use it for an escape."

Cappaletto asked, "You believe her? That this thing is a window into the past?"

"You don't believe in time travel?" Myell asked.

"When you do it, it's different," Cappaletto said.

"Maybe." He'd suspected rings could transport travelers to different eras long before he became prisoner of his own personal ouroboros. Why should only the blue ring travel in time? "What year does it go to, Ensign?"

Darling kicked more circles in the water. "That's the unreliable part. One trip through, you might end up in 1830. Another, you're in 1862. Or 1870. Or 1800. You don't want to go to 1800, though. It's pretty brutal, Dad said. The point is, it goes all over the place. No rhyme or reason anyone could ever figure out. It could change several times a day, or stay the same for a week. Every trip was a surprise."

Several thoughts competed for Myell's attention. It was possible he could direct the Painted Child in a more specific way than the Australian scientists ever had, but he couldn't be sure. It was also possible Homer had indeed broken the ring permanently, though maybe he'd used futuristic technology or a Wondjina trick to disable it until Myell could arrive and activate it. Myell wasn't sure it was advisable to take the children through to the wilds of nineteenth-century Australia, but he didn't think trying to take them and Cappaletto through the blue ring was a good plan either. Besides, the ring wasn't due for hours, and the Roon must be in the base by now.

Ammy coughed against Myell's skin. "I'm really cold."

"I know." He rubbed circles on her back. "Tom, here, take her."

Cappaletto took Ammy on his free hip. "You going in there?"

"Yeah. To see if it's even passable."

"I'll go with you," Darling said.

"No."

She slid off the catwalk. "You don't know where the entrance is."

The water quickly deepened. Myell shivered at the coldness of it as he was forced to start paddling to stay afloat. He was wary of underwater hazards that might snag or cut into his legs—not only the stalagmites, but discarded equipment benches or cabinets, more collapsed scaffolding, poles or pipes or consoles. Something soft and sinewy slid by his leg and he nearly gulped in water.

"Anything live down here?" he asked.

Darling swam forward confidently. "Crocodiles, you mean? Nah. Maybe snakes."

It was only a dozen meters or so to the Painted Child. Darling felt along the Sphere's exterior, judging, measuring. She unhooked a flashlight from her belt and switched it on. "The opening's right about down here," she said. "You good at holding your breath?"

"Good enough," Myell said.

Darling gave him a wide grin and submerged.

Myell followed her. The water was clear and he had no trouble seeing the beam from Darling's light as she scissor-kicked downward. The anxiety in his chest ratcheted up another step. He'd been right to worry about equipment—the floor below was littered with discarded machinery and what looked like a small birdie of some kind. An airship, maybe, good for short-distance hops. All those scientists and all this equipment, and they'd never been able to accomplish their goals with the Painted Child. Perhaps his were equally doomed as well.

It was a relief to see the arch ahead. Three confident kicks inside it, Darling was already ascending again. Myell followed. He broke the surface and saw the dome a good five meters overhead. Luckily, the air didn't smell bad. He did some rough calculations about enclosed spaces and suffocation. This wasn't a spaceship, but the principles were the same. Even with eight people treading water and putting out carbon dioxide, they should be safe enough until the Child's ring came.

If the ring came.

"So what now?" Darling asked, treading water.

"We wait," Myell said. "See if it works."

The cold water was leaching heat from him, but it wasn't so cold that he had to worry about hypothermia for any of them. He could only hope that the flooding wouldn't prevent the ring system from recognizing him as an authorized traveler, or, depending on Homer's fiddling, as Jungali.

"When Homer came through, did anyone try to stop him?" Myell asked. "Find out what he was doing with a pregnant woman in tow?"

Darling thought about it. "I'm not sure. I was just a kid. I think he told my dad that he was working for Team Space."

"He's not. And if you ever see him again, you should be very careful. He's dangerous."

And my son, he almost said. But he left that part out.

The low, muted, watery sound of the ouroboros cut through the air.

Myell couldn't help a relieved smile. "It's coming."

He and Darling swam underwater, resurfaced outside the Painted Child, and called to the others to join them. Nelson and Speed immediately jumped into the water. Cappaletto had both Ammy and Bell to carry, and it was obvious he wouldn't be able to swim with both children clinging to him.

"Gimme," Speed said, reaching for Bell. "She's my sister, not yours."

Cappaletto said, "No, take this one. She's easier."

Myell started back, intent on helping them, but a loud rumble from somewhere in the base above them made him stop and tread water. More rumbles followed—explosions muffled by rock and metal that made the lake around them slosh in response. He turned to Darling.

"You weren't supposed to blow anything up!"

"I didn't!" she protested. "They must have tripped the bombs by accident."

The explosions faded. Myell's fears of the domed ceiling caving in on them faded. Cappaletto said, "Not too bad, then," as he swam steadily toward the Painted Child with Bell clinging to his back.

Then a side wall collapsed. An enormous amount of water gushed into the cavern and crashed into the catwalk where the kids had recently been sitting. The unleashed torrent smashed aside the flimsy metal as it poured into the lake. More water punched through another section, angry and destructive and roaring like an old-fashioned freight train. The gush sent Nelson smashing into Speed, who immediately sank with Ammy still clutched to his neck.

Myell swam forward as fast as he could. It had been a long time—too long—since he'd done speed laps in the swimming pool on the *Aral Sea*, but his muscles remembered their form and panic supplied more than enough energy. He grabbed Nelson by one arm, yanked him out of swirling new currents, and propelled him toward Darling, who was yelling orders. Speed and Ammy had surfaced, both spluttering and choking, and Myell reached the little girl next. He grabbed her in a lifeguard's hold while reaching out for Speed.

"Come on! Swim this way!" he ordered.

Speed shouted, "Where's Bell? Where is she?"

Cappaletto still had her, but both were in trouble. The smashing river had pushed them several dozen meters away from the remains of the catwalk and was tugging them toward the far end of the cavern, where archways marked other chambers. Bell was limp in Cappaletto's arms, maybe dead, but he wasn't letting go of her.

"Bell!" Speed yelled. He elbowed Myell in the face and tried to swim that way. "Save her!"

Myell's mouth filled with blood from the hard smack of Speed's elbow against his teeth. He spat out some, grabbed the kid by the scruff of his shirt and held him back. "You can't help them! Here, take Ammy! Get inside before the ring leaves!"

"Let me go!"

"I'll get them!" Myell promised.

Darling had come their way. To Speed she said, "You can't swim that far and you know it. It's no use to her if you drown yourself. Come on."

The roof started to make a heavy groaning noise. If it collapsed and smashed the Painted Child, none of them would survive. Darling, Ammy, and Speed made it to the submerged arch before the first rocks started to fall. Myell wasn't so lucky. He was several meters away from Cappaletto and Bell when a boulder the size of a laser cannon smashed into the lake beside him. Another slab of rock, this one the size of a flit, hissed down and sent waves of water flying into the air.

"Go back!" Cappaletto yelled, struggling to stay afloat. "Get out of here!"

"You can make it!"

More rocks hailed down. The lights flickered and half of them died, leaving the chamber in enormous shadows with some weak yellow illumination. Another portion of underground river had tunneled through the rock high above and was showering down like a waterfall. The shock and cold of it all had Myell's legs and arms tingling, but he wasn't ready to give up yet.

"Come on!" he shouted to Cappaletto. "Move your ass!"

Cappaletto might have raised his hand to give him

an obscene gesture—it was hard to say with the whole cavern shuddering and shaking and roaring in its death throes around them. One last bit of defiance would have been in keeping with his character. But Myell couldn't be sure. A fist-sized piece of million-year-old rock missiled down from the loose ceiling and smacked Myell on the side of the head. The cavern exploded in pain and darkness around him. He never saw Cappaletto again.

CHAPTER **TWENTY-NINE**

Jodenny sat perfectly still in Lady Scott's parlor. Her hands were gripping the pads of the armchair and her dress felt like a wardrobe of lead keeping her pinned in place. The house, the street, and the two men in the room had gone utterly silent, as if the whole world were contemplating the death of Terry Myell.

"I'm sorry," Cohen said, from where he stood by the window. His voice was as distant as his gaze. "That's the last we saw of them. Chief Cappaletto drowning with my sister in his arms, and your husband knocked unconscious."

Osherman had an unlit cigar in his hand. He wouldn't light it around Junior, but he looked mightily tempted. Jodenny herself wished for a large glass full of whiskey or Scotch, anything that would burn and numb at the same time.

"Then what happened?" she asked.

"Cassandra made me go into the Sphere," Cohen said. "I kicked and fought her all the way, but even then, she was stronger than me. The Child's ring brought us to the caves in 1825. I tried to go back, but the ouroboros wouldn't come. It never worked again. We were all alone in the middle of nowhere. Stranded with no money or help."

Jodenny felt a dim new appreciation of Darling. It was an incredible accomplishment—not just surviving, but thriving in the fledgling colony given their disadvantages.

"I'm sorry about your sister," she said.

Cohen looked down at his shoes. "I was all she had in the world, and I let her down."

Osherman rose, found the whiskey, and brought back the bottle along with two glasses.

"Give me some," she said.

"The baby," Osherman replied.

"Give me some before I smash the bottle over your head," she said, trying not to think of the rock that had slammed into Myell's skull.

He got another glass.

Jodenny drank only a sip or two. Not only because of Junior, but because she didn't want to lose the questions still rattling around in her head. It seemed like it had been days since they'd skipped out on Lady Darling's funeral Mass and come here, but it couldn't have been more than an hour. Lady Scott and Professor Wallace would no doubt soon return, and this wasn't a story for their ears.

"I knew Darling lied to me," she said. "She told me Terry brought her and the others here through the blue ring, but it doesn't go that far. Supposedly he can't travel earlier than his own date of birth."

Osherman scowled. "She told you?"

"And you didn't," Jodenny said, with a little spite.

"I didn't . . ." he started, but then trailed off. Whatever he did or did not do, he wasn't willing to finish the sentence.

Jodenny fixed her gaze on Cohen. "Why did she lie about that?"

"I think she didn't want to tell you about the Painted Child," Cohen said, after a moment of thought. "Not until she knew you better. She's always been fearful someone would discover it out there. Especially since the gold strike."

"You said it doesn't work," Jodenny said.

"Not for us," Cohen admitted.

"I want to see it," Jodenny said.

Osherman immediately rose to his feet. "No."

She gave him her sweetest, most insincere smile. "No?"

"Do you know what a hundred miles of wilderness is like?" Osherman snapped. "When the road runs out, you have to go on horseback. When the horses can't go any farther, you've got to walk your way in. Through the jungle out there. Past the poisonous snakes and bandits and more dangers than you can count. Even if you weren't pregnant, I wouldn't let you do it."

Jodenny said, "*Let me?* You think you can stop me?"

He pointed a finger at her belly. "I think Junior can stop you. Because that's Myell's child and all it would take is one fall on slippery rock to kill her. Is that worth it? Just so you can go out there and see where he died?"

"He's not dead," she said firmly.

Cohen raised an eyebrow.

Osherman's chest heaved from the exertion of shouting. "How do you know?"

"Because I held his dead body on Burringurrah, and still he came back to me," she said. "If you haven't noticed, my husband is extraordinarily hard to kill. I won't believe it until I see his corpse again, and even then I'll always have hope."

She no doubt sounded crazy to them. She sounded crazy to her own ears.

"The gods favor him," Cohen murmured.

"It's not a favor to him," Jodenny said.

"You can't," Osherman said. He made an obvious attempt to calm himself down. "Jo, it's not physically possible. You're eight and half months pregnant. Just to get out there you're talking about carriages, horses, hiking through swamps, and climbing up and down cliffs. Even assuming you get there safely and without going into labor, you'll have to crawl through limestone caves on your hands and knees. How are you going to do all that?"

Jodenny didn't answer.

Silence in the room.

Cohen cleared his throat. "Actually," he said, sounding embarrassed, "I have an airship."

Cohen's home was a tidy brick cottage near the piers at Miller's Point. He lived alone with six cats that he'd named after Shakespearean heroines: Juliet, Ophelia, Viola, and three more whose names Jodenny didn't catch. She was too busy staring at the airship, which looked like a toy version of a Team Space birdie. There were only three seats under the tinted canopy. The ship was dented and the hull had discolored over the years, but the engine ports looked in good order and Cohen claimed that it was entirely airworthy.

"You fly it around Sydney and no one's ever noticed?" Osherman said, cranky and skeptical.

"It's got cammie shielding technology," Cohen said. "Makes it invisible. And it's very quiet."

"Wait," Jodenny said. "How did it get here?"

"It was in the Painted Child when we came through," Cohen said. "Submerged in the water, at the bottom. It came with us through the ring. But the fuel cells were depleted. It's taken me all these years to devise a solar power generator and recharge them. And the engine card was broken. Took me ten years just to get it working again."

He held up a slim silver card. Jodenny recognized it as the same kind that were used to authorize birdies to launch.

"How long would it take to get to the Jenolan Caves?" Jodenny asked.

"About fifteen minutes," Cohen said.

"You goddamned bastard," Osherman said.

The next thing Jodenny knew, Osherman had his hands around Cohen's neck and had backed him into the wall of the little cottage. She said, "Sam, stop!"

"You had this ship," Osherman said, through gritted teeth. "You had it and you didn't tell Cassandra. Jodenny nearly died on the trip here! All of us could have died. And you had this fucking ship."

Cohen's eyes went wide with terror as he tried to free Osherman's hands. "Cassandra knew I had it! She helped! But we just got the card fixed," he wheezed out. "Two weeks ago. I swear."

Jodenny tried to pull Osherman's hands away, but he was much stronger than her even when she wasn't pregnant. "What are you talking about? When did I nearly die?"

"I swear!" Cohen said. "It wasn't working!"

"Let him go," Jodenny insisted, pulling again.

Osherman let go so swiftly that Jodenny stumbled backward and fell on her butt in the dusty yard. She was too startled to say or do anything. Osherman swiftly bent over her, contrite.

"Are you okay?"

"I'm fine," she snapped. "You're insane! When did I nearly die?"

He sat down beside her. Cohen, still gasping for air, remained standing against the cottage.

"Cassandra knew Homer," he said. His rage had fled, replaced by weariness. "They first met when she was a child, stationed with her parents in the military base under the Jenolan Caves. To transport people—to transport us—he needed the Painted Child. My trip went fine, but you went into shock. He was frantic. I don't think he expected that to happen. Luckily Tulip and his people were there. They took you to Cassandra's farmhouse outside Katoomba, where she was able to save you. Then she brought you here. You were unconscious for most of it. But remember when you first woke up? How tired and sick you felt? That was why."

Jodenny stared at him. "What does Tulip have to do with all this?"

"His people guard the Painted Child," Osherman said. "For thousands of years. Cassandra's parents, when they were running experiments, never figured out the pattern of when the time portal would open back here in Australia. Tulip's people aren't sure, either. But they always know when someone's coming through. They say the gods come in their dreams and tell them. Sometime the gods tell them to stay away from the visitors, and sometimes they tell them to help. You were one they were told to help. Me, too, apparently."

"I hate you," Jodenny told him, struggling to her feet. She slapped aside his helping hand. "Truly and deeply. Has there ever been a time in our lives when you weren't lying to me?"

Osherman looked wounded. "Like you told me that you talked to Cassandra? How long have you known about all this and not said a word?"

She turned her back on him. "Mr. Cohen, I would be very much obliged if you took me to the Jenolan Caves now. I want to see this Painted Child for myself. Because if my husband is alive—and he is, I know he is—it's the only way I'm going to be able to find him."

Cohen straightened his hat, which had gone askew under Osherman's throttling.

"We should bring Tulip." His voice was still shaky, but his resolve was evident. "He's an excellent guide. His people have been exploring those caves for thousands of years."

"I'm coming, too," Osherman said.

Jodenny said, "No, you're not. This thing only seats three people."

Osherman held up the engine card.

Tulip didn't shriek when they took him up into the air over Sydney, but that was because his eyes were squeezed shut.

"You can look," Jodenny told him. "It's beautiful."

He shook his head. "Thanks anyway, missus."

The colony really was beautiful from high above. Jodenny pressed her forehead against the canopy to look down at the streets and houses. There was the Australian Museum. Beyond it, St. Mary's Cathedral. Hyde Park and the Royal Botanical Gardens were wide grassy areas, lush and green. Sydney Harbor was a glittering blue that led to the even bigger glittering blue and green of the Pacific Ocean. From up here she could see the city's shape and energy as it built up and out; spreading down the coastline and inland toward the Blue Mountains, which Osherman said were not mountains after all.

"It's a plateau eroded by rivers over the millennia," he said as he flew them westward. "And the haze looks blue because of gum tree oil."

She would have answered, but didn't feel like speaking to him any further than absolutely necessary.

Turbulence made the airship lurch. Tulip uttered a quick word or two and then shut up again. His eyes were still closed.

Osherman glanced Jodenny's way. She ignored him and fixed her gaze on the Blue Mountains, or Blue Plateau, or whatever he wanted to call it. Their journey took no longer than Cohen had promised. City gave way to countryside and river, then to dense wooded forest and jutting towers of rock. It took Osherman some time to orient himself to the landscape, and the onboard nav system, dormant all these years, wasn't much help with local geography. Finally they set down in a clearing near a stream that pooled under a small waterfall.

"Tulip," Osherman said, as the canopy lifted above their heads. "What do you think?"

Slowly Tulip opened his eyes. He climbed out of the airship, found his footing, and turned in a wide circle. When he nodded his approval, Osherman let out a sigh.

Jodenny refused Osherman's help getting out of the

airship. She reached out for Tulip's help instead, and he obliged. The brief flight had left her feeling queasy. Or maybe it was the heavy mourning dress she'd been wearing since Darling's funeral.

"I've had enough of this," she announced, and ripped the petticoat out from underneath.

She left the undergarment in the airship as Tulip led them toward the waterfall. Along the way he picked up a big stick to use as a walking aide. Osherman did likewise, and scoured the ground for one for Jodenny as well. She accepted it without comment.

"Are you going to give me the silent treatment for the rest of our lives, Lieutenant Commander Scott?" Osherman asked.

"I thought I might, *sir.*"

He looked and sounded aggrieved. "If I made a mistake trying to protect you, I'm sorry."

Jodenny let that comment pass without reply.

Tulip ignored their bickering. The forest here was lush but not as cool as Jodenny had hoped; sweat rolled down her back and she wished they'd had the foresight to bring canteens. They hiked along the stream a bit before entering a grotto. High walls of jagged rock opened to the sky. Lush greenery and thick flowers flourished everywhere, fed by a wide high waterfall that sent a fine mist floating through the air. Jodenny decided she could stay in this grotto forever, an oasis in the hostile wild land. Of course, the place was probably crawling with poisonous snakes and spiders, or plants with poison leaves, or some other morbid death risk.

Their time in the grotto was far too short for Jodenny's liking. Tulip dug under some fronds on the ground and pulled out pitch-covered torches stashed there on an earlier visit. He slung a coil of rope over his shoulder.

"He's well prepared," Osherman said.

Jodenny saw a ripple in the pool beyond the rocks. Two small stones were floating their way toward her. She stared, perplexed. How could rocks float on water? They were moving her way quite deliberately and leaving ripples behind them. Greenish rocks, with dark centers—

Not rocks.

Eyes.

A crocodile, swimming steadily toward them.

She let out a yelp and backed into Osherman, who retreated as well. The giant reptile glided ever more steadily toward her, its snout now visible over the water. Tulip, however, was unimpressed. He waved the torch in front of the crocodile, scolded it in his own language, and held his ground.

Jodenny's heart was beating so fast she thought she might die of a heart attack before the crocodile could chew through their bloody carcasses. In just a few cold seconds she saw how stupid it was to have ever left Sydney, how ridiculously ignorant she'd been of the dangers of the bush. How stupid to risk herself and Junior out here in the wild. It was hubris, hubris and denial, that had brought her out here—and now Junior, Osherman, and Tulip were all going to pay the price.

The crocodile lifted its snout, growled at them, and then veered toward the waterfall.

"You scared it off," she said to Tulip.

"It's not here to frighten us," he said. "It was sent to guide us."

With that, he followed the rock ledge under the falling water and disappeared into darkness.

Jodenny took Osherman's hand, squeezed it hard, and followed.

The darkness was disorienting, made only slightly better by the burning torch in Tulip's hand. The waterfall pooling outside the cave was channeled by rock into an underground stream. Mammoth limestone stalactites dripped down from the ceiling in pale pinks and gold colors.

Osherman asked, rather nervously, "How far down are we going?"

"Long way," Tulip said.

"Don't you remember?" Jodenny asked.

"No. I wasn't in very good shape when Homer brought me through."

Jodenny concentrated on not losing her footing on the slippery rocks. The air was humid but not too dank. The floor was wildly uneven with limestone deposits and jagged rocks. She didn't see how Aboriginals could come down here in their bare feet. She and Osherman needed both hands to get over some of the sharp formations, and though her dress kept twisting around her legs, she was glad for the fabric's protection.

Junior wasn't a fan of the climbing and voiced her displeasure by kicking, squirming, and punching Jodenny's insides. It was ridiculously difficult, being pummeled from the inside while she tried to keep her balance on the outside. Tulip led them deeper and deeper, down sloping caves away from the water and light of day. The formations grew larger in size and the passages narrower in width.

"You come down here often?" she asked Tulip.

"Since I was a child."

Osherman was out of breath. "For fun?"

"To talk to the gods," Tulip replied.

They were so far underground and so deep into the maze that Jodenny wished she'd left a trail of breadcrumbs to follow back someday. If anything happened to Tulip or Osherman, she would wander around lost down here for the rest of her and Junior's undoubtedly short lives.

"What gods are down here?" Jodenny asked.

"Rainbow Serpent, he made these caves," Tulip said. "Long time ago, in the Dreaming. He and the other, they were locked in battle. The serpent came this way, carved his way through the earth, made all this."

"What other?"

"You've seen them," Tulip said, stopping for a moment.

Jodenny massaged her lower back. "Not down here."

Torchlight played across Tulip's face. "The gods are everywhere, missus. You know that."

Osherman sat down, his shoulders shaking. Jodenny didn't like the clammy look of his face. "Are you all right?"

"Caves," he muttered. "Never liked them."

She empathized. It was easy to imagine getting lost down here. Helplessly disoriented and frustrated by the labyrinth that had been carved by water through here over millions of years. The weight of the plateau pressed down on her, steadily squeezing, though the air still smelled good.

"Let's go," Osherman said, and pushed himself up.

They resumed their trek. Jodenny was exhausted clear through. Junior had quieted down with just an occasional kick. The floor leveled off for a bit, and then dropped away into a staggeringly fearsome valley of enormous rock growths that looked impossible to traverse.

"You didn't tell me it would be so hard," she said to Osherman.

He squinted at her. "Actually, I think I did."

"That was a joke."

"Oh," he replied. "I must have lost my sense of humor."

The last part was the worst. A sheer drop of more than five meters led down to a valley of stalagmites sticking up like enormous daggers. The short way down was a series of ropes and vines that had looked well-worn with age. The longer way was a tunnel that had been worn away to a steep slide.

Osherman said, "We can still go back."

Jodenny studied the slide and the ropes. She turned back to the tunnel.

"We've come this far," she said. "We're going all the way."

Prior visitors had left some supplies among the rocks, including stubs of yellow candles. Tulip fashioned a loop that went over her shoulders and under her arms. He lit one of the candles from his torch and gave it to her to hold in the palms of her hands. He and Osherman grabbed their end of the rope securely.

"Be very slow," she told them.

The descent was smoother than Jodenny expected, though maybe their definition of *slow* didn't match hers. The roof of the tunnel was close and she kept one hand on her head to keep from banging it. If not for her candle and its small circle of light, she'd be in utter darkness. After about five meters of sloping progress, the rope stopped moving and she came to a stop.

Fear flashed through her, but she ignored it. She tilted her head backward. "What's wrong?"

No sound from above. No sound from below, either. Just the heavy press of rock all around here, the deep and abiding silence.

Claustrophobia wedged itself under her breastbone and began to grind its way toward her heart. Jodenny lifted the candle, trying to see back to the small circle of the opening. "Sam? Tulip?"

She tried not to think of all the ways they could have come to harm—a spider bite, down here? That crocodile. Surely it wasn't moving around down here.

"Hey!" she shouted. "Answer me!"

The rope abruptly loosened, plunging her downward.

CHAPTER **THIRTY**

J odenny yelped. She tried to slow herself but there was nothing to grasp on to, nothing that her poor abused fingers could grab for a handhold. The slide narrowed and twisted like a fun-park ride and she tried to pull her knees up, desperate to protect Junior. The candle tumbled from her hand and was lost. Total darkness, terror now, and she screamed involuntarily.

Already her descent was slowing, however. Within seconds she was left sitting on bare rock, her legs and butt tingling while she gasped for air.

Her whole body ached but she didn't think she'd been injured, and Junior was squirming in a way that indicated no harm had been done inside. Still, her heart was beating so fast she thought she might vomit, and she was trapped in the pitch darkness deep in the caves, and the silence was so vast it might as well have been a vacuum. For a moment she was almost sure she was in the middle of the cosmos before the stars were born. The formless void, with her riding a rock ledge like some kind of magic blanket. There was no beginning and no end, no point of reference to hold and map against.

Pragmatism returned. She pulled herself to her feet and called out Sam's and Tulip's names until she heard a shout back. The two men appeared out of the gloom a few minutes later, and Osherman checked Jodenny worriedly for injuries.

"I'm fine," she assured him. "What happened?"

"Rope got snagged," he said. "You're sure you're all right?"

Tulip pointed beyond Jodenny's shoulder. "There she is."

The Painted Child was nowhere near as impressive as she'd been led to believe. Sure, it was large—as large as any other Child Sphere in the Seven Sisters. Yes, it was covered with Aboriginal designs and figures. But the colors were muted with dust and age, nothing special in the torchlight.

Osherman tugged on her sleeve. "You're okay?"

"I'm fine," she said.

Tulip retrieved more torches from the side of the wall and lit them. Jodenny still wasn't impressed. Slowly she circled around the Child. In her mind it was supposed to have scaffolding and spotlights. This was just a big round chunk of stone, hollow, with a dark archway leading inside.

Osherman was watching her carefully. "Going inside?"

Jodenny stayed several meters from the arch. "No."
He waited.

Tulip sat on the rough ground and watched them.

Jodenny put her hand on Junior's bump. She was immensely tired of being pregnant, and this long hike hadn't improved her disposition. Osherman had been right—without the airship, she would never have succeeded in trekking out here from Sydney. There was no particular reason to tell him so, though. Nor would she tell him that her legs ached and her back hurt and she had heartburn, though she hadn't eaten in hours.

Cohen hadn't been happy about being left behind and she wished now there'd been room for him. He could have pointed out exactly where in the underground cavern he'd last seen Myell. Then again, maybe that was a detail she didn't need burned into her brain. For all her brave words she was afraid that he really wasn't coming back to her again. Surely the favor of the gods ran out at some point as they went and found new humans to toy with, new fools to send careening across the universe on fruitless quests.

"Are you happy now that you've seen it?" Osherman asked.

"No," Jodenny admitted.

He put a hand on her shoulder. She didn't swat it away. He said, "Let's go. It'll be sunset soon, and I'm not sure how that thing flies at night."

Jodenny stared past the archway. "No. I'm not leaving."

"You're what?" Osherman asked.

"Not leaving," she said. "Not yet."

Osherman's confusion deepened. "Why not?"

Jodenny dropped her gaze to her skirt. Her face warmed. "Because I think my water just broke."

* * *

Something rough and hard nudged Myell toward the surface.

"Do I have to do everything for you?" a voice asked.

He broke from water to air and gasped in breath. The back of his head hurt as if it had been cleaved open with an ax. The lights hanging from the ceiling blurred and swung in his vision. Cold water pushed and pulled on him from all sides and he wasn't sure he was even treading water correctly—it kept sluicing up his nose, and his ears were full of it, and he couldn't stop choking.

He was sure he'd heard a voice, though. Even more sure that someone had pushed him to the surface. "Tom?" he asked. Of Cappaletto there was no sign. "Tom!"

No Cappaletto, no Bell. Darling and the rest had also disappeared. The ceiling was still trying to collapse into the lake and more rocks glanced off his shoulders and arms as he tried to protect himself. He knew it would be easier to simply sink into the cold black water but he started swimming away. His legs and arms didn't seem coordinated; they flailed around like the floppy arms of a marionette cut loose from its strings. The Painted Child telescoped away in his vision, then was so close he could almost touch it, and then his face smashed up against something else entirely.

Anger surged through Myell. All he'd ever wanted was a nice career in the military. He'd fled Baiame not in search of adventure but instead some travel, a steady paycheck, the chance to find himself. The best part was falling in love and marrying Jodenny. The worst part? Moments like now.

His fingers scraped by a metal pole and grasped it automatically. The next thing he knew, he was pulling himself up on the twisted catwalk and vomiting up water. The lights above him were blurry and indistinct; half had gone out, leaving the cavern in shadows. But he could see some kind of movement and that cheered him—Cappaletto and Bell must have somehow survived, because there they were on dry ground, pointing to him.

Myell squinted. Funny how one adult human and one little kid could look like heavily armored Roon soldiers. Behind them, more figures scurried through an opening in the wall, and wasn't it funny that they too looked like Roon.

Still coughing up water, he clung to the catwalk and evaluated his position. The metal wreckage had been pushed by the river to a point halfway between the Painted Child and the Roon's spit of ground. The water was still rising, but the ceiling was no longer collapsing in a hail of missiles. If he stayed where he was, he'd eventually drown. If he swam to the Painted Child and made it inside, he might drown before the ouroboros came. The blue ring wasn't due for several more hours, during which time the Roon would be happy to torture him.

The alien soldiers were now shouting at him in their own language, and some were starting to wade into the water. He didn't think that rescuing him, wrapping him in a warm blanket, and serving up hot soup were part of their agenda.

Myell let go of the catwalk and started swimming toward the Painted Child.

Osherman asked, "Are you sure?"

"I don't know," Jodenny said. Her skirts were wet, yes, but she was still two weeks away from her due date. Fear made her shiver. She couldn't imagine giving birth in this dark cave in the middle of nowhere.

Osherman was pale in the torchlight. "Maybe you had an accident. You told me sometimes, near the end, it could happen."

"I didn't piss myself," Jodenny retorted. But the Digital Duola was reminding her that it was indeed a possibility. She wasn't having contractions, after all.

"Sit down." Osherman helped her and looked at her clothing. "You need to clean up, and we need a dry cloth."

She knew what he had in mind. While Tulip and Osherman both turned away, she wiped herself. In the meager light she couldn't tell if the liquid was urine or amniotic fluid, though it smelled more like urine. Jodenny ripped off part of her skirt and folded it several times to form a pad. She lay back on the rock, waiting to see what slid out next.

"Maybe Tulip can go get help," Osherman said.

Jodenny knew then that she wasn't the only one who was frightened. "Middle of nowhere, remember?"

He sat down beside her on the rock. "Contractions?"

"No."

"Pain anywhere?"

"No."

"Can I get you anything?"

"Sam," she said, as patiently as she could. "Go walk around. Explore. Bond with Tulip. I'm not going anywhere."

He didn't go far, but at least now she had some breathing room. Jodenny turned all of her attention into her own body. Junior wasn't moving much so she prodded her belly and got a tiny squirm in return. Maybe Junior was conserving energy for the ordeal to come. She certainly didn't seem in any hurry to come squeezing between Jodenny's legs.

Stay in there, Jodenny thought. *Now's not a good time.* Not in this dirty place where Myell had drowned, or would drown in the future. For all her faith, now that they were actually here looking at the Painted Child, she couldn't make herself believe he had survived what Cohen had seen. Not with rocks raining down on his skull and the whole cave collapsing into rubble.

She wasn't carrying a watch, and there were no convenient clocks hanging on the walls. Jodenny had no way of telling time. Maybe twenty minutes or so passed before she dared prop herself up and check the pad. No more fluid had come out.

"What do you think?" Osherman asked, returning.

"I think it's okay," she said.

He grinned in relief. Jodenny smiled back, her anger forgotten.

Tulip, who'd been sitting on a rock contemplating the Child, abruptly stood up and walked toward the part of the cave that led upward. A moment later, Jodenny heard the scrape and patter of approaching footsteps. She sat up with Osherman's help and turned to watch. Seven Aboriginal men in traditional dress—which was not much dress at all, mostly paint and belts—had climbed down the ropes and vines. Tulip went to them, and held an animated discussion before he returned to Jodenny and Osherman.

"These are my brothers and cousins," he said. "They dreamt of the gods. They say it's time."

Osherman asked, "What time?"

"Someone's coming."

Which is when Jodenny heard the low, haunting sound of an approaching ouroboros.

* * *

Right now," Myell said into the darkness of the Painted Child, "I'll go anywhere you want. Whatever year. I mean it. But it would be especially helpful if you send me where Jodenny is."

If it were just a question of using the blue ring, he'd carve her name on his arm. But this was the Painted Child's ring, and if dozens of Australian scientists couldn't figure out how to direct it, he didn't have a chance in this freezing darkness, with the water pushing him up against the ceiling. The Sphere wasn't impermeable: somewhere air was being pushed out of cracks or tiny holes. In a few moments he'd be underwater and a few moments after that he'd drown.

He guessed that left him alone with the gods. Certainly the children had disappeared, as had the abandoned machinery that had been on the floor.

"I don't think I'm asking for much," he said, and in his mind he was directing the words to Kultana. He reconsidered. Maybe asking for anything at all was like lifting planets or extinguishing stars; maybe because it was so easy to do, he never considered the actual enormity of it.

Still, he didn't have much choice. If the ring came, it was going to take him away *somewhere*. Better to Jodenny and Junior, wherever Homer had stashed them.

Homer. Wind-not-sea. He hadn't had much time to think about having a half-human, half-crocodile son, and there wasn't much time left to worry about it.

The water kept pushing him higher. The ceiling that had been an arm's length away was now so close he had to tilt his head back, and still the stone pressed against his nose. He only had a few gulpfuls of air left. He couldn't calm his own panicked breathing. His legs felt like useless blocks of wood, long tired of treading water. There was no grip for his hands, nothing to hold on to. When lights appeared in the water around him, he thought it might be the ouroboros. But they looked more like beams of flashlights. Roon flashlights. He could see bulky shapes in their illumination, all of them moving in menacing silhouettes.

Water engulfed him.

Time ran out.

CHAPTER **THIRTY-ONE**

Osherman said, "It's not him."

Jodenny started toward the Painted Child. "You don't know that."

"It can't be him," Osherman said, cutting her off. "It's probably Homer. Whoever it is, it's not safe."

She pushed past stalagmites and slippery stone.

"Stay here," he ordered, and hurried pell-mell across the jagged floor toward the arch.

The Aboriginals from Tulip's tribe had formed a circle and were chanting something loud and repetitive. Tulip had not joined them, but instead was there to help Jodenny.

"Sam!" She took a few more steps forward, but her legs were weak and she couldn't get far. If not for Tulip's sudden assistance, she would have collapsed to her knees. "Sam, who is it?"

Silence from inside the Painted Child. The cavern filled with chanting, swelled up with it, and Jodenny's heartbeat stuttered in her own ears. If the visitor was

Homer, she was going to kill him. If it was someone unknown from the future, she was going to tear her hair out with frustration. If it was—

Water poured out of the Painted Child. Cold water, rushing out from somewhere inside in a surge. The sudden tide chased after Jodenny as she retreated. For a moment she nearly panicked, thinking the entire cavern would flood, but the displaced water from the future spread itself out and trickled to a stop. Carried out on the last of it was Osherman, with Myell's limp body in both arms.

Jodenny was on her knees now, her skirts and hands wet, though she didn't remember falling forward. Osherman spread Myell on the ground before her. His clothes clung to him like icy pajamas and his lips were blue.

"He's got a pulse," Osherman assured her. He put his lips on Myell's mouth and blew air into his lungs. No response. More air. Myell jerked, began choking. His eyes flew open. Osherman rolled him onto his side and more water came vomiting out of him.

"You're okay, you're okay," Jodenny told him, close to his ear, her hands patting him all over. Her face was wet. She wasn't sure if she was dreaming or had gone totally insane, because here was the only thing she'd wanted all this time, and he was alive and breathing and throwing up against her legs, which was okay, more than okay, super okay, extraordinarily okay, and she was kissing his cheek and jaw and neck, anywhere she could find skin, only peripherally aware of Osherman leaning back on his haunches and exhaling shakily, as if he were the one who'd drowned.

Myell finally focused on her, and his hands found hers in a crushing grip. "You're here? You know me?"

"Of course I know you." The words came out bubbled with a laugh and a sob. "It's about time."

He arched up and kissed her, and she wasn't aware of Osherman at all anymore.

His lips were cold; all of him was cold. But he was heedless of it, because here was Jodenny in his arms, just as he'd prayed. She was much bigger than the last time he'd seen her, and somehow she managed to look beautiful and exhausted at the same time. Myell put his hand on Junior's bump and was rewarded with a kick.

"She knows you're back," Jodenny said, her eyes moist.

Myell forced himself to sit upright and look around. The cavern looked a lot different when it wasn't covered with catwalks or filling with water. The Painted Child looked dustier than it had in the last eddy. Sam Osherman was standing nearby with a tall Aboriginal man, and the expression on Osherman's face was inscrutable. A half-dozen other Aboriginals were gazing at Myell as if he were someone they'd been expecting.

"What year is it?" he asked.

Jodenny couldn't stop patting his cheeks, as if proving to herself he was really there. "1855."

"Homer?"

"Haven't seen him."

Myell turned his attention back to Jodenny. "You climbed all the way down into these caves?"

"Thought I'd go sightseeing," she said, and buried her head against his neck.

He held her for several minutes, rubbing her back, murmuring in her ear any words he could think of to ease her trembling. It wasn't about words, of course. It was about holding and being held, and of tragedy nearly averted. Again.

Myell swung his gaze to Osherman. "Thank you."

"Part of the service," Osherman said brusquely.

That Osherman could talk surprised him. It took a moment for him to remember the neural plug he'd been told about on the *Confident*. Tulip reminded them that sunset would be coming on fast aboveground, and it was best to get moving soon. Myell was still cold and soaking wet, and he was going to have spectacular bruises in the morning, but he was an enthusiastic supporter of any plan that got them out of the caves and up to fresh air and open skies.

As they made their careful way upward, escorted by half a dozen Aboriginals and Osherman, he grew increasingly appalled that Jodenny had hiked down here in her condition. The descent had been relatively easy in the military complex, but it was downright treacherous now. Surely she was exhausted. Climbing around couldn't be good for Junior, either. He helped as much as he could, but his own balance and strength weren't at their best, either, as proven when he slipped and landed hard on a patch of mossy limestone.

"We're halfway to the surface," Osherman said, hauling him back to his feet. He stripped out of his jacket. "Take off your wet shirt and put this on."

"I'm not cold," he insisted.

Osherman gave him an exasperated look. "Your teeth are chattering."

Jodenny, who had squeezed through a passage ahead of them, called back to see what was taking them so long. Myell swapped his wet shirt for Osherman's jacket and was slightly warmed.

"You're all she's thought about since she got here," Osherman said.

Myell didn't know what Osherman wanted from him. "Thanks for taking care of her."

Osherman motioned for Myell to precede him through the passage.

The last part of the ascent was a blur of magnificent stone formations and the increasing buzz of fatigue in Myell's brain. When they stepped out of the caves into a grotto of some kind, it took Myell's eyes several seconds to register the sight of stars in the dark trees above. Jodenny immediately sank to the ground and he joined her there, holding her in both arms.

"How do you feel?" he murmured.

"Never been better," she said. "You?"

"Great."

She traced the line of his jaw with her hand. "Liar."

"You lied first."

"Actually," she said, "you lied. On the *Confident*. And took off in that shuttle without me. We're going to have a long talk about that, mister."

He asked, "Is it too late for an apology?"

Jodenny kissed him. "We'll discuss it."

Tulip spoke to his people and then to Osherman in words Myell couldn't hear. The Aboriginals all disappeared into the dark forest. Osherman crouched low beside Myell and Jodenny.

"I don't think we should go back to Sydney," he said. "Cassandra kept a farmhouse near here. I think I can find it, and I know the housekeeper will let us use it. Do you trust me?"

"Yes," Jodenny said.

Myell nodded, though he wondered why trust was an issue. They didn't really have much of a choice. Then Osherman showed him the little airship sitting on the forest floor and confessed that he wasn't sure he could find Darling's house in the dark.

"We trust you," Jodenny repeated.

The seating was limited, but once aloft Jodenny dozed off against Myell's side and that was all right. Osherman was focused on the controls and the landscape below, which was lit mostly by the silvery light of a full moon rising in the east. There were so many stars that Myell lost track trying to count them. He was too tired to make casual conversation but full of questions.

"Darling?" he asked. "She's here?"

A muscle twitched in Osherman's cheek. "She was murdered."

A moment passed as Myell tried to absorb that. "The other kids?"

"They're not kids. They've been here thirty years."

"Oh," Myell said. "They're okay?"

"I need to concentrate on flying this thing," Osherman said.

Myell blinked down at the countryside below. He couldn't make out many details at all, but the flight console had a scanner that picked out individual homesteads and farms from the trees and foliage. After several minutes of orienting himself, Osherman let out a "Gotcha!" and set the airship down on a plot of land behind a long low building nestled against wooded hills. No lamps burned inside.

"This is the place," Osherman said. "You need help?"

"No, I've got her."

Jodenny was hard to rouse and harder to keep on her feet. By the time Myell had her inside, Osherman had lit three lanterns and started a fire in the main hearth.

The house was decorated with hand-carved furniture, thick rugs, and European paintings; Darling had done well for herself, Myell observed.

"There are two bedrooms down the hall," Osherman said, tending to the fire. "Take the one on the right. I lit a lantern in there."

Myell had never been happier to see a bed. The room was small but nicely done up, and the yellow lantern cast shadows on silver wallpaper. Jodenny sank on the bed with nary a protest and started to pull off her dress. Her fingers were clumsy and her voice was drunk with weariness.

"You have to be nice to Sam," she said. "He's been through a lot."

He kissed her nose. "Yes, ma'am. Love the dress."

"You should see what's under it."

"My firstborn child?"

"Petticoats." Jodenny stared down at her own bare legs once the dress was gone. Perplexed. "I swear there were petticoats. Where'd they go?"

"Are you hungry?"

"Thirsty."

He went to find the kitchen. All his bruises were making themselves known, and he knew that come morning he was going to be paying for them. Osherman had disappeared from the living room. Myell was too tired to wonder where he'd gone. The sink didn't have running water, but there was a hand pump that brought water in from a well or rain barrel. Myell sniffed it, decided it was all right for the time being, and brought it back to Jodenny. She was already asleep, her face mashed into the pillow.

Myell was tucking her in when Osherman brought in a serving tray. "The housekeeper lives just down the road. She gave me some cheese, these apples, some pie. She'll come up in the morning to cook breakfast."

"You've been here a lot," Myell said.

Osherman left the tray on the side table. "See you in the morning."

Myell bit into one of the apples, discovered he was famished, and finished it before his stomach began to revolt. He stripped off his own clothes, climbed into bed next to Jodenny and Junior, and was asleep before he could even figure out how to turn down the lantern wick.

Someone else took care of it, or else it burned itself out, because when he opened his eyes again the room was entirely dark. He was certain that he was back in the Painted Sphere with water rising all around him. He gasped for air, kicked his legs. Firm hands caught his wrists.

"Stop," Jodenny said. "Wake up. You're okay."

As his eyes grew accustomed to starlight through the windows, he saw that she was lying beside him with Junior's bump between them.

"What?" he asked.

"You were dreaming," she whispered. "Go to sleep."

He slipped underwater into more bad dreams in which he couldn't save Cappaletto or Bell. When sunlight hit his eyes he turned to the wall and pulled the bedspread over his head. He woke much later when the taste of butter reached his tongue. Pushing the blanket aside, he blinked at Jodenny sitting on the bed and smiling at him. She had been painting his lips with her finger.

"Humph?" he asked, as articulately as he could.

"Time for breakfast," she said. "There's a housekeeper

here named Mrs. Dunbar, and I think I love her. She made pancakes."

Getting out of bed was a good idea, but not as easy as he'd hoped. His whole body ached in bone-deep ways, and all his muscles had stiffened during the night.

"Maybe I'll bring it to you," Jodenny said, leveraging herself to her feet.

Shame got him to his feet and toddling after her. The house was larger by daylight than he remembered, which meant more walking, which meant more pain radiating up his legs and back. What he wouldn't give for a painkiller or two. The sight of the pancakes cheered him up, as did the smell of good old-fashioned coffee.

Jodenny watched him shovel food into his mouth, a fond smile on her face.

"Aren't you going to eat?" he asked.

"I had my turn," she said.

"Where's the commander?"

"After all this time, I think you can call him Sam."

Myell poured himself more coffee. "I think you can call him Sam. He's still Commander Osherman to me."

Mrs. Dunbar, round-faced and perfectly cheerful, bustled in with some fresh eggs. "It's good to have people in the house again," she said. "Lady Darling, she always said to treat Captain Osherman like one of the family."

"And now he's a captain," Myell mused.

Jodenny squeezed Myell's hand. "Not that kind."

"Will you be staying long?" she asked.

Myell's gaze drifted to the mantel clock he'd seen in the living room. It was almost ten o'clock. He was startled he'd slept that long. Jodenny's grip tightened on his fingers and he realized she hadn't been thinking of the clock at all.

"Yes," Jodenny said tightly. "We'll be staying for several days."

"I'd better see how the cows are doing," Mrs. Dunbar said.

She left the kitchen. Myell concentrated on his pancakes and tried not to flinch under Jodenny's stern expression.

"You're not going," she said.

He tried to think of something reassuring and soothing to say, but the words didn't exist. He settled for "Nothing's changed."

"Nothing's changed." Her cheeks turned red with outrage. "Nothing's changed?"

Myell had been warned that pregnant women could be mercurial, but he wasn't prepared for the full reality.

"I'll tell you what's changed," Jodenny said. "See this belly? It's changed. See my body? It's changed a lot. See the view outside these windows? This is nineteenth-century Australia. Does that sound like home to you?"

"It's not about—" he started.

But she was just warming up. "I've been stuck here with flies and open sewers, and do you know what a Team Space supply officer does around here? Nothing! She does nothing. She sits around and goes to tea parties and tries to save babies whose mothers are going to kill them anyway."

Myell shut his open jaw. "And she talks about herself in third person."

"It's not funny," Jodenny said.

"No." He pushed his plate aside. "It's not."

She didn't burst into tears, but looked close to the breaking point. Myell got out of his chair, came up behind her, and wrapped his arms around her so she could lean backward.

Jodenny sniffed. "When?"

"This afternoon," he said. "I'm probably back to every twenty-four hours or so."

She shook her head. "I'm not letting you go."

He didn't say, "You can't go with me," because that was as obvious as the sunlight streaking through the window. They both remembered what had happened when she went from Providence to the *Confident*. They couldn't risk that again, not so close to Junior's arrival. Not even if Junior dropped out in the next few minutes; who knew what the ring could do to a newborn?

Myell kissed the top of her head. It wasn't enough, of course, but it was all he had at the moment.

Osherman came in the kitchen door, stomping dust from his boots. "Well, we have a problem with the airship."

"What problem?" Jodenny asked.

"It's gone."

She sniffled. "Are you sure it's not just invisible?"

"Pretty sure, yes."

They searched the yard, but found no airship either visible or invisible.

"Maybe it drifted off," Jodenny suggested. "Like a balloon."

Osherman said, "I don't like it."

"Speaking of things you won't like," Myell said, steeling himself, "I need to tell you both about Homer."

The house had a shaded front porch and the day wasn't too hot out yet. A breeze washed over them as Jodenny sat in a rocking chair, Osherman leaned against a post, and Myell stood against the railing. He needed something to do with his hands and so he picked up a handful of pebbles and began pitching them, one by one, at a eucalyptus tree a few meters away.

"It started when I was with Commander Nam's team," he said. He told them about that long-ago day when he'd been rescued from the ocean by Free-not-chained, and later how she'd saved him from a shark attack, and how the rescue had been more intimate than he expected or wanted.

"Define intimate," Jodenny said, her expression dark.

"I was barely conscious," he said. "I didn't realize what she was doing."

Jodenny looked away. Osherman said nothing.

Next he told them about meeting Free-not-chained again, and the man-seal who'd told him about the son he hadn't expected. A son who was fully grown and in trouble with the Wondjina gods, and who just happened to be the one who'd stranded Jodenny and Osherman here in the past.

"Let me get this straight," Osherman said when he was done. "You have a son who's a half-crocodile. He angered the gods, stranded us here, lied and misled just about everyone, and now his mother wants you to intercede and release him from some kind of purgatory or curse."

Myell had no more stones to throw.

"I think that's about it," he said.

Jodenny covered her face with both hands. Her shoulders shook. Myell didn't know what to say or do. He went to his knees in front of her chair and put his hands on her knees.

"I'll fix it," he promised. "Whatever I have to do."

She pulled her hands down. Her expression was half amazement, half amusement. "They never mentioned this kind of thing in officer training."

A knot loosened its hold on Myell's heart. "You're not mad?"

"I'm furious," she said. "But not so much at you."

Myell kissed her soundly.

Osherman said, "I'm going to take a walk," and left.

Myell glanced after him, wondering if he should follow. Jodenny wrapped both hands around his head and pulled him tight. He breathed in the smell of her—cities and caves and places he hadn't been with her, hadn't shared.

Her lips broke free of his and she made a lewd suggestion against his ear.

"You're kidding," he said.

"You don't know much about pregnant women, do you?"

"We'll squish the baby."

"No, we won't." Her smile was wide and genuine and dirty. "We just need some pillows and some creative positioning."

He was still doubtful as she pulled him into the room, and even more doubtful once she'd shed her dress, but she was gorgeously lush in the morning light, all curves and soft skin and wide-eyed under his touch.

"I'll be back," he said. "Wherever it takes me, I'll come back. I won't leave you."

"Sssh." Her hands slid around his waist. "Right here, right now, it's only us. Stay with me."

So he did.

They slept until a dog barked somewhere, loud and obnoxious. Myell woke famished. The sun stood at midday and the hot air was still.

"Food?" he asked her.

"Great idea."

He slid out of bed, fumbled into his pants, and padded barefoot down the hallway. The house was empty and peaceful in the bright light. He was halfway to the kitchen when he saw Osherman sitting in the living room. A moment later he realized the man wasn't Osherman.

"Hello, Chief," the man said.

Myell squinted. He didn't recognize the stranger— not his pale face, his thin hair, or his well-cut clothes.

"Do I know you?" Myell asked.

The man patted the pistol that was resting in his lap.

He said, "You knew me when I was named Speed."

CHAPTER **THIRTY-TWO**

Jodenny was dozing off again. She thought she'd heard voices, but it was easy to ignore them and luxuriate in the comfort of the sturdy bed. When footsteps came down the hall she forced herself awake to greet Myell. Instead, Osherman walked into view. She grabbed the bedsheet and pulled it up to her neck.

He glanced her way and flushed.

"Where's Myell?" he asked.

"Not far." The sheet seemed woefully inadequate for the task of hiding, but Jodenny pulled it tighter anyway. "Why?"

"I talked to Tulip, and he had an idea or two," Osherman said.

He carefully avoided looking at her, which Jodenny

decided was ridiculous. They'd shared beds together, after all. In the permanent timeline, they'd been married. Still, logic had nothing to do with it.

"He was just here," Jodenny said. "Is he in the kitchen?"

Osherman went to find him. Jodenny got herself out of the bed, pulled her dress back on, pined for the luxury of a hot shower, and went after them. The living room was empty and Osherman was alone by the stove.

"Outhouse?" Jodenny suggested.

Osherman went out into the yard, and returned shaking his head. He scanned the countryside. "He can't have gone far."

"He wouldn't go anywhere," Jodenny protested. "Not on his own."

"Homer," Osherman said.

"Why would Homer take him away?"

"I don't know. But if not Homer, then who?"

A gunshot cracked through the air.

Myell risked a glance over his shoulder. "Where are we going, Speed?"

"The name's Cohen."

The dirt road wound past Lady Darling's farmhouse and through the deep woods. Flies hovered in the hot stillness. They were the only two people on the road. Maybe the only people for hundreds of kilometers, as far as Myell knew. He had only the vaguest sense of the surrounding geography—Cohen hadn't seen fit to give him a map. Myell's feet were bare and he was sweating in the heat. Cohen was also sweating under his hat and city jacket.

The pistol was unwaveringly fixed on Myell's back, sweat or no sweat.

"Tell me why you want to kill me?" Myell asked.

"I don't want to kill you," Cohen said. "You're going to drown yourself in the lake on the other side of this hill. It's not far, near where I parked the airship. Your stupid friends never thought to check if it had a recall device."

"Oh." Myell kept walking. "Why am I going to drown myself?"

A pistol shot whizzed over his shoulder.

Myell jerked and stopped walking, at the risk of a bullet through his back. "Bell," he said in sudden realization. "This is about Bell?"

"Keep going." Cohen's voice was brittle with anger. "I'm not kidding. I'll kill you here. I killed Darling for less."

"You killed her?"

"I had to. She was going to stop me from using the airship to go back through the Sphere and save Bell from drowning."

That plan was so fundamentally flawed that Myell lost his breath for a moment.

"It wouldn't work," he managed to say. "She didn't drown in the permanent timeline. She died with you and Darling and the others when you blew up the base. There's nothing there now but debris and rubble."

Cohen spat out, "According to *you*. Why should I believe anything you say?"

Damned if Myell was going to be Cohen's next victim, not because of some crazy plan and in the middle of nowhere with Jodenny and Junior so close by. He hadn't even had the goddamned chance to say goodbye. Myell turned and swung out. Cohen fired the gun again, sending the bullet in a wild trajectory by Myell's midsection. He didn't want to see if he'd been hit. He threw himself forward with fists and kicks, knocking Cohen into the dirt. The pistol fell aside with a solid thud.

Though Myell was sore and bruised already, he was still younger and stronger than Cohen. The boy who'd been known as Speed cringed at the blows, returned them slow and clumsy.

"You killed her!" Cohen was saying. "You let her drown!"

Myell landed a punch square on Cohen's jaw that made the older man's head snap back into the dirt. Myell grabbed the pistol and staggered upright, keeping it aimed at Cohen's chest. His knuckles sang with pain and his throat was tight with fury.

"I would have saved her," Myell said. He spat out a wad of blood. "All of them. Don't you think I would have saved all of them?"

Someone was running up the road toward them—Osherman, armed not with a gun but a knife. Jodenny was hurrying up the road after him, slowed by Junior. Myell wiped sweat from his eyes and kept the gun aimed at Cohen.

"Twig and Kyle," he said. Their names were bitter in his mouth. "Cappaletto, Adryn, Nam. Your sister. I couldn't save any of them."

Cohen's face was wet with tears and blood, and racking sobs shook his body. "You killed her."

"No," Osherman said, slowing to a stop beside them. His gaze was steady on Myell, his voice confident. "He didn't kill anyone. He just didn't save her."

Myell felt as if he'd been slapped. The sting was refreshing in its own way, a confirmation of everything he knew.

"Bell died when Darling blew up the base," Osherman said, still looking only at Myell. "I'm sure I died, bitter and old, on Providence. Jodenny, too. Cappaletto must have died in the Roon mines. Kyle and Twig had their own fates. Chief Myell gave us second chances, and there's nothing wrong with that."

Jodenny was still coming up the road, too far to hear them. Myell shook his head. "Second chances that didn't work out."

"Worked out for me," Osherman said. "Jodenny's here. Cappaletto died free. You think that doesn't matter?"

"I didn't save the fleet at Kultana," Myell pointed out.

Osherman shook his head in exasperation. "Oh, sorry. One single man didn't save all of mankind from an armada of invading ships. That's your crime?"

Cohen was still sobbing.

"It can be done," Myell said.

Osherman clearly didn't believe him.

"The Flying Doctor tried to stop me because it's possible," Myell said. "I still don't know how, but this isn't over."

Jodenny arrived. Myell took her into his arms, reassuring himself that she wasn't going to faint from the heat and exertion. She felt his arms and torso, looking for injuries that weren't there.

"I'm never letting you out of my sight again," she said.

"What about him?" Osherman said, his gaze on Cohen.

"He killed Darling," Myell said, feeling empty and drained. "He told me."

Osherman's face turned a mottled red. He held out his hand for the pistol. Myell glanced at Jodenny, who was watching them all with a stricken expression.

Something was going on here that Myell didn't quite understand.

"Commander?" he asked carefully.

"I'm not going to kill him," Osherman said firmly. "Give me the gun."

Myell hesitated some more. Flies buzzed in his ears and around his head. Osherman looked angry but not out-of-control homicidal angry. Slowly he handed over the pistol and walked away. He met Jodenny in the road and fell into her arms.

"You're okay?" she asked. Her hands again felt for injuries. "Are you hurt?"

"I'm fine," he murmured into her neck.

A pistol shot had them both whirling around in the road. Osherman had shot Cohen. Not a fatal wound in the torso or head but instead in the knee. Cohen rocked and screamed in agony. Myell wondered if a fatal shot wouldn't have been more merciful.

"That was for Cassandra, you son of a bitch," Osherman said.

The airship that had returned to Cohen in Sydney and then come back again was down to dangerous levels of power, but Osherman thought they could make it.

"Make it where?" Jodenny asked. She was clinging to Myell as if the strength of her grip could keep him safe from the blue ring. "Where is there to go?"

Osherman leaned against the ship. "Your crocodile girlfriend said you need witches or shamans, so I talked to Tulip. His people can call the Wondjina gods. They're gathering now at the Painted Child. If we hurry, we can make it before the blue ring comes again."

Jodenny frowned. "Why do we want to talk to the gods?"

"Not us," Myell said. "Me. To make an appeal."

"To save Homer?" she asked skeptically.

Myell's voice neutral. "To save mankind. To make the Roon vanish at Kultana. Just like they did on Burringurrah."

They tried to leave her behind, of course. Jodenny would have none of it.

"Besides," she said. "If you leave me here, Homer might show up. What would I do against him on my own? Me, pregnant and barefoot and helpless."

Myell had glanced at her feet. "You're not barefoot."

Osherman added, "You're hardly helpless."

She gave them both a cold smile. "And I'm not staying here, either."

The second trek down into the caves went faster than the first trip, for this time they knew the way and had a deadline careening closer with each minute. Jodenny knew she couldn't afford to slip and fall. Couldn't afford it for Junior or Myell. She sipped from the canteens they'd brought and let Myell help her over the tricky parts and yelled at herself because they had so far to go, and she was holding them up. She and her stupid fat ungainly body.

"We're almost there," Osherman said, so often she wanted to poke him between the eyes. But the trip was no easier for him, either. His breathing was short, and he kept glancing around at the walls as if expecting them to close in farther.

Tulip and the men of his tribe had already assembled by the time Jodenny, Osherman, and Myell made it to the Painted Child. The Aboriginals had started a small smoky fire, made markings in the dirt, and painted themselves with ocher. Jodenny wondered if that was how the Aboriginals of Shark Tooth's tribe had prepared themselves for sacred tests and ceremonies. Those people were separated from these by only a few hundred years. The saved and the almost-destroyed, just a Sphere's travel apart.

"What do I have to do?" Myell asked.

Tulip eyed his shirt.

Bare to the waist, Myell sat on a rock and let Tulip paint him with symbols. Jodenny itched to do the job herself but she didn't know the designs and she understood that women's magic was different from men's magic, at least to these people, and she couldn't afford to upset the balance. Osherman watched with obvious impatience, keeping an eye on his pocket watch.

"How much time?" she asked.

He shook his head.

The Aboriginals were chanting now. Jodenny didn't understand a word of it. Myell didn't either, judging from his expression, but he lifted his head and pinned her with a gaze.

"Whatever happens, don't go in there," he said.

She knew he meant the Painted Child.

"Promise me," Myell said.

She didn't recognize her own voice. "I promise."

"Don't let her, Commander," Myell said to Osherman.

Osherman's hand was white-knuckled on his watch. "After all this, you should call me Sam."

The Painted Child began to sing.

Jodenny hadn't expected that. She whirled in amazement as the colors across its surface began to glow with life. Corals and blues, green like deep summer leaves, yellow like the sun. She'd witnessed the First Egg in all its glory on Burringurrah but this was a more intimate display, filling her with warmth and building excitement.

Tulip said, "They're coming."

"The gods?" Osherman asked. His voice was higher than normal. "Right now?"

The torches all around them flickered and died. The Painted Child swirled in Jodenny's vision. In its rainbow depths she saw more Spheres, spinning around each other in exotic orbits. Junior had gone still in her womb, as if entranced by the vision of something she couldn't see.

Tulip pushed Myell toward the archway. "They're here."

Myell turned to Jodenny for one last, desperate kiss. "I'll be back," he promised.

Jodenny saw the Painted Child in his eyes. Felt the Painted Child swell inside her heart. Heard a great rushing, like the first winds of the world sweeping out of the core of the earth upward in a great rush.

The caves dissolved.

The plains of the Dreamtime stretched around Myell, but it was no Dreamtime he'd ever envisioned. The land was a jagged ocean of blue ice. The sky above was dark and starry, and full of exploding starships. The *Confident*. The *Melbourne*. Red and gold bloomed like deadly flowers low on the horizon. The best last hope of mankind died under the Roon onslaught, silent screams rolling across the icy landscape.

He expected to be alone but Jodenny and Osherman

were beside him, bewildered. The men of the Eola, Tulip included, sat in their own circle, unperturbed by the strangeness of their surroundings.

"This is Kultana?" Osherman asked.

"One version of it," Myell said. "An aspect."

Before them was an icy blue-white mound twice as large as any human body. A boomerang was jutting out of its side. The boomerang was reddish brown and looked like it was made of stone. Homer, forlorn, sat perched above it.

"Hello, Gampa," he said. "Gamsa. Good to see you."

Homer was dressed in drab brown clothing. His hair hung in dirty curls around his face, and his knees were drawn to his chest.

Myell said, "Wind-not-sea. That's your name."

"Once," Homer said.

Above their heads, Team Space and ACF starships continued to explode. Myell couldn't see bodies in the void, but it wasn't hard to imagine them floating in burned bits and pieces, char, limbs, dust. Admiral Nam was in that wreckage, as were Laura Ling and Chief Ovadia, and most of the chiefs who had welcomed him into the goat locker. The coffee and cake had been a long time ago, but he could almost taste chocolate on his teeth.

"They die," Homer said, his shoulders hunched. He tilted his head to the sky of destruction. "Over and over again. Everyone always dies. And I always watch."

Jodenny pressed herself against Myell's side. She was watching Homer with an expression on her face that said he wasn't trustworthy, maybe wasn't sane. But Myell already knew that.

Osherman said, "Can we stop it?"

"Nothing changes," Homer said.

"You don't care about saving that fleet," Myell said. "You don't care about humanity. You just want to save yourself from the fate you earned."

Jodenny said, "What do you mean?"

Myell looked away.

She pressed her hand against his arm, and Osherman said, "What aren't you telling us?"

"Look at what he's sitting on," Myell said.

Jodenny took in a sharp breath. Osherman took a step forward.

"Is that . . . ?" Osherman started.

The icy blue mound was a corpse. Oversized, clearly not human. Ossified and merging into the landscape in a slow eventual decay.

"Yes," Myell said. "It's Jungali. He killed his father. He killed me."

The red explosions in the sky faded to dark. No ships were left to destroy. The Roon fleet would be gathering up its prisoners now, and shipping them off to slow deaths in miserable mines.

"I didn't mean to," Homer said, from atop Jungali's corpse. "I came here to meet him, nothing more. But he wouldn't share. None of them would."

Jodenny's hand tightened around Myell's. "None of who?"

"The Wondjina. They're here." Myell scanned not the sky but instead the horizon, where blue and white clouds began to rush forward over the sea of ice. "They've always been here. Watching. Helping. Whenever mankind is in danger, they're there. It's where he knew he could find Jungali."

Osherman snorted. "Helping. What help were they? If they wanted to help, they would have sent the Roon away from this ambush, just like Jungali did at Burrin-gurrah."

Myell touched the boomerang. It was cold beneath his fingers. It felt like something pulled out of his own chest, unearthed and carved away and turned into a weapon.

"They care," he said. "They cared enough to build the Seven Sisters for mankind. To recruit the Nogo-main, who looked after us as long as they could. Jun-gali was the last of the Nogomain. And Homer killed him."

"He wouldn't share," Homer repeated. "He wouldn't give me what I wanted."

"What did you want?" Myell asked.

"Everything," Homer said softly.

Jodenny squeezed Myell's hand. He looked at her, at the odd sense of concentration on her face. Her lips were tight and she was breathing through her mouth.

He would have known what that face meant even without the Digital Duola in his head.

The storms on the horizon built skyward but came no closer.

Homer's face hardened with memory. "They impris-oned me here with nothing to do but count the stars in the sky and the cracks in the ice. No companionship or compassion. No conversation. No surcease. Only the hope that if I found you, and got you to come here of your own volition—if you agreed to sacrifice yourself again—then I would be freed. For that they changed time."

"Garanwa's station," Myell said. "You're the one."

"But you wouldn't do it," Homer said bitterly. "Only if it concerned *her*. Only if you could save *her*."

Myell took a protective step in front of Jodenny.

Osherman asked, "He sent you the blue ouroboros?"

"She did," Homer said.

Under their feet, embedded in the ice, blue ouroboros rings began to glow. A dozen, then a dozen more. Linked and glowing like lights under a dance hall floor.

"She who?" Myell asked.

Homer said, "The goddess of rain and the dead, Kultana. Can't you see her? She's in the clouds. She's staring at us."

More blue rings illuminated themselves under the ice, stretching from horizon to horizon.

"They forbid me to tell you the true story. Forbid me to bring you here myself. Every minute I appeared to you, I had to spend another decade on this ice. Every time I manifested with enough strength to touch someone, a hundred years. For saving you both—"

He pointed to Jodenny and Osherman.

"—a thousand years of isolation," Homer said. "But it was worth it, now that you're here. You can become Jungali again, Gampa. As a god, you can stop this battle. The gods can't resurrect themselves, but they can change history."

Above them, the stars reset. The Team Space and ACF fleet reassembled into silver points of light. The Roon fleet approached, gold and deadly.

Jodenny said to Myell, "Don't you even think about it. You're not sacrificing yourself again. Do you hear me?"

Beneath his fingers, the boomerang began to tremble.

CHAPTER **THIRTY-THREE**

Jodenny decided that of all the things in the world she hated most, contractions rated very high on the list. Her whole uterus rose up in spasm and she gripped Myell's hand tightly. He gave her a worried look. She tried to look reassuring but delivery was moving along much faster than it should. She didn't know how much longer she could stay on her feet, and had fleeting visions of Junior just sliding right out of her and crashing onto the icy blue ground.

But at the top of her most-hated list was the fear that Myell was believing Homer's threats and allegations. That maybe guilt was festering inside him for failures as a father—which was ridiculous. That her husband was about to sacrifice himself in a noble gesture to save the universe.

Over her dead body, she vowed.

The blue-gray clouds boiled on the horizon. Above their heads, though, the sky was a backdrop of darkness and stars, and the first ships began to explode again. Jodenny couldn't bear to watch.

"So what now?" Osherman asked. "We stand here and watch Team Space and the ACF get destroyed over and over again?"

Homer only had eyes for Myell. "You know what you have to do, Gampa. Father."

Myell pulled the boomerang from Jungali's corpse. One end broke off, leaving a jagged sharp edge. "No. That's my answer."

Jodenny saw the storms pause, as if watching.

Homer's expression collapsed. "You can't say no."

"You can always say no." Myell held the boomerang aloft. "Even to the gods. We'll find another way to save mankind. But it won't be here and now."

Jodenny felt her womb spasm again, a ridiculous pain that shot through her hips and up her spine. Despite herself, she cried out. This time the wetness streaming between her legs wasn't urine at all. She started to go to her knees. Myell was forced to drop the boomerang in order to support her.

Homer lunged for the boomerang but Osherman grabbed it first.

"I'll take that," Osherman said, and there was something wild in his voice.

Too late, Jodenny realized his intentions.

"Sam, no!" she said.

Osherman had already raised the broken shard. "Someone has to."

"You weren't chosen," Homer said.

A shrug in return. "Sometimes you don't have to be chosen. Sometimes you volunteer."

"Stop him," Jodenny gasped against Myell's ear.

Myell moved faster than even Jodenny expected. He and Osherman went down in a tangle of limbs. The ice beneath them cracked and burst inward, dumping them into a blue ring and out of Jodenny's sight and away, away, away from the here and now of Kultana.

The shock of breaking ice was nothing compared with the shock of grass beneath Myell's back, bright sunlight above, gasping onlookers, Osherman's fist against his face. Locked in struggle, smashing and head butting each other, they rolled across what appeared to be a soccer field, of all places.

"Someone call Security!" a voice yelled from nearby.

Jodenny's voice, stern and commanding, said, "Stop that right now!"

Myell pulled away from Osherman. His nose hurt and he could taste blood in his mouth. He sat on the grass, heaving for breath, while Osherman coughed into the dirt and gave off a groan.

"Who the hell are you two?" Jodenny demanded. Her hair hung in a glossy ponytail and she was dressed in a Team Space Academy sports uniform. Behind her, clutching soccer balls, were three members of her team. They all looked incredibly young in Fortune's bright sun.

"Just passing through," Myell said.

Jodenny picked up the fallen boomerang.

Osherman pulled himself upright and made an obvious effort to look official. "I'm Commander Osherman, and you need to give me that. It's not safe."

One of her eyebrows rose up. "It's a broken boomerang. What is this, anyway? Rock? Who makes them out of rock?"

The blue ring appeared on the grass less than a meter away. Myell was too damned slow to stop Osherman from grabbing the boomerang from Jodenny's hand and plunging into the ring. But he wasn't too slow to follow.

Jodenny was only five or six years old in this eddy. Pigtailed and gap-toothed. Grinning at them both as she held the boomerang in her hands.

"Can I keep it?" she asked.

"No," Myell and Osherman both said at the same time.

She gazed at them curiously. The lawn of the Simon

Street orphanage stretched wide and green around them. "What's it for?"

"For traveling in time," Myell said.

"For saving the universe."

"I'm keeping it," she said, and ran back toward the main building. "Sister Ann! Sister Ann!"

"Catch her," Myell said.

I buried you," Jodenny said. "Right here."

She looked a little bit pregnant and a lot scared, holding the fallen boomerang aloft in both hands like a baseball bat. The grassy hillside sloped underneath her feet and down toward the settlement of Providence. Behind her, treetops bowed in the wind and birds sang out in a sudden chorus.

Osherman pushed Myell off him and rolled aside. "Don't listen to him. Whatever he says, don't listen."

She stared at him. "You can talk? Since when?"

"Give me the boomerang," Myell said to Jodenny. "He's going to sacrifice himself with it."

Jodenny grimaced. "Why?"

"Because only the gods can change history," Osherman said quietly. "And there's a woman I need to save."

The reply made Myell pause. He searched Osherman's expression, looking for deception or fraud. He saw only grief and longing. Upon reflection, what Osherman wanted to do was no worse or better than what Myell had done for his Jodenny, time and time again.

This Jodenny shook her head. "I don't know who to believe."

"Kay," Myell said. "Give it to me. You've trusted me before, and you'll trust me again. I have no other reason to give you but that, and the fact I love you. I will always love you."

Osherman looked away.

She tossed him the boomerang.

Myell caught it.

Caught it, and handed it to Osherman.

Left alone on Kultana with Homer and the men of the Eola, the pain of contractions shooting through her, Jodenny crouched on the ice and groaned. Hands reached for her—Homer, concern on his face.

"Gamsa, what's wrong?" he asked.

"What do you think?" she bit out.

A humming sound filled her ears. Movement caught and blurred at the edge of her vision. She lifted her head, sure she was going to see Myell and Osherman returning to her, but instead it was the Roon in a black feather cloak and tall silver headdress. A silver ouroboros spun around its ankles. It smelled like something that had been dragged out of a musty grave—skin and bones and alien blood all rotting away. It held a silver weapon in one gloved hand.

Homer stood defiantly between the Flying Doctor and Jodenny.

"You're not allowed here," he said defiantly.

Its mouth turned into a rictus. "You think you're the only ones who have gods? Mine are just as powerful as yours. Even stronger, to smash through the flimsy walls of this construct."

Jodenny couldn't bring herself upright, as much as she wanted to. She felt light-headed and had the desperate desire to lie down, but at least the contraction was easing. It was no comfort at all to know that another would return in a few minutes.

By then, she and Junior might be dead.

Homer wasn't backing away from the alien. In that, if nothing else, he reminded Jodenny of Myell. He said, "Your weapon won't work here."

The Roon fired.

Sizzling bolts of silver dissolved around Homer and melted to the ground.

The Eola showed no notice; they were still sitting in their circle, chanting, and Jodenny wondered if their words were somehow keeping this so-called construct in place.

"This battle has already been won," the Flying Doctor said, as ships exploded like gruesome fireworks above its head. "Our civilization follows its own destiny independent of your wants and desires. I will not let you change the course of history."

"You can't stop us," Homer said. "Only your gods can. They sent you, but are they too afraid to come themselves?"

The Roon surged forward, as if to physically attack Homer, but it couldn't extend past the silver ouroboros.

"I thought so," Homer said.

The thing was, Jodenny mused, the Roon's argument had merit. The battle over their heads had indeed already been won. She herself would be pissed if mankind had triumphed over a foe and had the victory reversed by mysterious, omnipotent deities. She was still angry at Jungali for stranding the *Kamchatka*, after all, and that offense had at least been well-intentioned.

Seeing the Flying Doctor's side of things didn't mean she agreed with it, though.

No alien armada was going to triumph if she had anything to say about it.

"Homer, help me up," she said.

Carefully, one wary eye on the Roon, he reached down with both arms. When she was erect and steady, Jodenny took a careful step toward the creature.

"Would you negotiate a truce?" she asked.

Homer exclaimed, "Are you crazy, Gamsa?"

The Flying Doctor glared at her. "We do not surrender."

"Not a surrender," Jodenny said. Her insides were beginning to cramp again, and she pushed both hands against her belly. Just a moment more. One more. "An agreement. You already have what you wanted—control of the Wondjina network. You don't need to eradicate mankind and other species as well. There must be a way to exist side by side and not kill each other."

The blue-gray clouds on the horizon slowed.

The exploding ships overhead faded.

"There will be no coexistence," the Flying Doctor said. "My gods will pound yours to dust."

Another contraction in Jodenny's womb tore through her. The pain was so vicious, so unexpected, that she almost missed the sound of Sam Osherman's voice behind her.

"Your gods will fail," Osherman said.

Myell and Osherman had returned.

One of them was dead on the ice, a boomerang through his heart.

The new god standing above Osherman's corpse sounded like him but was larger all around, from the broad expanse of his shoulders to the long stretch of his face and legs growing taller with each passing second. The rain clouds on the horizon rushed forward to circle around his head. Though his gaze was on the Flying Doctor, some part of him focused on Jodenny as well. She could feel his warm attention, a touch of concern.

Homer said, "Jungali."

Myell moved away from the new god and took Jodenny into his arms. She clung to him, bereft. Osherman's death was a loss she hadn't prepared for at all.

The Flying Doctor said, "I reject you and all your kind."

"Too late," Jungali said.

The god raised a white-hot hand.

The blue ice plain of Kultana flickered away. Gone as quickly as it had come, with no more exploding spaceships to mark the sky. Instead Jodenny found herself kneeling on all fours in the underground cave with the Painted Child before her. The worst pressure of her entire life was ripping through her body. She screamed. There was nothing easy about this, nothing calm or soothing, nothing at all worth recommending—but then the huge weight and shape of Junior's body was moving through her into Myell's hands, and Jodenny sobbed with relief and gratitude and grief.

Which was how Junior Scott Myell came into the world in the Jenolan Caves, New South Wales, Australia, in the year 1855.

CHAPTER THIRTY-FOUR

Mrs. Dunbar at Lady Darling's farmhouse had no misgivings about letting them stay on, or at least none that she voiced around them. Jodenny couldn't help but feel like a trespasser. Osherman had left behind money for Mrs. Dunbar's salary, though, and for a nice side payment to her brother the local police constable as well. With no heirs to claim the estate, Jodenny and Myell and the baby had some time to recuperate.

"Are we really going to call her Junior?" Myell asked one morning as they lay in bed. The baby had just finished feeding off Jodenny's breast and was dozing, her pink lips happily sucking her own thumb. Jodenny brushed at wisps of dark hair and planted a kiss on Junior's fat little cheek.

"You said we named her Lisa."

"We don't have to name her Lisa this time," Myell pointed out. "We could name her Kay."

Jodenny thought a moment. "I'd like to call her Sam. Samantha."

Myell leaned forward to kiss them both. "Samantha it is."

They didn't talk about Osherman and his sacrifice. They didn't speculate as to Homer and his fate, though Myell sometimes gazed unseeingly at the wallpaper and Jodenny thought he was thinking of icy blue plains. They had no plans for the future, or at least none they shared with one another.

When Samantha was one week old, Jodenny woke to

rain at midnight. Myell was already out of bed and standing at the window.

"There's a Wondjina in the backyard," he said. Somehow he managed to sound casual about it.

Jodenny pulled on her bathrobe and lifted Samantha out of the dresser drawer they'd been using as a make-shift crib. "Is it Sam?"

"I don't think so."

The baby fussed and kicked but settled down against Jodenny's shoulder. Jodenny held her tightly, one hand supporting her tiny soft head, and joined Myell by the curtains. Lightning illuminated the figure in the field—a woman just about as tall as St. Mary's Cathedral, with black skin and green eyes and a belly curved with pregnancy.

"I'll go," Myell said.

"We'll all go," Jodenny corrected him.

He grimaced.

She said, "It's not like the door's going to stop her if she wants to come in, right?"

"I suppose," he said doubtfully.

They pulled on rain slickers and shoes and stepped into the yard, which was already a morass of mud. The goddess watched them approach with impassivity. Water leaked from her breasts and streamed between her muscular legs.

"Kultana," Myell said, with a bow of his head.

"Once-Jungali," the goddess replied. "Your absence is keenly felt."

Jodenny didn't like the sound of that. Her free hand snaked out and grabbed Myell's wrist. Lightning slashed across the sky in long jagged tears, accompanied by thunderous booms, but the rain against her face was soft, almost gentle.

"He's not going back," Jodenny said.

The goddess turned her attention to Jodenny for just a moment. An invisible spotlight scorched through her. Hard and bright, uncovering every flaw and crack. She felt burned by it but also curiously renewed. Destroyed and reborn at the same time, one moment spinning endlessly in time. The goddess's gaze swiveled back to Myell and Jodenny wondered how he could withstand the scrutiny.

"A sacrifice was made," Myell said.

The goddess was silent. Ominously dreadfully silent, while the wind around them moved and Samantha began to fuss inside Jodenny's coat. Jodenny thought centuries were speeding by with each passing moment—the entire continent of Australia spinning forward in time, landscapes flourishing and dying under merciless skies— but Myell's pulse beneath her fingers kept her grounded. She strengthened her grip. If he had any intention of stepping forward, he'd have to drag her with him.

"The sacrifice was accepted," Kultana said. "Even now he steers the helm. He asked for you to be sent this gift."

The goddess's belly shifted again and lit up from the inside. An illuminated blue-and-green sphere spun inside her. It descended between her legs until it was resting in the mud—smaller than the Painted Child but large enough to accommodate Jodenny and Myell and a dozen of their closest friends. This blue sphere sang out, filled with sunlight and the sound of ocean waves breaking on shore.

Myell sounded suspicious, which Jodenny thought was prudent. "What gift is this?"

Kultana's voice echoed across the landscape. "It is the gift of travel, to take you anywhere you want. It is the gift of time to follow your dreams. It is the gift of language, so that you may speak to your enemies and understand them. It is the gift of harvest, so that your children and their children will enjoy bounty."

The goddess, her belly diminished, began to rise upward into the dark clouds.

"Wait!" Jodenny said. "The Roon! Were they turned back at Kultana? Did Sam save humanity?"

Kultana gazed down silently, her countenance both beneficent and terrible, and disappeared into the storm.

"I think he did," Myell murmured. "I think everything's okay, for now."

She wished she could be so sure. Slowly the rain eased away. Jodenny undid the coat to let Samantha enjoy fresh air. The baby scrunched up her nose and turned her head unerringly toward the Blue Sphere, which sang out with promise.

"Are we going to use it?" Jodenny asked Myell.

He kissed her and kissed the baby.

"Not tonight," he said.

They trudged through the mud and back into the house. The Wondjina gift glowed and sang through the windows until dawn.

EPILOGUE

He woke on slimy cold rock, in what smelled and looked like an underwater cave. His skin itched from scrapes and salt water, and he had a headache that hurt like a bastard. He had the desperate, panicky feeling that he'd failed to do something important. Failure was nothing new to him, as his family and former commanding officers could attest, but this was entirely different.

He lifted his head and spat out the vile taste of seawater.

"Hello?" he called out.

His voice echoed in the dank caverns. A pool of water nearby rippled as a silver fish broke the surface and darted away again.

A moment later, he tried again. "Is anyone here?"

A seal broke the surface of the pool and hauled itself onto the nearest ledge. As it moved, its flippers turned to long arms. The tail split into muscular legs. A naked man with a wild red beard stood upright and gazed benevolently downward.

"You can call me the Sea King," the man said. "Also known as Sea Unchanging and Sea Eternal. I rule all the oceans and all the creatures in them. And I have a job for you."

Tom Cappaletto grinned. "Mother always told me I'd lead an interesting life."